Praise for th

IF TWO ARE DEAD

RICK MOFINA

/ll MIRA

/II MIRA™

ISBN-13: 978-0-7783-6859-5

If Two Are Dead

Recycling programs for this product may not exist in your area.

Mira
22 Adelaide St. West, 41st Floor
Toronto, Ontario M5H 4E3, Canada
MIRABooks.com

Printed in U.S.A.

This book is for all my nieces,
especially those who have been asking
when I'm going to dedicate a book to them.

*Secrets, silent, stony sit in the dark palaces of both our hearts:
secrets weary of their tyranny: tyrants willing to be dethroned.*
                              —James Joyce, *Ulysses*

1

The wipers swatted in near hysteria at the rain distorting Luke Conway's view.

Close to midnight, very little traffic, but it was coming down hard. Gusts sent branches and pieces of trash whipping across his path. Peering into the gloom, Luke weighed his wife's words as she spoke to him over the phone.

"He's sick and needs us there," Carrie said, her voice tinged with static.

"And he helped me with the job," Luke said.

"I know," Carrie said. "And I want him to see Emily—"

She paused, her silence over Luke's hands-free app underscored by the thrumming wipers. He glanced at his phone, which was illuminated with a photo of Carrie, her smile radiant as she held Emily, their one-year-old angel. He considered their situation. Soon, he'd fly back to California and they'd finalize everything on their house in LA, dispatch the movers, then fly back together to Texas for the next chapter of their lives.

Luke was eager to have Carrie and Emily with him in their new home. He'd be glad to stop living out of his suitcases, sleeping alone on a foam mattress and eating cold pizza for breakfast.

But he knew this call wasn't about him; it was about Carrie's fear around moving back to Texas.

"It's going to work out," he said. "And Anna supports you. She said it wouldn't be easy."

"I know there are issues," Carrie said. "I knew it when I made the decision to move back. I know Dad thinks it's a big step and doesn't want us to come, like he's trying to protect me or something."

"Right."

"But it's the right thing to do, for all of us. Emily will get to know her grandfather. I want that to happen. And Dad needs it."

"That's right."

"So how was today?" Carrie asked.

"Good. I just went for a beer with some of the guys."

"And you're driving? Luke!"

"One light beer. I swear. Had a burger, too."

"Still, you need to be careful."

Luke winced, Carrie's caution hanging in the air before she added, "You know what I mean."

"They invited me. I want to fit in with the new crew."

"What did you guys talk about?"

He nearly said cold cases and serial killers, but caught himself.

"Football."

"Of course." Carrie switched the subject quickly. "I was looking at the pictures you sent of the parts of Clear River I haven't seen in a while—the town has changed so much."

"You'd hardly recognize the place."

"Our neighborhood looks nice."

Luke had rented them a house in Cedar Breeze, a contemporary suburb of Clear River, a small city in East Texas situated about ninety minutes, give or take, northeast of Houston. Cedar Breeze had emerged about the time Luke and Carrie had both left Texas. Now it was a pretty community of beautiful homes along streets shaded by pine, oak and cedar trees.

"Hang on," Luke told Carrie, slowing and signaling, then leaving US 59 for a state highway. He continued a short distance before getting onto River Road, a ribbon of blacktop that meandered through an expanse of countryside, the road dipping and rolling along a small patchwork of rural properties and forests.

The wind continued scattering broken branches and loose refuse, some of it knocking against his car. He went by Fawn Ridge, a new subdivision of cookie-cutter houses in various phases of construction. At the entrance, joggling in the wind, was one of the billboards promoting a dream community for families. No one had moved in yet. Instead of families, Fawn Ridge was occupied by lines of equipment and fortified by mounds of dark earth, pallets of lumber and sod.

The development had devoured a sizable portion of the land. The black windows of its empty houses stared out at the sprinkling of old houses and barns standing faithfully nearby, like weary soldiers surrendering to the new world.

But with tonight's downpour, Luke saw little of it.

"Was that thunder?" Carrie said. "Maybe we should hang up?"

"I've got the road to myself."

The rain was overwhelming his wipers. But as Luke came to a small valley where the road curved, he saw what no one driving nearly forty miles an hour in a storm should ever see.

Is that a person on the road, running toward me?

It happened before Luke could react. Before his brain issued the order to lift his foot from the gas to stomp the brake, before his jaw opened, before his hand spasmed on the wheel, before he could form the cognitive command to swerve, he heard and felt the heart-sickening thud.

In that one millionth of a second, in the streaming watery chaos, he thought he glimpsed something—*a face of a woman, a flash of color?*—streaking over his windshield.

"No!"

His stomach spasmed, his pulse hammering in time with the wipers as he stopped on the shoulder with Carrie's voice calling from the dark.

"Luke?"

As he glanced at his mounted phone, every instinct screaming to call 911, his thoughts ran as wild as the storm.

I've hit a woman with my car! On River Road near Fawn Ridge! Send an ambulance!

But Luke didn't call.

He stared at his phone, at the faces of his wife and daughter, hearing and feeling Carrie's anguish, feeling his life ending as seconds ticked by with shards of truth piercing his thoughts.

He'd been at a bar, drinking. Driving a little too fast. And maybe he'd hit a woman.

Maybe I killed her.

He'd be charged. He'd need a lawyer. He'd lose his job.

I could go to prison. I could lose Carrie. I could lose Emily.

2

The wipers continued moving in a frenzy.

"Luke? What is it?"

"I hit something—"

"Are you okay?"

"I'll call you back."

Luke dragged a hand across his mouth, looking around for headlights, for anyone nearby.

He saw nothing through the water-streaked windows.

Rifling through the glove compartment, he found his flashlight, activated his hazard lights, grabbed his phone, then got out. He pulled up his jacket collar and pulled down on his ball cap. The rain bubbled on the pavement like a simmering cauldron as he began searching.

There was no woman near his SUV.

"Hello! Hello!" he called out.

Nothing.

In the roaring deluge he trotted behind his car, down the middle of the road, ten yards, thirty, almost a hundred.

"Where are you? Are you okay?"

Nothing.

He moved quickly to the right shoulder and got down into

the grass and bramble. In near panic he raked his flashlight side to side, rain glistening in its bright beam. He sloshed through small marshes amid the fast-food trash, plastic garbage bags and wind-blown debris from the Fawn Ridge construction crews.

"Hello!"

No sign of the woman.

He scoured the right shoulder all the way back to his car.

Nothing.

His heart racing, alarm flaring as he adjusted his fingers around his phone.

Call 911. Get help now.

But he couldn't.

He examined the road's left shoulder, hurrying the same distance, then back again through the roadside bushes to his car.

Nothing.

He got down on his knees and looked under his SUV.

Nothing.

He went around to the front, checking for damage. From what he could see in the pelting rain, his windshield was intact. No cracks and no blood.

He directed his flashlight to the car's nose, his eyes widening at a crumpling, a small dent and scratches on his front bumper.

A stinging stream of bile erupted in his throat.

Taking a few steps back, processing what was unfolding, he stared into the darkness, the rain hissing around him. In all this time, no one had driven by. *No one saw.* The only witnesses were the empty new homes and the distant old buildings.

"Hello!" he called again into the night as he jogged back down the road, calling out, thinking that maybe she'd crawled off hurt toward one of the houses. "Hello!"

Nothing.

He trotted back to his SUV, stood in the middle of the road and stared at his dashcam.

It had died in New Mexico on the drive from California,

and he hadn't gotten around to replacing it yet. He'd checked the fuse, the connection, the charger and the memory card, but it hadn't done any good—it was broken.

Whatever had happened, his airbags hadn't deployed, likely because he didn't hit a solid fixed barrier, like a wall, or a parked car.

But I hit something. Or someone.

Feeling his phone in his hand, finger poised to tap out 911, his breathing quickened. Once he hit those three digits, he'd set in motion the unstoppable mechanism that would destroy his already fractured life.

His conscience screamed at him. *Call 911 now!*

But another part of him weighed the situation.

Wait. Hold on. Think. Just think.

Luke clenched his eyes. Did he, in fact, hit a person? Maybe it was all in his head? The storm had tossed all sorts of things against his car. Maybe it was an animal, or debris, trash, a chunk of a billboard torn free by the storm? It was the only possibility—there was no woman that he could find, no body.

I couldn't find the woman. There is no woman.

Luke lowered his phone and felt rain trickling under his collar, soaking his skin. He got into his SUV and startled when his phone rang. Carrie was calling.

"What happened? What did you hit?"

"Trash or something, I think, blown around by the storm."

"You scared me to death."

"Sorry. It surprised me."

"Are you hurt? Where are you?"

"No, I'm not hurt. I'm just driving home."

"Are you sure you're all right?"

"I'm just really tired. I'll call you tomorrow. Promise. Kiss the baby for me. Love you guys."

"Love you, too."

He sat there shaking, staring at his phone, his breath growing shallow, his conscience prodding him.

Call 911. Get help now.

But if he called, if the worst had happened… *No. I can't go through this again.*

He looked at his home screen, at Carrie and Emily. He couldn't bear to put them through the ordeal, not with what Carrie was facing. Not with what he'd left behind in LA. But what about the woman?

What woman? I looked everywhere. Maybe my brain's playing tricks on me?

Suddenly his eyes flicked up, and through the wipers and the rain he saw a twinkling, like distant stars: the headlights of an approaching car.

He bit down on his bottom lip, knowing that drivers who left the scene of an accident involving a serious injury or death could be charged with a felony and sent to prison.

But there's no victim. No scene, it's all in my head.

The car was nearing him, his wipers ticking, his conscience jabbing him.

Call 911.

So much was at stake.

He had to decide right now.

Inhaling deeply, Luke switched off his hazard lights, shifted from Park and continued driving the short distance home.

3

Cedar Breeze was a mile farther down the road.

The storm hadn't let up.

Thankfully, Luke saw little traffic and no emergency lights, and heard no sirens, as he navigated around bits of windblown debris and tree limbs to get to his neighborhood.

He was numb as he parked in his driveway and went inside. His movements and breathing echoed in the near-empty house as he pulled off his wet clothes and took a shower. Welcoming the stinging needles of hot water, he scrubbed his skin as if he could erase the incident.

But he couldn't.

His guilt and questions were unrelenting.

Just like LA.

Had he left an injured woman to die in the rain?

Why would a person be running toward his car in a storm? It happened so fast, the rain obscuring his vision.

He had to stop thinking like that.

Maybe all he hit was a piece of trash?

After showering, he pulled on sweatpants and a Los Angeles Rams T-shirt, went to the living room and switched off the lights. He lay down on his foam mattress and stared out the big window. Lightning flashed; watery veins slithered down the glass as he searched the night.

Maybe I imagined the whole thing?

His police psychologist in Los Angeles had told him he would face a range of reactions, like intrusive imagery, flashbacks, distorted memories and impaired judgment. *With treatment and time, you can return to the job.*

True, he was able to return to work, but he wouldn't have been able to handle LA much longer—the move back to Texas was for him as much as it was for Carrie.

Thunder rumbled as Luke took stock of his actions tonight. No way was he drunk, not after one beer and a burger. No way was he speeding. And he'd intended to call it in.

Intended?

The road to hell is paved with good intentions.

He cast around the house, practically bare. Down the hall, the baby's room; next to it, his and Carrie's bedroom. Near him in the living room, a rocking chair Luke had bought at an antique shop near Houston. A surprise for Carrie, it had a big bow and was waiting in the corner for her.

So much was on the line.

His new job, their battle to overcome the past, to make their family closer, stronger.

Carrie's dad. Her chance to heal. My shot to put my problems behind me.

Now it was all at stake.

His conscience would not release him from the incident. He'd wanted to do the right thing. But he'd found no one. There was nothing to report.

Time swept by; the rain let up, and eventually sleep came in snatches.

Suddenly, he woke with new, terrifying thoughts.

What if he had in fact struck a woman and she had called

911? What if she'd emerged and flagged down the car that was approaching when he left?

No, he told himself, *there's no woman. The storm hurled trash at you—that's all.*

His nerves continued rippling until he fell back to sleep.

Luke woke after sunrise.

Sorting his thoughts, the memory of last night hit him.

Massaging his whiskered face, his pulse picking up, he checked his phone. A few spam messages and ads. No critical emails or alerts.

He stiffened.

Out of the corner of his eye, through his front window, he'd glimpsed a figure.

Someone's in my driveway, looking at my car.

Concern whirled through him as he opened his door to the humid air. The storm was over, the morning clear.

Stepping into his driveway, he found a stranger standing behind his SUV, studying the leafy tree limb wedged under its rear end.

Luke threw a glance to the pickup in the driveway next door—the driver's door was open. Then he looked at the man. He was wearing a blue short-sleeved shirt, jeans and sunglasses. Midforties, short hair, average build, an inch or two shorter than Luke. "Can I help you?" Luke asked.

"Hi, neighbor. I was heading for work when I saw that broken branch stuck under your Chevy Blazer there."

Luke pulled the branch free and tossed it onto his front lawn.

"There you go," the man said. "I was afraid you wouldn't see it and was going to ring your doorbell. We haven't met yet. Greg Ronson."

He was all smiles, bright teeth, a firm handshake.

"Luke Conway."

"Sorry for coming onto your property like this, Luke. That was a helluva storm."

Absorbing the explanation, Luke responded, "Yeah, it was."

"I've been away on business and my wife, Roxxie, tells me you moved in ahead of your family and you're from California?"

"That's right."

"Whereabouts?"

"Los Angeles."

"Well, we won't hold that against you." Greg chuckled. "What did you do in LA? If you don't mind me askin'?"

Luke hesitated.

"Hey, sorry," Greg said. "I'll go first. I'm with Texeter Diamond Industries—it's oil and gas equipment. I'm in accounting."

"I was an officer with the LAPD."

Greg's eyebrows peeked above the frames of his sunglasses. "You don't say. And who are you with here?"

"The county. I'm a deputy."

"How 'bout that. Welcome, Luke. Happy to have you as my neighbor. Say, maybe when your family gets here, Roxxie and I will have you over for a barbecue?"

"Well, I work weekends, shifts." Luke glanced to his SUV. "And when my family and the movers come, we'll have a lot on the go."

"I understand," Greg said. "Whenever the time is right."

"Sure, and thanks."

"You bet." Greg turned, then stopped. "One thing, though."

Luke braced as Greg kept walking backward to his truck while pointing at him and winking.

"We got more Cowboys and Texans fans than Rams fans around here."

Luke smiled and nodded, watching Greg climb into his pickup.

Once the truck disappeared around a corner, Luke took a breath. Feeling his tension melt, he looked at the tree limb. He hadn't noticed it last night. There you go. It had to be some of the debris he'd struck. Moving to double-check the damage, he walked toward the front of his SUV. Conditions were better now in the morning light.

His windshield was clear. Good. He studied the front bumper. Left side was fine, but the passenger side had a small indentation with scrapes. And the headlight on the passenger side was intact but the cover was fractured.

Could this be consistent with hitting debris, a piece of billboard or a tree?

He squatted for a closer inspection.

A faint ticking sound rose with a breath of wind, shifting his focus to the grille on the passenger side.

Then to a flash of pink, lifted by the soft breeze.

As if waving to him.

It was a piece of fabric.

A gum stick–sized fragment of frayed pink fabric bearing a single pink button. It appeared to have been ripped from clothing. It must've folded out of sight in the rain, then dried to emerge.

Like an accusation.

Carefully, Luke removed it from the mesh, placing it in the palm of his hand before closing it into his fist.

It began in his gut with a low grumbling of terror, erupting to a stabbing in his chest and throat, everything turning to haze. He made it back inside in time to reach the toilet, where he vomited, coughing and gasping.

When he'd finished, he washed his face with cold water, his heartbeat and the truth thrashing in his ears.

You hit someone.

He recalled the flash of a woman's face.

You hit a woman and left her to die.

No. No, it never happened.

The screaming in his brain evolved into the ringing of a

phone. A million thoughts and fears racing, he found his cell in the living room and answered.

"Yes?"

"Hansen at the office. You up, Luke?"

"Yes, sir."

"We need you to start early today. Can you do that?"

"Yes, sir."

"We need you to get in as soon as possible. We're going to support Clear River. They've got a body, an unidentified female."

"Where, sir?"

"North edge, not all that far from you."

4

Luke met himself in the mirror.

Fear etching his face, he raked his hand through his hair staring at what he'd become. He was no longer a husband, a father, a law enforcement officer.

Now he saw one thing.

A suspect.

He shut his eyes and felt a clamp of panic. He thought of Carrie. He thought of Emily growing up here, playing in the backyard, learning to ride a bike. He envisioned their new life before his guilt clouded it.

But wait, just stop. Stop this!

How did he know he wasn't being paranoid about something that never happened in the storm? How did he know he wasn't reading something into it because of the incident in Los Angeles? Seriously, how could he make a connection between last night and an unidentified dead woman?

But he had to convince himself, he had to be certain. Reaching into his pocket, he withdrew the damning evidence he'd plucked from his SUV's grille.

He looked at the slip of pink fabric with the button.

This will prove it.

★ ★ ★

Luke got ready, then headed for the sheriff's office.

On the way, he took long, slow breaths. At his locker he moved quickly, getting into his uniform, buckling his duty belt. He unlocked his gun and studied it before he holstered it, suited up and signed out a marked unit. Ruby, the civilian office manager, tilted her head, assessing his face.

"What happened to you, Luke?"

He touched his chin where the blood from small cuts had coagulated.

"Shaved a little too fast."

"Looks like you crawled through barbed wire."

Luke grimaced and headed out to his car. The death scene was near, located inside the northern edge of Clear River. It fell within the jurisdiction of the Clear River Police Department, with support from the county sheriff's office.

Emergency vehicles, lights flashing, were clustered at a strip mall parking lot. Shingles, wooden crates and take-out bags were scattered along the street from the storm. Traffic was inching by. A Clear River cop stood in the middle of the road waving rubberneckers through.

Luke stopped on the shoulder.

Hesitating, he slid the plastic sandwich bag holding the fragment of fabric from his pocket. Looking at it, thinking how it held everything for him, he tensed before sliding it back into his pocket. Then he got out, striving to remain calm.

Investigators were concentrated on the parking lot near a mini-mart. It was flanked by a diner and an auto accessories shop. The businesses were closed, the area cordoned with yellow tape.

The victim was in the middle of the lot, covered by a tarp.

Luke found his supervisor Don Fowler huddled with other senior officers next to a line of police vehicles outside the tape. Scrolling through his phone, he turned to Luke, nodding.

"All right," Fowler said. "Here's what we have. Deceased is

a white female in her twenties. Clear River detectives say she attended a house party last night, argued with her boyfriend then wandered into the storm, possibly under the influence."

Luke glanced at the yellow tarp covering the body. Clear River crime scene people and medical examiner staff wearing coveralls worked next to it, photographing and analyzing the scene.

"Luke?"

"Yes."

"You with me?"

"Yes, sir."

"I said we'd like you to take the east side of the road, go north door-to-door canvassing for witness statements, any camera footage. Log it, and deliver what you get to Clear River PD downtown."

"Yes, sir," Luke said. "Do we have a possible cause, a timeline or what she was wearing? It may help."

"No." Fowler shook his head. "No indication yet on cause. No other information than what I gave you, which is not to be shared. It's background." He turned to the forensic workers. "They'll tell us more when they can."

Luke got his tablet from his car and started north toward a gas station on the east side, Fowler's words echoing in his mind.

…wandered into the storm, possibly under the influence…

Luke estimated this scene was a little over two miles from Fawn Ridge, the spot where he'd struck something. Could someone have walked that distance in a storm after they'd been hit?

He didn't want to believe it.

But he knew from traffic courses he'd taken with the LAPD that the body reacts to trauma by producing a lot of adrenaline to cope with injuries. And there were cases where injured people, even those hurt badly and in shock after a crash, had wandered a great distance.

It was possible.

Luke's stomach knotted, thinking how he needed to know what the dead woman was wearing, when a roaring staccato noise combined with air brakes filled the air. A semitrailer growled to a halt near the strip mall. Luke looked back at the traffic cop in the distance waving at the rig to keep rolling through.

Since he was closer, Luke trotted toward the cab, noticing the words *Ramble Tamble* on the plastic bug deflector.

"You can't stop here, buddy," Luke called up to the driver's open window over the grumble of the idling diesel. "Keep moving."

The door opened. The driver climbed down quickly, a bearded bear of a man. His face was in torment, embodying urgency; ignoring Luke, he hurried toward the scene.

Luke rushed to block him.

"You need to move your truck, sir."

"That's my daughter!" The man, nostrils flaring, pushed against Luke. "I was going to Dallas—I got word she didn't come home!"

The man was strong, like a defensive tackle, forcing Luke backward as other cops ran to help.

"Let me see her!"

The officers and deputies, four including Luke, eventually got the truck driver to the back of an ambulance at the scene where detectives talked to him.

For a moment, Luke saw him raise his head to the sky, shaking it with a hoarse, pained groan.

Luke looked away.

Having come face-to-face with the father's agony, fear roiled in Luke's heart, nearly erupting when he turned to resume his assignment. That's when fate intervened, as if his conscience had reached out, pulling his attention to a snap and a sudden gust. It lifted the side of the tarp, and like the previous night, he saw a flash—this time he saw the woman's body, her shoes, her jeans.

And her pink top.

5

"I remember the ground under me vanishing, my legs pumping in midair and…it's like the river shoots up to swallow me… then I'm choking, flailing in the rushing current, my body pinballing between the rocks, then…it feels like a hammer striking my head, everything goes dark…and I wake up in the hospital… and my father's looking down at me…"

Carrie Conway stopped, let out a slow breath and stared off at the painting on the wall—a serene garden that she found comforting. She'd gone as far as she could in today's session, recounting a shred or two of muddied memory from the nightmare she'd been wrestling with for years. She accepted a tissue from Dr. Anna Bernay, her psychologist, who said, "You've done well in these past months."

"All I know is the last true memory I have, the one before running, the river, the hospital and my dad—" Carrie paused "—the last thing I remember is school. Something happened at school."

Carrie looked down at her hands.

"Why can't I remember more? So much of it is still a blank page for me."

Dr. Bernay repositioned her glasses. "With this being our

last in-person session, let's look back on it all. As you'll recall from previous sessions, we discussed your condition: a type of dissociative amnesia, which doctors suspect arose from the head injuries you suffered while escaping. Your mind is blocking details. It's a protection mechanism, keeping you from revisiting the trauma, or learning the truth about it. Healing happens in stages and everyone's process is different. For some, it takes weeks, others, months. And in cases like yours, it can be much longer."

"But why is that?"

"Your case is complex. You entered the woods with two girls who were murdered, but you fled and survived. And the case remains unsolved, the killer never arrested. You're also experiencing survivor's guilt, and prolonged traumatic bereavement. But, Carrie, despite all of this, despite having a lot to deal with over the years, you've made progress."

Touching the tissue to the corners of her eyes, Carrie said, "I'm anxious about moving back to Texas, where it all happened. My dad insists we shouldn't come home."

"He's being protective, which is perfectly understandable."

"Yes. But he's sick. We don't know how much time he has, but sometimes I really don't know about this move, about what could happen."

Dr. Bernay leaned closer to her.

"It's all right to feel unsure. But I'm confident that you will be able to handle it, Carrie. When you get back to Texas, try to build a good support system while drawing on your familiarity with the community. You'll have your dad, and maybe you can reconnect with old friends while making new ones."

Dr. Bernay paused, nodding at her notes.

"But real challenges and risks remain," she said. "Returning to where the attack happened, visiting familiar places, could also unblock painful memories and more disturbing details. And while possibly providing you with answers, some that could even be beneficial to the outstanding case, this could also un-leash new fears and anxieties given the nature of the incident."

"It scares me that the killer hasn't been caught."

"Remember, there are ways you can feel safe," Dr. Bernay said. "One obvious step is installing a home security system."

"Luke will take care of that."

"Yes. I'd also suggest you draw on your supportive network, reach out to the people you trust. Building on positive relation-ships with people in the community will foster a new sense of belonging and safety. It may even give you a feeling of resil-ience, a sense of control. This could all make you more confi-dent about living in the community again."

A moment passed. Dr. Bernay removed her glasses and looked up from her tablet. "And you have me." She smiled. "We'll have regular video sessions. You can text me whenever you feel the need to talk."

"Thank you, Anna."

"It's going to be okay, Carrie."

6

Carrie wanted to believe that moving back to Texas would be okay.

I'm doing it for Dad, for Luke, for Emily.

And for me.

This was what she told herself as she pulled away from Dr. Bernay's building, a glass rectangle in downtown Los Angeles. Stopped at a light, Carrie thought of Luke. She'd texted him this morning. He'd said that he'd been called in early to help at a scene and everything was good.

Unlike last night.

He'd alarmed her, hitting something driving home from a bar in a storm. He'd assured her everything was fine.

But he sounded different. Like he was afraid. Maybe he experienced a flashback.

Carrie couldn't sleep for much of the night. At one point she'd woken in a panic. She could never lose sight of the fact that Luke had his own reasons for leaving the LAPD and the city. She hadn't raised this with Anna in today's session, but now she wondered if his hitting something was an omen around their return to Texas.

She weighed her thoughts.

I'm just anxious. Moving back is my decision and it's the right decision.

A horn sounded behind her. The light had changed.

Carrie continued onto the freeway. Half an hour later she was in Montecito Heights, a quiet hilly neighborhood with views. She parked next to her aunt's Tesla in the driveway of their modest, cottage-sized bungalow, got out and sighed.

The For Sale sign was gone. Soon the movers would come. It wasn't perfect, of course, but she and Luke had had a good life in California where Emily was born. *Yes, a good life*, she thought, memories stirring before she blinked them away.

Stepping inside, she put her keys on the entry table and went to the living room. Emily was on the floor playing with her plastic stacking rings. Her eyes brightened when Carrie swept her into her arms with a flutter of coos and kisses.

"How was she?" Carrie asked her aunt Pearl.

"A perfect little cherub."

"Did she eat?"

"I gave her some cut-up fruit and toast."

Carrie tickled Emily, making her giggle.

"What a good girl," Carrie said, then smelled the baby's bottom. "Oh, someone needs freshening up."

Carrie got the change bag, spread the blanket on the floor, placed Emily on it and got busy while Pearl rose from the sofa to make tea.

"How did it go with your shrink?" Pearl said.

Carrie smiled. Aunt Pearl was a woman without pretense who hit you with absolute directness.

Long divorced, Pearl had never had kids or remarried. *Not going to dance that dance again*, she always said. Her failed marriage to a screenwriter happened after she'd arrived in California from Texas to pursue acting, mainly getting commercials and small parts in shows and movies.

Always working, she rarely visited Clear River County except for holidays, and for Carrie's mother's funeral. Carrie remembered how Pearl had consoled Carrie's dad, Vernon, who was Pearl's brother. He'd looked like everything inside him had shattered, and Pearl sat alone with him, talking softly. She consoled Carrie with a crushing hug, whispering: *You're strong, you'll survive this.*

Pearl's words proved prophetic when a few years later, Carrie, then aged seventeen, emerged as the sole survivor of an attack that still traumatized her. Like her mother's death, the incident had shaken her father.

In the time that followed, Carrie struggled through her senior year. Wanting to protect her, Carrie's dad urged her to move to California and live with Pearl, who'd insisted. Becoming a second mother to Carrie, Pearl helped her enroll in college in LA to study graphic design.

After graduating and finding a position with an agency that produced promotions for TV and movies, Carrie got an apartment in Burbank on Glenoaks Boulevard.

She liked being on her own.

She had friends from school, work and her neighborhood. But at times, walking alone on the street, shopping or parking her car, she felt she was being watched. Sometimes, she even thought she was being followed by a man, an indistinct stranger, always distant, always turning away whenever she stared in his direction. Her suspicion never deepened enough to warrant calling police. Maybe it was fallout from Texas—the embodiment of her fears. Or maybe it was life in a big city.

Whenever Carrie had mentioned it to her father during his visits or calls, their conversation inevitably devolved into his questioning her about the attack in Texas.

"What do you remember?"

"Nothing. I can't remember details."

"What about Donnie Ray Hyde?"

Her father always brought up Donnie Ray Hyde, who was

on death row in Texas for committing another murder. Investigators suspected Hyde, a drifter, had also been the perpetrator in Carrie's case. But with no hard evidence, they couldn't charge him.

"I don't remember, Dad. I told you."

"Not a single detail?"

"Dad, please. I don't want to discuss it."

"Nothing that could help the case?"

"I can only remember running, then the river. Don't you think I'd tell you if I remembered more?"

"I'll always be concerned."

She knew he would. He was being a father and wanted her to take precautions. Still, she'd made it clear she was not getting a gun for safety—"I don't ever want to touch one again, Dad." Carrie had agreed to carry pepper spray to ease his concern.

That concern eased further when she met Luke Conway, an LAPD officer, at a reception for a promo her agency had done for the city. He was in uniform and had a shy smile. They had a small-world moment when she discovered he was from a Texas town near Clear River. He swore he'd first seen Carrie years earlier, when she was a teen working at Whataburger. After meeting in California, they hit it off, dated, got married, bought a house and had Emily.

They were living their dream.

Until the incident with Luke. It didn't matter that the investigation by the DA found he was justified. It had changed him.

It was around this time that Carrie's father called to say he'd been diagnosed with colon cancer. Stunned, she dropped the phone, collapsing on the sofa. After picking up the phone, her fingers shaking, voice trembling, Carrie asked her father for more information. Reluctant at first, he sounded strong, telling her his condition had progressed and he was receiving treatment. Then, his voice calm, resolved, he said: "Doc tells me it's advanced and I got about two or three years."

Carrie flew to Texas with Emily, Luke and Pearl to see him. He was thinner but not in pain. Looking at her dad, Carrie once again confronted what she, her father and her husband, like everyone in the world, were facing: the fragility of life.

Seeing Emily on her father's lap during that visit, Carrie realized she had to move back to Clear River, even if only temporarily, so he could spend the time he had left with his family near. Carrie and Luke took a long walk that ended with them making the decision to move. Carrie had a teleconference call with her manager, then one with the agency's CEO.

"You have our full support for your situation, Carrie," she said. "We're prepared to facilitate you working for us remotely."

When they told Carrie's father the news, he hesitated, his eyes clouding.

"You really want to uproot your lives to come back here?"

"Yes," Carrie said.

"You're sure about this? I mean with all that—you know."

"Yes, Dad. I thought you'd be happy."

He swallowed. His eyes brightened, then he smiled at Emily and said, "All right. Well, now, how 'bout that."

Aware of Luke's wish to leave the LAPD, Carrie's father said he was confident he could get him on with the county.

"Even with my history?" Luke asked.

"You were cleared, weren't you?"

"I was."

"The county will look beyond that. They need deputies. Now, you'd see a drop in pay from the LAPD."

"Fine with me, Vern," Luke said. "It would be a new start."

When Carrie and Luke arrived back in Los Angeles, they got things rolling, starting with Luke's application for deputy with Clear River County. He sailed through the process and got the job. The county provided a relocation bonus, health plan and other incentives because of his qualifications.

The sheriff's office wanted Luke to start right away, so he

moved to Texas first, staying briefly with his father-in-law, while Carrie tied up loose ends in California. And through video calls, she helped Luke find the rental house in Cedar Breeze.

Now, as Carrie finished changing Emily and the kettle's whistle subsided, Pearl continued asking about today's session.

"So, what did Dr. Bernay say?"

"We went over the move."

Carrie related points while sitting on the sofa next to Pearl.

"I see," Pearl said when she'd finished. They sipped tea as Emily played. "Want my two cents?"

"Sure."

"Vern needs you back home."

Carrie searched Pearl's face, void of makeup. She looked at her aunt's auburn hair, gray at the temples, into her hazel eyes, then hugged her.

"We'll miss you," Carrie said.

"I'll miss you all like crazy." Pearl's voice weakened. "In fact, to deal with it all, I'm heading off on a six-month around-the-world cruise, right after you move."

"Wow. Really?"

"It sounds cold, but I had a long talk with Vern. You know we never saw eye to eye on things. I offered to put off the cruise and move in with him for a spell—he didn't want that. He'll be happy to have you back in Texas. So he insisted I go."

"Sounds like Dad."

"You keep me posted. We should be able to keep in touch."

"Six months, my gosh."

"Residuals have been good. I've been saving."

They soon finished their tea, and Pearl watched Emily while Carrie began collecting items.

She cast about the house, looking for the things she wanted to pack herself before the movers arrived. In a short time, she came to an unmarked cardboard box. Carrie knew what was in there. She'd wanted to burn the contents, but felt compelled—

no, she felt a duty—to keep them. She traced her fingers over the folded flaps. The box held news stories, mostly from Texas papers, chronicling her tragic case. Even though Carrie couldn't remember much, the news articles detailed what was known to have happened.

It had been thirteen years now.

Three teenage schoolgirls walked into the woods at the edge of Clear River, Texas. Two were murdered. The sole survivor, found unconscious on the riverbank, remembered little about the crime. That girl was Carrie Hamilton, daughter of Vernon Hamilton, Clear River County Sheriff.

7

Going house to house, business to business, Luke glanced back at the grief-stricken truck driver standing with the investigators.

Luke distanced himself, pressing on with his assignment.

He stood on doorsteps and asked residents if they'd recalled seeing anything unusual the previous night. He entered stores, asking employees at a computer shop, a diner and a gas station the same questions. He got names and numbers of staff who were around last night. And he asked if anyone had security camera footage.

But while taking down preliminary statements and tapping in notes, his moistened fingers began slipping on his tablet. Several times at each location he had to ask people to spell their names more than once, or repeat information they'd already provided.

"Last night?" one man said. "Hell, no, I didn't see anything, not in that storm."

An older woman stroked the cat she held in her arms and looked toward the scene. "A dead woman down there? Dear Lord," she said, shaking her head. "No, I didn't see anything."

He came to a house where a man and woman answered the door together. They were husband and wife—they hadn't noticed anything but still had their theories.

"I bet she was shot," the husband said. "A drug deal."

"Yes, a murder. Was she murdered?" the woman asked.

"We can't speculate," Luke said. "I don't know."

Finished with his last canvass, he walked to his car. Nearing the scene, he looked at the tarp covering the woman's body. He stared until the sudden yelp of a siren, a city unit pulling out, shifted his thoughts. He got into his car and radioed dispatch. A few minutes later, in keeping with instructions, he drove to Clear River Police Department headquarters downtown.

Along the way, Luke's mouth went dry as he was assailed by images of the woman under the tarp and the storm.

Stop. Keep your mind on what's real.

He seized his water from the front seat and drank, fear swirling through him. The day after tomorrow, he had to go to California.

Then I'll fly back with Carrie and Emily. The movers are scheduled; it's all coordinated.

His chest tightened, thoughts and buildings blurring. He forced himself to stay calm upon arrival at Clear River PD. He parked, then entered the new one-story brick building.

Inside, Luke was directed to the Criminal Investigations Division, where he reported to Sergeant Gary Raeburn.

"Appreciate the county's help," Raeburn said.

"Not much in these statements. Nobody was really out last night, with the storm and all."

"Yeah, we figured."

"Get Ready N' Go Gas will provide security footage—with a warrant. I called the clerk who worked the night shift. He doubts there's anything there, but worth a look," Luke said.

"No problem, we'll take care of that. We'll make a public appeal for anyone to come forward, and for dashcam footage."

"Think you'll get anything you can use, what with the storm?"

"Technology's getting better. We can enhance these things. Thanks again." Raeburn gave a small wave.

"Can I ask you something?"

"What's that?"

"Do you have anything more on a timeline, or her clothing?"

Raeburn's smile faded as he looked at him.

"How did you know it was a woman?"

"My supervisor told me when he called me in? And a distraught man arrived at the scene concerned about his daughter."

Considering Luke's response, Raeburn said: "I see. Word's getting out. What's your interest in the timeline and clothing?"

"You know, if tips come our way, we can filter them out, save you a lot of trouble."

Raeburn stuck out his bottom lip.

"Let me ask the detectives." He made a call and began relaying information to Luke while on the phone. "She left the house party around midnight…Right…They looked for her but she wandered off in the rain…Right…"

Luke's stomach tensed as Raeburn continued.

"Wearing sneakers…Jeans…Right…A pink top…"

Pink.

His heart ready to burst, Luke slid his hand into his pocket, feeling the plastic bag holding the small piece of fabric.

"…it's a pink pullover hoodie…over a black T-shirt with a US flag…Right…Thanks." Ending the call, Raeburn turned to Luke. "You got that?"

Luke had shoved the plastic bag deep into his pocket and was busy tapping notes into his phone.

"Yes, sir, I got that."

Later, driving through the city, he pulled the bag with the piece of pink fabric bearing a single pink button from his pocket and tossed it into the wind.

8

Most days, people couldn't tell if Vernon Hamilton was a happy man or an angry one.

Like today, at Bush Airport in Houston, waiting at carousel number 4 in terminal C. The arrivals board confirmed his daughter's family's flight from LAX had landed right on time.

But Vernon's thoughts were not evident under his thick silver mustache. They rarely were. Except for when the edges drooped in displeasure. For the times he might be happy, his eyes crinkled, like when the pentas in his late wife's garden bloomed and drew the hummingbirds.

Concealing feelings had given Vernon a face as inscrutable as those on Mount Rushmore. An expression carved over time from all he'd seen. First with the Highway Patrol, then as a Texas Ranger, then as a county sheriff. It had also evolved as he'd been widowed and tasked with raising his daughter as a single father, helping her through the adversity she was coping with to this day.

When her mother had died suddenly, Carrie was devastated, leaving Vernon to believe, and hope, it was the worst thing she would ever face. But a few years later, Carrie was nearly killed in an attack in which two other teens from her high school were murdered.

Vernon winced internally because that was a painful time for Carrie and for him. He was glad he got her out of the county to live with Pearl. He wanted her to put Texas in her rearview mirror and build a good life. A solid life. And she did that with Luke and Emily.

He was of two minds that Carrie had made the decision to move back home. He was fearful about the risk of her conjuring up ghosts. *Dangerous ones.* Still, he had to admit, having her and her family with him in the time he had left, well, that suited him just fine.

Vernon looked around at the busy, expansive terminal with its polished floor, standing there in his boots, jeans and blue gingham shirt. He no longer had his silver star pinned on his chest, but he wore his white Stetson. Not everybody in Texas wore a cowboy hat, but Vernon did. He liked that it kept the sun out of his eyes, but he had to admit, wearing it might've been more of a throwback to his days as a Ranger and sheriff, a last grasp at authority.

"Oh, no!"

Vernon turned to the adjacent carousel where a woman was tussling with several bags while corralling two toddlers. She appeared to be alone, and her attempt to stack her bags on a cart was failing. He moved with surprising quickness for his sixty-seven years, offering to help.

"Oh, please," she said.

He restacked the bags securely on her cart.

"Thank you, sir, you're very kind."

He touched the brim of his Stetson and nodded as a new stream of passengers flooded the area. Surveying faces, he found Carrie's as she hurried to him ahead of Luke, who was holding Emily. Vernon opened his arms and Carrie rushed into them in a long, strong embrace.

"Oh, Daddy," she said through tears before stepping back, giving her father a once-over and a shaky smile.

"And there's our little angel," Vernon said, looking to Emily as Luke passed the baby to him. Vernon's eyes crinkled at the corners as his granddaughter reached for his hat.

He put it on her and she nearly disappeared under it. He tilted it so he could see her little face.

"Welcome home," he said.

Minutes later, bags were dispensed onto the carousel. Luke loaded theirs onto a cart and they navigated their way to the terminal garage and Vernon's Ford F-150 with the crew cab.

Vernon unlocked the doors and indicated the new baby car seat base in the back. "It's the one you told me to get," he said to Carrie's delight.

After Carrie buckled Emily in, Luke got into the back with the baby, while Carrie rode up front with her father. As Vernon wheeled the Ford from the terminal along the parkway, they made small talk: the flight was smooth; Emily slept; she was a good flyer except for the descent, when she'd fussed a bit.

Passing the Sonic Drive-In and the Waffle House, Carrie gave an update on Pearl—she was well and might come for Thanksgiving after her cruise. The subject shifted to the new house in Cedar Breeze and logistics about the move. Their conversation was pleasant, but working through traffic, Vernon sensed that Carrie was assessing him. And by the time they got onto US 59 for the drive to Clear River, their conversation went beyond small talk.

"You look thinner, Dad."

He nodded.

"So, how're you feeling?" she asked. "I mean, really feeling?"

He lifted both hands slightly from the wheel, giving a casual shrug, then replaced them. "Fine."

"No pain, discomfort?"

He shook his head slowly.

Several long seconds went by with Carrie processing his response, studying his face, his wrinkled neck and his age-spotted hands. Finally, she patted his shoulder.

Miles later, as they left greater Houston, Vernon found Luke looking at him in the rearview mirror. His son-in-law asked: "Vern, have you heard anything new through your channels on the woman found at the strip mall at the north end of town?"

"Like what?"

"Anything on cause?"

"Word is blunt trauma."

"Really?"

"I'm hearing she was under the influence, could've been from falling, or from something else." Vernon held Luke in his gaze for a moment, forcing Luke to look away. "Why you interested? It's a city case."

"We supported them. I canvassed."

"Hmm. Well, I heard nothing more than that." Luke nodded before Vernon added, "But my pals at the county tell me you're doing a good job."

Surprised by the compliment, Luke smiled. "Good to hear, Vern. I can't thank you enough for putting in a good word and all."

"Weren't nothing. You were plenty qualified."

"Yeah, but with my issue—" Luke gazed out the window.

Finding Luke's doleful expression in his mirror, Vernon said: "Forget it, Luke. California's in the past." He turned to Carrie. "And what about you? How're you feeling?" Then echoing her: "I mean, really feeling?"

She took in a long breath, then let it out.

"Anxious about moving back here because of—you know."

"I do."

"I can't wait to see the house, though—it looks nice."

"And your therapist, what did she say?"

"She said I could handle this, and I'll continue sessions with her online."

"So, after all this time, it still helps?"

"It does. She said by being back here, maybe I could remember more about what happened."

"Maybe it's just as well you don't remember."

"Why?"

"It was such a terrible thing you went through. I mean, do you really want to relive it?"

"Some days I want answers."

"And other days?"

"I don't know. Dr. Bernay said remembering could be traumatic. But also that I could get control of it by standing up to the past."

After listening, Vernon was silent for the longest time, sorting through Carrie's concern. Finally, he said, "You know, I appreciate what you two did, picking up your lives like this. You didn't have to do this, and if you change your minds, that's okay."

"Dad, we want to do this."

He looked at her, then in the mirror at his granddaughter, and the corners of his eyes crinkled.

"I'm glad you're home."

Carrie patted his arm and the cab went quiet but for the baby's soft chatter.

Vernon leaned his elbow on the door frame, cupping his chin in his hand. Staring ahead at the road blurring under his wheels, he thought back to his doctor telling him his condition was terminal.

You won't feel any pain, he'd said.

No, no pain.

Just the torture of the secret I've been carrying all these years.

9

The next morning, the hiss of air brakes, a sharp creak, then muffled conversation signaled the arrival of the movers.

When Luke went to greet them and get his SUV out of the driveway to give them room for unloading, he froze.

Vernon, who'd come to help, was squatted at Luke's front bumper, inspecting it.

He turned to Luke.

"Just happened to be looking at your front end, got a little dinged up. What happened here?"

"That. Yeah," Luke said. "Got hit with debris in that storm a few nights back. It was pretty intense."

"You going to tend to it? Guys at JB Paint and Body are good."

"I'll do it when things get settled."

Vernon stood, becoming aware that the crew was waiting. "Guess you'll want to get the show started."

Unloading went smoothly with Carrie and Luke directing the crew on where to put items. For much of the time, trading off with Carrie, Vernon held Emily or kept her amused out of the way in the yard. The movers finished by early evening, and after Luke gave them each a seventy-five-dollar tip, they climbed into the rig and pulled out.

Most things had been placed well enough for the family to have supper together. Vernon was partial to Chinese food, so Carrie called for a delivery order. She got Emily strapped into her high chair, found plates and cutlery, then set the table. After the order came and they began eating, Carrie nodded to her rocker in the corner.

"Did you see the chair Luke got me, Dad?"

"I noticed." Vernon looked at it. "What kind of wood?"

"Oak," Luke said.

"Should last a long time."

Vernon's words hung in the air, Carrie and Luke reading the subtext as Vernon reached a hand out to Emily. She took hold of his pinky finger while eating the chicken Carrie had cut up for her off her tray.

"It's a beautiful chair," Carrie said. "I love it."

"Seems to me—" Vernon spooned fried rice from a container "—that you had two cars in California."

"Luke drove our SUV here, and I sold our small car to a friend in LA just before the move."

"With the baby and all, you'll need a second car," Vernon said.

"We're going to look for a used one here," Luke said.

"I've got a friend who runs a car lot in town, Randy Ringo's Auto. He buys late models from rental car companies. I'll talk to him, see if he'll give you a deal on a good SUV, if you like?"

Luke and Carrie traded glances.

"That'd be great," Luke said.

"Consider it done."

Vernon drank some of his iced tea, then said, "And you were saying you want a home security system installed?"

"I'm looking into that," Luke said.

"Well, a big local company, Pace-M-Tec, does the schools, businesses, residential. I know the people there and can get someone to come over."

"If it's not too much trouble," Carrie said.

"No trouble. You both have your hands full."

"All right, that'll be good, Vern," Luke said.

"Thanks, Dad," Carrie said.

Vernon paused eating. "And I think Carrie should have a gun."

"No, Dad."

"Because," Vernon continued, "some folks in this town can't help thinkin' what they think about what happened, Carrie. They won't let it go. Just a precaution."

"No."

Looking at her in silence, fear clouded Vern's eyes.

"I've got the spray," she offered as consolation. "And I've got my own cop in the house."

Vernon nodded, ending the discussion with: "It's my job to look after you."

"We know, Dad."

As they continued eating, Carrie stole subtle glances at her father. His hair had thinned and whitened. For a second, she thought his eyes were tinged with a degree of something she'd seen only twice before. Once, when she'd stared into them after waking in her hospital bed after the attack.

And before that, when she was in school…

…*in Mrs. Holbrook's geography class, where Mrs. Holbrook was guiding everyone while they labeled and completed their charts of the earth's geological periods. Carrie was detailing the Cenozoic era and the evolution of humans when Mrs. Holbrook said something that had nothing to do with the chart.*

"*Carrie Hamilton?*"

"*Yes.*"

Mrs. Holbrook asked her to go to the classroom door where Principal Taylor was waiting, her face a mix of sadness and concern. The principal took Carrie's hand and escorted her to her office, where Carrie's father stood, his big hat in his hands, his hair slightly mussed, his face creased. She looked into his eyes, which were reddened, clouded with desperation and fear as he lowered himself to her, his voice creaking like it had broken. His Adam's apple rising and falling as he took her hands, battling to say what he had to say.

"Carrie, sweetheart, this morning your mother..."

He'd hit a wall.

"What about her?" Carrie looked at him, then at Principal Taylor, whose face was a mask of sorrow, then back to her father.

"What about Mom, Daddy?"

"Sweetheart, she's gone."

"Gone where?"

"Carrie." Her father found his voice. "She died. She had a brain seizure and fell down the stairs."

The principal's office spun with Carrie's screams...

Now, as Carrie watched him playing tenderly with Emily's fingers, she saw it again in his eyes, as brief as a falling star: the desperation and fear for all the things they knew.

But when his eyes crinkled at Emily, they were bright and strong, making Carrie demand answers from heaven on how her father could be dying. It only underscored that it was right for her to move back home and confront whatever waited for her here.

With supper done, Carrie put Emily to bed. Luke and Vernon cleared the table, then they all settled into the sofa and chairs amid the clutter of the living room, talking until night fell and it was time for her dad to leave. Luke brought Vernon his hat, and he gripped Luke's shoulder warmly, then he hugged Carrie and kissed her cheek.

"I'm glad you're here," he said. "I'll help with everything I can."

"We know, Dad."

"Thank you," Luke said.

Vernon took a long look at them, then left.

Sometime in the night, while Luke snored, Carrie heard Emily, awake and fussing in her room.

Carrie dragged herself from bed. In the ambient light she bumped around unpacked boxes, feeling her way in the unfamiliarity of the new house to the kitchen. She prepared a bottle, got Emily, then returned carefully to the living room, sitting in her new rocking chair, absorbing its comfort. Feeding her baby and rocking, Carrie's weary mind reflected on the last few days and the changes in their lives.

Doubt flared.

It was right to move back.

Her father needed them here for the time he had left.

But every horrible thing in my life happened here, in Clear River County.

Holding her baby and rocking in the dim light, Carrie knew they were coming, she felt them coming, inching at the edges of her memory like wolves in the darkness creeping toward the firelight.

Carrie looked toward the window.

Nothing there but the night.

But in her mind, as if disinterred from the far reaches of memory, she saw them as they were that day.

Erin Eddowes and Abby Hall.

10

Luke pressed his phone to his ear and lowered his voice.

"No, I don't have a name or date of—"

The woman at the hospital cut him short. "We protect our patients' privacy."

"Yes, I underst—"

"Do you have a warrant?"

"No, nothing like that. I'm checking on a potential victim of a crime."

A few seconds of silence passed before the woman broke it.

"The details again, Deputy?"

Luke surveyed the patrol room in the sheriff's office once more, ensuring no one was near enough to overhear.

"White female, aged twenty to forty. The time frame on the date I gave you, at 11:30 p.m., to twenty-four hours after that."

"Still vague. Anything else?"

Luke glimpsed a figure—*someone in uniform*—passing through the patrol room, disappearing at the edge of his periphery. Luke lowered his voice again.

"Bear in mind the time frame," he said. "It was an anonymous tip from a person who saw a woman in distress, maybe injured, walking along River Road near Fawn Ridge. Do you have any admissions or walk-ins that fit?"

A burst of typing on a keyboard came through the line, punctuated by clicks. Luke imagined the hospital official likely scowling as she searched.

"No," she said.

"You're certain?"

Sighing with exasperation, she said, "In that time, we had a woman in her seventies with a reaction to medication; a man who fractured his hand; a teenage boy with abdominal pain; and an infant with a fever. That's it."

"Thank you."

That was the last of the four hospitals serving the county. He'd made the calls surreptitiously, between his duties. He'd also checked with EMS for the county, asking if paramedics had treated, or transported, anyone fitting the description.

Again, the response was negative.

Luke leaned back, his chair creaking, and dragged his hands over his face.

What's happening to me? The LAPD psychologists warned me about all the issues around post-traumatic stress—altered thinking, paranoia, guilt, self-recrimination. Is that what this is?

Am I imagining the whole thing?

I couldn't find any woman, and there's no match for anyone hurt. The fabric could've been from a rag, or something tossed in the storm. It could've been from something earlier.

Right?

I feel like I'm losing my grip.

"Luke?"

He looked up at his boss, Sheriff Ellerd, standing before his desk.

"You good?"

"Yep. A little tired."

"Got a minute to talk?" Ellerd said. "In my office."

11

Clear River County Sheriff Bob Ellerd eased into his high-backed tufted leather chair.

Covering the wall behind him was a Texas flag, along with awards, citations and framed photos, some with Ellerd and politicians, and one with Ellerd and Vernon Hamilton.

Luke took a chair across from the desk.

"I wanted to chat a bit before you go back out on patrol," Ellerd said, turning to his computer monitor. Momentarily keeping his eyes on it, he said, "Dispatch tells me you requested a history of calls in East Division for the tenth, reaching into the eleventh."

Luke was silent.

Ellerd looked directly at him and asked, "Why?"

Luke felt his gut spasm. Swallowing, he cautioned himself to stay close to the truth.

"Well—" he cleared his throat "—I was off duty driving home, it was storming and I thought I spotted someone in distress. I stopped, got out and looked but didn't find anyone. That's why I was asking. So now I think it was a tree limb, an animal or something."

Luke then thought of the car damage seen by his neighbor

and Vern. He added: "I know I hit some branches in the storm, scraped up my car."

Ellerd stared at him without speaking for a long moment.

"If you saw someone needing help, you should've called it in," Ellerd said. "We could've sent someone out to check."

"But I looked and didn't see anyone. And with the storm, I didn't want to tie anyone up."

Ellerd continued staring.

"A word of advice," he said. "Next time you need dispatch to do a search for you or get a specific history, go through the sergeant or lieutenant. All right?"

"Got it."

"Don't get me wrong. You're okay to search our data banks, DMV and criminal records as part of your job on your own. But we've got to log every specialized or custom search we do for our monthlies, the annual and audits."

"Understood."

Suddenly recalling how Vern had questioned him about the damage to his SUV, Luke's focus went to the photo of Vern on the wall, and Ellerd noticed him looking.

"Yeah, that's Vernon up there. Man, we go back." Ellerd smiled. "He brought me along when I started as reserve, then jailer and moved my way up. Supported my run for sheriff. And here I am in my second term. Probably run for a third."

Luke nodded.

"I know he's your father-in-law, put in a good word for you. But the fact is, being with the LAPD, you were qualified and we had a spot to fill. And I'm glad to have you. Wish we could pay you more but my hands are tied."

"It's okay. I get it."

"As I mentioned when you started, you might find things a bit slower, the culture a little different. You've been with us a short while but you're doing fine."

"Appreciate that, sir, thanks."

"What am I sayin'? You're local, raised over in Dixon, right?"

"That's right."

"And are you and Carrie all settled in now?"

"Almost."

"That's a pretty part of the county. You got a nice little bit of twisting road out there. I mean, it's our job to know every inch of our yard, isn't it?"

Luke hesitated. "It is."

"But it's changing fast. We got more new developments, like Fawn Ridge, eating up the rural areas with those big new hotel-size houses. I'm ramblin' on."

"That's okay."

Ellerd sat straighter and leaned forward. "Before I let you get back to it, I want to ask, how's Carrie?"

"Good, she's doing good," Luke said in that socially super-ficial way people say "Good."

"It can't be easy for her, coming back home here, thirteen years after it happened."

"No, but we wanted to come back, you know, with our sit-uation and Vern's situation."

Ellerd paused.

"Yes, it seems like the right thing, given all the circumstances and Vern's diagnosis." Ellerd rubbed his chin. "Listen, can you please let Carrie know that if she remembers anything about the case, we'd be happy to talk to her."

"I'll let her know."

"It may be a cold case, but it's still open. I got two good de-tectives handling it, Blake Mallory and Eugene Cobb." Ellerd smiled. "Blake's due to retire soon and would love to clear it. Anyway, I'll tell you, there's always pressure to solve a case like this. It's an awful thing for the families to bear—they need a resolution, you understand?"

"I do."

"Hell, I want to clear it." Ellerd studied his palms. "We looked at a number of people, but the killer could be dead, in prison or living free among us. There were all sorts of theories, all kinds of speculation at the time."

Ellerd shook his head slowly.

"They even looked hard at Carrie," he said. "They were just being thorough, leaving no stone unturned."

Ellerd stared at nothing, as if looking into the past.

"Abby Hall and Erin Eddowes. Both seventeen. Good girls from good families. Loved. Popular in school."

Ellerd directed a question at Luke.

"I understand from Vern that Carrie's had therapy over the years, to help her cope, or heal, as they say?"

"That's right, and it has helped her."

"Maybe now, being back here, she might remember something—any detail, no matter how small, might help us solve this case."

"I guess time will tell."

Ellerd crossed his arms. "You got that right," he said. "Two girls were murdered and Carrie's our only living witness."

Later, after his shift ended, Luke walked through the parking lot to his SUV.

Glancing at the damage, grappling with his mystery, he heard a low rumbling.

"Hey, Luke."

He turned to see Deputy Clayton Smith at the wheel of a shining blue Mustang fastback. Luke followed Clay's gaze, which lingered on his Chevy's front end before shifting to Luke.

"We're going to Willie's. Join us."

"Thanks, Clay, but I should be going home. Beautiful car. Is that a '67?"

"It's a '68. I saw you come out of Bob's office earlier. Looked like he was giving you a hard time. Come out, just for one."

Luke gave it a thought, deciding he could text Carrie.

"A quick one."

★ ★ ★

His eyes adjusting to the darkened bar, Luke spotted Clay at a table with two other deputies.

Johnny Cash's "Ring of Fire" mingled with the smell of beer and deep-fried food on the cool air as Clay kicked out an empty chair for Luke.

"There he is," Clay said.

"Hey, Luke," Lonnie Welch said, resuming his conversation with Garth Reeger, who gave Luke a stiff nod. "They never caught the Zodiac and never caught Jack the Ripper." Lonnie took a swig of beer. "And they never would've caught BTK."

"But they did," Reeger said.

"His ego got the better of him," Clay said.

"Right," Lonnie said. "Son of Sam was on his way to immortality until the NYPD's police work stopped him."

"Got him on a parking ticket," Clay said as their server emerged. "What'll you have, Luke? On me."

"Thanks, Clay—a Bud Light."

"That's what I'm saying," Lonnie said, "Green River, Bundy, Dahmer, Gacy—they all messed up. It's a rare animal that can elude justice."

"What about right here?" Reeger said, shooting Luke a cold look, then the others. "Wild Pines. Still unsolved."

Reeger took a swig of his beer, then studied his bottle on the table. "What do you think happened out there in the woods with those girls, Luke?"

"I don't know, Garth."

"Any theories?"

Luke's beer came, and he nodded his thanks. "Nope."

"You must have one or two, Mr. LAPD. Mr. Son-in-Law to the former sheriff. Your wife was there. You two must've talked about it."

Lonnie and Clay traded an uneasy look.

"Knock it off, Garth," Clay said.

Luke picked up his beer, took a small drink, then set it down. "I should go."

"Stay put, there, Luke." Reeger stood, tossing crumpled bills on the table. "I gotta go. See y'all."

Watching Reeger leave, Lonnie said, "Ignore him. He thought his cousin was getting your job."

"That's right," Clay said. "So, how're you and Carrie doing? You grew up over near Dixon, right?"

"I did."

"Must be strange moving back. How's it going?"

"We're settling in, taking it one day at a time."

"Was Bob giving you a hard time?" Clay said.

"Not really." Luke shook his head. "I love your Mustang."

"I like restoring cars. Got a few in the works out at my place."

"So, Luke—" Lonnie leaned closer "—I'm sorry, I got to ask, did Bob tell you about Cobb and Mallory?"

"He did."

"I heard they're hoping with Carrie back, she'll remember something."

Luke nodded.

"Didn't she have a serious head injury?" Clay said. "Messed with her memory and everything?"

Luke nodded again.

"Don't mean to pry," Clay said.

"Yes, you do, Clay." Lonnie chuckled. "Luke, did you know Clay here's studying to make detective, maybe take the slot when Mallory retires?"

"I did not know." Luke raised his bottle, saluting Clay.

"We'll see about that," Clay said, looking at his beer. "I saw the little bit of damage to your Blazer there. Let me know when you want to get it fixed. I know guys."

Luke raised a palm. "That's mighty kind, Clay. But it's not serious, and with all we got going, I'll get around to it. Thank you."

"Anytime."

"So," Lonnie said, "everyone knows they really looked hard at Carrie for Wild Pines. Then Donnie Ray Hyde, sitting there on death row, surfaces as the one who likely killed those two girls. You guys think it'll ever be solved, what with Hyde's execution coming up?"

"Who knows? Time will tell," Clay said. "What do you think, Luke?"

"I really don't know." Luke shook his head slowly, staring at his half-finished beer.

12

Driving on a country road a few miles from town, Carrie adjusted her grip on the steering wheel.

I need to do this. Dr. Bernay said I could handle it.

Taking a breath, she first thought of other things, like the pictures Pearl had sent from Honolulu. *Sailing for Suva, Fiji. Hope all is good there. Hug the baby, Vern and Luke,* Pearl wrote with a photo of her toasting the sunset on the Pacific.

Missing her aunt, Carrie wished they could be together. *Especially because of where I'm going today*, she thought as she navigated her almost-new, low-mileage, blue Ford SUV.

She and Luke had used the money from selling their second car in LA, and some from the sale of their house, to buy it. Her father and Randy Ringo helped with plates and registration. Carrie had had it about a week now and liked that the new-car smell lingered. She looked into the baby back-seat mirror they'd installed, seeing Emily buckled into her rear-facing seat, content and humming to herself.

Carrie was grateful to have the second car; it gave her freedom to run errands and do what she needed to do.

Her destination was coming up, pulling her attention back

to what lay ahead. Repositioning her hands, she slowed down, turning at the mouth of a narrow paved road.

She traveled through an open wrought-iron gate, passing under its ornate iron arch that bore the words: Oak Rock Cemetery.

Over ten acres of well-kept lawns bordered by precision-cut hedges and shaded by oak and pine trees. Carrie knew that Oak Rock was the county's oldest cemetery. Her history teacher once brought her class here to see the weatherworn crosses and markers of people killed at the time of the Civil War.

Driving slowly along one of the twisting roadways lacing the grounds, Carrie reached the section where her mother was buried. She stopped, shut the engine off and got Emily into her stroller. Moving along the soft grass, she was pierced with a sliver of apprehension.

It's okay, she told herself, glancing around.

Nobody had followed her. No one was in the immediate area. She had pepper spray in her purse. And the groundskeeper she saw in the distance would hear her if she needed help.

It's okay.

Arriving at her mother's grave, Carrie stared at the granite headstone for a moment before kneeling at it. She traced her fingers over its letters, summoning memories, feeling them coming gently with images and the beginnings of music and…

Her mother, at the sink, the radio going with a song. She's excited, calling, "Vern, get in here!" Her mother and father dancing like a dream to Solomon Burke's "Cry to Me."

Now here was Carrie much younger, going with her mom down to Reddick's pecan orchard and roadside stand. Carrie helping her in the kitchen. Her mom made the best pecan pies in Clear River County but declined to try for a ribbon at the fair. "Oh, no, I'd never win, sweetie."

Then her mom's joy at getting her real estate license. Watching her father lift her mom in a victory hug, taking them all out to celebrate for a steak dinner at Braddson's Sunset Grill.

And when her mother worked, she dressed so fine, her hair and makeup perfect, her perfume fragrant. Always going out, showing properties. Then came the dark times, when through the closed bedroom door, Carrie heard the late-night muffled arguments between her mom and dad. He'd grown jealous of her always going out, making connections, always having meetings and drinks with men, some of them rich. "It's my job. What about your job, Vern? You're out at all hours, and you could get killed." Doors slamming, Carrie running down the stairs, her father leaving. Carrie seeing her mother and the crumpled edges of the tissue she squeezed in her fist.

Over the years, their arguments subsided, her parents adjusting, or maybe resigned, to things as they were, until that day Carrie's dad stood in Principal Taylor's office holding his hat, the earth shaking under Carrie's feet. Her screams. The numbness of the nightmare that followed, kissing her mother for the last time as she lay in her casket, her skin as cold and hard as stone. Carrie's tears falling on her mother's face. Watching them lower her into the ground, feeling so raw, as if a claw had raked its talons across her heart.

Emily cooed, pulling Carrie back to the moment. She kissed her daughter, reached under the stroller's seat into the basket for the collection of flowers she'd brought: white lilies, daisies and baby's breath. She placed them at the base of the headstone.

"I miss you, Mom," Carrie said aloud. "This is Emily, your granddaughter. I wish you had the chance to hold her. I'm sorry for not visiting as much as I should have. There were things I had to deal with. But we're back now, all together with Dad… and…time's working against us."

Carrie paused.

"Mom, if you can hear me, please help me find the truth."

She patted her mother's stone, stood and braced for what was coming.

Carrie pushed the stroller from her mother's section, across the curve of roadway to the next section. Threading grave sites, she came to one. The headstone was blue pearl granite. The name was Abigail Elissa Hall, and the stone bore the dates of her birth and death with her portrait etched in the center over the words:

Our Daughter. Taken Suddenly. Always In Our Hearts.

A minute of silence passed as Carrie stared at Abby's grave. Then she reached into the stroller's basket for a single pink rose. She placed it at the base of the headstone, then made her way to the next grave site she needed to see.

The stone was a granite silver cloud, bearing the name Erin Lee Eddowes; the birth date showed she was the same age as Abby. The same date of death. And a color photo of her smiling, looking radiant. The inscription:

Gone Too Soon. Eternally Loved.

Carrie gazed upon the stone for about a minute before placing a pink rose on its base. A breeze lifted her hair and she corralled the loose strands, thinking hard, thinking how…

…*it's been thirteen years since Abby and Erin were murdered…but I survived. Why?*

Carrie looked across the cemetery toward Abby's stone.

Why did we go in the woods that day?

You were never my friends.

13

That afternoon, Carrie stopped to pick up some things at River King Grocery in Clear River.

Paying close attention to prices, she realized most items were less expensive than they were in Los Angeles. Eggs, bread and milk each cost less—a good thing, and she'd welcome all the good she could get after her sobering visit to the cemetery.

While shopping to the strains of the store's soft background music, Carrie weighed her psychologist's advice to let things unfold naturally with everyday matters. She was doing that now, finding joy in cheaper groceries for her family.

"Well, this is nice," Carrie said to Emily, who was strapped into the child seat. "Even the rice costs less here."

Placing two packages in her cart, she noticed a woman nearby. They'd happened upon each other in previous aisles, with Carrie catching the trace of her stare each time. Carrie continued to the next aisle, stopping to select salad dressing. Putting a bottle in her cart, she turned to see the woman suddenly standing beside her.

"Excuse me. I'm so sorry, but are you Carrie?"

She looked the same age as Carrie. She had nice hair and makeup, and there was something familiar about her. Carrie was trying to place her when the woman said, "Carrie Hamilton?"

"Yes, but it's Carrie Conway now."

"Oh, my goodness! Carrie, it's me." The woman placed her hand to her own chest. She had beautiful nails. "Lacey! Lacey Lee! We went to high school together!"

Recognition dawned.

"Oh, my gosh, Lacey! Yes! Hi!"

They gave each other an awkward hug.

"So, it's true," Lacey said. "Clay told me it was happening."

"Clay?"

"My husband, Clayton Smith. I'm actually Lacey Smith now. Clayton's a deputy. He works with Luke. That's how I knew you were moving back."

"Ahh, I see. Yes, it's true. We moved back."

"You look good, Carrie." Lacey lowered her gaze to Emily. "Oh, and this must be your precious little one. What's her name?"

"Emily."

"Welcome to Clear River, Emily. What an angel. She's so sweet."

"Thanks," Carrie said. "I love your hair and nails."

"You're too kind." Lacey grinned with a modest wave. "Had it all done at the Always Charming Salon."

"They do nice work."

"They better. I own the shop."

"Oh, wow."

"It's a little place in town. Got one in Lufkin and one in Nacogdoches. But we're busy and we have fun. Drop by some time, we'll give you a discount."

"That'd be nice, thank you."

"Were you working in movies and TV in California?"

"I did graphic design for program and film promotions. Still do—the company's been great, arranged for me to work remotely."

"How long have you been back now?"

"Not long, a couple weeks."

"Clay said you guys were in Cedar Breeze?"

"We are."

"Looks pretty there. I was going to drop by, but I figured you were busy."

"Yeah, still got things to unpack, still settling in."

"Listen." Lacey blinked several times. "I'm sorry about Vern."

Carrie paused, realizing that in a small town few things were kept secret.

"I mean, with him being the former sheriff, most all people at the sheriff's office know."

And likely everyone at your hair salons, too, Carrie thought, nodding with a weak smile while caressing Emily's hair.

"I mean," Lacey continued, "I'm sure it's the best thing that you're back even though—"

"Even though" hung in the air when Lacey stopped herself, and Carrie looked at her to finish. Lacey cleared her throat. "It must be hard for you, what with your dad's condition and, well, you know, with all that you went through back then with the case, and it still being unsolved."

The warmth of their meeting started to melt, with Carrie turning from Lacey to Emily, brushing her cheek.

"Nice to see you, Lacey. We should be going," she said.

"I'm sorry for prattling on. I didn't mean anything by it."

"No, it's okay, really."

"Wait. We're having a party at our place this weekend. Why don't you and Luke join us? So many people will be happy to see you and catch up. Please, come."

Carrie looked around, pushing down the emotion rising in her, and began to shake her head.

"That's lovely, but I don't know."

"It would be really nice if you could come."

In hesitating, she noticed Lacey's overflowing cart. Lacey followed her gaze and they both smiled.

"You got a lot of stuff there, Lacey."

Lacey rolled her eyes. "Tell me about it. This is my second trip to the store in two days. We're catering, but I like to have plenty of extras. We're good at parties."

"I'll talk to Luke and let you know."

"Good. You can reach me through the shop."

Lacey gave her a hug, then a wiggly finger wave to Emily.

At home later, as Carrie was feeding Emily a spaghetti dinner, she told Luke about her day.

"Guess who I ran into getting groceries?"

Luke didn't answer. He was engrossed in his phone.

Wiping Emily's face, Carrie turned to him and, from what she could see, he was scrolling through news sites.

"Hello?"

"Sorry." He put his phone down. "Who was it?"

"What's so important?"

"Nothing. Who did you run into?"

Carrie let a few seconds pass.

"Lacey Smith. Clay's wife."

"Oh, yeah. You went to school with both of them. Clay was telling me she has a couple of hair salons and they're doing well."

"Lacey invited us to a big party at their place."

"A party?" Luke's face softened as he took stock of Carrie. "What did you say? Do you want to go? I mean, how do you feel about that?"

As Carrie resumed feeding Emily, she considered Dr. Bernay's suggestion that embracing new experiences and creating memories could give her a sense of control, make her more confident about living in the community again.

"I think going to the party could be a good thing."

14

Vernon Hamilton's car radio spurts—dispatch is calling.

"Four-Six in South Division requests you attend Memorial, Code Three."

"What does he have?"

"Stand by."

Vernon inventories recent calls his people handled in SD: two traffic stops; a hiking injury in Wild Pines Forest; a possible burglary in Tagallet Mobile Home Park. Did he miss anything? Keying his microphone, he responds.

"Ten-four, on my way… Seventy-Five to Four-Six, what do we have?"

Seconds later Bob Ellerd, the deputy in Unit Four-Six, texts: Carrie taken to Memorial.

That's all it says.

His engine roars, fear knifing through him. His daughter—the only family he has left. He arrives in minutes, trotting through Emergency, the smell overwhelming, the PA system announcements ringing in his ears. He spots Ellerd, face taut with concern, telling him Carrie's going to be okay. A doctor takes him aside, unable to explain what happened, telling him Carrie has a concussion, multiple fractures, lacerations, contusions. She's in shock.

"But she's stable."

Seeing her unconscious in bed, bandaged, bruised…tubes, monitors blinking… Vernon holds her hand, his heart twisting. What happened? He steps into the hall, joining Ellerd in the corner with a man in his fifties who has mussed hair, a blanket draped over wet clothes. Leon Bryant, a mechanic, is repeating what he knows as Vern stands over him.

"I was fishin' in the big creek in Wild Pines when I heard screams. Upstream I saw something big coming down the water to me, knocking against the rocks. Lord, I think, it's a woman, a girl—I'm thinking she's hiking and fell in. I pulled her onto the grass. She was bleeding and banged up good, but she was breathing and I called 911."

Vern asks: "Did you see anyone near?"

"No, sir, I was concentratin' on the girl. I pray she'll be okay."

Vern pulls Ellerd aside.

"Take Bryant to the office. Get detectives to run him, question him, search his vehicle, verify his story. Get more people to search the woods. I'll get out there as soon as I can."

Ice clinked as Vern sipped whiskey from his glass, tasting the smoky sweetness. He was home alone at his desk, thinking back to that day, thirteen years ago.

Preferring cool darkness, he'd closed the shutters. His face was lit by his computer screen, which threw soft light on the paneling of his study. The light reached his wall-mounted guns, citations and plaques, his shelves lined with books on investigative techniques of homicides, FBI studies, serial crimes and criminal histories. The light also reflected off his glasses as he looked at his wife, Doreen, smiling from the photo beside his monitor. Next to it, bottles for his prescriptions, and another photo of Carrie, Luke and the baby. He loved that picture and was looking forward to watching Emily this weekend while Carrie and Luke went to the Smiths' party. More time with his granddaughter meant the world to him. It warmed him to have them all home, and he appreciated the big step they'd taken.

It was important. Because time was slipping away.

But it was also terrible that they were here, because part of him did not want Carrie back in Texas. Not now.

He resumed opening computer files with his notes, copies of recordings on the murders of Erin Eddowes and Abby Hall. These were not the official case files. These were personal files he'd made back when he was sheriff.

Leon Bryant's version of events had checked out and detectives had cleared him. Leon was a good man who'd saved Carrie's life, and at that time, Vern had thanked him.

But there were still many unanswered questions. Back then, detectives were hoping Carrie could help them fill in the blanks after she'd recovered.

But they'd hit a wall.

Her injuries included a fractured skull, with bone nicking her brain causing some bleeding. Her recovery took longer than expected. And after her release from hospital, she still couldn't remember details about that day. At that time, Ben McGraw, one of the county's lead detectives, advocated various avenues, including hypnosis, which yielded little information. They polygraphed Carrie twice and each time the results were inconclusive. Vern soon learned that some investigators had begun to quietly regard Carrie not as a victim who'd escaped, but as a suspect who'd fled. It was about this time that the district attorney cautioned him.

As sheriff, you have a role in this case. But ultimately you have to let your investigators do their work and keep your emotions as a father out of it, Vern. Yes, you can oversee it, but keep your hands off. Do not taint or sway how this goes.

Vern had ensured that while he was sheriff, the investigation went by the book.

Now he pushed through his notes. Abby, Erin and Carrie were from the same high school, but Carrie was a junior. Abby and Erin were seniors who traveled in popular social circles, trafficking in fashion and gossip for status, according to school friends who knew them. They'd said Carrie hung out with a low-key group and was quiet, especially after her mother's death. Some said Carrie gave off "a narc vibe" because her dad was sheriff.

But no one knew why the three girls were in Wild Pines Forest that day. And other than circumstance, the investigators had no solid evidence linking Carrie to the double homicide. Only Vern and the detectives knew the key evidence that was never made public, information only the killer would know— which they held back to protect the case, and to assess the tips they'd received and suspects they looked at.

And they looked at a lot of suspects.

Austin police pointed them to a taxi driver from their city who'd allegedly harassed and stalked women. Austin detectives said he'd moved to Clear River. The man was located, questioned and ruled out. Clear River County detectives looked at recently released violent felons and registered sex offenders. All were alibied. They looked hard at Abby Hall's uncle, who, a month before the tragedy, allegedly groped Abby at a family gathering. Abby's young cousin stepped forward to say she'd witnessed it; Abby had slapped her uncle, making him so furious "he clenched his jaw and turned red." The uncle told detectives he was drunk and being playful, then proved he was in Galveston on business at the time Abby and Erin were murdered.

Vern took another sip, angry, and fearful, at what came next as he opened another file.

In the weeks that followed, conspiracies swirled about Carrie: she was faking her injuries; there was a cover-up because her dad was sheriff. What about the sudden death of Carrie's mother years earlier? What did Erin Eddowes and Abby Hall know about Carrie? Relatives and friends of the murdered girls wanted an arrest. Carrie received threatening anonymous emails and calls.

Local, state and national news outlets covered the tragedy, which remained enveloped in mystery.

Carrie's face, and Vern's, appeared with those of Abby Hall and Erin Eddowes on news sites under headlines like: **SURVIVOR CAN'T REMEMBER WHO KILLED HIGH SCHOOL TEENS; SHERIFF'S DAUGHTER SOLE SURVIVOR OF DOUBLE HOMICIDE;** and **TEXAS MURDERS ENSHROUDED IN MYSTERY.** The *Dallas Morning News*, *Houston Chronicle*, *Washington Post*, CNN, NBC News and *USA TODAY* were among those who profiled the case.

Time passed.

Through it all, Carrie struggled, but she managed to finish her senior year.

Given what Vern knew about the case, his concern for Carrie's safety did not diminish. He was happy to arrange her move to Los Angeles to live with Pearl. It broke his heart to see Carrie go, leaving him alone with ghosts, but he took comfort in getting her out of Texas so she could get on with her life.

Carrie graduated from college, got a job and set out on her own as the case grew cold.

Then they got a break.

It was close to four years after Carrie left.

Donnie Ray Hyde, a thirty-year-old drifter, was convicted of murdering sixteen-year-old Jenna Dupree in Tyler, Texas. Jenna was heading home from work when Hyde killed her in a wooded area. Hyde received the death penalty but was later linked to the murders of Erin Eddowes and Abby Hall after investigators in Tyler placed him near those crimes. But the evidence was circumstantial and Hyde denied involvement, most likely to aid his appeals against the death penalty for murdering Jenna Dupree.

That was then.

Vern took another drink.

He knew that inmates waited on death row in Texas for

years. Hyde's time was growing much shorter because his appeals, even one that went to the US Supreme Court, had failed. Vern went online and called up the latest news report on Hyde's status from the *Tyler Morning Telegraph*.

Hyde's execution date was this month.

Through his attorney, Hyde had turned to the Texas Board of Pardons and Paroles, seeking to have his death sentence commuted to life. His last chance.

The board's decision was expected anytime now.

Rubbing his chin, Vern sat up, reached for his phone and called an old friend, Cam Holloway, a lawyer who was a board member.

"Hey, Vern, you old sonofagun. I heard about your condition. Damn, I'm sorry." Holloway sounded like he was outdoors.

"You play the hand you're dealt. Say, Cam, where are you?"

"Houston. On a fairway with a view of the skyline."

"I won't keep you from your game, but I want to ask you which way the board is leaning on Donnie Ray Hyde's petition for clemency in the Tyler murder."

"We have to be confidential about cases before the board."

"I'll keep it confidential."

A long silent moment passed.

"As a favor," Vern added. "You're going to be deciding soon."

Another moment passed before Holloway broke it.

"This is confidential?"

"Absolutely."

"The governor's office has indicated that the governor has seen no new evidence to challenge the jury's verdict that Hyde is guilty. His death sentence should be carried out."

"What are his chances with the board?"

"He has no chance of a favorable decision from the board."

"None. That's it?"

"That's it. In fact, Hyde will be notified very soon, and our decision will be posted."

"Thanks, Cam."

"Take care and God bless, Vern."

After the call, Vern sat forward, thinking of what he needed to do. He decided the next call he'd make would be to someone he knew with the Texas Department of Criminal Justice. He needed to get in touch with Donnie Ray Hyde's spiritual advisor.

Vern needed to talk to Hyde before it was too late.

15

Pickup trucks and SUVs already jammed both sides of the road as well as the laneway curving through the property by the time Carrie and Luke arrived at the party.

"Lots of people," she said.

As he parked, Luke could sense Carrie's apprehension.

"We don't have to go," he said. "Because Emily's fine with your dad." He grinned. "We could sneak off to Whataburger."

Thinking how she needed to take control, Carrie squeezed his hand. "Let's go to the party."

The Smiths had a sprawling bungalow on a couple of wooded acres of countryside at the edge of town. They had a lush lawn and thriving flower beds shaded by magnolia and willow oak trees. Clay greeted them at the door, wearing a Hawaiian shirt and holding a bottle of Lone Star.

"Well, hello!" He looked at Carrie, smiling, and hugged her before patting Luke's shoulder. "Welcome. Come on in. Glad you could make it. Lacey's in the kitchen. We'll get you fixed with a drink, and there's plenty of food."

The house was filled with the hum of conversations from people scattered in knots in the foyer and the living room, which led to the patio doors. The crowd had spilled outside, more people gathered around the pool with its brilliant turquoise water. The aroma of barbecue wafted inside. Catering staff worked at the smoking grill and tended to more tables of food. Inside, the open kitchen area was also packed with guests, more food and drinks.

"Hey, Lace!" Clay called. "Look who's here!"

Lacey emerged from the group clustered at the kitchen island. She was wearing a bright floral sundress, and she rushed over, embracing them.

"Carrie! Luke! You've come! So many people want to see you!"

Heads turned, Carrie and Luke's arrival rippling through the party, creating whispers and stares.

"Can I get you a drink, Carrie?" Lacey asked.

"Maybe a little red wine? And thank you for having us."

"All right. Clay, take care of Luke." Lacey seized Carrie's hand, pulling her into the kitchen crowd.

Clayton yanked a Lone Star from a tub of ice and handed it to Luke, saying: "This way."

Inching through the crowd to the pool, they were continually intercepted by people, with Clay introducing Luke each time. In the whirl of handshakes and small talk, Luke scanned the party inside and out, recognizing deputies and staff from the sheriff's office.

In the kitchen, Lacey passed a glass of wine to Carrie.

"You know, hon," Lacey said, "they say on average, around 10 percent of people come back, or stay, where they grew up."

"Is that right?"

"Mmm." Lacey drank from the beer she was working on. "But in Clear River, it's like a quarter of the people never left. And look at you—here you are! You might remember some folks from school. Oh, here's Sarah, Sarah Curtis. Works at the salon with me."

"Hi, Sarah."

"Hi, Carrie. Lacey says you worked in Hollywood, in movies."

"I create graphics for TV and film promotion, that kind of thing."

"Ever meet anyone famous?"

Another woman moved closer to listen.

"A few times."

"Who? What were they like?" Sarah asked.

"Well, Tom Hanks was warm, friendly. Emma Stone's sharp, very funny. And Conan O'Brien's down-to-earth. And tall."

"That's so cool," Sarah said as the woman next to her touched Carrie's shoulder.

"Hi, Carrie. Sofia Vera, from English lit."

It took a second before Carrie recognized her former high school classmate.

"Yes, Sofia!" Carrie hugged her.

"I teach drama and fine arts at Clear River High."

"Really?"

"Yes, I'm dying to hear all about LA and Hollywood. Maybe you could drop by the school sometime for coffee?"

"That would be nice, Sofia."

"Lacey says you have a baby girl now?"

"Yes, her name is Emily. Dad's watching her at home now."

"That's so sweet. Show us pictures."

Setting down her wine and pulling out her phone, Carrie scrolled to photos of Emily, which drew more women closer. As they cooed, Carrie glimpsed two women across the room, shooting her icy stares.

Outside, the humid air carried loud laughter mingling with the smells of grilled meat and the pool. Some men, further along in their drinking, collected around Luke.

A man he didn't know wearing a blue Texans T-shirt stepped up to him. "Clay says you were with the LAPD."

"Yes."

"He says you grew up here near Dixon but met Carrie in LA?"

"That's right."

"What are the odds?" The man glanced around for consensus, drinking his beer and shaking his head. "Two people grow up in East Texas but meet in California and get married."

"Fate, I guess. I first set eyes on Carrie when she was still in high school working at the Whataburger here in town."

"Damn, son. I think you have the start of a country song there."

As the party progressed, Luke drank moderately, grabbing food when he could. The alcohol flowed, and so did the talk, moving from politics to football. Then Luke spotted Tom Beale, a Clear River detective who'd worked the case of the dead woman near the mini-mart. Luke reminded him how he'd helped.

"Right, I remember seeing you on scene," Beale said.

"What's the status?"

"It's been cleared."

"Cleared?"

"Yep. Not suspicious. She argued with her boyfriend at the party, ingested a lot of drugs and took off. Cause of death was an overdose."

"I heard blunt force."

"That was the original thought, but the trauma was all superficial. She must have fallen a couple times before she ended up at the scene."

"That's sad."

"Yeah."

Luke gave it a moment as relief washed over him, but only temporarily because his uncertainty of what really happened that night gnawed at him. Suddenly, someone nudged his shoulder. Turning, he saw Garth Reeger, who started poking him with a finger extended from his beer-holding hand.

"I forgot to ask you something, Luke."

"Sure."

"My sister-in-law Annie's a nurse at Memorial and she told me that not too long ago you called, searching for a victim."

Luke's pulse picked up. A couple other people from the sheriff's office, including Clay, listened as Reeger went on.

"Annie said you were asking about a white female—you had the time and date." Reeger paused to drink some beer. "I also heard you wanted dispatch to give you a call history for East Division covering the same time period as your hospital call."

Reeger let that sink in, then asked, "What're you up to in my division, partner?"

Luke felt everyone's eyes on him.

Stay calm, stay with the facts, he told himself.

"A few weeks back, I was driving home from The Old Stirrup—" Luke nodded to the deputies listening, Lonnie Welch and Shelby Slade. "You were there. It was storming. I thought I saw someone stumbling, hurt, near the road. I stopped, searched around, didn't see anyone. That's why I was asking. Nothing came of it. I figure it was trash, an animal, maybe. It was a bad storm—I hit some branches on my way home."

Lonnie nodded. "I saw your Blazer dinged up in our lot."

"Yeah, I've been meaning to get it fixed."

"You got a dashcam?" Shelby said.

Luke shook his head. "It broke on my drive from California."

"That was a helluva storm," Shelby said. "It took my shed door. What about you, Clay? Any damage?" Shelby pointed his chin to the trees, the lane to a garage and outbuildings where Clay worked on his cars.

"No, no damage, just a lot of crap in the pool," Clay said.

Luke thought that might be the end of it, but Reeger's attention remained welded to him. And whatever was behind his intoxicated eyes was not friendly.

"Know what else we all heard about you?" Reeger fingerpoked Luke again. "You got into some kind of trouble while on duty in LA and that's why you had to leave the LAPD."

A moment passed.

"It's complicated, Garth. I don't like talking about it."

"I bet." Reeger gulped more beer.

"That was investigated and he was cleared," Clay said. "Maybe you should back off, Garth."

Ignoring him, Reeger went on. "And we all know how Vern Hamilton's still tight with Bob Ellerd and most everyone else. Guess being married to Vern's daughter didn't hurt with getting you on with Clear River."

Luke remained silent.

"And she comes home, after all these years, Carrie Hamilton, the sole survivor with memory loss." Reeger took another swallow of beer. "Maybe there's a streak runnin' in the family."

"Knock it off!" Clay said.

"What do you mean, 'a streak runnin' in the family'?" Luke asked.

"You ain't heard the rumors about Vern?" Reeger shook his head, smirking. "You're one helluva investigator, there, partner. And, you know—" Reeger turned to the others from the sheriff's office "—y'all know that Barlow Botner from Polk and Neil Vance from Angelina were up for Luke's job here, until the great Vern Hamilton pulled strings."

"That's it. You're cut off, Garth. Let's get Jill to drive you home."

"Whatever," Reeger said as Clay wrangled him away to another group.

"Don't pay any mind to him, Luke," Shelby said. "Garth shoots off his mouth when he's lubricated."

"Most folks know about Vern being ill, and they get that he wanted his family here," Lonnie said.

At that moment, Clay made his way back to the group, clasping his hand on Luke's shoulder.

"Don't think twice about Garth. A while back, contractors reported theft of building materials from the construction sites at Fawn Ridge. So far, Garth's investigation has gone nowhere. It's likely why he got territorial about your queries."

Luke hadn't known about the theft, but something more pressing was on his mind.

"I want to talk to you," he told Clay.

They went to a corner of the yard offering privacy.

"What are the rumors about Vern?"

Clay's brow creased, and he glanced around, not wanting anyone to hear them over the din of the party.

"When Doreen died, the medical examiner, a friend of Vern's, concluded that she'd had a brain seizure and her neck was broken from falling down the stairs. But the talk was that Vern had a temper and thought Doreen was stepping out on him. So maybe her death was suspicious."

"Really?"

Clay nodded.

This was a revelation to Luke. He stared at Clay, who added: "Luke, nothing came of it. It's just a nasty rumor."

Luke's gaze scanned the guests, searching the kitchen, and he finally spotted Carrie, his heart breaking for her.

Clay said, "Come on, I'll show you guys my cars."

16

Across town from the party, at Carrie and Luke's home in Cedar Breeze, Vern sat in the rocking chair feeding his granddaughter a bottle of milk.

Emily gazed up at him while sucking away, her eyes bright as stars. He loved her sweet smell, her perfect tiny features. Holding her was the best medicine. When she was done eating, he placed her tenderly on his shoulder, like he had many years ago with Carrie, patting her back softly until she burped.

Then he walked with her in his arms for a time before carefully putting her down in her crib. He stood over her for a moment, smiling, watching her fall asleep.

Moving through the house, he looked approvingly at the control panel of the new home security system, with its exterior cameras and alarms. He was pleased he'd helped them get the premium package installed.

Satisfied, Vern wanted to assess the things weighing on him, things he had to take care of.

But first, he wanted a Diet Coke, so he went to the fridge. Next to it, pinned to the wall, was a large calendar with a picture of a forest. Some dates bore handwritten appointment

times, including one for Carrie's upcoming video session with
Dr. Bernay in Los Angeles.

That notation went to the heart of issues on Vern's mind.

Can Carrie still not remember anything?

Surely, she must've told her psychologist something about the
case, he thought. During her sessions, she must've remembered
a detail, something that could be helpful. He went to Carrie's
home office area, scanning her bookshelves. Maybe she kept a
journal during her counseling and wrote things down. He slid
out a few notebooks and flipped through them. Nothing there
but notes about various projects for her job.

Besides, he thought, replacing the notebooks and glancing
at her laptop, if Carrie kept a journal, she'd likely have it on
her computer. And he wasn't going to attempt to snoop there.
He already felt like he was invading her privacy.

He returned to the living room, took out his phone, scrolled
to a specific thirteen-year-old video recording and tapped Play.

He lowered the volume.

It was his copy of the first interview with Carrie after she
was released from the hospital. It was done in the small, stark
interview room at the sheriff's office. Detectives Eve Trainor
and Ben McGraw were the leads then, but they had since moved
out of state; Trainor went to Cleveland, and McGraw moved
to New Zealand.

Thirteen years ago, Vern thought again.

At that time, Carrie, just a high school junior, looked so
small, so fragile. Her face and arms were spotted with scrapes,
her head still bandaged. Even though she was not considered a
suspect, the DA had said, *These things can always take a turn*, and
insisted Carrie be Mirandized. Vern got her an attorney, Susan
Guinn, who came up from Houston. She was expensive. But
Vern wanted her sitting next to Carrie during the process because he agreed with the DA.

Things can always take a turn.

Watching the old interview still tore Vern up; he'd never get over seeing his little girl sitting at that plain table in a hard-backed chair, in that room with white cinder blocks. The same room where they questioned killers, rapists, drug dealers and other criminals.

The video played, with Eve Trainor taking the lead.

"Carrie, why did you go into the woods with Abby and Erin?"

"I don't remember."

"Do you have any recollection of seeing someone else in the woods, someone other than Abby and Erin?"

"I don't know."

"Is it possible another person was with you or was waiting there?"

"I don't know."

"In the time leading up to that day in the woods, do you recall any conversations, any dealings with Abby and/or Erin? Anything at school, at the mall, an event, anything?"

"I know they were seniors, and popular. I didn't hang out with them."

"Can you think of a reason why you three might go into the woods together?"

"No."

"Was it to do drugs, or deal drugs?"

"I don't think so."

"Was it to get drunk?"

"I don't think so."

"Was it a sex thing?"

"No, that couldn't be it."

"Was it about other kids at school?"

"I don't know."

"Boyfriend stuff?"

"I don't know."

"Did anyone accuse anyone of something?"

"I can't remember."

"Did it have anything to do with anything satanic, witchcraft, or any fads, experiments, anything like that?"

"I don't know."

"Do you remember anything that was said?"

"No."

"Did any of you have a weapon at the time?"

"I don't remember."

"Do you recall seeing a weapon?"

"I don't know."

Ben McGraw, who's been reclining in his chair with his arms folded, leans forward.

"Okay, Carrie, then tell us what you do remember."

Her hands, webbed with red scratches, fly to her face.

"I remember running through the forest, that I'd never been so scared in my life. Running so fast, branches whipping me, just running and running until the ground was gone and I was flying, falling into the river, gasping, swallowing water, thrashing in the current smashing against the rocks, like something hammered my head, then I woke up in the hospital…and I can't remember." Carrie's voice breaks to a squeaky whisper. "Then people were telling me that Abby and Erin are dead, that they were murdered."

"Why were you scared?" McGraw asks.

"I don't remember."

"Was someone chasing you?"

"I don't know."

"Carrie." McGraw looks at her. "Look at me."

Slowly she lifts her eyes to his.

"Carrie, were you scared because of something you did?"

"I don't know."

Carrie drops her face into her arms on the table and sobs, with Guinn rubbing her back.

The detectives exchange glances.

At that moment, Vern's phone flickered and vibrated with

an incoming call, pulling him from the video. "Hello?" he answered.

"Vernon Hamilton?"

"Yes."

"Vince Azure, Donnie Ray Hyde's spiritual advisor, following up on your request."

"Yes, Pastor."

"Your request came right after the board's recent decision. His appeal has been rejected. I relayed your request to him. You can appreciate that he's not in the best frame of mind."

"I understand."

"However, with that said, Donnie Ray's agreed to see you."

"Thank you."

"You'll hear back from me, or more likely someone from TDCJ, with the date and time of your visit."

Vern allowed himself a moment to respond.

"I'll stand by. Thank you."

17

Luke realized this was a diversion, an escape from the pool scene, as he walked with Clay and the others to see Clay's cars.

To get to the garage, they had to go about seventy-five yards along the narrow paved roadway meandering from the house.

Ambling in the cool shade of the woods, Luke retreated into his thoughts, contending with Reeger's ridiculous claim that Vern had killed Carrie's mother.

Luke refused to believe it as his concern pinballed to Carrie surrounded by women in the kitchen. Then to his own crisis. The questions that came up went straight to his ambiguity and fear that he might have hit someone.

These guys know I hit something, damaged my SUV, called hospitals. They know about LA. On top of that, the psychologists told me I'd have issues with post-traumatic stress. Is that it, then? I'm imagining that I saw a woman in the storm. There's no solid evidence. No real proof of anything. Why do I think something happened? But if the others found out that I'm still dealing with PTSD, they'd consider me unfit for the job. I've got to figure out what really happened, to prove it to myself. And I've got to be careful.

"Luke?" Pulled from his problems, he turned to Clay, who repeated: "I said sorry Reeger's been such an ass to you."

"I'll get over it."

They came up to the garage with its adjacent carport sheltering several vehicles. Squinting, Shelby did a quick inventory.

"Did you get another one, Clay?"

"Got a deal on a '76 Trans Am. Guy in Lubbock had it sitting on his ranch."

"What've you got in your collection now?"

"Out here, I got the Nomad in the garage." Clay fished out the key for the gate of the metal fence securing the carport. Opening it, he gave a tour, for Luke's benefit, of the aging cars in stages of deterioration, parked in two rows of three.

"That's a '74 Dodge Challenger; over here is the Firebird Trans Am. Beside it, the GTO—having trouble finding parts for that." Clay flipped up a tarp on one. "A '57 Thunderbird."

"I love it," Lonnie said.

Clay pointed to his 1967 Mercury Cougar GT, then the 1969 Dodge Coronet Super Bee at the end as his group inspected the cars, cooing admiringly.

"Some classic stuff here," Luke said.

"I like hunting for parts, rebuilding them. It's like therapy from the stress of the job," Clay said, leading them from the carport and locking the gate. "Guys, go to the front of the garage."

Clay unlocked the side door and stepped inside. A few seconds later, the big door rose automatically, releasing the rumbling hum of the Nomad. Clay, at the wheel, eased it out. Keeping the motor running, he got out and popped the hood. For a long moment, the men marveled at the purring 265 cubic-inch V8, Lonnie and Shelby smiling like dads staring at a newborn as Clay raised his voice.

"Needs more work yet before the raffle," he said, dropping the hood, returning the car and locking the garage.

"You're raffling the Nomad?" Luke asked as they started walking back to the party.

"Lacey's involved with our church fundraisers. We can raise quite a lot. It's all good."

"Very nice." Luke nodded.

"It's the whole thing about giving back. Lacey's shops are doing well. I inherited my dad's hardware stores."

"And what're you two driving?" Shelby asked.

"Lacey's got her Caddy; I got the Mustang and my truck. We're fortunate. But not blessed like Luke and Carrie."

"How so?"

"You have a baby daughter; you're back here with family. Things might not be ideal right now, but you really have something, something to hang on to."

Luke looked at Clay. "So do you and Lacey."

"We do. But we don't have kids like you do."

"Do you want kids?" Luke asked.

"There was a time, but then we accepted it's not really in the cards for us."

"That's a tough break."

"It's okay. Lacey stays busy with her business and charities. I came into some money from Dad's hardware business. Worked there part-time in school, learned the art of repair work from the older guys there. Don't get me wrong, I know I've got it good, and I had it good, ever since Lacey and I were sweethearts in Clear River High School."

"Hey, Luke," Lonnie said. "Did you go to Clear River High?"

"No, I went to Rosedale Eastern, across town. After my folks died, I moved out West, went to college there, then got on with the LAPD."

"And now here you are," Shelby said.

"You came back with Carrie, leaving everything behind to deal with things here," Clay said, putting a friendly hand on Luke's shoulder and exchanging a look with him as they neared the house.

18

At the party, Carrie was encircled by women in the kitchen. Glasses in hand, contents spilling, voices growing louder, laughter and subjects overlapping. Opal Wells was reminiscing about their time together in high school history class.

"Remember how we teamed up for the presentation about Benjamin Franklin, his life and words of wisdom? I remember one of my favorites: 'A penny saved is a penny earned.' There was one you liked—what was it? Remember, Carrie?"

Lacey was watching carefully.

"Gosh, I don't know, Opal."

"We did our presentation right before—" As if she'd arrived at a cliff, Opal stopped herself cold.

Most everyone in the room knew what Opal was alluding to: "right before" Abby Hall and Erin Eddowes were murdered.

"Y'all know what?" Melissa Pruett chimed in loudly. "I saw on the news recently that Donnie Ray Hyde's going to be executed real soon for killing Jenna Dupree in Tyler. As I recall, he was a suspect for Abby and Erin."

"That's right," Grace Cox, a cousin of Sheriff Ellerd, said. "Our boys looked hard at him. But they couldn't prove he did it."

Lacey turned to Carrie. "Honey, I'm so sorry, this talk must be upsetting."

"Can't be helped. I understand."

Carrie sipped wine as two women she didn't know slowly shouldered their way to her.

"We wanted to welcome you home and tell you how much we admire you, Carrie." The first woman, the one with a ponytail, touched her arm.

"Admire me?"

"For moving back for your dad, with his condition and all."

"And for being so brave," said the second woman, whose hair was short.

"Brave?"

"To come back when the killer's still out there," the woman said.

"It's just such a shame that Abby and Erin don't get to come back, isn't it? They don't get to talk about old times and show baby pictures, do they?" the ponytailed woman said, a hint of something sharp in her tone.

Without speaking, Carrie glanced to Lacey, then at the women, trying to figure out who they were.

"You promised you wouldn't do this," Lacey said to the women.

"Oh," the ponytailed woman said, "forgive me, I'm Nicole Hall. Abby was my big sister."

"And," the second woman said, "I'm Lauren Eddowes. Erin was my cousin."

The blood drained from Carrie's face.

"Then again—" Nicole turned to Lauren "—I guess it wouldn't be brave to return if you knew who the killer was, would it?"

"Not at all," Lauren said.

Nicole turned on Carrie. "You know what happened that day, don't you, Carrie?"

She began shaking her head. "No, I don't. I can't remember anything."

"All this time, Carrie, you've known," Lauren said.

"You need to tell everyone the truth!" Nicole said.

Lauren thrust her phone toward Carrie, showing her a photo of Abby and Erin. "Let's go down memory lane, Carrie."

"No, please."

Lacey inserted herself between Carrie and the women.

"Put your phone down. Back off, girls, that's enough. Come on."

Nicole and Lauren moved away just as Luke emerged, standing next to Carrie, catching the wake of tension.

"Everything all right?" he asked.

Carrie nodded and took a sip of wine, then quietly she said to him: "I would like to leave now."

Minutes later, after saying their goodbyes, they were in their SUV.

Driving home, Carrie looked through her window, watching houses and streets floating by, the air heavy with her silence until Luke spoke.

"We knew moving home wouldn't be easy. But we'll get through it."

He turned to Carrie, who was now looking straight ahead.

"Maybe..." she started. "Maybe we can make this move temporary, just until..."

"Until what?"

"Until Dad—" She turned to the window. "I don't know," she said, brushing the tears rolling down her face.

19

The aftershocks of the party rippled for days.

Connecting with people and the past had not been easy, Luke thought as he patrolled his sector in North Division.

We knew we'd face this sooner or later. Going to Lacey and Clay's party was a first step.

But it was a painful one, both for Carrie and himself, especially with Reeger's animosity toward him. The rumor that Vern had killed his wife was one Luke kept to himself and wished he'd never heard. To top it off, Luke's conscience was eating at him for all of his sins.

All of it, pushing down on all of us.

On the surface, Carrie seemed to be coping. She'd resumed work and her virtual sessions with Dr Bernay.

As for a silver lining, at least this week, Reeger was away on a course in Austin and Shelby Slade was swinging up from South Division to cover Reeger's territory in East Division. Shaking it all off, Luke focused on his car's monitor and his next call, a theft at a drugstore. It was at the edge of North Division, taking him through town. He was nearly there when the call was canceled.

That's when he happened by the Whataburger.

Looking at the A-frame roof, the orange-and-white color

scheme, he fell back through time to that summer night when he was seventeen.

He'd finished his chores on his family's small farm near Dixon and pocketed the pay his father gave him. He was saving for his dream—buying the beat-up 1996 Corvette Stingray at Phil Dooley's dealership—but it was a stretch. He had to be content for the moment to use the family's old pickup, an ancient Dodge.

Lonely and bored, he did what he did most Saturday nights: drove around by himself. This time he went into Clear River. Hungry, he stopped at the Whataburger to eat. He was thunderstruck by the girl with the bright smile serving him.

Luke overheard a worker call her "Carrie." Finishing his burger, he asked after her and learned what high school she went to, that her dad was the county sheriff. Being shy, Luke never spoke to Carrie, but he drove home in the Dodge that night with his heart swelling. He couldn't stop thinking about her and visited the same Whataburger a few more times, hoping to see her again. He even drove to the big Halloween dance in Clear River. Amid the music, crowd and lights, he searched for her in vain.

Not long after that, the story broke about the murders in Wild Pines Forest. Like most everyone, he'd soon learned that the sole survivor, found near death in the river, was the sheriff's daughter, Carrie Hamilton. Luke was stunned. He didn't know her. He wanted to help her. But there was nothing he could do.

Time went by.

His life unfolded and after high school, a buddy who had moved to California urged Luke to join him there. As a young man, Luke was eager to leave the farm and Texas, so he moved to Los Angeles. He never got the Stingray. Instead, he used his savings to study criminology at college, working part-time as a security guard before getting on with the LAPD.

A few years later, at a function for a community program led by the department, he met Carrie Hamilton, whose agency was handling promotion. Neither he nor Carrie could believe the odds of them meeting. They talked about growing up in East Texas. It was incredible, like the first time he saw her.

Only now, he wasn't so shy.

They started dating. Carrie told him about surviving the double murder and nearly dying in the river. How she remembered little from all those years ago. He said he was aware of her tragedy from media reports at the time. She'd told him that, outside of her sessions with a psychologist, she didn't like talking about her past, and he never pressed her on it.

He told her that he never knew his real mother—she'd given him up. His adoptive parents, Royce and Rhona Conway, were older, stern churchgoers. By his midteens, Luke often felt they used him like a workhand on their farm. Sometimes he resented it; other times he was just grateful to have a home. Then Royce and Rhona died in a motel fire while attending a wedding in Longview. It was a hard time for Luke, leaving him with complicated emotions. Wanting to leave the farm, he eventually moved to Los Angeles, where he met Carrie all over again.

They kept dating, fell in love, got married and bought a bungalow in Montecito Heights. Then they had Emily, who was the sun in their world. *Everything was going well,* Luke thought, *until—*

...the woman lying on the street, blood oozing...

Luke pressed a hand to the back of his neck, telling himself he'd been cleared. But it didn't matter.

He couldn't forgive himself.

The air burst with a sudden crackle of his radio.

"Dispatch, twelve-o-nine."

Luke picked up his microphone.

"Twelve-o-nine, Dispatch."

"Luke, can you see a Kent Purcell at the site office at the Fawn Ridge development?"

He hesitated, then said: "That's East Division—I thought Shelby was covering the East?"

"He's tied up with a traffic hazard at the Loop near Pinecrest Acres. I'll send you the info for Fawn Ridge. It's a status thing."

"Ten-four."

Luke had hesitated to take the call, not just because it was Garth Reeger's area. But also because it was the location where Luke had thought he'd struck a woman, who could've staggered off. *Stop worrying. It didn't happen. You imagined a woman,* he told himself. At the party, the update from the Clear River detective confirmed that the woman found dead in town couldn't be connected to his incident.

What more do I need? I didn't hit anyone. It was all in my head. Paranoia. Just like the shrinks in LA said.

Minutes later, he was rolling through the familiar countryside, coming to the billboard of dreams and one of the entrances to the new Fawn Ridge subdivision.

He drove along emerging streets, busy with tradespeople working on houses that were in varying stages of completion. He navigated around mixer and dump trucks, finally finding the double-wide trailer that served as the jobsite office. He climbed the wooden ramp and knocked on the door.

"It's open," a voice called.

Inside, the air conditioner hummed. The place smelled of cut lumber and coffee. Several people sat at a table, reading plans. Above them, a map detailing building lots covered one wall. At one end of the trailer, Luke saw a tangle of cords, computers, monitors for a closed-circuit TV system and file cabinets, as well as a microwave, fridge and coffee maker.

A man sitting at his terminal saw Luke and said, "Kent?" to the man at the planning table, the one talking on his phone. He turned and held up a finger to Luke.

"Today, Miles," Kent said into his phone. "We need that load today or we're done. Read your contract."

Ending his call, the man's attention went to Luke.

"Kent Purcell." He shot out his hand. "Assistant supervisor."

"Luke Conway."

"Conway? Our front office told me Reeger was handling this."

"Right, well, he's in Austin. I guess wires got crossed."

"The front office was hoping Reeger could give us an update or hand us a report on the investigation. Can you do that?"

"No, I'm sorry. My understanding is that it's still under investigation."

"Damn. It's been over two months now. It was forty thousand in material and tools. We gave Reeger video we had from our cameras. Front office says the insurance claim is an issue."

"I'll advise him. He'll be back Monday. Sorry for the mix-up."

Purcell pressed his lips together and broke eye contact. "All right, sorry you had to come out. This could've been handled with a phone call."

"Wish I could've been more help." Luke had just turned to leave when an idea—a risky one—stopped him. He looked to the end of the trailer where the closed-circuit TV system was. "While I'm here, can you tell me how long your security system keeps recordings?"

Purcell directed Luke's question to the man sitting at the computer. "A long time, right, Dean?"

Dean swiveled in his chair.

"Yeah, we can go back as far as six months."

"Do your cameras pick up traffic on River Road?"

"The one near the south entrance does."

"Would it be possible to go back several weeks and see what's there?" Luke asked.

"Sure, I can pinpoint it." Dean shrugged. "Got a date and time?"

Luke gave him the date he drove home from the bar and the time he would've been on River Road.

"Why're you asking?" Purcell said. "This related to us?"

"I don't know," Luke said. "We had an unverified tip that maybe a person in distress was seen at that time near here along River Road."

Luke knew he was taking a risk, *a big one. But this could prove that I imagined hitting a woman because of my trauma.*

Dean tapped away on his keyboard, then pointed at a monitor showing footage. Luke and Purcell stepped closer. The small TV screen offered a fuzzy full-color view of the road, obscured by sheets of rain, glistening like a snowstorm.

"Can't see much," Dean said. "I'll speed it up."

A blip of light streaked by. Dean reversed the footage, ran it again slowly.

Luke flinched.

Details were hazy, but it was clear enough to see an eastbound vehicle passing by. It was impossible to see a plate, though, or determine the model or make before it vanished.

Luke swallowed.

That's me, he thought. *It has to be.*

But the footage did not encompass the range to show him colliding with a person. Dean continued running the recording, branches and debris skipping across the road. Then a shadowy figure appeared, a small, intense light raking in the storm before disappearing.

"That's interesting," Dean said. "Is that a person looking for something? What's up with that?"

The recording continued with nothing but the storm and windblown limbs and trash bouncing across the rain-soaked road. Dean accelerated the footage, but then something flared by.

He reversed the footage and ran it again a few times. Even slowed down, it was an enigmatic flickering. But in the sequence, there was an illumination from a car's approaching headlights, a blip of color, a flash forming and a figure rising from the ditch before vanishing from the frame. For a long, troubled moment, Luke was frozen, stunned.

Ice prickled at the base of his scalp.

The blip of color was pink.

20

"Some people hate that I'm back."

"I understand," Dr. Bernay said from Carrie's laptop monitor. "But we expected challenges."

Carrie also raised her anxiety around having accepted Sofia Vera's invitation for coffee. She was supposed to meet her at the high school later that day.

"I think," Dr. Bernay said, "revisiting the location where a number of your issues originated is a good step."

"It won't be easy."

"True, but neither was moving back or going to Lacey's party. And you did both. Keep building on your successes."

Carrie turned to Emily, who sat on the floor nearby playing with her toys, happy for the moment to stay in one spot.

"Carrie, you said you had concerns about Luke?"

"He's kind of distant, even with small stuff. He seems preoccupied."

"Allow him time to adjust to the move, his new job. Remember, he's carrying his own trauma."

"I want to help him but he internalizes so much."

"Give it time. Look at the positives. Luke wanted to move,

wanted the new job. And, of course, there's your dad, with Emily. This is also a time to be cherished."

"Yes." Carrie brushed a tear. "It's beautiful to see him with her—he just lights up."

"Keep taking these small steps. Like going for coffee at the school today. It's a welcoming gesture that will help you re-connect, give you a sense of belonging."

Carrie reached down and stroked Emily's hair.

"One day at a time," Carrie said.

"Yes, but," Dr. Bernay cautioned her, "be ready for the po-tential to unearth memories. Even disturbing ones."

Clear River High School was a two-story building, built circa 1970.

There were plans to build a new school with a big foot-ball stadium—in keeping with the community's passion for the game, Carrie thought as she parked in a visitor's spot. She buckled Emily into her stroller, took a breath, then went to the secured door and used the buzz-in system. After identify-ing herself over the intercom, an armed guard escorted her in.

Instantly, the smell of polished floors, the portrait wall of administrators and the glass case holding prizes won for school glory pulled her back to adolescence. She went to the office, where Sofia Vera was waiting at the counter, looking at her phone. Upon seeing Carrie, a couple of the staff nudged each other, exchanging glances. One, who Carrie recognized from Lacey's party, gave a small wave.

"Hey, Carrie." Sofia hugged her, then bent down to Emily. "Hi, sweetheart. Having fun visiting with Mommy like a big girl?" Then to Carrie, "Let's get you signed in and get your visitor badge, then we'll go to the cafeteria."

The halls were deserted now that the school day was over, the faint echo of a basketball bouncing on hardwood and the squeak of running shoes underscoring the emptiness.

They went through the student common area, where Carrie slowed to a near stop. Abby Hall and Erin Eddowes stared at her from the framed photographs of a memorial display, pulling Carrie to them with their pretty clothes and pretty-girl smiles.

Noticing Carrie's disquiet, Sofia said, "They put this up after you'd graduated and moved away. Their families set up a memorial college scholarship. I hope it doesn't—"

"No, it's okay. That was a nice thing for the families to do."

They rounded the corner to the open doors of the cafeteria. While no one was there, they could hear activity in the kitchen.

"Have a seat. The coffee's on me. How do you take it?"

"Thanks. A dribble of milk."

"How about a juice box or something for Emily?"

"Thanks, but I'll give her a bottle and she'll be happy. She might even nap in the stroller. She's good that way."

Carrie took in the rows of empty tables and seats. The room seemed so much smaller now. A moment later, Sofia returned with two ceramic mugs bearing the school's crest.

"I like having the place to ourselves," Sofia said.

"Yes, it's calm, peaceful."

"It's so good to see you." Sofia put her hand over Carrie's.

"It is nice. How're you doing?"

"I got divorced last year."

"Oh, no, I'm sorry to hear that."

"It was for the best."

"And kids?"

"No kids. That was part of it. Anyway..." Sofia smiled. "I've been seeing Kendrick, who moved here from Atlanta after his wife passed away from cancer. He's a good man who wants kids. He's got his own trucking company. We're taking it slow."

"You look great, Sofia."

"Thanks, Carrie. But what about you? Your dad's got to be happy to have you back home."

"He is. It's good for him to see Emily."

Sipping coffee, Sofia blinked, choosing her words.

"You know, we were so young back then, but with your mom's passing, then what happened in the woods…whenever I thought of you over the years, I just wanted to hug you."

"Oh, thank you."

"And thank you for meeting me at the school. I'm actually finishing up grading papers, and leaving notes for my sub. Then Kendrick's picking me up. We're driving to Houston tonight, then flying to Seattle for a short holiday."

"Sounds like fun."

Sofia paused, peered into her coffee and said: "I have to confess a secret."

Carrie tensed. "A secret?"

"I wanted to do this before I left. This is embarrassing."

"What is it, Sofia?"

"I've written a screenplay, a rom-com, about high school teachers."

And there it is, Carrie thought.

"Congratulations."

"Writing one has been a secret dream and, well, seeing how you worked with movie people in Los Angeles, I wanted to ask if you know anyone in the business who could help me. Oh, gosh, Carrie, tell me if I'm out of line."

"No, it's all right." Emily started fussing. Carrie fished a prepared bottle from the bag under the stroller and gave it to her. "But I don't know. Just about every second person in LA has written a screenplay. It's tough."

"I know, but I thought I'd ask."

"I have a friend at an agency. No promises, no guarantees, but I could touch base with her."

"Really?"

"I can ask if she'd be willing to look at it."

"That would be fantastic! Thank you!"

Sofia's phone rang as she moved to hug Carrie.

"It's Kendrick. I'm sorry—I have to take this."

Carrie waved her off. "No problem."

Sofia left, talking on her phone, disappearing into the common area, leaving Carrie to stroke Emily's hair while she drank from her bottle.

Again, Carrie took in the room's emptiness, this time the subtle, lingering aroma of cafeteria food stirred something buried deep in her memory, seizing her with a haunting sensation that wrenched her back to when she was seventeen and...

...in the cafeteria, packed for the lunch period, the chaos of conversation is deafening, but she's pretty much alone eating at the table with Opal Wells and some junior girls who don't have many friends. They blend in with others at neighboring tables—nerds, geeks, unpopular kids and freshmen. At one end are the brainiacs, then rows across, tables with jocks, cheerleaders, and the upper echelon of seniors and super popular kids who rule the school—they're talking about a wild upcoming party... Carrie spots Lanna. She's an unpopular junior in the chess club with braces, acne and a speech impediment. Lanna stands alone with her tray, scanning for a seat... One is free but it's in the exclusive zone of popular seniors, who reign over everyone...

Lanna steels herself before moving slowly, as if stepping onto a minefield, navigating to the empty seat near Abby Hall. As she arrives, a backpack thuds onto the seat. "Taken, Rama-Lanna-Ding-Dong," says one of the senior boys.

But Abby Hall says, "No it's not. Kirk, move it. Sit, Lanna." Lanna looks at her as if seeking assurance, like she's checking it's okay, checking they're not going to kick the chair out from under her. "Go ahead, sit." Abby grins. The scene attracts glances and giggles from the other popular kids, who, like wolves, are knowingly anticipating a response to Lanna's daring to set foot in their realm.

Placing her tray down, Lanna sits. She eats while reading a book, her head bowed, bothering no one. Abby smiles, elbows Kirk. The wolves strike; he snatches Lanna's unopened milk carton from her tray.

"Hey," Lanna says, reaching in vain for it as he passes it to Abby,

who passes it to Erin Eddowes beside her. Erin holds it up like cap-
tured treasure, wiggling it to taunt Lanna, igniting the group's laugh-
ter before passing it to the boy beside her, who passes it to the girl next
to him. Lanna protests in vain as the chortling group passes her stolen
carton farther from her.

Unable to stomach the hurt on Lanna's face, Carrie makes her way
to the end of the table, where one of the senior boys unwittingly puts
Lanna's carton in Carrie's hand. She strides to Lanna and returns
her milk, noticing two empty seats across the room. "I'll get my tray,
Lanna. Let's sit over there." Then to the group, Carrie snaps: "That
was a juvenile, shitty thing to do!"

One boy mutters, "Yo, Carrie's Five-O. Her dad's the sheriff."

"Busted by the cafeteria cop," a girl says.

Another chimes in, "Narc."

"Whoa, Carrie." Abby flashes a beautiful queen bee smile. "Honey,
just chill."

Erin joins in. "We weren't going to keep Rama-Lanna's stupid milk."

"It's just a little harmless joke," Abby says.

"Are you going to take us in, Sheriff?" Erin says, extending her
wrists together to be handcuffed.

Carrie stares at them with a growing intensity that prompts one of
the boys to warn, "Look out, she may be marshaling her evil powers."
But his grin soon fades, as do the smirks on the faces of Abby, Erin
and the others, then Carrie leaves…

Now, sitting in the unoccupied cafeteria, surfacing from the
past, Carrie heard her name being called.

"I said, are you okay?" Sofia asked. "You're so pale."

"Oh. Yes," Carrie said. "I was lost in my thoughts."

Turning to Emily, Carrie grasped the near-empty bottle of
formula.

"Want to trade numbers and emails so I can send you my
script?"

"Absolutely." Carrie reached for her phone. "This has been
so nice, but I should be getting Emily home."

Later, in the privacy of her car, after buckling Emily into her seat, Carrie hesitated to start the motor.

She stared at the school, covering her face with her hands.

The cafeteria memory with Abby and Erin was crystalline. It's happening.

It was the memory of the time leading up to when the three girls went into the woods.

The time leading up to Abby's and Erin's deaths.

What did I do?

21

Vernon winced as he guided his Ford F-150 along the road, winding through the countryside toward death row.

Gritting his teeth, he rode out the brief waves of pain. He'd taken his pills; it would pass. He changed his grip on the wheel as he neared Livingston. Gazing at the landscape dotted with pine and oak trees, he went over the cases again.

On the last day of her life, Jenna Dupree was working part-time as a cashier at HealthTown Drugs in Tyler. After her shift ended, she got on her bicycle and took a shortcut through tall grass on the path that led to her house.

Store security camera footage had recorded Donnie Ray Hyde, a thirty-year-old drifter, talking to Jenna in the store earlier. Jenna was unaware that Hyde, a stranger, had followed her on the path. He attacked and murdered her, taking a few personal items before concealing her body in the grass and submerging her bike in a creek.

The next day, Hyde was found sleeping in a park and arrested. Evidence found with him, and at the scene, led to his conviction and death sentence. But during their investigation, Tyler detectives discovered social media messages and photos that put

Hyde in Clear River County at the time Erin Eddowes and
Abby Hall were murdered.

Hyde's brother, Brophy, who did time for robbing a gas station, lived in Tagallet Mobile Home Park near Wild Pines Forest. The pattern of the Wild Pines killings was similar to that
of Jenna's murder. And scrutiny of the evidence at Wild Pines
suggested Hyde was at the crime scene.

"All circumstantial," Will Young, the district attorney, told Vern
and the investigators. "You have circumstantial dots. You need
something stronger—direct evidence, or Hyde's confession—to
connect them to our Wild Pines case."

Clear River detectives interviewed Hyde in prison several
times. He denied killing Abby and Erin. He claimed to be
drinking with Brophy in their single-wide that day. It was a
flimsy alibi, but it was all investigators had. Through his attorney, Hyde agreed to a polygraph in prison. The results were
inconclusive—without Hyde's confession, they had no case.

Will Young and the investigators figured that Hyde had refused to admit to killing Abby and Erin because he didn't want
to hamper his death sentence appeals in the Jenna Dupree case.
But now, left with no hope for a reprieve, Donnie Ray Hyde
would be executed in a few weeks.

Vern's truck's turn signal ticked like time on a clock as he
slowed to enter the Allan B. Polunsky Unit.

It was a vast dismal complex of dull gray buildings trimmed
with tranquil blue. Sprawled over some fifty acres, the unit
was bordered by multiple razor wire security fences, a range
of surveillance sensors and armed guard towers. Here, death
row inmates awaited execution in small individual cells, some
with a sliver of a window.

After reporting to the guard staff, clearing the security process and slipping on his visitor's badge, Vern went to the visiting room for death row offenders. It was a stark area with a

polished floor, plastic hard-backed chairs and drab white walls, all under bright fluorescent lighting.

Death row inmates were not permitted to have contact visits, which meant using security cubicles, divided by a thick Plexiglas window, and talking through telephone handsets on either side. Vern glimpsed the white collar of Pastor Vincent Azure, a bulky man with white hair and pugnacious features sitting across from Hyde, holding a handset. Vern got into a chair, scraping it into position as they made quick, cordial greetings.

"Good, so here we go," Azure said into the phone. "Donnie Ray, I'll leave you two to speak in private for a spell, then I'll be back."

"All right."

Azure and Hyde then pressed their hands on the glass.

"Be strong," Azure said. "Remember what we discussed, son."

Hyde nodded.

When the pastor left, Vern took up a handset and studied Hyde sitting inches from him in prison-issued white clothing. The last time they looked at each other was years ago when Hyde was being questioned by Clear River detectives. Now Hyde's hair, flecked with gray, had thinned, and his face carried tiny folds and creases from his time on death row. Vern took stock of him. He had Hyde's information committed to memory.

Born in Kilgore, Hyde had a grade eight education and had held various jobs: laborer, warehouse worker, gravedigger.

"It's been a long time, Sheriff," Hyde said.

"A long time. Thank you for agreeing to see me."

Hyde gave a hint of a smile.

"Nobody has thanked me for anything in a while." Hyde waited, then said, "I agreed 'cause I was curious. Pastor Azure says you think that before I go, I might want to unburden myself. Why? I ain't killed nobody."

"Jenna Dupree?"

Hyde dragged his hand hard over his face. "I made my peace

with that, wrote her family a letter. They'll get their payback when they send me to the other side."

Vern said nothing.

Hyde's eyes narrowed; his cordiality cooled.

"I shoulda got life, not death. My trial was a farce, just like my case before the board. Did they, or the governor, even look at it?"

"Son, every appeal concerning your trial has failed. You know the board rarely grants relief if there's no compelling reason, like errors in trial proceedings, or new solid evidence. And in your case, they found no compelling reason. It's done."

Hyde fell silent.

"It's over for you. You know it. And Pastor Azure has been preparing you for the end."

"So why did you come?"

"To help you."

"Help me with what?"

"This is the time to clear your conscience, to make peace with your soul."

A few seconds passed.

"Son, let's get to the truth. We know you were in Clear River County when Abby Hall and Erin Eddowes were murdered. And we know you were in Wild Pines Forest."

"I was in the county with Brophy having beers that day. I done told everybody that."

"There's no need for you to hold back the truth now," Vern said. "The fact is, you went into the woods. And there were three of them, weren't there? Three girls."

Hyde was silent.

"How did you get three girls to go into the woods with you? Did you force them? Wait for them? Follow them? How did you take control?"

Hyde said nothing.

"Only the killer would know what happened," Vern said. "And this looks a lot like Jenna's murder."

Hyde rubbed his chin. "No, I wasn't with them—I was with Brophy."

"But your brother lied to alibi you, didn't he?"

"No, I was with him."

"But one girl survived—you know that."

Hyde looked at him. "Your daughter."

"That's right."

"But she hurt her head and don't remember nothin', all the news said that."

"*You* were there and *you* remember. You know things only the killer would know. You've denied the truth for too long. Now is the time to set things right. Now, I want you to listen closely to me because this is your only chance. I'm going to tell you what we think happened because we're running out of time and I need to hear your response. I need the truth."

For the next twenty minutes, Vern recounted the detailed scenario investigators adhered to, a scenario that had never been made public. As Vern went over the case, piece by piece, Hyde absorbed every aspect in silence.

When Vern finished, he gave Hyde a moment, then said, "Let's talk about your people, Donnie Ray. Your deadbeat dad died from too much drink; Brophy died five years back in that shoot-out in Georgia. All you have is your mother."

Hyde looked away, blinking. "I'm all she's got left."

"Ain't that the truth. I did some checking on her situation in Kilgore. Seems she's in a bad way. She can't afford to claim your body. You'll end up in the ground at Joe Byrd."

"She wanted me in Kilgore, next to my dad and Brophy." Hyde looked into his empty hands and shook his head.

"Son, you might be able to help her before you go to the other side. But only if you clear your conscience, make a positive step."

"What difference will it make?"

"Your mother might get a little help."

Hyde stared at him.

"I want you to think long and hard after I leave," Vern said. "It's all in your hands. Time is ticking down to make this right, son."

22

Carrie arrived home from the school unable to think clearly.

After unbuckling Emily, she got her into the house, changed her and then put her down in her room for her nap. Carrie checked the time, then went into her office.

She needed to go over notes for her work video call coming up with clients in California. Struggling to keep busy, she tried to get past her visit to the school, but it was all she could think about until she sat stock-still, covering her face with her hands.

It's happening, just like Dr. Bernay said. The cafeteria memory with Abby and Erin was crystal clear. They bullied Lanna, and it made me so angry—I—I— What happened? I know that's a memory of the days leading up to the woods and their deaths. What did I do?

Carrie's fingers were trembling.

Take it easy, she told herself. Dr. Bernay had said that healing would happen in stages, that she had to gain control, that she could handle it.

The doorbell rang, startling her.

Carrie went to the control panel of their home security system and looked at the small monitor for the front door camera. A woman stood at her porch. She looked to be in her midthirties, wearing a sleeveless denim top, dark hair pulled into a ponytail, sunglasses perched on her head, bag slung over her shoulder. There was a white SUV behind her, parked on the street in front of the house.

"Yes?" Carrie said through the system.

"Hi, I'm Denise Diaz with the *Clear River Chronicle*. I'd like to talk to Carrie, Carrie Conway."

"What's this about?"

"Are you Carrie?"

Carrie squeezed her eyes shut for a half second, then glanced down the hall, relieved Emily's door was closed. Steeling herself, she went to the front door and opened it. Denise Diaz straightened slightly as the two women assessed each other. The reporter was pretty, in a rugged way; she had a nice figure and was Carrie's height.

"Are you Carrie?"

"Yes. How did you find where we live?"

Denise's face held the look of a sharp-eyed journalist who'd seen much of this world.

"Word got to us that you had moved back. Carrie, I'd like to talk to you about the case. It's still unsolved. It's been thirteen years. The killer hasn't been arrested. I'd like to do a feature on it that would include your reflections."

Carrie began shaking her head slowly.

"A story with your input could jog someone's memory. It might even lead to solving the case."

"No, I'm not prepared to talk about it."

"I understand, but please, think about it, Carrie. Listen, I apologize for showing up like this at your door, for not calling ahead or sending a message. But I wanted to ask you in person."

"It's still no. I'm sorry." Carrie grasped her door handle. "Excuse me, I have to go."

"Hold on." Diaz reached into her bag, then handed Carrie a business card. "Just think about it, please, Carrie."

Carrie took her card, then retreated into her home.

Inside, she closed her fist around the business card and slammed her back to the door, clenching her eyes shut.

23

Rising from the ditch in the downpour, the woman's spectral figure vanished in a heartbeat.

But the image remained, seared in Luke's conscience.

He contended with it at his desk in the patrol room while finishing reports at the end of his shift. For in the days after copying the few seconds of construction site security video, he'd replayed it secretly on his phone, staring in disbelief at the evidence that blew away all doubt as reality came crashing down.

I struck a woman with my car and left the scene.

I didn't imagine it. I'm not losing my mind.

He was holding the horrible truth in his hands.

Oh, God, I should've reported it that night, called dispatch, turned myself in. But this is not about me. Not anymore. It's about the woman. She's real. And I've got to be sure she's okay.

Luke thought of scenarios.

Had someone helped her? Had she fallen injured into the brush? Without help, she'd be dead after all this time, making him guilty of a serious crime. How could he face Carrie, Vern, Emily, himself, with the shame he'd bring on his family? He'd lose everything.

I'll go to prison.

So why was he sitting there? He should report what happened, request a full grid search of the area. Call in canine units, drones, helicopters, whatever it took. But what if after he drew all this attention, they didn't find anything? They'd label him unstable, and, taken with his history in LA, they'd deem him unfit for duty.

No matter what I do, I'm finished. No, I'll do this myself.

He couldn't let go of the desperate belief he could fix this.

Yes, there was his public admission to being on the road and striking something. His vehicle was damaged. There was the fragment of fabric he'd found and discarded. There was the video.

But no victim had been found.

Maybe she was helped. Maybe she survived. *It's been so long since I left the scene. Anything could've happened.* He had to continue investigating.

I'll see it through and get answers. Then I'll surrender to face my fate.

His thoughts spun as he took a deep breath and let it out slowly. *God, I hope she's okay.* He resumed digging, looking at an avenue he should've tried earlier, his keyboard and mouse clicking. The department's page for missing persons opened.

First, the scarred face of a white male stared out, age fifty-nine, missing for fifteen years. No, can't be a male.

Next, another white male. No.

He scrolled down to another male. No.

Next, the pretty face of a Hispanic female teen from the county. Missing for thirty-five years now, last seen in Austin. After considering this case, Luke didn't think it fit and scrolled on.

Next, he came to the case of a white woman, aged twenty-eight, missing from the county now for ten years, making her thirty-eight. She was last seen in El Paso. She'd called her father in Clear River to say she'd met a man named Bobby, and was never heard from or seen again.

Luke wasn't sure this one fit either.

The remaining cases were males. The page only held a handful of missing person files for the county. He could try the Texas Department of Public Safety page for the whole state, or search nationally. The possibilities were infinite, he was thinking when a shadow fell over his monitor.

"What're you up to, there, Luke?"

Clay Smith was standing behind him, reading over his shoulder.

"Just looking at old cases."

Clay moved around Luke's desk to his own, letting a few seconds pass while examining Luke. "Why?"

Luke closed the pages on his screen. "Thought I'd familiarize myself with them."

Clay looked at him, as if searching for deception.

"Something wrong with me doing that?" Luke asked.

"I'm just curious about your interest in missing person cases. They're cold and we got detectives for that," Clay said.

"Like I said, to be familiar."

"Right," Garth Reeger scoffed from his desk. "I'll tell you why, Clay. Mr. LAPD there wants to stick his fingers into everything. That's why he was poking into my stolen property case while I was gone."

"I wasn't poking into your case, Garth. Dispatch sent me."

"Sure, Mr. Fortunate-Son-in-Law."

"You know," Luke said, "there is a possible way to solve your theft case."

"Did I ask for your help?"

"Just saying, there's something you could try, Garth."

"You fixin' to make me look bad?"

"Hey, Reeger, back off," Clay said. "Dispatch sent Luke over while you were in Austin. Just handle your business."

"Is there a problem here?"

All eyes went to the front of the patrol room where Sheriff Ellerd had been watching them.

"No," Clay said. "We're all good here."

Ellerd was scanning his deputies, quelling the tension, when Irene from the front desk emerged.

"Sheriff, we got Will Young at the DA's Office on hold. Says it's urgent he talk to you."

"I'll take it."

Ellerd went to his office, closed the door and picked up his phone. Through the glass window, Luke and the others saw Ellerd say a few words before his expression became grave.

Ellerd was still on his call with the district attorney when Luke left the office.

Walking across the parking lot, Luke wondered if the call was about him, if his hit-and-run had been discovered.

You're being paranoid—the call could be about a thousand other things.

But Luke's guilt overwhelmed him. The video had changed everything. It proved his crime.

Looking at his SUV, he considered the unrepaired damage. It was a small amount, but now it screamed at him, like a tell-tale admission. Maybe, on a subconscious level, he didn't want to repair it until he resolved the incident.

It was a sunny afternoon as he drove home.

But rolling along River Road near Fawn Ridge, images came back to him, and he saw the woman's face as she streaked over his windshield.

It was real.

Just like LA.

The house was quiet when he entered.

He saw Emily's door was closed—an indication Carrie had put her down for a nap. Luke walked through the house, look-

ing for Carrie, eventually finding her outside in a chair on their
backyard deck. A closed book on her lap, she seemed deep in
thought.

"Hey. How was your day?" he asked.

"I'm thinking that maybe moving here was a mistake."

"Why?" He sat in the chair across from her. "What happened
today?"

"I went to the school to see an old friend and some memories came back."

"What sort of memories?"

"Bad ones."

"Well, Anna said this would happen with the move. And a
lot has happened. Maybe if you talked to me, or her, about it,
it might help?"

"Not now, maybe later." She shifted in her chair, changing
the subject. "How was your day?"

"My day?" He looked off, shrugging with something behind
his eyes. "Just fine. I'm a little beat."

"I haven't started supper. What do you want?"

"Maybe we can go out after the baby wakes up?"

"Sounds good."

"I'll get cleaned up. Are you sure you're okay?"

Carrie nodded.

In the bathroom, Luke looked in the mirror and realized that
he and Carrie were each adrift. Both haunted by their tragedies.

It was coming back to him again. He saw the woman's face
blurring over his windshield.

I've got to find her. She has to be okay.

His knuckles whitened as he gripped the sides of the sink,
staring at himself.

I cannot have the death of another woman on my hands.

24

Denise Diaz had returned to the paper.

The *Chron*, as locals called it, was once housed in a prominent three-story building downtown, next to the courthouse and city hall.

But the evolution of the newspaper business had pushed it from its brick edifice into a strip mall, between a paint store and a pet shop, across from the IHOP at the edge of town. The *Clear River Chronicle* was now in a leased unit just big enough to hold the desks for its nine-person staff, including the cramped office of the editor. With a print circulation of 4,500 and an online presence, the weekly was holding its own in a rocky business.

One wall of the newsroom displayed front pages and awards. On the counter at the reception desk sat a large aquarium treasured by editor Lynn Grant. It held her beloved tetras, guppies and blue bettas. She'd fixed a sign to it that warned: *DO NOT TAP GLASS!*

Denise was working at her corner desk.

She'd joined the *Chronicle* four years ago, after applying for an opening.

You're overqualified and you'll be underpaid, Lynn—a no-nonsense woman whose arm bore a tattoo of her late husband, Merle—

had told Denise during the interview in a booth at the IHOP. *But the job's yours.*

Denise had a long relationship with journalism, but the industry was in decline. Denise had to move to survive, enduring layoffs and buyouts at newsrooms from Seattle to Dallas.

In her time, she'd covered everything from cat shows to school shootings. Along the way, she married a news photographer, whom she divorced when he cheated on her. She'd think of him sometimes, usually while driving home with an old song on the radio underscoring that hers had been a lonely life—that is, until she'd found her one true love, Harvey, her golden retriever. He was always there for her, never let her down. They'd rescued each other. Still, she accepted that she was married to her job, and being a reporter was in her blood. She lived to tell stories and was always on the hunt for good ones.

Soon after she started at the *Chronicle*, Denise mined the paper's archives for items that might have anniversaries coming up, or require follows or updates.

She'd already been familiar with one of the region's biggest mysteries—the unsolved murders of Abby Hall and Erin Eddowes. Although the case had happened years before she'd joined the paper, Denise took over the story. She devoured the *Chronicle*'s earliest reports. Then she read coverage by the big Texas and national news outlets, becoming an expert on the case.

Over her years at the paper, while watching the case grow colder, Denise would check with police for leads. She did small stories, waiting for the right time to do a fuller piece. She was considering a feature tied to the upcoming execution of Donnie Ray Hyde. He'd been considered a suspect but had always denied involvement. Her focus shifted when word reached her that Carrie Hamilton, the sole survivor of the double homicide, had returned to the county.

Denise had put out calls to her sources for help finding Carrie, and for developments on the case. If she could get an exclusive interview with the survivor and weave in Hyde's upcoming execution, she'd have a strong feature.

But it was not to be.

Now Denise sat back in her chair, considering another approach. The *Chronicle's* front door opened, accompanied by the yip of puppies from the pet store. Lynn had returned—she quickly spotted Denise and made her way to her desk.

"How did it go at Cedar Breeze, Denise?"

"She turned me down."

"What was the sense you got from her?"

"She was surprised, but she took my card…so maybe."

"Let her ponder it, then try again."

"I want to know what happened in those woods."

"Everyone does," Lynn said. "With her dad being sick, and her husband's issue in Los Angeles, Carrie's got a lot going on, and I hear not everyone's happy she's back."

"Yeah, I can't imagine coming home to face your ghosts after all these years."

"And we know Hyde just lost out with the Texas Board of Pardons and Paroles and the governor."

"Yes, no surprise there. I'll write something up on that."

"I'm going to try to free you up to really dig into this story with the new Carrie-is-home angle. Maybe tie it to Hyde's upcoming execution."

"Exactly what I was thinking."

"I'm counting on you to deliver."

Denise's phone rang. Lynn nodded to it. "I'll let you get that."

Lynn left and Denise picked up her phone. The number was blocked but she recognized the voice of one of her sources, returning her call.

"Your timing's uncanny," her caller said. "Something has happened in the unsolved murders."

"You mean Hyde striking out with the board? Everyone knows that."

"No, something much bigger."

"Really, pray tell."

"Listen, you're not getting this from me. You can't even say it's from an unnamed source, or on deep background. This is just on the wind, okay?"

"Okay."

"What I'm going to tell you is absolutely true."

Pressing her phone harder against her ear, Denise grabbed her pen, listening and taking notes. When the call ended, her heart beating a little faster, Denise called Will Young at the Clear River County District Attorney's Office. Having been repeatedly reelected to the position, Young was encyclopedic on local criminal history. Fortunately, she'd caught him outside of court and he took her call.

"I'm seeking your response, on the record, to what the *Chronicle* has learned."

"Go ahead."

After Denise relayed what she'd heard from her source, there was a moment of silence before the DA spoke.

"What you've stated is correct."

"All right, can you tell me how—"

"No, I'm sorry, but I cannot elaborate."

The call ended. Denise paused, then placed a call to a law office in Livingston and left a message. Then she placed another call to the county sheriff's office. While waiting, she began typing up the information she had. She was drafting a lead when her phone rang.

"Ridley Martin, returning your call."

After outlining what she had, Denise asked Martin, a criminal law attorney, for his response.

"Your understanding is accurate, but I'm afraid I can offer your paper nothing further at this time."

Thanking Martin, Denise typed up her notes. Then she went to give her editor an update.

"Get as much reaction as you can and get writing," Lynn instructed. "Let's get this up on our site ASAP."

Back at her desk, Denise took a moment to think of the enormity of what she had. Collecting herself and concentrating, she began writing her breaking story.

Convicted killer Donnie Ray Hyde, a drifter from Kilgore, has confessed to killing Abby Hall and Erin Eddowes, both 17, of Clear River, the Chronicle *has learned.*

Hyde made the admission to the district attorney's office through his lawyer in the days before his scheduled execution for the murder of 16-year-old Jenna Dupree in Tyler, Texas.

Hyde's confession came after the Texas Board of Pardons and Paroles, and the governor's office, rejected his request to have his death sentence commuted to life, thereby removing his last and final chance for mercy...

25

A TV news van from Lufkin was the first to arrive in front of Carrie's house.

Soon, media cars and trucks from East Texas, Houston and Dallas lined the street. Neighbors stared from windows, watched from doorsteps and driveways. Reaction to the *Chronicle*'s breaking news of Donnie Ray Hyde's confession to the murders of Abby Hall and Erin Eddowes had been swift.

Carrie peered through the crack between her living room curtains, holding Emily in her arms like an anchor in the tumult. She looked over at her father, who stood at the kitchen counter, talking on his phone. Not long before the story broke, he'd received a call from Bob Ellerd, who'd learned from the DA that Hyde had confessed. Things moved fast once the *Chronicle* got tipped to it and Vern had rushed over to the house, taking steps to shield Carrie from the upheaval emerging around them.

She had not asked for his protection, but everything snowballed after the flutter of calls he'd made to Ellerd, which brought Luke home, still in uniform, along with Deputy Smith. Clay had summoned his wife, Lacey, who came along with Carrie's old high school friend from the party, Opal Wells. Ev-

IF TWO ARE DEAD

eryone was reeling from the news, and Carrie was just trying to comprehend it all.

"We're here for support," Lacey said.

The doorbell rang.

Luke and Clay answered it, stepping outside and, raising their palms respectfully, getting the newspeople to move from the property back to the street.

Carrie joined the others in the kitchen, where Vern remained absorbed in a quiet, intense conversation on his phone. She tried reading his somber expression. Lacey and Opal were scrolling through their phones, constantly looking up toward the sheer curtains and the street.

"This is incredible," Lacey said.

"Everyone always thought it was Donnie Ray," Opal said. "After all these years, it's over, the mystery's been solved. How're you doing, Carrie?"

"It's all so unexpected."

"Maybe you should have some tea? I could hold Emily for you?"

"Maybe later."

Lacey went to the front window, checking on Luke and Clay, then returned.

"Those press people are relentless. We should get you and the baby into a hotel in Houston," Lacey said. "Just until all of this settles down."

"Thank you, Lacey. But no, we'll stay."

Luke came back into the house alone and took Carrie aside. Still holding Emily, she followed him into her office and closed the door behind them.

"How're you holding up?" he asked.

"I don't know. I can't believe it's happening."

"Look, they want a statement."

"A statement?"

"We can keep it short."

Carrie adjusted Emily on her hip. "But I don't know what to say."

"I'll help you. Just one or two sentences. I'll go back out and read it to them. It should satisfy them and they'll go away."

Carrie looked at him.

"It's a tornado right now," Luke said, "but things will calm down and we'll sort it all out."

Struggling to make sense of it all, Carrie worked with Luke on a few sentences that he tapped out on his phone. Then he returned to the street and, under the glare of TV news camera lights, with phones and microphones extended or aimed at him, he read his wife's statement:

"I pray this brings a measure of comfort for the families of Abby, Erin and Jenna, and everyone touched by the crimes. I also pray it marks the end of a long nightmare."

Clay and Luke remained outside as the cluster of media people began breaking up.

Finishing his call, Vern went to Carrie and hugged her.

"Are you okay?" he asked.

"I can't believe this is happening. Why did all the press come here? It's not about me, Dad."

"It's about everyone involved. I've been making a lot of calls. I spoke with Bob Ellerd and he said the same thing's going on with media with Abby's and Erin's families and with Jenna's in Tyler."

"What I don't understand is how? How did this all happen? Why did he confess? Why now?" Carrie asked.

Vern rubbed his temple. "I went to see him."

"You went to see him on death row?" Carrie asked.

"I did."

"Why?"

"He'd always been a suspect—*the* suspect. He'd exhausted every appeal. I spoke with his spiritual counselor, who set up the visit. I spent time with Donnie Ray, explaining this was his only chance to tell the truth and unburden himself, clear his conscience, cleanse his soul, you know. And he did. He gave the district attorney a confession with details only the killer would know."

Carrie stared at her father in awe, her mind blazing back through time, back to her school cafeteria, to standing up to Abby and Erin, then running for her life through Wild Pines Forest and waking in the hospital.

"But I don't remember anything about what happened," she said.

"Carrie," Vern said. "You can stop trying to remember now. He confessed."

She looked at her father. "So, it's over? Is this how it ends?"

Vern searched her face.

"No."

"What do you mean?"

"I've been talking to the TDCJ about the execution, how victims and their family members will be permitted to watch."

"Watch him die?"

Carrie covered her mouth with her free hand, her eyes widening as she shook her head.

26

"This is a surprising turn of events," Dr. Anna Bernay said, her face creasing with concern on the screen.

Carrie had already related the background on Donnie Ray Hyde's confession and the process to view his execution, now less than a week away.

The day after the story broke, Carrie had requested a virtual session to discuss whether or not she should see Hyde put to death.

"Certainly, it's a major development, and it's arisen suddenly," Dr. Bernay said. "What are your thoughts on it all?"

"It's overwhelming. I'm on edge. I do not want to go. The idea of watching someone die right in front of me—it's just—I don't know how anyone can do that."

"Without a doubt, it could be distressing."

"Dad doesn't want me to go. He wants to protect me. But part of me feels, as the survivor, I should do it, as a way to honor Erin and Abby. But in my heart, I know I can't."

"I see. Let me ask you—do you remember Hyde, or anything about him?"

"No."

"Nothing at all?"

"No. But, as you know, I started remembering a little about Abby and Erin when I visited the school. A clear memory came back, about being in the cafeteria and confronting the girls over their bullying of Lanna."

"Visiting the location triggered the event, as we anticipated. We knew the move back would give rise to memories, and Hyde's confession, coupled with his execution, is a huge turn."

"Yes."

"But it can be addressed."

"How?"

"A number of ways. We can identify it, and his execution, as a landmark event, the beginning of the end. And with that, it can be considered an opportunity to heal the past.

"As for witnessing his execution. Your reluctance is understandable. If you do not want to do it, then under no circumstances should you be compelled or feel the need to do so. Do not diminish your reaction in any way. There are real risks. Research has shown witnessing an execution can be psychologically traumatic, that witnesses have experienced dissociative and anxiety symptoms and acute stress."

"Like what exactly?"

"Some witnesses have reported that afterward they felt detached from other people. Other witnesses have said they saw things that weren't real, or had nightmares. The experience could leave you with an unwanted image you cannot erase."

"Would any good come from me witnessing Hyde's death?"

"Carrie, as the sole survivor to the tragedy, you are inexorably linked to it. Attending this final moment could bring on a finality. As you mentioned, you could regard it as a duty to the young girls who died, as the sole survivor bearing witness to the last chapter of this horrible tragedy, which could be a path to healing."

Carrie took a long moment to absorb what Dr. Bernay had offered.

"I'm afraid there is no right or wrong decision here," Dr. Bernay added. "There is only *your decision* and I think you know what it is."

27

The day had come.

Convicted murderer Donnie Ray Hyde was escorted from his cell on death row in handcuffs to a prison van.

It rolled from the Allan B. Polunsky Unit near Livingston through the East Texas countryside bound for Huntsville, a little under an hour away.

Hyde's final journey.

He'd mentally prepared for this day, using the drone of the wheels on the asphalt to seek calm.

Hyde had been assured that all was in order for his mother to claim his body for burial next to his father and his brother, Brophy, at a cemetery in Kilgore. Hyde also saw to it that his property, a few Batman comic books and his radio, along with some money in his inmate trust fund, would be distributed to his friends, other men on death row.

He'd told TDCJ officials that he did not want his ailing mother to witness his execution. Only Ridley Martin, his lawyer, and Vince Azure, his spiritual counselor, were on his witness list.

Hyde regretted how he'd messed up his life. He would not blame God if He cast him into the fire for all eternity.

The van traveled along farmland, bordered by snake-infested swamps with birdsong rising from the treetops. Then, in what seemed to be no time at all, Hyde felt the speed decrease as they navigated through Huntsville to the prison in the heart of town. Soon, they came upon the Huntsville "Walls Unit." Built in the mid-1800s, with its imposing brick walls of two-story buildings and guard towers, it gave off a forbidding aura.

This was the location of the execution chamber.

After some maneuvering in the courtyard, the van stopped. Doors opened.

Taking quiet, deep breaths, Hyde, his handcuffs clinking, was escorted from the van into the chamber, known to inmates as the death house. It was a confined area, containing a handful of empty cells, beige in color. The area smelled of soap, fresh linen and lost hope. Inside, Hyde was strip-searched, given new prison clothes, then placed in the cell farthest away from the door to the execution room.

This was Hyde's death cell.

Guards continued updating Hyde's watch log, which they'd started days earlier. They noted his activities every thirty minutes in the days prior to his execution and now, with hours remaining, every fifteen minutes.

Executions were scheduled for 6 p.m.

Beyond the bars of Hyde's death cell, almost within reach, stood a small table covered with a white cloth, a Bible and a landline phone. Hyde was permitted to make calls for good-byes. He called his mother, barely able to summon the words to talk to her for the last time.

They reminisced about his childhood before he eventually moved the subject to what was about to happen.

"I'm sorry for all the people I hurt. I'm so sorry I brought all this on you, Mama."

"You'll always be my boy. We'll all be together soon."

Later, Hyde was visited by his lawyer, then his spiritual counselor. Throughout their visits, Hyde could not resist staring at the two other phones on the wall of the death house: one was a direct line to the Governor's Office; the other, direct to the Attorney General's Office. The lines would remain open during the process in the event of a last-minute stay.

So far, they had not rung.

In keeping with his last-meal request, Hyde was brought a cheeseburger, fries, Dr Pepper, apple pie and vanilla ice cream. Later, Hyde was offered the chance to shower in the small stall near the cells. The guards explained how many of the condemned want to cleanse themselves before death.

Hyde showered and was given another set of fresh clothes.

It was nearly 6 p.m. when the warden and prison chaplain arrived. Hyde could not help but look at the phones on the wall while the warden spoke.

"All legal relief has been exhausted, Donnie Ray."

Hyde looked at the chaplain, then the warden.

"It's time, son," the warden said.

Hyde was handcuffed and slowly taken from his cell. He stopped to stare. A few paces away was the massive beige steel door to the execution chamber.

Hyde had heard all the stories: how at this point some men cried out; how some felt their knees buckle and had to be steadied by guards.

The huge door opened.

"The Lord is with you," the chaplain said. "Be strong."

"Face it like a man," the warden said.

Numb, Hyde found himself inside the small death chamber, staring at the waiting gurney. He was helped onto it by the guards. His handcuffs were removed and he lay on his back. The tie-down team secured his body to the gurney at eight points using thick caramel-colored leather belts, two of which secured Hyde's extended arms on the armrests. The armrests were encased in white medical tape, filling the chamber with an antiseptic smell. A medical officer then affixed an IV to Hyde's arm and a monitor cable to his heart.

Hyde gazed around the small room; its brick walls were robin's-egg blue. The curtains were closed at the barred viewing window. He stared up at the bright light above, then heard witnesses shuffling softly into place near him on the other side of the curtained window.

Soon, Hyde would see the faces of the murdered girls.

28

Vern's jaw tensed when the viewing window curtains opened.

Donnie Ray Hyde, strapped to the gurney, turned his head, meeting the gaze of the witnesses standing a few feet away on the other side of the glass.

In that moment, Vern recalled what a retired warden had told him about mothers who watched their sons being executed, how they'd release a banshee cry that haunted anyone who heard it.

Vern knew that Hyde's mother was not present. Hyde did not want her to see his death. It was just as well. And Vern was relieved Carrie didn't want to be here. Witnessing this would exact an enormous new psychological toll on her. It could trigger all sorts of memories.

Things she doesn't need to remember.

Not now.

Carrie was safe, away in another room with Luke.

Watching the process unfolding before him, Vern knew this was the beginning of the end. It was his job to see it through, to bear witness.

He knew Texas law allowed for five journalists to view executions: one from the local paper, the *Huntsville Item*; two from wire services; and two from the communities where the crimes had happened. A TV reporter from a Tyler station was present for Jenna's case. And Denise Diaz with the *Clear River Chronicle* was there for Abby and Erin's case.

When he'd arrived at the prison, officials took Vern into a room where staff from the Victim Services Division briefed him—along with the families of Abby Hall, Erin Eddowes and Jenna Dupree—on the procedure before escorting them to the viewing area.

Now everyone was in place at the viewing window, the victims' families, witnesses for the condemned and the press all separated by curtained walls, never seeing each other during the execution process. When they saw Hyde through the glass, relatives of Abby and Erin, who were wearing blazers, opened them slightly and pointed to themselves, a gesture that puzzled Vern.

Hyde only blinked when he saw them.

Looking upon him, Vern concentrated, struck by how human Hyde appeared. Not like a killer, or a monster, but vulnerable. Hyde's eyes were filled with fear.

Suddenly Vern's attention was pulled to the warden, standing next to Hyde.

"Do you wish to make a statement, son?"

Hyde swallowed hard, summoning the remnants of his composure, clearing his throat. He lifted his head slightly, turned to all those at the window and searched their faces.

"I am sorry for what I done. I am sorry for the pain I caused."

Hyde turned back, looked up to the ceiling light.

"Anything more, son?" the warden asked.

"No, sir."

At that point, the warden looked at the IV tubes fixed to Hyde that ran through a small port into the executioner's room. The warden then signaled the unseen, anonymous medical officer to begin administering the three drugs. The first would sedate Hyde. The second would relax his muscles, collapse his diaphragm and lungs. The third would stop his heart.

Hyde's body quivered; the color of his face changed, then his eyes closed.

At the moment of Hyde's death, Carrie was in another part of the prison.

Sitting in a barren meeting room with Luke and a Victims Services staff member, she retreated into her thoughts. Nearby in the death chamber was the man who'd murdered three girls.

And tried to kill me.

Imagining Hyde dying on the gurney, Carrie was cast back…

…to the frightened eyes of a school friend…in the cafeteria… Abby and Erin tormenting Lanna… Carrie's anger erupting… Abby smiling… "Whoa, Carrie, honey, just chill. It's just a little harmless joke." Erin extending her wrists. "Are you going to arrest us, Sheriff?"…

…running through the woods…running for her life…the ground under her vanishing… She's in the air…falling…the river swallows her…flailing…fighting for air in the violent current bouncing between the rocks…smashing her head… Waking in the hospital…her father looking down at her…

Suddenly Carrie's attention was pulled to Vern and others in the group of the victims' relatives, accompanied by Victims Services members, filing through the room.

This stage of the execution process had ended.

Carrie took a breath. Just knowing that Hyde had confessed, that he'd been executed, was as far as she could go.

It has to be enough for me.

"Are you okay?" Luke asked.

"I don't know."

Shaken, she turned her focus and distress to her father, who was looking down on her.

"You watched him die."

Vern studied her.

"It was important to see this through to the end." He rubbed her shoulder. "It's done. It's over."

Carrie looked at him.

"It'll never be over, Daddy."

29

After Hyde was declared dead and his death certificate signed, his body was loaded into a waiting hearse backed up to the same door of the death house where he had entered alive.

A local funeral home would prepare his remains for transfer to Kilgore.

Carrie and the families were led in a somber procession from the prison, across the street, to an area outside near the administration building. TV news vans and satellite trucks were parked in the distance.

People from Tyler, Clear River and across Texas had gathered with signs advocating their support for Hyde's execution. Nearby, separated by police and prison staff, a smaller group opposed to the death penalty carried placards and lit candles.

A few yards away, dozens of journalists had assembled. The families had agreed to a brief press conference, and they joined the group gathered around an impromptu podium, heaped with microphones under the glow of TV lights.

First to speak was an official with the Texas Department of Criminal Justice, who summarized how Hyde's death sentence was carried out. Next up was one of the wire service reporters who'd witnessed the execution. Referring to the notes he'd taken, he gave a careful account of the execution. He detailed Hyde's appearance, his demeanor, how he'd turned to look at everyone present. He recounted how Hyde had apologized with his final statement, reading word for word from his notes as other reporters recorded it.

The victims' families and their supporters had formed a large group. With them were friends of Jenna Dupree and investigators from Tyler. Relatives and friends of Abby and Erin stood nearby, along with detectives from Clear River County, deputies and friends. Clay and Lacey Smith, along with others, were also there.

The reporters began by asking Jenna Dupree's family for reaction. Her uncle came to the podium.

"Our anguish at losing Jen will never ever go away," he said. "But we're relieved to know Hyde can't hurt any more innocent people."

Then the first question for Abby's and Erin's families came from a TV reporter from Dallas.

"Why was it important for you to be here?"

Nicole Hall, Abby's sister, glanced around. Being closest to the podium, she stepped up to it and, with all the news cameras aimed at her, took a breath.

"To see justice done," Nicole said. "I think all of us take some comfort that we've reached some sort of finality."

A Houston newspaper reporter asked: "What did it mean for you when Hyde expressed remorse for his crimes?"

Lauren Eddowes, Erin's cousin, stepped forward. "It took so long for us to reach this point," she said. "For years we've lived with the pain of not knowing the truth, and—" Lauren glanced at Nicole, then they both glanced at Carrie, blinking apologetically. "There were so many unanswered questions, so many hurtful rumors. So, yes, we're glad he confessed and it's finally over."

Carrie covered her mouth with her hand. The gesture from

Lauren and Nicole, who'd behaved so coldly and accusatorily to her at Lacey's party, had taken her by surprise.

Another TV network reporter indicated the framed photos of Abby and Erin that many held, as well as the T-shirts Lauren and Nicole were wearing, which displayed the faces of the murdered teens. A few friends of Jenna also wore T-shirts showing her picture.

"Lauren, Nicole," the reporter said, "can you tell us a little about why you wore those T-shirts into the execution?"

"Well," Nicole said, "we weren't permitted to take photographs into the viewing area."

Lauren said: "We had these shirts made so that their faces would be the last thing Hyde saw."

"Did Hyde see them?" the reporter asked.

"Yes, he did," Nicole said.

Luke studied the faces of the girls in the framed photos and on the T-shirts.

Faces of the dead.

Suddenly waves of raw emotion unleashed horrible images… the face of the woman he'd killed in Los Angeles… Then, in Clear River, driving home that night, the storm…*the face of a woman hurtling over his windshield*… Thinking of Hyde dying on the gurney, all of it churned in Luke…

"You were there when Abby and Erin were killed," Denise Diaz of the *Chronicle* was now saying to Carrie, pulling Luke from his thoughts.

Carrie had moved to the podium, surveying all the news cameras.

"We know from the witness list that you didn't see Hyde's execution. Why did you not want to be there?"

"I just couldn't do it."

"This was the man who'd tried to kill you."

"I didn't want to witness his death."

"I'm wondering," Diaz continued, "if being here today brought back memories of that day in Wild Pines Forest?"

Carrie was silent for a long moment. Vern stood next to her, putting his arm around her as she began shaking her head slowly.

"No," Carrie said. "I remember very little."

"Not even after today?"

"She nearly died in the attack," Vern said. "She suffered a serious neurological injury, impairing her memory to this day."

"I understand," Diaz said. "But on another aspect, Carrie, you were the sole survivor. Three of you entered the woods that day. But you were the only one who came out alive. Early in the case, investigators considered you a suspect. Does Hyde's confession and his execution today bring you any solace, any relief?"

Carrie took a breath. "It's been a nightmare and now it's over."

Diaz continued while paging through her notebook. "This is for the Clear River investigators—it's my understanding that Hyde confessed after he was recently visited on death row by Vernon Hamilton, Carrie's father and Clear River County's former sheriff, who oversaw the initial investigation. Can you tell us how Hyde's confession came about when he'd always denied having any involvement in the case? And I also understand that investigators had no hard evidence linking Hyde to the case. Could you elaborate on what changed?"

Vern's jaw muscles bunched as he traded a glance with Sheriff Bob Ellerd, who made his way to the podium.

"I don't think," Ellerd said, indicating the families, "that this is the proper time and place for this discussion."

But national network reporters from Dallas and Houston, eager to piggyback on Diaz's expertise on the case, pressed Ellerd to respond.

Exchanging glances with Vern and Will Young, the Clear River County district attorney, Ellerd rubbed his chin before he spoke.

"Donnie Ray Hyde was always the primary suspect. His polygraph was inconclusive; his alibi was weak. After his death sentence for killing Jenna Dupree, he launched appeals. As long as he had any hope of succeeding, he would not cooperate with our case. But once all of his appeals were exhausted, he confessed."

"Sir," a reporter from NBC said, "can you or any official here tell us what Hyde said in his confession?"

Ellerd turned to the DA, who indicated for Hyde's lawyer, Ridley Martin, and Vince Azure, his spiritual counselor, to join him.

"I can tell you," Martin said, "that Donnie Ray waived his attorney–client privilege after death."

"We can also say," Young added, "that he provided information only the person who killed Abby and Erin would know."

"Can you elaborate?" the NBC reporter pressed. "What sort of information?"

"We're still assessing it," the DA said. "But there is no indication that anyone other than Donnie Ray Hyde is responsible for the deaths of Abby Hall and Erin Eddowes."

A reporter from CNN then asked Vince Azure: "As his spiritual counselor, can you tell us why Hyde made the last-minute confession?"

"He told me he wanted to leave this world knowing that he'd told the truth. He wanted to cleanse his conscience, do the right thing, maybe give the families some peace."

At that point, the TDCJ official took to the podium. "I think this concludes things."

Reporters called out more questions, but the official closed it down with: "Thank you, everyone."

As the various groups began leaving, Lacey and Clay joined Carrie and her father.

"You did good, Carrie," Lacey said, rubbing her shoulder.

"You sure did," Clay added. "It's over now, all of it."

"That's for damn sure," Vern said. "This puts it all to rest."

Carrie offered a weak smile, looking for Luke.

He'd stopped and was staring hard at the imposing "Walls Unit."

30

Carrie didn't answer her front doorbell.

In the quiet of the passing minutes, she heard murmuring voices on her doorstep. Then, after a long moment, car doors slammed and an engine started.

Checking the monitor of her home security system, she saw the vehicle pulling away, a van from a Houston TV station.

Following the execution, she'd received a stream of messages and calls from news media. Some showed up at her house. It had been several days now, and thankfully the flow had ebbed. The Houston crew was the only one to come to her door today.

Carrie had declined all earlier requests, including those from CNN, the *New York Times* and *Dateline*. She couldn't bring herself to talk about the case.

At times, to ease herself, she thought of the most recent photos from Pearl, and her postcard asking Carrie: *How's everybody?* It hurt Carrie to keep the truth from Pearl. Sooner or later, she'd learn what had happened. For now, not wanting to spoil her aunt's cruise, Carrie was reluctant to tell her how she was still coming to grips with the aftereffects of Hyde's execution. Vern had stressed that it was the end. But for Carrie, it felt like a beginning, like something indefinable had opened, and she wished she could talk about it with Pearl.

It didn't feel like something she could bring up with Luke—as much as he appeared to have resumed his routine, Carrie still felt he was withdrawn, distant. A few times at dinner she'd had to repeat herself to pull him back into the conversation.

And she felt a similar distance from her father. Visiting with him, she sensed that a calm had come over him. A finality. *Is it acceptance of his own mortality?* Whenever she asked him if his condition was causing him discomfort, he'd give her the same answer: *No pain, darlin'.*

Carrie would smile, watching him play with Emily. But in her heart, she wasn't sure she believed him. She wasn't sure of anything anymore. Today, during a video call with clients, she'd lost track. People had to go over subjects more than once because she couldn't focus.

Nights were the worst.

And tonight was no different.

Again, sleep was a fugitive.

She didn't want to take sleeping pills in case it interfered with her ability to hear Emily. Not wanting to wake Luke beside her, she got her book light and resumed reading *Les Misérables* until she grew drowsy. Placing the novel on her night table, she settled into sleep, but she was soon haunted with thoughts of Hyde.

The man who killed Jenna Dupree, Abby and Erin.

The man who tried to kill me.

He confessed to everything.

I should remember him.

I should remember what happened in the woods.

In her torpid state between consciousness and sleep, Carrie heard a voice deep inside her. Far off but strong, pressing her to keep casting back, keep trying to remember, because it was the only way she could resolve the questions that tormented her.

She recalled being angry with Abby and Erin in the cafeteria.

But why did we go into the woods? Where was Hyde? What happened?
She remembered running for her life...falling into the cold water...choking,
flailing in the current...struggling to breathe...waking...

...in the darkness of her bedroom.

The blue illuminated digits of her clock glowed: 3:15 a.m.
She turned to nestle against Luke, but there was nothing.

His side of the bed was empty.

He was gone.

No light in the bathroom.

He wasn't working.

Carrie slipped from bed and went to Emily's room.

The baby was gone.

31

Midafternoon in Los Angeles.

Luke and his partner, Nick Hernandez, are in uniform, in a marked black-and-white LAPD SUV on patrol.

The shift has been quiet so far when they pick up a broadcast, alerting patrols to a suspect vehicle. The plate and description: a 2019 blue Chevrolet Silverado with a smashed right taillight. Lone occupant, driver is a white female in her thirties, possibly armed with a gun. Extreme caution advised: vehicle is related to a fatal shooting.

Minutes later, an LAPD helicopter broadcasts, "Eyes on the vehicle, high speed, eastbound."

The officer continues updating coordinates.

The vehicle then enters Luke and Nick's division.

The helicopter broadcasts: "We'll get other units to respond, Code Three."

Nick, at the wheel, spots it. Luke grabs the radio, identifying their unit and location.

"We've got a visual on the vehicle. She's moving."

The officer in the chopper responds: "Watch your traffic, driver reportedly armed."

Nick activates their siren and lights. The Silverado accelerates, clips vehicles. *It weaves to the wrong side of the road, racing through red lights and stop signs.*

Nick and Luke are the primary unit, but second and third units, lights and sirens going, join the pursuit. It lasts for three miles before the Silverado slides, brakes screeching into the rear of a dump truck loaded with gravel.

Airbags deploy.

Luke radios updates. He and Nick, weapons drawn, hurry to the pickup. Nick takes the driver's side, Luke the passenger side. There's movement from the sole occupant, a female. Nick shouts: "Get out of the vehicle! Get on the ground!"

The woman springs out, brandishing a semiautomatic rifle, and opens fire, hitting Nick, putting him down and instantly swinging to Luke, shooting and missing as he returns fire. He strikes her, sending her to the ground, her gun sliding away.

Luke restrains the suspect and secures her weapon, radios updates, rushes to Nick. He's groaning, but alive. His new body armor stopped the rounds that hit him; he indicates through clenched teeth that he's okay.

Luke goes to the suspect, staring at the woman lying on the street, plastic cuffs on her wrists, blood oozing from her wound...brilliant puddles growing on the pavement. The whomp-whomp-whomp of the chopper above—radio transmissions, distant sirens—everything is muffled, like he's underwater. People on the street, faces contorted... phones pointing like accusations... Looking down at her...dropping to his knees...his hands on her chest...applying compressions... Her eyes open wide, her head nodding like a rag doll, but he doesn't stop. Paramedics take over...but he knows...standing over her, his hands dripping with her blood...he knows...she's dead...

It emerged that the woman, a thirty-five-year-old mother of a little boy and a little girl, was struggling with addiction. Upon learning that her husband was cheating on her with her best friend, the woman went to her friend's home and caught them in the act. She shot them both dead before fleeing. While driving, she phoned her brother, telling him what she'd done and that she wanted to die. He alerted police; he'd tried to convince her to surrender.

It was futile. She refused to stop.

Later, the LAPD's investigation had cleared Luke, finding that the suspect was ultimately responsible for her own death.

But official exoneration would never erase the fact that he had killed a woman, leaving her two children orphaned.

Nothing could diminish his anguish at taking a life.

Now, in his living room, past 3 a.m., rocking in the darkness with his sleeping daughter on his chest, the woman's face haunted him again…

…her head nodding like a rag doll…eyes open wide…eyes that smiled on her wedding day…at her children at Christmas, at birthdays…

Then Luke saw the woman he'd struck on River Road, her face blurring in the rain over his windshield.

Another life.

Careful not to wake Emily, Luke got his phone from his pocket. He replayed the construction site video he'd copied. In the brief flicker, he saw the rain-streaked blip of pink, a figure rising from the roadside before disappearing. The construction guys had no idea what they'd seen.

But Luke knew.

He'd struck a woman.

Why don't I report it? Am I so traumatized I can't think straight?

Luke shut his eyes and winced. How long had it been now?

No victim had been found.

But the evidence hammered at him like the beating of a telltale heart. The damage to his car. The fabric he'd tossed. The video.

Is the woman alive?

I need to find out what happened to her. Then I'll turn myself in.

Luke thought of Hyde's execution, knowing that he'd confessed, ending the nightmare.

Luke considered Carrie and Vern, all they'd suffered, all they'd endured over the years. Carrie's torment, folks turning against her, suspecting her. And people turning against Vern, with the ugly rumor about how his wife died. Then Vern's diagnosis— *his death sentence.*

Even Hyde had cleared his conscience.

Admitted his guilt.

"Luke?"

At the edge of the ambient light, Carrie's face appeared.

She looked at him holding their sleeping daughter, stepped closer and touched his shoulder.

"What is it?"

He remained silent.

"Honey," she said, "you're acting like you did right after the shooting, when things were so bad, when you were not okay. Are you okay?"

He tensed and for an instant he wanted to bare his soul. He wanted to tell Carrie what he did on that rainy night they talked on the phone, tell her what he was hiding.

But all he could do was utter: "Hyde's execution just drove home the truth for me."

"The truth?"

"I'm a killer, too, Carrie."

She stared at him for a moment, then said: "It's the shooting again."

He nodded.

"Honey." Carrie stroked his hair. "You were defending yourself, keeping people safe, doing your job."

Luke shook his head.

"I'm as guilty as Hyde for what I've done."

32

The song floated like balm over the speakers in the darkened bar in Clear River. Waylon Jennings, longing to get back to the basics of love and a pain-free life in Luckenbach, Texas.

The music played while, in a quiet corner, several men were gathered at a table, huddled over a skyline of glasses and bottles. And as the song revered a simpler life, they talked quietly about death.

"What was it like, watching Hyde go to his maker?" Clay Smith asked Vern Hamilton.

Vern glanced round at the faces of men from the sheriff's office and police. In their line of work, they'd confronted death at highway wrecks, where bodies were entwined in twisted metal, deaths at shootings, fires, drownings and suicides. But Vern was the only one here who'd witnessed an execution.

He stared into his beer, as if it would carry him back to the viewing window in Huntsville, then shook his head thoughtfully.

"Like watching someone go to sleep. It looked peaceful."

A pensive air fell over the men as they each absorbed his account.

"Peaceful," Clay repeated, shaking his head. "A shame he

didn't suffer like the girls he killed. It's good he's in the ground. Good riddance, I say. It's done."

The group punctuated Clay's words with another pull on their beers, a subtle toast to the end of a violent chapter in the county's history.

"How'd you do it, Vern?" Eugene Cobb, a detective with the county, asked. "Every time Blake and I approached him, he shut us down." Cobb had chiseled features, but his recent divorce had carved lines into his groggy face, making him look older than he was. "You go see him at Polunsky in Livingston and prod him to confess? I mean...wow."

The edges of Vern's silver mustache drooped and he traded a quick glance with Sheriff Bob Ellerd, then Blake Mallory.

"He'd always been a suspect," Vern said.

Ellerd nodded and drank some beer as Vern continued.

"As you know, it started when Tyler detectives put Hyde near the woods at the time of the murders. All the similarities with Jenna Dupree, and some physical evidence left at the scene, were consistent with Wild Pines."

"But you had nothing strong enough to charge him?" Clay said.

"No, not at the time," Vern said.

"But before Hyde surfaced—" Garth Reeger nodded, his focus landing on Vern "—they were looking hard at your daughter for the murders."

All eyes turned to Reeger, who was regarded as a pariah by most at the sheriff's office. He hadn't been invited to join the group. He happened to arrive at the bar and, upon greeting his colleagues at the table, was, after a brief hesitation, permitted to pull up a chair, momentarily changing the mood. Reeger had mostly remained silent and the others tolerated his presence. But now, as he engaged in the conversation, Ellerd saw Vern's jaw tensing.

"That's right, Garth," Ellerd said. "Eve Trainor and Ben Mc-

Graw, the first leads, were convinced that Carrie had a falling-out at school with Abby and Erin and resolved it in Wild Pines Forest."

"And what was the cause of death?" Reeger asked.

Ellerd, Vern, Cobb and Mallory exchanged glances.

"That's never been revealed," Mallory said. "It was always held back to protect the case."

"If it's over, there's nothing to protect," Reeger said.

"Most people always speculated it was gunshot wounds," Ellerd said. "That turned out to be the cause, of course."

"So, when Hyde confessed, you recovered the murder weapon?" Clay asked.

"No," Ellerd said. "Hyde said he threw it and the casings somewhere in the Sabine River, in the Piney Woods. It's never been recovered."

Clay saw that Vern appeared pensive, lost in his thoughts.

"Damn, Vern, you been through hell with this for so long," Reeger said. "Carrie not remembering anything? Maybe that's a blessing."

Vern stared at Reeger.

"She nearly died running for her life," Vern said. "A bone chip from her skull cut into her brain."

"It was good that you got her to California," Clay said.

After a gulp of beer, Reeger nodded in agreement. "It sure was," Reeger said, nodding. "She marries Luke, of the LAPD. They make you a granddaddy. Then Luke comes to work here, for lower pay and a slower pace after his troubles in LA. Kinda like on-the-job therapy."

"You got a point to make, Reeger?" Vern said.

Reeger drank again. "Just that Luke Conway is something, all right."

"What the hell are you talking about?" Vern said.

"I'm talking about him sticking his nose in my zone. In my

investigation. He just seems awfully interested in things near Fawn Ridge and River Road and I can't figure out why."

"Drop it," Ellerd said.

"Is this why you came here?" Vern said. "To make insinuations about my family?"

"I'm just saying, something's a little off with Luke Conway."

"I said drop it, Garth," Ellerd said.

"Garth." Clay turned to Reeger. "You got a mighty short memory, buddy. Fact is, Luke was assigned to cover for you while you were in Austin. The construction folks at Fawn called to ask why you were draggin' your ass on the theft of forty thousand in material and tools from their site. And, as I recall, Luke suggested he might know a way you could solve it. But your ego shut him down."

Reeger's face reddened as he bit back on his anger, then downed the remainder of his beer.

"I'm just sayin' there's something not right," Reeger said, reaching into his pocket. He tossed some bills on the table. "Not right."

Once Reeger had left, the others shook their heads, some of them smiling.

"Yep, something's not right. With Reeger," Clay said.

The men passed another hour talking and slowing their drinking. At one point, Vern, being the proud grandpa, took out his phone and showed off pictures of Emily.

"Vern," Mallory said, "it's got to feel good having Carrie back home with your grandbaby and Luke, especially with all this awful Hyde business done."

"It's the best medicine, given the time I got left."

"Yeah," Clay said, "colon cancer. That's a hell of a thing, Vern. A hell of a thing."

"You play the hand you're dealt."

"How you doing these days?" Ellerd asked.

Vern shrugged. "No pain, just living every day."

"Well, your detective instincts and skill are as sharp as ever," Mallory said. "I'm amazed that after all these years, you succeeded in getting Hyde to confess."

Vern peered into his beer.

"Sometimes when a man is close to death, his sense of what's right and what's wrong becomes crystalline. It can become more than his conscience can bear."

Mallory had the least to drink and was the designated driver, taking the others home in his pickup with the crew cab.

After arriving home, alone in the dim light, Vern went to his office. Sitting at his desk, he looked at his framed pictures of his family while reflecting on the conversations at the bar.

In his tired, semi-inebriated state, he considered Luke. Vern understood fully the regret and trauma Luke carried. Then, looking upon Doreen's smiling face, the melody of her favorite song came to him, along with memories of holding her while they danced in the kitchen.

Then her job, their arguments, his suspicions.

Her death.

How it'd cleaved him, left him a broken man.

Those vile rumors that he'd killed Doreen.

Vern swallowed hard.

Lord, he missed her.

Then Carrie, the lone survivor in the woods. He thought about how he almost lost her. Making sure she moved away, to live with Pearl in California. Her meeting Luke, becoming a mother.

The doctor, telling him he was terminal, running out of time.

Hyde's confession, clearing the case.

The girls were shot. The gun never found.

The questions at the bar echoed in his mind: How did he get Hyde to confess?

Sometimes a man's conscience becomes more than he can bear.

Vern took stock of his study, his citations, plaques, guns and books on investigative techniques.

And sometimes, the truth will remain buried even if I have to take it to my grave.

33

"No, Donnie Ray didn't want me to witness it." Mary-Ellen Hyde's voice weakened. "He knew I couldn't bear it." She set a mug of coffee on her kitchen table in front of her guest.

"Thank you," Denise Diaz said.

Mary-Ellen sat as though the world was on her shoulders.

"You say he didn't suffer? It was like going to sleep?"

"Yes."

Eyes glistening, Mary-Ellen gazed out the window over her chipped sink. For some forty years, she'd lived in this two-bedroom frame home with a leaky roof, blistered paint and a sagging front porch propped up with cinder blocks. It sat on a patch of dirt and grass in the northwest part of Kilgore.

It had taken Denise a little under two hours to make the drive from Clear River that morning. Lynn, her editor, was reluctant to let her go, but Denise told her it was important. Determined to tell the full story of the murders in Wild Pines Forest, she wanted to talk to as many people connected to the case as she could. Hyde's mother had welcomed her into her home.

"It's been a hard life," Mary-Ellen said. "Jack, my husband, drank and gambled. His family had problems with the law, drugs, booze, everything. Jack said they inherited misfortune. 'It's in our blood,' he'd say."

Mary-Ellen looked at her hands, gnarled with arthritis.

"Must be true because trouble always found Brophy and Donnie Ray wherever those boys went," she said.

"I don't deny that Donnie Ray, that he—" Mary-Ellen paused, unable to voice the correct word "—that he *hurt* that little girl in Tyler. He told me. He said it was like being under some spell and it wasn't really him doing the hurting. He said the girl appeared in his prison cell at night, standing at the foot of his cot, asking him why."

Mary-Ellen shook her head slowly. "Lord only knows. But I can tell you this: in all my visits with him over the years, when I could make it to Livingston, Donnie Ray never once admitted to hurting those two girls in Clear River County. What he did in Tyler was wrong, to be sure, and he got convicted for it. Paid for it. But confessing like he did, at the last minute, to hurting two more girls? I just can't believe it. I know he done wrong, and my heart breaks for the families, but for him to take away three girls. *Three?* I don't believe it. That would make him a monster."

She touched a tissue to her eyes.

"We had a hard life. What's done is done. Now my boys are in their graves next to their daddy. Lord, I hope with all my heart that Donnie Ray's death brings peace to the families of those girls."

Mary-Ellen thought for a long moment, then her face creased into the hint of a mournful smile.

"Funny how not long after Donnie Ray's passing, some good fortune came."

"What do you mean?"

"The other day, I got word that some of my financial difficulties got straightened out, on taxes and other debts. It was a godsend."

"Isn't that interesting."

"Strange how things go."

Mary-Ellen looked to the window and the blue sky as they talked more about how she planned to bring fresh flowers to the graves of her husband and sons.

Wrapping things up, Denise collected her recorder and notebook. Then she took photos of Mary-Ellen in Hyde's childhood bedroom as Mary-Ellen cradled a picture of him when he was ten years old.

Of course Mary-Ellen couldn't accept Donnie Ray's eleventh-hour confession, Denise thought later, after ordering a club sandwich in a Kilgore diner. What mother wants to accept giving birth to and raising a serial killer?

Or, in Mary-Ellen's words, a monster.

It was strange that Mary-Ellen had received word of financial relief at the time she was mourning the end of her family. *Weird how life unfolds*, Denise thought, pulling her notebook and phone from her bag and placing them on the table of her booth.

She was under pressure because Lynn had cleared her to chase the story. With a small staff, it meant others had to pick up extra assignments, including Lynn, who was handling things Denise would've done.

Her food came and she ate while reviewing her work. She'd already talked to Abby's and Erin's relatives. There were a few revelations there, she thought as she struck them off her list.

Next, she was headed to Tyler to interview Jenna's family as well as the investigators who'd tipped Clear River County to Hyde.

She also wanted to talk to the first lead detectives on the Clear River County murders: Eve Trainor and Ben McGraw. She'd tracked down their contact information and sent messages but hadn't heard back yet.

Aspects critical to the story remained a challenge. She was

having trouble getting her hands on the entire file, which held
reports, statements, forensic tests, Hyde's confession—everything
related to the Wild Pines murders. She'd asked for it over a week
ago.

No word on the status.

Denise was concerned. Scrolling through her contacts on her
phone, she pressed a number knowing that her ID would come
up at the other end.

It rang twice.

"Hello, Denise."

"Hi, Sheriff. It's been a week."

"Well, it's like I told you." She heard the squeak of Ellerd's
office chair as he leaned back. "I'm not sure we can release it."

"Really?"

"We're looking into a few things first."

"What few things?"

"Just a few things."

"Sheriff, the investigation's over, isn't it?"

"Well, yes."

"So there's nothing outstanding to hinder prosecution of
any sort. Hyde's confession was assessed and accepted, correct?"

"Yes."

"I would like a copy of the file. I've assured your office that
the *Chronicle* will pay for the copying costs, or for the time it
takes to give us a digital copy. It's been more than a week now."

"We're looking at your request."

"You know I have other options, Sheriff. It might take me
longer, but I'll make a formal request for the entire file under
the Texas Public Information Act, compelling you to release it
under the law. And if you still don't release it, or if you with-
hold parts of it, the *Chronicle* can go to court and make an appeal. Think of the media attention that will bring down on your
office. You know that's our legal right under the law, Sheriff."

A moment passed between them.

"I know the law, Denise. I never said we wouldn't release it. I just said we're looking into a few things."

"How much longer?"

"No more than a day or two, at most."

"All right, Sheriff. Thank you. I'll keep checking."

"Oh, I know you will."

Ending her call, Denise exhaled, sipped her diet cola, then ate more of her sandwich. While chewing, she gnawed on her need to get the case file. Why was Ellerd stalling? What few things could they still be looking into? It shouldn't take long to copy it. Not much had changed over thirteen years. The only new addition was Hyde's confession.

Accessing the file was critical to the story Denise was going to write. She wanted to take readers back to that day in Wild Pines. To do that, she needed two things: the case file and an interview with the only living witness, Carrie. With those two pillars, she could fill in the blanks, tell the full story of the mystery that had gripped the county, the state and the country for thirteen years.

And she had to get it out before anyone beat the *Chronicle* to it. *This tragedy happened in our community*, she thought. *We have to tell the definitive story. It's a matter of journalistic pride.*

Denise had reached out to Carrie for an interview. No response. Denise had then contacted Luke, Carrie's husband. Again, no response. Finally, a few days ago, a message came from Vern, Carrie's father.

Carrie doesn't want to talk about the case. We refer you to the statements she made at the press conference in Huntsville.

Denise did not want to reuse those older comments that were already public. She wanted an exclusive interview with Carrie about that day, with the aim of getting as many untold details as Carrie could remember. Denise was aware Carrie had suffered a head injury in the attack, leaving her with a spotty memory—it was what gave rise to rumors and suspicions about her—but Denise wanted as much as she could get. She wanted to tell the whole story. And for that she needed to talk to Carrie.

She leaned back in her booth seat.

Maybe she needed to show up at Carrie's house again. Or follow her, approach her, plead face-to-face. Maybe that was what it was going to take. Denise collected her things, paid her check and headed for her car.

Being persistent was part of her job.

34

After his shift, Luke headed home along River Road, his gut stiffening as it did each time he neared the new subdivision at Fawn Ridge.

This is where it happened.

Today, instead of quickly driving by, he slowed, taking in the few distant houses and storage buildings dotting the gentle slope to the right. Set far from the road, they were scattered amid clutches of forests and fields.

What if she'd stumbled to one of those places?

His signal clicking, he turned onto the dirt road leading to the nearest house. Along the way, he struggled with his thoughts.

I'm grasping at straws. Putting off what I should've done from the start. But I can't turn myself in.

Not yet.

He needed answers. His urgency to end the mystery had increased in the wake of Hyde's admission—he'd seen how it had brought a horrible part of Carrie's and Vern's lives to a close.

Vern.

Vern was a force unto himself, he thought.

I got this deputy job because of him. He moved heaven and earth to help me, all while dealing with his own terminal condition. And he triggered Donnie Ray Hyde's confession.

And what do I do after killing a woman in LA?

Shaking his head, he looked out the window.

I hit a woman on this road. I'm not losing my mind. I didn't imagine it. Please let her be okay. Somehow, I'll find out what happened to her, then I'll make this right.

Luke came to a stop in the driveway next to a white clapboard house. It had a tin roof and roomy front porch with wicker rocking chairs. Boards creaked when he stepped up. The intermittent whirring of a sewing machine could be heard through the screen door when he knocked.

A woman in her seventies wearing a print dress answered, gray hair tied into a knot. She had nimble hands, fingers that moved gracefully when she removed her glasses, letting them drop by the chain around her neck. A trace of concern tugged at her while she assessed him standing there in his uniform.

"Sorry to trouble you, ma'am."

"No trouble." Her eyes caught the nameplate on his breast pocket. "Is something wrong, Deputy?"

"Several weeks back, or longer, we had an unconfirmed report of a person needing help on the road there." He turned to point, then turned back. "Near your property."

"Oh, my, was it an accident of some sort? People drive so fast along that road."

"Possibly. But no one was found. No one was taken to the hospital. No other reports. And, like I said, nothing could be confirmed, and it was some time ago."

"So maybe a false alarm?"

"Do you recall seeing or hearing anything unusual on the road during a storm a while back?"

"Goodness, no, I don't think so."

"Did anyone come to your door needing help? Anything like that? It would've been late, around eleven thirty."

"Eleven thirty?" She shook her head. "No, we usually turn in about ten, then I read for a bit."

"So, nothing?"

"Wait, a deputy did come by."

"When?"

"Oh, maybe two or three months ago. He was asking about somebody stealing lumber from those new houses." She shook her head. "That big development is eating up our countryside. We didn't notice anything then either."

"You said 'we'?"

"Me and my husband, John."

"Could I talk to him?"

"He's in Beaumont visiting his brother."

Luke nodded, thinking. "Ma'am, would it be all right if I look around outside your place?"

"Look for what?"

"Well, maybe there's an indication of someone passing through or something."

"Look all you like." She almost laughed. "But the only things passing through are rabbits and possums. Go ahead, I'll fix you a glass of lemonade."

Luke walked to the outbuildings, first coming to a shed without a door. Stepping inside, he was hit with a pungent, vinegary odor. Noticing feathers dotting the floor, he took it for a former chicken coop.

Nothing here, he thought, moving to a small garden thriving with tomatoes, onions and peppers. He looked for possible shoe impressions, but he couldn't discern anything.

Near the garden's edge, he saw overgrowth laced over the boards covering the mouth of an abandoned well. He moved them. A damp earthen odor escaped. He withdrew his flashlight and probed the darkness. He looked for a body, or signs of one, anything matching the fragment of pink fabric he'd pulled from his grille.

Nothing down there.

Moving on, he surveyed the pasture that backed up to woods. *What do I think I'll achieve doing this? I'm avoiding the inevitable.* Realizing this cursory look was futile, he returned to the house. The woman got up from a chair on the porch and handed him a sweating glass of lemonade with ice.

"Did you find anything?"

"Thank you. No." He smiled, touching the cold glass to his temple. "You might want to see about plugging that well." He took a big gulp.

"I've been after John to do that."

Luke nodded, took another sip.

"This is good, thank you." He set the glass down. "I've taken up enough of your time. I'm sorry, you are?"

"Clara. Clara Price. And you?"

"Luke Conway. Thanks, Clara. I'll be moving on."

Seeing Luke off, she said: "A little warning."

He stopped, turning to her.

"If you're going to check my neighbor's property—" She nodded to the right. "Raylin T. Nash, there, gets kind of ornery if you intrude on his privacy."

"I'll remember that. Thank you again."

Driving along the lane, sorting his thoughts, Luke glimpsed through the trees: movement at the mouth of the roadway. Was it just a car passing by on River Road?

Or is somebody watching?

35

Working at her desk at the *Chronicle*, Denise Diaz's computer chimed with a message.

A response from Ben McGraw, one of the original lead detectives. He'd retired in Auckland, New Zealand.

I'm glad it's over. For the sake of the families and everyone impacted by the case. That's my only comment.

Wow, not much there, Denise thought, adding it to her notes. She'd already transcribed her interviews with the family and friends of Jenna Dupree. And the detectives in Tyler. The relatives and friends of Abby Hall and Erin Eddowes had also given Denise strong interviews, and they shared more photos of the girls, some taken right before their deaths. It would all stand in painful juxtaposition to the interview and photos she'd obtained from Hyde's mother, Mary-Ellen.

Denise's keyboard and mouse clicked steadily. The story was coming together, but it still lacked two key components: the case file and an interview with Carrie. The last time Denise had gone to Carrie's house in Cedar Breeze, her SUV wasn't there. No one appeared to be home.

Biting her bottom lip, she paused. Maybe she'd drive by again. If Carrie wasn't home, she could park out front and wait, or even follow her. Denise needed Carrie's cooperation to make this story work.

And she needed that case file.

She'd sensed that Lynn was growing concerned. Leaving her on the story was straining the resources of the *Chronicle*'s small news staff.

A new message pinged.

Maybe it was Carrie, she hoped. Or even Vern, or Luke Conway, who'd so far declined to be interviewed.

No, it was Eve Trainor, the other county detective to first investigate the case.

Hi Denise: Sure, I can help with your story. How about a quick video call two hours from now? I should be clear then. Let me know if that works for you.

Denise answered, Thank you, Eve. It works.

Bolstered by Trainor's warm response, Denise finished off her notes, collected her phone and laptop, then told Lynn she would continue working from home.

"I hope we're going to see a good story from you soon," Lynn said.

"It's coming together—slowly, but it's coming."

Along the way home, waiting at McDonald's to bring home some food, Denise begged the gods of desperate news reporters to smile on her.

At home, after eating and cleaning up, Denise made coffee and reviewed her notes.

Soon, Eve Trainor's face appeared on her laptop's screen. She had high cheeks with a few wrinkles at her eyes, putting her in her late forties, early fifties, Denise thought.

"Hi, Denise."

"Hi, Eve. Thank you for making time to do this."

"No problem."

"I'll get details later, but you're in Cleveland, Ohio, now, with a private investigation agency?"

"That's right," Eve said. Then jumping right into the subject, "I have to say, I was a bit surprised with Hyde's confession."

"Why?"

"Ben McGraw and I were really looking hard at Carrie Hamilton, Vern's daughter."

"How did Vern take that?"

"He was torn up. He'd recently lost his wife; then Carrie nearly died fleeing the attack; then we suspected her of killing Abby and Erin."

"That's a lot to bear."

"Still, Vern was largely hands-off. It was our investigation and he told us to follow the evidence wherever it led and make the case."

"So why was Carrie a suspect?"

"She was the last one seen with the girls and they'd had a recent confrontation," Eve said. "In homicides, the answer is usually the obvious one. The simplest one. The one that makes sense. And our team, especially Ben, couldn't shake his belief that Carrie did it."

"But she was never charged."

"We needed solid evidence to back it up."

"And it wasn't there?"

"The DA said it was circumstantial. We knew Carrie had argued with Abby and Erin in the cafeteria. We knew they traveled in different social circles at the school. We knew that subsequent to the cafeteria run-in, there was a big Halloween party at the dance hall. Carrie, Erin and Abby attended, but we couldn't establish if the girls talked to each other there. Then the day after the party, Abby, Erin and Carrie go into the woods. But only Carrie comes out alive."

"What did the evidence tell you?"

"Well, a gun was used but none was ever found."

"And you questioned Carrie?"

"Extensively. But she couldn't give us answers, said she couldn't remember. She was polygraphed, hypnotized—nothing worked. Ben accused her of not being truthful. He tried to get her to confess that things got out of hand when she tried to settle a score from the cafeteria. He told her he knew it was an accident."

"And?"

"Nothing. We consulted the doctors. Carrie's spotty memory was consistent with her head injuries. They were serious and genuine. She was not faking it; she couldn't remember details of what happened."

"You couldn't present a case against Carrie that went beyond a reasonable doubt?"

"That's right. Then we got a tip from detectives in Tyler after they'd charged Donnie Ray Hyde for the murder of Jenna Dupree."

"And your case took a turn."

"A big turn. Tyler people established that Hyde was in the area at the time of the murders. His pattern was the same and there were other pieces of evidence."

"Such as?"

"He had guns in his possession, bought on the street after a gun shop burglary in Fort Worth."

"Including the murder weapon?"

"We never found it. I understand he got rid of it. I believe it came down to a crime of opportunity for him and the girls being in the wrong place at the wrong time. We believed that he'd been drinking, doing drugs at his brother Brophy's place in the mobile home park, wandered to Wild Pines, encountered the girls there, forced them deeper into the woods at gunpoint. Also—I'm not sure I should tell you…"

"Tell me what?"

"It's never been revealed."

"The case is over. Hyde's been executed. Whatever it is will likely come out."

A long moment passed before Eve decided.

"I'm sorry, Denise. All I can say is that this case is disturbing and heartbreaking for everyone. I know the families will never have closure, whatever that is. But maybe they'll take comfort that after all this time, there are answers and it's finally resolved."

After ending the call, Denise sat back in her chair, processing the new pieces of information. She'd got more than she expected from Eve. *But what is it that's never been revealed?*

She was sipping the last of her tepid coffee when her computer pinged with a message from Sheriff Ellerd.

The case file is ready for you to pick up.

36

Carrie strapped Emily into her car seat and buckled the seat belt, double-checking the connections before kissing her daughter.

Straps and buckles. Hyde strapped to the gurney.

Driving from her neighborhood, her thoughts whirled; the anguish of being that close to the execution still burned. The aching to remember what happened in the woods was unrelenting. She needed to get control, ground herself in the routine of everyday living, but the unknown consumed her.

And she felt pressured.

Partly because the media interview requests, which had waned over the years, had started up again. She'd declined new ones from CBS and Reuters. But the most persistent was Denise Diaz of the *Clear River Chronicle*—she did more than send messages and call. Once, when returning home from errands, Carrie spotted Denise's white SUV parked at her house. Carrie detoured and drove around the neighborhood to avoid her. She was not ready to talk to reporters, even one from her local paper.

That's why she'd welcomed Lacey's invitation for a session today at her salon, seeing it as a way to ease her anxieties. Driving across town now felt normal. She had the day off, and her father had agreed to watch Emily.

He lit up when they arrived, taking his granddaughter into his arms as Carrie slipped off the baby's diaper bag.

"Everything's here," she said, "diapers, snacks, toys, fresh clothes."

"Good."

"I fed her, changed her. Thanks for doing this."

"No thanks needed. All part of my grand plan." Vern tickled Emily. "So glad to have y'all home."

"How're you doing, Dad?"

"No pain, darlin'. Holding this angel is my medicine. And how're you and Luke doing?"

"Okay, I guess."

"Okay?"

"No. He's been busy at work…and quiet. And I—"

"And what?"

"I don't know." She drove her fingers into her hair. "It's the not knowing. Even after Hyde's execution, it's still a nightmare that won't end."

"It's over, Carrie."

"But I need to remember what happened."

"No, you don't. You have to put it behind you."

"I'm trying, but I can't."

"What does your doctor say?"

"That I have to sort this out on my terms, whatever that means." Carrie waved away the subject. "I gotta go. I'll be a couple of hours, at most."

Carrie kissed Emily.

Before she turned to leave, Vern said: "It's behind us. Live your life."

The Always Charming Salon was pristine, smelling more of lavender than chemicals and perfumes.

Amid the sounds of hair washing, blow-dryers and low conversations, Lacey looked up from the list of appointments on her tablet to greet her.

"Well, hello, Carrie. I'm delighted you came."

A few heads turned as Lacey moved around the counter, leading her friend to an empty chair.

"Got this one waiting for you."

"Thank you," she said, nodding to a couple of women who'd been at Lacey's party.

"My pleasure."

Carrie settled into the chair, meeting Lacey's gaze in the mirror.

"Your hair has nice body."

"Thanks."

"What'll it be today? And this is on the house."

"No, I'll pay."

"Honey, it's on the house."

Carrie smiled, taking a moment to appreciate Lacey's gift. "Thank you. I was thinking just a trim."

"All right, a shampoo and a trim, it is."

Lacey brushed Carrie's hair and placed a towel and gown on her, then they headed over to the sink. The warm water and scalp massage melted her tension. It was soothing, just what she needed. After her shampoo, Carrie was upright, back in front of the mirror, when Lacey voiced a thought.

"It's so cool that Luke is from here but you met in Los Angeles."

"Small world."

"LA's such a big town. How did it happen?"

"He worked on his folks' farm near Dixon, then went out to California, got on with the LAPD. I was doing a promo for the LAPD and we met at a work function."

"It's so romantic, like you were meant to be together."

"Same with you and Clay? High school sweethearts. An East Texas love story."

"You bet." Lacey laughed.

Grace Cox, Sheriff Ellerd's cousin, leaned over from the chair to Carrie's left. "Are y'all settled in at Cedar Breeze, Carrie?"

"Hey, Grace. Pretty much."

"It's such a nice new community out there," Grace said.

"I like how they kept most of the trees," Lacey said, toweling Carrie's hair to prepare for a wet cut.

"We really like it," Carrie said.

"And how's your dad?" Grace asked.

"He says he's good."

"He must be happy having y'all together, with his grandbaby. And Luke getting on with the county," Grace said.

"Well, I think it's a blessing you moved back from California," said the woman in the chair to Carrie's right.

Carrie couldn't turn her head because Lacey had started cutting her hair. But glancing in the mirror, she saw Opal Wells.

"You must be so relieved Donnie Ray Hyde confessed," Grace said, "that it's finally over, after all this time."

"I don't think it'll ever really be over," Carrie said, "but the years have been hard."

"The not being over part's so true," Opal said. "I still see TV trucks prowlin' through town. Word's going around that the *Dateline* people are working on a story."

"Is that right, Carrie?" Grace said. "I'd think they'd want to talk to you."

"They've reached out to me. I've gotten a lot of press calls, but I said no to all of them. I don't want to talk about it. I don't remember much, and the fragments I do remember are—well, I don't want to talk about it."

"You'd do well to think of other things," Opal said, "like memories of our time in high school."

Memories of our time in high school?

A chill coiled up Carrie's spine, her head snapped in midcut to Opal: "What?"

"Opal!" Lacey said. "Did you not just hear what Carrie said about remembering that time?"

Opal's cheeks reddened. "No, not that! I'm sorry! I'm such a dope! No, I mean fun things, like the Halloween party at the dance hall, or that Benjamin Franklin project we did together. We got an A-plus. I rarely got one, so it felt special. Remember?"

"I remember."

"Gosh, I was so proud of that," Opal said. "It was about his Poor Richard days, and his witty sayings, like, 'Early to bed and early to rise, makes a man healthy, wealthy and wise.' There were some quotes you really liked."

"Sure, it was a good presentation." Carrie found it weird that Opal remembered. Then again, Carrie often got good grades in high school, so maybe the Ben Franklin project didn't stand out the same way for her as it did for Opal.

"I've still got it packed away somewhere," Opal said.

"Good for you," Lacey said.

"Maybe I'll dig it out."

Over the next few minutes, Lacey finished Carrie's cut, and after blow-drying her hair, she began touching it up.

"Carrie?" Grace's voice held the weight of a serious question. "Did you ever hear from Nicole and Lauren, Abby's and Erin's relatives?"

"In what way?"

"They were so in-your-face at Lacey's party. Did they ever apologize?"

"Sort of. At the press conference after the execution."

"I thought they might have made a formal apology to you, given how the nasty rumors and accusations died with Hyde in Huntsville."

"It doesn't matter," Carrie said. "This has taken a toll on everyone."

"It took a lot of courage to go to Huntsville," Lacey said. "You were so brave to put it to rest."

In those moments before she got up to leave, Carrie accepted how the women of the salon, her old friends from school, had assumed the role of a chorus in her tragedy. Staring at herself in the mirror, admiring her hair while forcing back tears, Carrie managed a weak smile.

But inside, she was screaming.

37

Emily's little fingers flipped the page to pictures of kittens frolicking with butterflies.

She smiled, making Vern's eyes crinkle as he held her in his lap while reading her the story. Emily twitched when his phone rang, and he calmed her.

The call was from Bob Ellerd.

Carefully, Vern placed Emily at his feet on the floor with her book and picked up the phone.

"Bob."

"Is this a good time, Vern?"

"Just doing a little reading."

"Want to give you a heads-up. The case file's gone out the door to Denise Diaz at the *Chronicle*."

"That so? The entire thing?"

"Everything. I talked to the DA, and we're compelled to release it. It was just a matter of time."

"I figured."

"Some things in there might open old wounds for you, for Carrie."

"Most all of them have been open a long time, Bob."

"Whatever Denise writes, it won't be much more than a

rehash of things. Still, nobody likes to have someone looking over their shoulder."

"Most folks don't understand investigative work."

"It was all done by the book. I know it and you know it."

"That's right."

"I'll let you get back to reading."

"I appreciate the call, Bob."

Tucking his phone in his pocket, Vern watched his grand-daughter chattering at the pictures in her story. Grunting, he lifted her back on his lap. Looking at her face, her eyes, he saw Carrie's face, Carrie's eyes, pulling him back to the day at her school in Principal Taylor's office. On that day, his words were mammoth jagged boulders, rammed so tight in his throat he could barely get them out to tell her that her mother had a brain seizure, fell down the stairs and died.

Carrie's scream had pierced him, like the silent one in his heart when he saw her in her hospital bed on that day of horror in Wild Pines Forest...

...unconscious, her bruised face bandaged, the tubes, the monitors... Only after the doctor repeatedly assures him she's stable does he release her hand and break away, driving from the hospital to the woods...fear eating at him... What was she doing in the woods? Was she alone, despondent about her mom, using drugs or drinking? Was it a boy? Was she attacked?

Or was it something else?

Arriving at the scene, his radio a riot of transmissions from Bob Ellerd and other deputies in Wild Pines...telling him where to enter... A deputy waiting at the edge...guiding him...light dimming in the cool forest... earthy smells...going deeper...branches tugging and slapping... Meeting another deputy pointing, not touching... "We found this here..." A woman's sneaker...not Carrie's...more static-filled radio blasts...

"This way, Sheriff."

Branches pulling, scraping...as if the trees are pleading...do not go farther...a bird screeching...the air ominous. He comes to Ellerd, who is squatting, turning to him. Ellerd's face sober, he moves aside to reveal a body...white, female...twisted clothing blood-streaked...a shoe missing... Ellerd stands and leads him a few yards to a second body... white female...blood-soaked clothing...legs in a running posture as if felled in midflight.

What in God's name happened? Taking a breath, assuming order in the chaos... "Looks like they were shot," a deputy says. They must protect the scene...anything and everything is evidence...fibers, hair, shoe impressions, broken branches... Bring in Forensics...medical examiner... assign detectives...search for casings...a weapon...other victims...video or photographs...measure...sketch... Some deputies cannot hide their anguish. In a small community people know people...even without official confirmation they know the dead...

Abby Hall and Erin Eddowes...

More help arrives...working the scene...grid searching...metal detectors...a dog... Tape is stretched around trees...along the presumed trail—do not contaminate the scene, protect the scene—but he feels eyes cast toward him...hears the whispers...detects trailing glances. Word has spread...something monstrous emerging from a mist...the specter of suspicion... Carrie was here...pulled from the water...in the hospital. The girls are from Carrie's school, two dead but she survived... she's part of this...

What in God's name happened?

Everything's in motion...procedures are being followed. He needs to get back to Carrie at the hospital. He signs off with Ellerd...stepping back alone through the forest...the yelp and squawk of radios echo... his mind on fire with questions...he needs answers from his daughter...

Moving through the brush...branches yanking and hitting him... he steps on something...stops...looks down. What's this? Cannot believe what he sees...reflexively reaching for his radio to alert the others while lowering himself...catching his breath... He freezes, examining what he's found, and tiny hairs on the back of his neck stiffen... He does not use his radio...he tells no one...

Vern felt gentle wriggling in his arms.

His granddaughter's soft babbling pulled him from the forest to her, her little smile and eyes brightening as she flipped to another page in her book.

Suddenly he saw Donnie Ray Hyde, heard his last words before his execution.

I am sorry for what I done. I am sorry for the pain I caused.

Vern swallowed, then smiled at Emily.

"It's all right, sweetheart." He kissed the top of her head. "It's all behind us."

38

Carrie got to her car, her nerves pulsing.

Still disturbed by some of the talk at the salon, she wasn't ready to collect Emily. In that moment, driving through Clear River, she wished that she and Luke had never left California. She missed the life they'd had there.

It wasn't perfect, but it was a good life.

She knew returning to Texas to be with her dad and give Luke a fresh start had been the right thing to do. But Dr. Bernay wasn't wrong when she said it would be difficult, that it could even unblock painful memories. So far, Carrie had faced ugly gossip, media scrutiny and an execution. Her struggle to heal had been troubling, her memories of the tragedy coming in excruciating drips.

Dr. Bernay had believed she could handle it.

But Carrie wasn't so certain.

Holding on to the wheel, she thought of Thomas Wolfe's book *You Can't Go Home Again*. Surveying the old center of town, she saw how some things were the same. There was city hall, the courthouse, the bank and the old *Chronicle* building. She looked at the storefronts. Fondly, she took in Clear River Fix-It Hardware, which was once owned by Clay Smith's family. Now it was Billie's Pizza. There was Dyment's flower shop, now an accounting office; Tracy's Diner was now a boutique; and Sue's Bakery was now a coffee shop, reminding Carrie how quickly life could change.

Since her move back, each time she passed through downtown was bittersweet, almost haunting. And it was even more acute today with comments from the salon echoing in her mind. Opal, fixated on their Franklin project and his clever sayings, as if she were mired in the past, telling Carrie to remember "our time in high school." *That's the whole problem, Opal.* Then Lacey and Grace saying how she must be relieved since Hyde confessed, how after his execution she should be able to "put it to rest."

How can I ever put it to rest without knowing what happened, why Erin and Abby were killed and why I survived?

Carrie left the downtown, smiling when she passed the Whataburger where she'd worked and where Luke said he'd first set eyes on her. She couldn't remember meeting him there.

She kept going, eventually finding herself at the edge of downtown and parked at the old dance hall with something stirring...something about Abby and Erin. Yes, there was the incident in the cafeteria that day when their group, the older seniors, bullied Lanna... *Rama-Lanna-Ding-Dong.* Carrie had defended her, stood up to them.

Then...

At school, after the scene in the cafeteria, Abby and Erin shot Carrie icy stares between classes in the hallways. She'd let it go, tried to ignore them. But what happened next?

Now Carrie looked at the old dance hall, a big white wooden building that went up in the 1900s. Staring at it, something flicked in her subconscious, pulling something to the surface.

The old dance hall.

Carrie held her head in her hands.

It was coming to her.

Yes, after the standoff in the cafeteria, there was the Halloween party at the dance hall. Everyone dressed up. There was
music, lights flashing on dancing zombies, vampires, werewolves,
ghouls and monsters.

Then what?

Carrie's memory stopped there.

Feeling lost, she looked at the old building, as if expecting it
to conjure up the answers she needed.

It was futile.

Frustrated that the dance hall memory had faded before
yielding more information, she drove off. She glimpsed cars
and traffic in her rearview mirror. Then she glanced at the baby
back-seat mirror and Emily's empty car seat. High school was
long over; she was an adult, a mother, a wife. Why couldn't
she put it all behind her and live her life?

Some part of her needed to remember.

She drove aimlessly while grappling with her torment, her
heart beating faster when she stopped at the edge of Wild Pines
Forest.

She hadn't been back since it happened.

A tornado raged through her—scenes of her mom and dad
arguing; her mother's death; the cafeteria; the dance hall monsters; Hyde's execution; Ben Franklin's quotes; voices telling
her, *Put it to rest.*

From the driver's seat of her car, Carrie looked into the woods.

Where Erin and Abby died.

Where I almost died.

Were the answers buried in there?

Go in. Hyde's dead. It's safe now. Go in.

But she was frozen. Her heart pounding because she was...
*running for my life, the ground under me vanishing at the cliff...my legs
pumping in midair...the river shoots up, swallows me...flailing in the
rushing current pinballing in the rocks then...like a hammer striking my*

head, everything goes dark...the abyss...and I wake in the hospital...
my father looking down at me...

What happened in the woods?

Carrie pounded her fists on her steering wheel.

Why can't I remember?

After a long moment, regaining composure, she caught her breath.

Was that car parked far off in the distance the same one that she'd glimpsed near the dance hall?

Is someone following me?

A soft vibration sounded and she reached for her phone.

Denise Diaz was texting her again.

Carrie's finger was hovering above Delete, but she hesitated, the words coming clear on the screen.

I've obtained the full case file. It sheds light on the murders. Please talk to me.

39

After making fresh coffee, Denise returned to work at her kitchen table.

For much of the previous night, and all this morning, she'd studied the case file. The sheriff's office had released it to her on a USB flash drive. The amount of information was massive.

And disturbing.

With Harvey keeping her company, lying at her feet and gnawing on a chew toy, Denise had worked through the night, her kitchen lit only by her laptop screen. The crime scene photos of the bodies of Abby Hall and Erin Eddowes had jolted her. Sharp color images, taken from every angle. Some were close-ups. The amount of blood was alarming. As an experienced reporter, Denise had faced graphic situations, but these photos underscored the ferocity of the murders. Moving beyond them, she went through every item in the file.

She'd scanned the scene work, measurements, videos and hundreds of photos, the case logs, reports and time frames. She moved on to the autopsy reports. Cause of death was gunshot wounds. She looked at the inventory of evidence collected and forensic analysis. Odd, no shell casings were recovered at the scene. Even after a grid search and a sweep with metal detectors, not a single shell casing, which meant the killer must have collected them. *Smart*, Denise thought. There were statements and interviews. Details on the investigators' questioning of Carrie.

She looked through interviews of people who knew the girls—friends, relatives, other students. She looked over reports on canvassing and the investigation of known offenders, including registered sex offenders residing in the area. Scores of tips had been followed.

The time between the dates of summaries got longer. An update noted slow progress after indicating that Carrie had moved from Clear River County to Los Angeles. Years passed, then detectives in Tyler alerted their colleagues in Clear River to Donnie Ray Hyde as a person of interest for the unsolved double murder.

Hyde had already been convicted of murdering Jenna Dupree in Tyler. He acknowledged being in Clear River at the time Abby and Erin were killed. His pattern fit and his alibi was weak. But Hyde had long denied involvement in their deaths. Denise remembered looking at him on the gurney in Huntsville, hearing his last words.

I am sorry for what I done. I am sorry for the pain I caused.

In his confession, Hyde said that on the day of the murders he'd been drinking, doing drugs at his brother Brophy's place. He said he'd wandered into Wild Pines and encountered the girls, forced them deeper into the woods at gunpoint. Said he was overcome, possessed by dark urges to kill—like with the girl in Tyler. He shot Abby and Erin, but Carrie got away. He figured she died in the river. Went back, got his casings and fled, relieved to learn later that Carrie's brain injury had robbed her of memory. He tossed the gun and casings somewhere in the Sabine River.

When Denise reached the end of the file, it was 2 a.m. She'd finally stopped working and went to bed.

Now, this morning, she'd been going over all the material

again. She worked slowly, making careful notes, piecing together a fuller picture of the crime for her story. The assessments, comments and theories she found in some reports were revealing, especially how deeply Ben McGraw believed Carrie had killed Abby and Erin.

Absorbed in her work, Denise heard a soft noise as Harvey joined her in the kitchen.

"You're finally up, are you?"

Harvey yawned, his paws clicking on the floor. He went to the door and waited, a sign he needed to go out.

"Hang on."

Denise pulled on a sweatshirt, got his leash and bags, and gave him a big hug before they went outside. Not long after Denise had started at the paper, she'd heard a woman at the pet store talking about a dog abandoned in the trash before ending up at the Clear River rescue shelter. He was still just a pup when his sad eyes took Denise's heart hostage.

Whenever she couldn't be home, her neighbor Melvin Sprague, a seventy-five-year-old widower, took care of Harvey. Although, it was more a case of Harvey taking care of Melvin.

When Harvey had finished his business, they returned home and Denise freshened his water bowl, got him some food, then got back to work. Looking again at the forensic reports, she saw how most of the shoe impressions collected at the scene were partials. But they were consistent with Abby's, Erin's and Carrie's footwear. A fourth partial was collected; it was larger and indicated another subject was present.

Investigators looked at the phones and computers belonging to Abby, Erin and Carrie. They found nothing linking all three girls. Whatever led to them being together in the woods had to have been communicated verbally, or by other means.

Denise then found a note containing information that had never been released, appearing to be holdback evidence. Something only the killer would know...and it was consistent with Hyde's confession.

It concerned action the killer took at the scene.

Reading it gave her pause.

Chilling, Denise thought.

Rubbing her temple, she absorbed her research. She now had one of the two major pillars: the case file. This was shaping up to be a strong investigative feature. But she needed the second pillar.

Denise stared at her phone.

Come on, Carrie, come on. This time, say yes.

40

Reaching into her oven, Carrie removed the baked mac and cheese she'd made for her family's dinner.

She smiled at Emily, bibbed in her high chair and singing, which she did when she was hungry.

"Almost ready, sweetie. It needs to cool," she said, fixing a steaming bowl for Emily and putting it in the fridge.

Carrie glanced at her phone on the counter and, for the umpteenth time, considered the text from Denise Diaz at the *Chronicle*. She hadn't responded, but this request was different. Not just an interview. Denise had the case file, and it shed light on the murders.

Maybe talking to her would help me.

"I'm going to do it." Carrie turned to Luke, who was sitting at the table, scrolling on his phone, saying nothing.

Present, but not with her.

Frowning, she reflected on texting with Dr. Bernay yesterday about whether she should meet with Denise. It could result in Carrie learning painful investigative details. But otherwise, she might never find all the answers, Dr. Bernay had said.

Carrie glanced at Luke, still staring at his phone. She scooped a heap of mac and cheese for him, banging the serving spoon on his plate.

He snapped to attention.

The baby started to whimper.

"Where did you go, Luke?"

He put his phone down. "I'm sorry."

"I said I've decided to talk to Denise Diaz at the *Chronicle*. What do you think?"

He considered her question.

"With all you've been through already, is it a good idea to talk about it with a reporter?"

"I texted Dr. Bernay about it." Carrie caressed the baby's cheek, soothing her.

"What did she say?"

"She said I've made progress, that it could still be challenging, but it's up to me. I think it could help me get answers." Carrie got Emily's bowl from the fridge, spooned a sample, tested it. It was cooler. She started feeding her. "You've been so distant lately."

"I'm sorry. I'm dealing with some things. But, Carrie, it breaks my heart to see all you're going through."

She looked at him for a long moment. "What things?"

Working on his dinner, staring down at his plate, he didn't answer.

"Is there something you're not telling me, Luke?"

He searched her eyes without answering.

She read his face before asking: "Do you think we made a mistake moving back?"

He looked away.

"Maybe."

"Maybe?"

Luke was silent.

"Is it your new job?"

"No, I'm just tired. It wasn't a mistake. We had to come back, for your dad, for you, Emily, the job. We had to do it."

"Is it the shooting? Because, Luke, this feels like right after the shooting. You're not talking to me again."

"No, it's not about LA."

She turned to him when she heard his fork clink as he set it down. Then he looked at her as if he was about to tell her something important.

Something hugely important.

Luke rubbed his hands into his face, pressing his knuckles deep. "I guess we're both battling ghosts," he said.

Carrie took a long breath as they let a moment pass, and then Luke shifted the subject.

"Do you want me to go with you when you talk to the reporter?"

Carrie shook her head.

"Are you going to tell your dad?"

"No. I need to do it myself. But I'll get him to look after Emily. He'll like that."

They left it there, finishing their dinner with small talk and watching Emily.

Slowly, they each retreated into the silence of their own troubling thoughts.

41

"This will be hard to look at, Carrie."

Denise opened her laptop and cued it to the folder containing the crime scene photos.

She'd arranged a room for them at the Clear River Public Library. They were alone with the door closed. Denise had drawn the blinds on the exterior window. The interior glass window opened to the main section where, far across the room, preschool children sat on the floor for story time. A librarian was reading *Where the Wild Things Are*. Denise angled her computer. Only she and Carrie could see the monitor.

"Are you sure you want to start with this?"

Carrie hesitated, then nodded.

"All right, brace yourself."

A few keystrokes and clicks, then images exploded on the screen and Carrie drew a sharp intake of breath.

Photo after photo of the body, a female, splayed on the ground in the woods. Her blood-drenched clothing partially torn away, she was missing a shoe and her hair was a confused mass, her face turned. In close-ups, her half-closed eyes looked to the earth as if she were ready to sleep.

This was Abby.

Denise continued, slowly clicking through the next series of crime scene photos, which showed the second body, discovered several yards from the first.

Erin.

Again, her clothes were mangled, in disarray, saturated with blood.

So much blood. Too much blood.

Her legs were sprawled, frozen like she was midstride while running. Her head was turned as if looking back before death, her mouth slightly open. Through the hair webbed on her face, Carrie met her eyes, empty of life yet staring with laser accuracy into hers.

Telegraphing the truth.

You were with us. You were here—

But I don't—I can't...

Alarm clanged in the back of Carrie's mind...propelling her back years...back to...the woods...and...

...gunshots...branches clutching her...running for her life...

A hand on Carrie's shoulder.

"Are you okay?" Denise asked.

Carrie clawed her way back, composing herself.

"Yes."

"Do you want to keep going?"

Carrie glanced to the story circle, the children absorbed with the Wild Things. She reached for her thermos of water, drank some, then breathed deeply.

"Let's keep going."

Denise used a sharing app to connect two pairs of headphones to her laptop so they could listen and watch the recorded interviews together. For close to forty-five minutes, they watched the most intense segments of Eve Trainor and Ben McGraw questioning Carrie about the murders. Then they removed their headphones and, bringing up reports, statements and her notes, Denise walked Carrie through a timeline.

"You didn't really know Abby and Erin, right? They were seniors and you were a junior?"

"Yes."

"The whole thing first began with the incident with them that day in the cafeteria." Denise referred to her notes and various case reports on her screen. "What do you remember about that?"

"They were picking on a shy girl, Lanna."

"Lanna Fendelson."

"They were calling Lanna names, taunting her. It upset me and I confronted them."

"You were then targeted, teased for being the sheriff's daughter. They called you 'narc,' bumped you in the hall, that kind of thing."

"Yes."

"And not long after that—" Denise clicked to statements from other students "—there was the Halloween party at the old dance hall, which you attended in costume."

Carrie nodded. "Everyone was dressed up. I went as a witch."

Looking at her notes, Denise said, "Did you talk to Abby and Erin? They were there."

"I can't remember."

"Was there any tension? Any problems with anyone?"

"I can't remember. I don't think so."

"Somehow, a day later, the three of you ended up in the woods. Do you recall why?"

Carrie shook her head.

Denise bit her bottom lip, thinking, consulting a report.

"They checked Abby's phone, Erin's phone, your phone, and computers belonging to all three of you, and found no communication relating to your meeting in the woods. Was it discussed or planned in conversation, or through an intermediary? Was it spontaneous, a chance meeting?"

Carrie shook her head. "I don't remember."

Denise looked at Carrie, tapped her pen to her chin.

"As you know, detectives had some theories and—" she nodded to the screen "—they believed you went to the woods to settle a score with Abby and Erin."

"I don't know. I can't remember."

"The cause of death was gunshot wounds, and you had access to your father's guns—"

"Donnie Ray Hyde confessed."

Denise stared at Carrie, attempting to decipher her tone. Carrie drank more water. Then keys clicked. Denise opened Hyde's official confession on her laptop. After they'd reread it, Denise exhaled, summing it up.

"Hyde said he was drinking and doing drugs with his brother, wandered into the woods with his gun and was overcome with dark urges. He said he put on a mask. Do you remember seeing anyone?"

Carrie held her head in her hands. "No."

"Carrie, has this case material helped you remember anything?"

Her thoughts swirling, she turned to the reading circle.

The children were gone now.

What do I remember?

Carrie thought of the librarian reading *Where the Wild Things Are*. She remembered that it was a story about a boy sailing to an island where monsters lived…and something monstrous had happened to her. As memory pulled her back again to Wild Pines Forest, she was…

…running for her life…off the cliff edge…the river rising, swallowing her…the rushing current slamming her against rocks…everything going dark…waking in the hospital…to a face looking down at her…

"Dad."

Carrie's hands flew to her mouth, stifling a whimper, maybe a revelation.

"What is it, Carrie?" Denise asked. "Something about your father?"

Carrie shook her head.

"I remember being scared to death, running through the woods and falling in the river, losing consciousness, then being in the hospital with my dad looking at me."

That's all she could say right now. The full truth was that a memory, *a new one*, was emerging—hazy but so horrifying that Carrie had blocked it.

"Are you okay?"

Carrie nodded.

"It seemed like you were having a breakthrough. Do you want to keep going?"

"Yes."

"All right, I'd like to try something that could help." Denise's face, creased with concern, searched Carrie's. "But only if you think you can handle it."

42

Denise stopped her Chevrolet Trax at the fringe of Wild Pines Forest, on a slip of dirt near a thicket.

There were no other vehicles or people around as she turned off the engine.

Reaching into her bag, she took out her phone and her notebook, paging through her handwritten entries, maps with distances, sketches and various notations.

"This is where you entered, according to the case file." She turned to Carrie in the passenger seat.

Carrie's gaze into the forest was haunted, as if holding some terrible secret, sensing some horrible dread.

"Like I said at the library," Denise continued, "if we walked through the scene, step-by-step, like a re-creation, it might stimulate your memory."

Carrie said nothing.

"Are you still okay to do this, Carrie?"

Carrie stared blankly into the darkened woods, unable to move. Setting foot inside now with Denise would be her first time since the murders. As she dwelled on it, years of therapy with Dr. Bernay swept through her.

Carrie knew that to avoid the event was a defense mechanism that would leave her hostage to her fears.

Possibly forever.

But to confront it, here and now, with all of its frightening memories, she could conquer those fears, and, maybe, just maybe, arrive at *the truth.*

You might find you're stronger than you thought. Dr. Bernay's words echoed, and Carrie steeled herself.

I did not move my family back to Texas to surrender.

"Let's go in," she told Denise.

As they entered, Carrie followed Denise, thinking how the reporter had become Carrie's version of Virgil from *The Divine Comedy*, guiding her through her very own Hell.

Moving deeper into the forest, the light dimmed under the canopy of trees. Carrie breathed in the pine, mingling with the earthy patchwork of evergreen shrub, letting go, trying to remember. They hadn't gone far when Denise stopped at a large rock, consulted her notes, then pointed.

"They found partial shoe impressions here from a fourth person. The poor quality made analysis difficult, but they were larger and inconsistent with yours and the other girls'. Hyde had been following you, according to his confession and the case notes."

Denise looked directly at Carrie. "Did you see anyone here, other than the girls?"

Carrie took stock of the area.

"I don't remember."

They moved on for some distance, then Denise checked her notes before stopping at a large rotting log.

"Abby's sneaker was found here, indicating the three of you had likely been accosted and fled. Do you remember this point?"

Carrie shook her head.

They progressed for another few minutes. Branches swished,

brushing against them, breezes whispering through the treetops as they came to where two tall trees had formed a V.

Denise stopped.

The air tightened with expectancy.

"This is where they found Abby."

Denise looked at Carrie. "Do you remember what happened here, Carrie?"

Abby was murdered here.

The image she'd seen of Abby's corpse on Denise's laptop in the library was seared into Carrie's mind.

Abby's body spread on the ground, one foot shoeless, her jumbled clothes sopped with blood, her eyes nearly closed, frozen, dreamless.

Standing here in the spot where Abby died ignited remembrance in Carrie, illuminating a dark corner where a memory crouched before coming to life.

Abby and Erin wanted to talk to me.

That's why we came to the woods.

"Carrie?" Denise prompted.

"It's not clear."

"But you just remembered something?"

Carrie nodded. "Yes, but it's not clear."

They moved on, birdsong sounding in the cooler air, with beads of sweat moistening Carrie's brow. They hadn't gone far when Denise stopped again.

"They found Erin here."

The crime scene photo burned in Carrie's mind.

Erin on her side. In a runner's posture, the earth permeated with her blood, soaking her disordered clothes, her messed-up hair, her empty eyes staring like an accusation.

Nothing was there now, only undergrowth.

"Do you remember?"

Carrie spasmed at gunfire echoing from the past.

"Carrie?"

Returning to the present, she said, "I ran that way."

Denise looked to where she was pointing.

As they moved forward, Carrie was pulled back, remembering the terror, her heart hammering, pulse thundering, branches whipping, slicing into her, running until she was falling.

They had come to the cliff's edge.

Carrie stared down at the river rushing far below.

Battling to breathe…smashing her head…the hospital and her father…

Lightning flashed in her mind, launching a memory, rocketing from that day. Unable, perhaps not wanting to stop it, Carrie shook her head.

"I can't be here."

Turning, she walked back quickly, with Denise hurrying to keep up.

"Carrie, what is it?"

She didn't answer.

Several long minutes later, the distance from the cliff had grown and the river's rush had faded. They'd returned to the tranquil area of the forest. There was only the sweep of branches as Carrie continued back, until Denise stepped ahead of her.

"Carrie, please. You remember now, don't you?"

Carrie drove her fingers into her hair.

"What is it?" Denise asked. "Is it Hyde? Do you remember seeing him? How it happened?"

She shook her head.

"What is it, Carrie?"

Carrie heaved a huge breath, staring at nothing, then everything in her past, as if some monster was waiting.

"Abby and Erin wanted to talk to me. They said that they needed to talk here. But I was afraid."

"Of what? What did they want to talk to you about?"

Carrie held her head, unwilling to release the shard of truth that was piercing her.

"Was it about your confrontation in the cafeteria?"

She couldn't tell Denise because she couldn't comprehend what it meant. It was only a fragment.

Abby and Erin want to talk to me...but I can't understand why... Why here? Why now?

"Carrie, it might help if you tell me—"

A branch cracked.

They both caught their breath.

Something, or some*one* was near, unseen in the forest.

"What was that?" Denise said.

Several seconds of silence passed before Carrie said, "I think we better leave."

43

Luke's radio spurted with a request while he patrolled his sector.

"Payroll needs the signed hard copy of your benefits sheet. Deadline's today, Luke."

Chiding himself for forgetting the paperwork, he took up his microphone. "It's at home. Permission to swing by my place and get it? It's quiet in my zone."

Seconds later, dispatch radioed approval. Luke headed for his house in East Division. Once he got there, he found his form in an envelope on the shelf by the door with a sticky note from Carrie: *Don't forget.*

The house was empty. Carrie was out and Vern had Emily. Driving on River Road, coming back near Fawn Ridge, tightening his hold on the wheel, he thought how the sheet would be insignificant once he came clean.

That's when he glimpsed the property next to Clara Price's place, across from the new subdivision.

Much of the fencing was overtaken with shrubs and branches, and hanging on sections of fence were signs that read Private Property, Keep Out and No Trespassing. But the gate, usually locked and chained, was open. On impulse, he took it as an invitation to make another effort to resolve his crime.

He turned down the property's dirt road, his car tottering along the rutted pathway. It ended at a clearing with a sprinkling of buildings: a couple of aging sheds, a Quonset hut and a double-wide trailer that cried out for a power wash of its filth-laced walls.

This place belonged to Raylin T. Nash.

Clara Price, his neighbor, had cautioned how Nash didn't care for visitors.

Luke wheeled his marked patrol car next to an orange Ram 5500 flatbed tow truck with RTN Towing, Clear River on the doors. Stepping outside, he first heard Tammy Wynette singing at low volume on a radio. Then came the tinkling of a long chain dragging on the ground. Then guttural growling as a large mixed-breed dog with a bone clamped in its jaws met him.

"Git back now!"

The command came from the depths of the shed. Old tires were piled in small towers, car batteries scattered nearby. An engine hoist stood to the side; a neat stack of new lumber peeked from a blue tarp. Inside the shed, Luke saw a workbench, a number of tools, a grease pit. A film of grease and sawdust covered the floor.

A man emerged from the open door, shirtless under his stain-smeared denim overalls. His muscular arms were sleeved with tattoos, his unshaven face stubbled. He stepped into the light, wiping his hands with an orange rag.

"Git!"

The chain tinkled and the dog sauntered off, disappearing around the shed.

The man eyed the patrol car, then Luke. "Need a tow?"

"Excuse me?"

Studying his rag, the man said: "You're new. I have a towing contract with the county." He nodded to his truck. "They usually just call. Where's the wreck?"

"Oh, right. No, I don't need a tow."

"What, then?"

The two men were the same height and build.

"Raylin Nash?"

He gave a short nod.

"Was hoping you could help me."

Nash's eyes narrowed. "With what?"

"Some weeks ago, the night of a bad storm, we had a report of a person in distress on River Road, right up there near your place."

"That so?"

"Do you recall seeing or hearing anything?"

"Ain't seen nothin' like that."

"No one come down here, looking for help?"

"Nope."

"Would you volunteer to let me look around?"

His lower jaw moved; he stuck out his bottom lip and scratched his stubble.

"Got a warrant?"

Luke took a moment, then inventoried all he could see, including the partially covered stack of new lumber, the tools on the bench. It appeared a couple were new power tools. One looked like a nail gun.

"A warrant?"

"That's right." Nash turned and tossed his rag toward a multi-colored heap of rags and old clothes, faded denim, dirty T-shirts, torn colored clothes.

"Now, why would you ask me that?"

"Because if you want to stick your nose in my private property, that's the law."

"Right. I just wanted cooperation, not a confrontation."

"Don't want no trouble either."

"Thanks for your time. Before I go, your lumber there, looks new." Luke nodded to the workbench. "So do some of those power tools."

Nash hooked his thumbs on his suspenders, sneering.

"I know what you people are thinkin'. Deputy Reeger came onto my place a long time ago, sniffing around after things got stolen from the construction. He knows I got it all in Lufkin. I showed him the receipts to prove it."

Luke let a moment go by while he decided whether to believe Nash. "Good to know. You enjoy the rest of your day."

As Luke moved to his car, the tinkling chain approached. Faster than before, and this time Nash did not call the dog away. Seconds after Luke closed the driver's door, the dog rose on his hind legs, pawing at his door frame, teeth bared, snarling and barking.

Luke glanced at Nash, whose thumbs were hooked in his suspenders, a grin cutting across his face as Luke eased his car away and back along the road.

44

Waiting at the IHOP for take-out coffee, Denise thought back to being with Carrie in the woods a couple days ago, the noise they'd heard.

They'd seen nothing. At first Denise had figured it might be a news competitor spying on them. More likely an animal or falling branch, they reasoned after they'd left the forest.

Now, waiting in the IHOP, Denise's phone vibrated.

A message had come through her public contact address.

Just read your story. So sad, but so informative, Gloria T. wrote.

The message was one of many compliments she'd received from readers since the story went up on the paper's site last night. The print edition was delivered across the county earlier this morning.

Grabbing her coffee, she crossed the street to the strip mall and the *Chronicle* office.

Her younger fellow reporters were already there. Marco Barnes raised his mug.

"Epic piece of journalism," he said as Denise got a copy from the newsroom stack.

"Yes," Kelcey Field said. "First-rate work."

"Thank you, colleagues. And thank you for taking up the extra story load."

Denise went to her corner desk to study her work. Flagged as an exclusive, her article ran under the headline:

MURDER IN WILD PINES FOREST
Unraveling the Heartbreaking Mystery

Dominating the front page, her story ran a few thousand words, spilling inside, filling two ad-free pages—a "double truck" in news terms. Denise had just started reading when Lynn, her editor, arrived at her desk, pushing her glasses to the top of her head.

"Giving you time for this paid off," Lynn said. "Good work."

"Thanks."

"We're getting calls from national outlets. The wires are reporting on it. We're looking at syndicating it."

"That's great."

"You did us proud, Denise. Some networks want to interview you. The exclusive with Carrie was new information, and the little old *Chron* beat the big guns who were poking around—the *Times*, the *Post*, CNN, everybody." Lynn knocked her knuckles on her desk. "Good stuff."

Denise returned to the story and her coffee. She looked at Carrie's photo with the cutline *Haunted Sole Survivor*. Getting her to talk had been a coup. Denise had tried to get her to remember as much as she could. Going over the files with her had helped. So did walking through the crime scene, until Carrie became overwhelmed.

It seemed that she was on the brink of recalling more—but Denise thought she was holding back.

I wonder what she might have remembered.

Still, Denise had plenty of material. After two days of writing at home, she'd pulled it together, hammering out the most exhaustive story yet on one of the darkest chapters in Clear River's history. It didn't answer all the questions, but still, she was pleased with the result.

She'd given the timeline: Carrie's confrontation with Abby and Erin; then the costume party; then the woods.

Sipping coffee, Denise thought of Carrie struggling to recall why the three of them ended up together in the woods. In the story, Denise detailed how the detectives had suspected Carrie, believing she had a vendetta against Abby and Erin. The investigation revealed that the girls died of gunshots fired from a Glock, a common police weapon. Being the sheriff's daughter, Carrie had access to such a firearm from her father's collection. And her father had even instructed her on how to use a gun.

Given the situation, it was clear to Denise why they'd thought Carrie committed the murders.

But no weapon and no casings were ever recovered at the scene. All of Vern Hamilton's weapons were accounted for; ballistic tests on his Glocks were negative. Testing Carrie for gunshot residue was ineffective because she'd been in the river.

Denise moved on to her story's next key aspect, the one she felt Eve Trainor had declined to reveal. Denise had found it buried deep in the case files. It was a theory suggesting the murder scene was staged to look like the work of a serial killer, with missing items taken as trophies. These included shoelaces, articles of clothing, identification and jewelry. They were never recovered. The theory held that Carrie would know how to disguise the scene. Denise found this aspect intriguing. No weapon or casings found. Items taken from the victims, *in a possible staging.*

She read on, to the detectives' interviews with Carrie's high school classmates, coming to one with Opal Wells. They'd asked Opal if Carrie was capable of violence, or seeking vengeance, after the confrontation in the cafeteria.

"No, not at all," Opal had said at the time in her statement.

"I was there sitting with Carrie the day Erin, Abby and their group were bullying Lanna. Carrie saw what was happening and told them to stop. Carrie's a good person, so smart. She helped me with my homework and we worked on projects together. I always felt sorry for her because she was so quiet after her mother died."

When Denise interviewed Opal for the story in her home, she supported everything she'd said in her police statement years earlier. However, Opal struck Denise as being a tiny bit unsophisticated and naive—she recalled how Opal had rummaged in vain through closets for a school project she'd done with Carrie.

Denise continued reading how the circumstantial evidence at that point was insufficient to charge Carrie. Her spotty memory was a challenge. Carrie moved to California; the case grew cold. Years later, Donnie Ray Hyde emerged as a new suspect, ultimately confessing to the murders before his execution.

In his confession, Hyde admitted to being "out of my mind on drugs and alcohol, wanting to know what killing three together would be like." He confessed to wearing a mask, killing the girls and chasing Carrie, trying to kill her before she fell from the cliff. Hyde said he'd collected shell casings, took items from the dead girls, then got rid of them and the gun. He was relieved reading news reports that Carrie's injuries had blocked her memory, and as time passed, he grew ever more confident he would never be linked to the case.

It was remarkable, Denise thought, how after he was visited on death row by Vern Hamilton, a man who had his own death sentence, the case was closed. Obtaining his confession was attributed to Hyde's exhaust of appeals in the Dupree case—and wanting to cleanse his soul.

Denise read on, to her eyewitness account of his execution in Huntsville and her interview with his mother, Mary-Ellen, in Kilgore. The story also went into the lives of Hyde, Jenna

Dupree, Erin, Abby and Carrie. The layout of the article was well-done with an array of photos—high school yearbook pictures, photos of Erin and Abby taken on the day they were murdered, before they went to Wild Pines Forest. There were pictures of Jenna Dupree as well as Vern and the detectives. The story also featured photos of Hyde, a file image of the gurney in the execution chamber at Huntsville, and one of Hyde's mother in his childhood bedroom.

At the story's end, Denise took readers back into the woods with Carrie battling to remember, to unravel the mystery of how she and the others ended up there.

"Abby and Erin wanted to talk to me. They said that they needed to talk here. But I was afraid."

Afraid of what, and why, will likely never be known, Denise had written, *because on that ill-fated day, the three young women crossed paths with a killer, in a forest that may never give up all of its secrets.*

45

Standing at her kitchen counter, Carrie closed her laptop and covered her face with her hands.

Luke put his arm around her. "You finished it?"

She nodded.

"How're you doing?" he asked.

Carrie released a shaky breath. "Not so good. I'm kind of spinning, you know?"

Luke's concern deepened.

"I'll call off work, stay home with you."

She waved away his offer. "No, I don't want you to do that. Thank you, but no."

"Carrie—" Luke paused, thinking, then indicated her laptop and the story. "Did talking to the reporter help?"

She didn't answer him. Luke saw worry bordering on fear in her eyes. Then Emily cried out from the other room and Carrie went to her.

Alone in the kitchen, Luke was still sorting out what he'd read that morning in the *Chronicle*. Fixing fresh coffee, he struggled with his own thoughts. The article noted how Carrie was considered a vengeful suspect; how at the time some thought the investigation was biased because her father was the sheriff.

The story related how Carrie had nearly died in the attack, had been robbed of her memory. And how, later, Vern received his terminal diagnosis. Man, if reading about all of this was difficult for Luke, it must've been brutal for Carrie, and for Vern. And what amazed Luke was how, as the article stated, Vern, after all those years, convinced Hyde to confess when a clock was ticking down on both of them.

Carrie and Vern were enduring so much.

Too much.

And how am I helping?

Yes, they'd moved to Texas because it was the right thing to do. Carrie needed to be with Vern, and Luke needed to leave his ghosts behind in LA. But since they'd been here, he hadn't been supportive because he'd been so consumed with what might have happened on River Road.

Pain shot through the back of his neck. Guilt stabbed at him over and over until he was sucked back into the swirling torment of his own catastrophe, the one that would soon further devastate his family.

At that moment, Luke's new burner phone vibrated. He'd received a text from Derek, a friend in Los Angeles he'd reached out to confidentially for help.

Hey pal. No guarantees, but I owe you.

Really need this. Thanks, Luke texted back, then let out a long breath.

Maybe there's hope. If I can just resolve it my way.

Carrie came in holding Emily. Luke went to them and nuzzled his daughter, kissing her then Carrie, who seemed better than when she'd left the room.

"I didn't expect the story to hit me so hard," she said.

"It must have been a gut punch."

"Worse."

"Are you going to be all right?"

"I don't know."

They let a moment pass.

"I'll take Emily to see Dad this morning." Carrie looked at Luke, fear lingering in her eyes. "I need to talk to him."

46

Alone at home, Vern Hamilton was concentrating on his computer monitor.

He'd closed his wooden shutters, muting the light in his study. As he read to the end of the online edition of Denise Diaz's story, his body sagged. This was not the rehash Bob Ellerd had anticipated.

It was an in-depth investigative article, and it was good.

She's nailed everything.

He sipped his glass of whiskey, then dragged the back of his hand over his lips.

Well, almost everything.

Vern looked at the framed photo of Doreen next to his computer, then the one with Carrie, Luke and Emily. He glanced at his prescription bottles. Ice rattled as he drank, scrolling the article, words and photos reflecting in his glasses like a running river, carrying him back to that day...

The doorbell rang.

Vern wondered who it could be until he saw Carrie's car through the window.

He opened the door to see her standing there with Emily in her arms.

They went to the living room.

"How're you today, Dad?"

"Physically, or mentally?"

"You know what I mean."

The edges of his mustache had drooped, his expression sober. Across the room, through his study's open door, Carrie saw his glass by his computer and caught the smell of alcohol when he let out a breath.

"Why didn't you tell me this story was coming?" Vern asked. "That you talked to the reporter and went back into those woods with her?"

Unshouldering her bag, Carrie put Emily down, then withdrew a picture book, *The Very Hungry Caterpillar*, and gave it to her.

"I'd heard she was nosing around," Vern said. "But not a word from you. Why?"

"You would've tried to talk me out of talking to her."

"You're right. Because it's behind us. Why do this?"

"She had the case files and I needed answers."

"Why? You don't need to remember. You should stop this. It's over."

"Not for me. I've gone back to that day so many times, trying to remember. Dad, it's like the day you came to my school to tell me Mom died."

His jaw tensed and he raised his head slightly.

"It changed me," she said. "It changed both of us."

Vern blinked at his own dark thoughts.

"And that day I went into the woods, the not knowing, is always with me."

She stared hard at her father.

"Can you understand? I need to know why we were in the woods."

Vern rubbed his chin and asked: "Did you get the answers you need, going back there with the reporter? Did you remember?"

Carrie paused.

"A few more pieces came back."

Vern tilted his head. "What pieces?"

"Abby and Erin said they needed to talk to me in the woods."

"You said that in the story."

"Why would they want to meet me secretly?"

"You don't remember?"

"No, it hasn't come back to me. Do you know?"

Vern stuck out his bottom lip.

"Why would I know? It could have been a world of reasons. You should put a stop to this remembering stuff. It doesn't matter now."

"It matters to me, Dad. I want to know why we were there. Why did they want to talk to me?"

"I don't know."

Carrie shifted the subject. "You went to see Hyde on death row. Why?"

"Time was running out. All the evidence pointed to him, like the story says."

"How did you get him to confess?"

"All of his appeals had failed. I told him this was the time to clear his conscience."

Carrie looked at Vern, processing his answer when soft chattering drew them to Emily. She'd pattered into the study. Carrie went after her, getting a pen and paper from her father's desk, letting Emily sit on the floor and scribble.

Carrie took in the room; the air held Vern's cologne, loneliness, heartbreak and resignation to his condition. She saw the photos beside his computer. Being in this room stirred Carrie's childhood memory of how she used to toddle into the study and crawl up onto her dad's lap.

Carrie's mind went to other memories. When she was a little older, she'd sometimes find his homicide textbooks open. As a little girl, she was chilled by the graphic photos of murder victims—shot, burned, drowned, stabbed, eviscerated. But she was also fascinated and engrossed, reading details until her mother found her. Doreen always put the books up out of reach, then scolded Carrie's dad.

For heaven's sake, Vern, do not leave these things lying around for Carrie to see!

She glanced at her dad's bottles of medication, then turned to him. Vern had joined them in the room, lowering himself into the sofa chair, his eyes crinkling as he watched Emily.

"Are you taking your pills, Dad?"

"Yes."

"You shouldn't be drinking, period."

"You're right—it might kill me."

"Dad." Carrie raked her fingers through her hair. "I know the story could raise those disgusting rumors of how a lot of people thought Mom died because you—hurt her. I'm sorry. That must've been painful."

Vern pushed back a surge of anguish.

"I admit that I was quick to anger with her at times. I had my reasons. But despite what small minds in a small town whip up, I did not hurt her."

Carrie was weighing his response when he turned to face her.

"In some ways, you're like me, quick to anger."

"What?"

"You argued with those girls in the cafeteria. They were older, more popular, but you got in their faces over their bullying."

"It wasn't anger so much as doing what I thought was right."

Carrie surveyed Vern's study, the plaques, citations and mounted guns, the shelves lined with those books and journals of horrendous criminal histories. She scanned titles like: *Criminal Investigative Analysis*; *FBI Academy: Serial Offenders*; *Forensic Techniques*; *Homicide Investigation*; and *Crime Scene Processing and Investigation*.

"Why can't I remember why they wanted to talk to me, Dad?"

"You don't have to remember. Hyde confessed. It's all buried. You don't have to remember."

"Yes, I do. Because I nearly died, too."

47

Luke got to the sheriff's office long before his shift started.

Suiting up, he set aside his concerns about the story's impact on Carrie and Vern.

I've got to solve my own crime, on my own time.

That Derek in LA was helping had given him a boost. But Luke still had more to pursue on his own. Alone in the patrol room, he logged on to his computer and continued his clandestine investigation.

The few minutes he'd had with Raylin Nash had yielded a bad vibe. Before leaving Nash's property, Luke had memorized the plate on the Ram tow truck and was now running it. He got the man's full name, Raylin Thurman Nash, from his registration. Then his driver's licence, photo and particulars. Entering commands, he ran Nash through various data banks, then saw something that made him sit up straight.

He'd gotten a hit.

Nash was the subject of a protective order filed a year ago by Brenda Gwen Jones, his ex-wife. She'd alleged physical abuse, threats and harassment. The court ordered Nash to keep at least five hundred feet away from Jones, who resided in Sellron just north of town.

After thinking for a moment, Luke ran Brenda Gwen Jones's name through the system. Obtaining her driver's license, photo and address, he submitted her information to more data banks.

No complaints, no warrants, no record.

Clean as a whistle.

Luke then ran her name through the local, state and national systems for missing persons.

Nothing.

He got his phone, scrolling to the blurry clip of the construction site security video from the storm. His stomach tightened as the hazy shadow figure rose from the ditch.

No way to tell if that's Brenda Gwen Jones.

No way, without technical help, to tell who it is.

Or was.

That was why he was counting on help from Derek Springer.

Derek was a tech wizard with the LAPD who'd played softball with Luke. When Derek's nephew got into trouble, Derek reached out to Luke, who took the kid on a ride-along, giving him a hard look at where his life with gangs would end up. It worked, and Derek, an expert with facial recognition, pledged his allegiance.

Now Luke was calling in his favor. He'd sent Derek the fuzzy video of the woman rising from the ditch. For an instant, like a camera flash, she was illuminated from a car's approaching headlights. It gave Luke hope that facial recognition might work. Maybe the mystery woman hadn't been hurt badly and had somehow left the area. Or maybe she'd been under the influence. Maybe she fell out of a vehicle, or was fleeing a domestic situation, or was involved in a crime.

Or maybe she was abducted.

His pulse picked up a little.

Remember, another vehicle approached the scene.

Luke looked at the fuzzy footage of the figure in the storm. He would not allow her to become another ghost in his life;

he would find her and help her, however long it took. He only hoped it wasn't too late.

He cued up Nash's face on his screen. There had to be a way to quietly keep digging deeper into this so he could end it. Luke considered how Nash's property was adjacent to where he'd struck the woman—close to the new houses. Luke had seen new lumber and new power tools at Nash's. But he claimed to have receipts from Lufkin. Still, there was that heap of old clothes, including some that were pink.

Is it enough for probable cause, enough to support a warrant? What if I linked it to the thefts at the new houses? But that's Reeger's case. Do I want to try that just yet?

Other deputies began arriving in the patrol room, so Luke closed his files, logging out of data banks.

"Hey, Luke," Lonnie Welch said. "How about that story in the *Chron*. Everybody's talking about it."

Luke nodded as Lonnie went on.

"My cousin works at the IHOP across from the *Chron* and heard now NBC and CNN might be on the story. Did you hear that?"

"All I know is that Carrie's getting a lot of calls from the press."

"That story's got so many details on the case," Lonnie said, turning to Clay Smith and Garth Reeger.

"Carrie still can't remember things?" Clay said.

"No," Luke said. "It's in the story."

"That injury was a silver lining of sorts for her," Reeger said, "wasn't it?"

"What?" Luke said.

"Well, back then, they looked hard at her being the killer." Reeger locked on to Luke with an icy stare.

Luke stared right back.

Reeger added: "The case was unsolved all this time, right up until after she moved back, and until Donnie Ray's execution."

Sensing tension, Clay intervened, saying: "But Hyde was a suspect and he confessed."

"Whatever." Reeger kept his eyes on Luke. "What I'd like to know is, what're you doing in so early?"

"Excuse me?"

"Irene out front says you got in well before the shift. I'm curious." Reeger indicated Luke's computer. "What're you up to? Why so early? No need to make an impression. You already got the job, *son-in-law*."

"Wow," Lonnie said.

"Back off, Garth," Clay said.

Luke did not pull away from returning Reeger's stare.

"I don't report to you," Luke said. "But if you have a pathological need to know, I was catching up on work, Garth."

"Pathological?"

Luke said nothing.

Lonnie and Clay exchanged glances, unsure where this was going.

"I heard you stopped at Raylin Nash's place," Reeger said. "Are you still sticking your LAPD nose into my zone, on my investigation?"

Luke let a moment go by.

"Yes."

The patrol room fell silent.

"I was patrolling my division," Luke said. "I went home to get a form for personnel, then I had an idea."

"You had an idea?"

"I stopped to check on something on Nash's property, which, as you know, Garth, is close to where forty thousand dollars of material was stolen. *In your zone*."

The muscles in Reeger's jaw bunched as he took a step toward Luke, who didn't budge.

"Easy, Garth," Clay said.

"Did you know," Luke said, "Nash has a stack of new lumber and new power tools?"

"I checked it out. He bought it in Lufkin," Reeger said. "You offend me."

"I offend you?"

"I questioned Nash. He has receipts. I cleared him. Tell me, why the hell are you so fixated on my case!"

"Hey!"

All attention shifted to Sheriff Bob Ellerd watching from the edge of the patrol room.

"What's going on here?"

No one spoke for several seconds.

"Well?" Ellerd said.

Reeger nodded to Luke. "The fortunate son here is interfering with my case."

"Which case?"

"The stolen material from Fawn Ridge."

"Is that true, Luke?"

With every eye in the patrol room on him, Luke had to think quick.

"You know we live near there, and I had an idea that could help Garth with his case."

"What's that?" Ellerd said.

"We could obtain information from cell phone towers close to Fawn Ridge, from around the time of the theft. Phones are always pinging from towers. It could help us identify which phones were in proximity at the time of the theft."

Ellerd began nodding, saying: "Did you try that, Garth?"

"No, sir—it means getting a warrant."

"I know that technique," Ellerd said. "It's effective."

"The LAPD uses it," Luke said, "to help pinpoint who was in a given area during shootings."

Ellerd looked at Reeger. "Do you have any serious leads?"

"I'm working on it."

Ellerd turned back to Luke.

"As I recall, you thought you'd encountered someone in a storm in that area, and you were calling hospitals? Could it have been someone scoping the construction site?"

Luke swallowed.

"Might've been."

"In any case, I like your idea. We'll try it," Ellerd said. "Luke, help Garth write up our request to the judge for a warrant to get the information from the cell tower folks. I want it done by end of day."

Reeger's jaw dropped.

"You want to solve your case, don't you, Garth?" Ellerd said.

Reeger said nothing.

"Good. Now, get to work, everybody."

48

Luke was walking a tightrope.

All through his shift, he grappled with what he'd launched in that morning's dustup with Reeger.

Luke had been pressed; he'd needed to think fast.

So, under the guise of helping Reeger's case, he'd urged for the cell tower warrant to pursue his own.

It was a risk.

But one he had to take. Because, sooner or later, the truth would come to light. For now, he still had control of it.

At the same time, his guilt over striking the mystery woman, and for failing to support Carrie, was eating him up. He could barely focus on his duties.

Just like it was in LA.

Much of his day he responded to calls: two silent alarms; a welfare concern; a loose livestock complaint; and a minor traffic accident. Later that afternoon, he was cleared to end his patrol early so he could return to the office and work on the warrant. Reeger waited with a laptop in the meeting room, his jaw firm, telegraphing that he was cooperating under duress.

"Exactly how does this cell tower BS work?"

Sitting next to him, Luke outlined how cell phones are always communicating with cell towers to find the strongest signal. The records sought in their warrant would show that a specific phone, or phones, were communicating with a specific tower.

"With that information," Luke said, "we can confirm that a person's phone was in a location at a given time."

They got the names of the service providers operating the towers closest to Fawn Ridge. In their request, they provided perimeters, location, date and time covering the forty-thousand-dollar theft from Fawn Ridge.

"That should do it," Reeger said.

"Wait," Luke said. "Let's extend it to include the location, date and time of the storm, when I thought I saw someone on River Road near the subdivision."

"Why?"

"Like Ellerd said, it could've been someone scoping the construction site."

Luke gave Reeger the date and time. When they'd finished, they sent the request for the warrant to their supervisor to look over before it would be sent to the clerk for the court. With that done, they'd need to wait out the next steps in the process, which could take a few days. Reeger, his cheek twitching, said little and left without looking at Luke.

At his own desk in the patrol room, Luke worked on completing reports. But his misgivings wrenched him back to the ramifications of the warrant.

Sure, it was possible the action would yield a phone linked to the theft from the construction site. It could even be a phone owned by Raylin Nash. It would deepen the need to take a look at him for the theft. But Nash lived close to the site, which could make it difficult to prove anything.

Luke's greater concern was his own situation.

His phone would come up. But that was to be expected, as he'd already related that he was in the area.

No, something else terrified him.

If the woman he struck had a phone, the warrant would yield a number; it could be traced to her, or her family.

Luke felt his heart beat a little faster.

On the other hand...

What if she was fleeing someone? What if she got picked up? What if Nash picked her up?

He'd seen a car approaching at that time.

And if the driver, or a passenger, had a phone, the cell tower record could yield another avenue of pursuit for Luke.

He clenched his eyes shut for a moment.

I'm walking a tightrope without a net.

After finishing his shift, Luke changed, then headed to the parking lot, where he noticed Clay Smith standing near his Chevy Blazer.

"Hey, partner," Clay said. "How'd it go today?"

"Helped capture a fugitive donkey, among other things."

"Speaking of asses, how'd it go on the warrant with Reeger?"

"It went."

Clay took a moment, staring at Luke.

"Listen, I know what's going on."

Luke swallowed.

"What's going on?"

"Lacey told me that Carrie's having a hard time with all the news attention on the murders. Like it just won't end for her."

Luke nodded with a mix of relief and guilt. "Yes, she's set on remembering what happened."

"I don't get it. Hyde's dead; the case is over."

"I know. I don't think talking to that reporter at the *Chronicle* helped. It seems to have opened up wounds."

"Is she remembering more?"

"A little, maybe. I'm not sure."

"Why're you here? You should be with her. I'm sure Ellerd would give you some personal time."

"Carrie wants to deal with it on her own."

"You ought to think about helping her—" Clay pointed his chin to the office "—instead of this crap with Reeger's case."

"Just trying to keep busy, keep my mind off things. You know?"

Clay looked at him.

"I get it. If you want to talk over a beer, let me know."

"Appreciate that, Clay."

Luke got into his Chevy. Before starting it, he watched Clay walk off.

Then he placed his hands on the wheel, gripping it tight to stop them from shaking.

49

Sitting next to network news anchor Haylee Hunt, Denise clasped her hands together and interlaced her fingers, her knuckles whitening.

Denise inhaled, looking out to the woman with the headset, who was standing beside a camera aimed directly at Denise.

Haylee patted Denise's arm. "Ignore all this hullabaloo. We're just going to have a conversation."

Giving her a taut smile, Denise couldn't believe how quickly everything had moved. Once she'd agreed to be a guest, the network flew her to New York. They'd put her up in a nice hotel the night before her live interview with Haylee at its world headquarters in Manhattan. Now, amid the bright lights, cameras and busy studio crew, Denise watched the headset woman's hand signals. Counting down, going live to millions of viewers in five…four…three…

Intro music played, then faded.

"Welcome back," Haylee said into the camera. "It's been more than thirteen years, but the murders of two teenage girls is a tragedy that continues to reverberate in the rural community of Clear River, Texas."

The wall-sized video panel behind Haylee and Denise displayed the pages of the *Chronicle*'s story with enlarged insets of photos of Abby, Erin and Carrie as teens. Haylee summarized the murders, then referenced Denise's story.

"New light has been shed on this heartbreaking case through the exceptional work of the local paper, the *Clear River Chronicle*. What makes the *Chronicle*'s reporting outstanding is that despite efforts by larger media outlets, this small paper was first to interview the tragedy's sole survivor. The *Chronicle* also revealed new information on the case. But a caution, this story contains disturbing details. Here with us now in New York to discuss the story," Haylee said, turning to Denise, "is Denise Diaz, the journalist who wrote this riveting account. Denise, welcome."

"Thank you."

"You've covered this case extensively."

"Yes, but not when it broke thirteen years ago. I got into it after joining the paper about four years back."

"What drew you to it?"

"Many things. I immersed myself in it when it was an unsolved mystery, and I found it disturbing."

"And the case was recently solved when Donnie Ray Hyde made his stunning confession before he was executed for another murder. You witnessed his execution. What was that like?"

"Unsettling. I think it was for all the witnesses."

"You interviewed Hyde's mother, who refuses to believe her son was a multiple murderer."

"Yes, but that's understandable. Hyde did confess after Carrie Hamilton's father, who was sheriff at the time of the murders, recently visited him on death row."

"Like many who've followed this case," Haylee said, "I'm wondering—didn't you find that timing odd? That Hyde confessed so soon after Vernon Hamilton visited him on death row?"

"I did. But Hyde's attorney, as well as his spiritual advisor, noted that the confession came after Hyde's appeals had run out for the murder he was convicted of, Jenna Dupree; they said he wanted to clear his soul.

"I read Hyde's confession, and Hyde had facts only the person who'd killed Abby Hall and Erin Eddowes would know," Denise added.

"Years before Hyde surfaced as a suspect, Carrie Hamilton, the sole survivor and the daughter of the local sheriff, had been considered the leading suspect."

"Yes, primarily because she was the last to see the girls and they'd argued prior to the murders. But the case against Carrie was circumstantial. In his confession, Hyde admitted that he'd attempted to kill her."

"As your story states. Yes, very intriguing. But no weapon was ever found, no shell casings. Items were missing, as if the scene was staged," Haylee said. "And what about Carrie's injuries? Some have speculated that her diminished memory was a convenient way to evade telling all that happened."

"It definitely fueled rumors and conspiracies. But the case file contained signed statements by doctors that a chip of skull bone had nicked her brain. And there was the trauma of the murders and her near death in the river. The evidence suggests her problems with memory are legitimate."

"Denise, Carrie's never spoken publicly on the case; I should mention that we invited Carrie, her father, Vernon, and Clear River investigators to participate here with us, but they declined. So how did you get your interview with Carrie?"

"A series of events—key among them is that I'd obtained the case file. Carrie agreed to go over it with me and revisit the scene, which she hadn't done since it happened. It was traumatic for her. She still doesn't remember much, but our return to Wild Pines Forest may have helped her remember a bit more."

"Well, you and the *Clear River Chronicle* are to be congratulated on an outstanding piece of reporting."

"Thank you."

"It's testament to the importance of local newspapers. And we've learned that there may be plans to submit it for consideration for a Pulitzer in the category of local journalism."

"My editor has suggested that."

"Amazing," Haylee said. "Now, one final thing before we have to go. We've learned that based on your reporting, publishers have approached you about a book, and a producer is interested in developing a TV miniseries?"

"It's all preliminary, but yes, I've talked with a literary agency. It's all overwhelming. But what's most important is that the victims of this tragedy not be forgotten, and the truth, the full truth, about what happened be known."

"Absolutely. Thank you for being with us, Denise." Haylee turned back to face the camera. "Again, I urge you to read her story in the *Clear River Chronicle*, online at the site provided at the bottom of your screen."

After the show, a car service from the network took Denise to Newark Liberty International Airport for her return flight.

Adrenaline rippled through her as they left Manhattan, taking the Holland Tunnel and surfacing in Jersey City. Along the drive, her phone exploded with messages from people who'd seen her appearance, read her article or both. She was looking at them when her editor called from Texas.

"Denise, that was fantastic," Lynn said. "Good Lord, the traffic to your story is nearly crashing our site. We're getting thousands of visits. *Thousands*."

"Wow."

"And we've just surpassed over one thousand new digital subscribers."

"That's great."

"You were so good, so poised."

"I was so nervous."

"You did good. Oh, the *New York Times* wants to send a reporter and photographer from its Houston bureau to do a story on you, the paper and the case, once you get back."

"Guess I'm getting my fifteen minutes."

"You earned it. Nice work. Have a safe flight back."

After moving through airport security and settling in at pre-boarding for her flight to Houston, she worked on unwinding. A few travelers did a double take, but she was left alone to resume reading posts and messages. They continued flowing in.

Such a tragedy for those girls and their families, Denise.

I'm from California. You didn't go into the story deep enough; Carrie's husband killed a woman when he was with the LAPD.

Saw you with Haylee Hunt. Great work Denise.

Come on, the sheriff's daughter? Fought with the other girls in the cafeteria. It's a no-brainer. She did it.

Well-written story, Denise. Good job on this terrible tragedy.

You don't have the real story. That's not what happened.

Just read your excellent report and thinking how Carrie lost her mother, was almost murdered, and now her father's dying. How much is a person supposed to bear?

Hyde confessed at the last minute. Something doesn't smell right.

Great investigative reporting—hope you get that Pulitzer!

The messages kept coming as Denise buckled into her seat and shut her phone off. The plane seemed to taxi forever before it rocketed down the runway and lifted off. During the flight, Denise tried to relax, but the questions Haylee Hunt had asked and comments that followed gave her pause.

Is this story really over?

50

Carrie put Emily down for a nap, then closed the bedroom door with growing desperation.

Seeing Denise Diaz on national network news had left her questioning everything in her life.

Kneading the back of her neck, she went to the kitchen to prepare coffee. Denise's TV appearance with Haylee Hunt had caused a flood of new media interview requests. It also unleashed a torrent of hateful comments online.

Carrie is the killer.

Reeks of hick-town police coverup.

Hyde is a patsy. Carrie did it.

The onslaught of offensive postings concerned Lacey and Grace, and they'd reached out with support.

Are you okay? Lacey had texted. A few of us can come right over.

Carrie's dad was at a doctor's appointment. Luke was at work because she'd told him not to stay home. She'd wanted to be alone. But now, Carrie was feeling like she was against the ropes and Lacey's offer had come at the right time.

Not long after the coffee was ready, Lacey and Grace arrived with a round of hugs.

"Opal is tied up," Lacey said. "She can't make it."

With Emily asleep and Carrie watching the monitor, they went to the living room, keeping their voices low.

Carrie found comfort being with them.

"It's like the whole world has read the story or seen the network piece," she said. "Everything about me and my family has practically gone viral. And it victimizes Abby, Erin and Jenna again."

Lacey and Grace nodded.

"It's selfish," Carrie said, "but I'm feeling raw, exposed, under attack."

"That's not selfish," Lacey said. "Hyde tried to kill you, too."

"Some of the stuff online is horrible," Grace said. "You can't pay attention to idiots and creeps."

"Even with Hyde's confession and death," Carrie said, "with the case solved, I don't know."

"What do you mean?" Lacey asked.

"The conspiracies, the accusations and the attacks online leave me struggling with my own questions."

"But it's over—you've got to move on," Lacey said.

"I can't. Not until I remember everything."

"Would it help to talk about it with us?" Grace said.

Carrie looked at them: women she'd known since they were girls.

"Honey," Lacey said, "talk to us. We grew up together."

"We were all there in the cafeteria that day," Grace said. "Me, Lacey, Opal, Clay and so many others. We all know Abby and Erin were acting like bitches."

"Grace!" Lacey scolded her.

"Well, that's what people said, Lacey, and it's true. Lord, they didn't deserve what happened, but when you stood up to them like you did, Carrie, all of us thought it was a good thing."

Lacey put her hand on Carrie's arm. "Talk to us, honey."

Looking at Lacey and Grace, Carrie felt they were the only friends she had at that moment. And now, with the case out there, maybe she could open up a bit. It was a risk, but they might know something that could help.

"I remember that Abby and Erin said they needed to meet me in private. In the woods," Carrie said. "Do you know why?"

Lacey and Grace traded glances, then Lacey stared blankly into her coffee cup.

"No," Lacey said. "But remember Violet Engstrom? Tall, red hair, in our year?"

"Her family moved," Carrie said.

"To Canada, after graduation." Lacey glanced at Grace. "I don't know if this was in the police report; I mean, after the murders, they questioned everybody, but Violet told me something about seeing Abby and Erin at the Halloween party at the dance hall."

"Did you see anything about that in the police files, Carrie?" Grace asked.

"No. What did Violet tell you?"

"She said she saw Abby and Erin outside the hall, and they looked rattled."

"Rattled?"

"That was her word: *rattled*," Lacey said.

"Did she say why?" Carrie asked.

"No, she didn't know."

"Does it mean anything?" Grace asked. "Does it help?"

"Maybe. I don't know."

Like a curtain, a brief silence fell over them before the monitor came to life with Emily's cries and Carrie left to tend to her. Once the baby was changed and dressed, Carrie brought her to the living room.

IF TWO ARE DEAD

Lacey and Grace fussed and cooed over her before taking it as a cue to leave. Carrie thanked them for their support, loving them for it. But once they'd left, her gut knotted, questions mounting.

51

Across Clear River County, Clay Smith's attention flicked to the vehicle that had just rolled into the Chevron west of town.

Chewing on the last of his Cheesy Pepper Jack Tornado, Clay headed to his patrol car with a cold can of Coke as an orange Ram flatbed tow truck creaked to a halt at the pumps.

The driver was lifting the nozzle when Clay approached.

"Hey there, Ray."

Ray Nash of RTN Towing nodded at Clay in uniform.

"Deputy." He smiled. "Got a job for me?"

"Not at the moment." Clay touched the Coke to his forehead.

A second or two passed, both men enjoying the highway breezes and the shade of the gas station's canopy.

"While I got you," Clay said, "maybe you could help me out. Unofficially."

"What's on your mind?"

"I understand my new colleague, Luke Conway, paid you a recent visit?"

"He did."

"Mind telling me what that was about?"

Scratching his stubbled chin with his free hand, Nash half smiled to himself.

"What's it worth to you?"

Clay's warmth dropped a few degrees as he eyed Nash. "I believe we have an understanding, Raylin."

Nash shrugged, watching the pump, easing on the nozzle, slowing the flow.

"He asked about some sort of a report of somebody out on River Road, in that storm a few weeks back."

"What about it?"

"Wanted to know if I'd heard or seen anyone, that kind of thing."

"That's it?"

"He asked if he could look around my place. I refused."

Clay digested the information. "And that was the end of it?"

The nozzle clanked as Nash replaced it, then screwed on and tightened his truck's gas cap.

"That was the end of it. Why you interested?"

Clay turned to search the horizon.

"Something happened with the new deputy out there on River Road that night."

"Like what?"

"Something." Clay clamped a friendly hand on Nash's shoulder. "Thanks, Ray. Good seein' you again."

52

Denise Diaz navigated her Chevy Trax around potholes while avoiding the dogs running loose in Tagallet Mobile Home Park.

Flies circled the trash bins she passed as she looked closely at the numbers on the trailers. Coming to unit 33, she parked in front. Observing it, her thoughts went back to the murders as she contemplated the case.

Hyde's brother, Brophy, had lived there, where Hyde said they drank and did drugs until he went into the woods and murdered Abby and Erin.

A loud growl vibrated Denise's car window. She saw the dog—ears down, strings of slobber swinging from its jaws. Then she saw the unwelcoming face of a woman eyeballing her from the steps of a neighboring unit.

Denise left the trailer park, driving less than a quarter mile to Wild Pines Forest, stopping for a few minutes at the entrance, then moving to the spot where Carrie had been rescued. Denise didn't know exactly what she hoped to accomplish by stopping at these places.

Earlier today, she'd been on a regular assignment, interviewing people who were restoring a historical building that had burned months earlier. But while returning to the newsroom, something drew her back to the murders. Ever since her article and everything that followed—her TV network appearance, her interview with the *New York Times*, the talk of a book and TV miniseries—Denise had found it difficult resuming the life of a small-town news reporter.

It wasn't so much the fanfare of her brush with fame; it was the steady flow of questions and comments her article had generated. During her interview with the *Times*, the reporter had noted the case was a strange one.

"A lot of twists," he'd said. "Carrie, the sheriff's daughter, is a suspect, then Hyde emerges, and after denying involvement for so long, he makes a last-minute confession."

The *Times* ran its feature, giving rise to more comments and questions. Some were outlandish, some congratulatory, others cast conspiracies. In its wake, Denise began doubting if her reporting on the murders was complete.

She couldn't let it go. Still, she wasn't certain what to do about it as she arrived in the newsroom. Trying to focus on something else, she wrote up the historical building item, which took little time.

She got a coffee, then went back to her desk, thinking as she sorted through all the comments on her murder story. She went way back to early ones that came immediately after her live interview with Haylee Hunt in New York.

Scrolling through them, she wasn't sure what she was looking for.

Saw you with Haylee Hunt. Great work Denise.

Well-written story, Denise. Good job relating this terrible tragedy.

Just read your excellent report and thinking how Carrie lost her mother, was almost murdered, and now her father's dying. How much is a person supposed to bear?

You don't have the real story. That's not what happened.

The last one came from someone using the name FactorRex31, and it hit a nerve.

Do I have the real story?

Denise then went to a new wave of recent comments that had followed the feature about her and the story in the *New York Times*, stopping on one in particular.

Diaz is giving DRH too much credit.

Again, that was FactorRex31.

Denise gave the comments little currency. Like trolls, just someone being an armchair quarterback. But comments like those fueled her doubts. Taking a hit of coffee, she began typing, opening her folders on the case. Jumping from Hyde's confession to forensic reports, crime scene photos to her interview with Mary-Ellen Hyde. She scanned them quickly, reconciling them with some of the comments until it dawned on her.

Something doesn't add up.

She tapped her finger on her mouse.

Some pieces just don't fit.

After turning things over in her mind, she went to her contacts, then called Barry Fitzsimmons at Communications for the Texas Department of Criminal Justice. He'd set up the media witnesses at Hyde's execution. Once she'd reached him, she made a request. Taking a moment, he said he'd have to check.

Denise reread more files in the time it took him to get back to her.

"This is preliminary," Fitzsimmons said. "We still need to confirm a few things, but we should be able to accommodate your request. I'll get back to you with a day and time."

Denise thanked him.

Pleased with her small success, she went to Lynn Grant, who was feeding her fish.

"Gave your fire story a quick read. Looks good. We're going to need you to do a feature on a local artist. Her paintings and sculptures are going to be showcased in Chicago. I'll send you the info. Take lots of photos."

"About that, Lynn. Something's come up. I want to go to Livingston."

"What's in Livingston?"

"Death row."

Lynn looked at her. "Is it the story?"

"Yes."

"Denise, you did a fantastic job on a big story. But we're still a small paper."

"Listen, I can't put my finger on it, but something's not right. I've got to do more digging."

Lynn was weighing her request.

"Tell you what," Denise said. "I'll do the artist story first, as soon as possible. Then I'll go to Livingston."

Letting out a long breath, Lynn nodded. "Okay."

53

Denise placed her notebook and pen on the counter of her side of the cubicle in the death row visitation room of the Allan B. Polunsky Unit in Livingston.

Staring at her from the other side of the Plexiglas window, framed by the confined booth's scarred casing, was multiple-murderer Darnell George Sharp, aged forty-one.

She'd discovered his name in the case records.

A brief notation said that he had known Donnie Ray Hyde on death row, where Sharp was awaiting execution for murdering four people: his ex-girlfriend and three members of her family in Lubbock. Sharp had declined to talk to Clear River detectives when they were investigating Hyde years ago. But he'd agreed to Denise's request for an interview. It took a couple of days to arrange through the warden's office, his prison chaplain and Sharp himself.

Now here he was. Dressed in prison whites, arms laced with tattoos, bearing a chin curtain beard and shaved head, his eyes shining like dark ball bearings.

He pointed to his handset and Denise picked up hers.

"Thank you for agreeing to see me, Darnell."

"I don't get many visitors, ma'am. It breaks up my day." He gave her a shy smile.

"I hope it's been explained to you that I'm here to ask you about Donnie Ray Hyde."

"Yes, ma'am, it has."

"I understand you have an ongoing appeal, but I'm not here to report on your case."

"Yes, ma'am. That's fine."

"Okay, so we're both on the same page."

"We are, ma'am."

"You knew Donnie Ray while he was here?"

"I did."

"But you refused to talk to detectives from Clear River about their investigation of his connection to the two murders there?"

"I was not inclined to assist them at the time. In here, word gets around, and not in a good way. But he's gone now, so..."

"Did you know much about the Clear River case from Donnie Ray?"

He didn't answer.

"Darnell, did he ever talk to you about the murders of Abby Hall and Erin Eddowes, the girls from Clear River?"

He adjusted his hold on his handset and shrugged.

"I see," Denise said. "Shortly before Donnie Ray's execution, he confessed. Shortly before he confessed, he was visited by Vernon Hamilton, the former sheriff in Clear River. Were you aware of that?"

"Yes, ma'am."

"Did Vernon reach out to talk to you?"

Darnell shook his head.

"Can you tell me—I mean, under the circumstances, this may seem like a stupid question—but what was Donnie Ray's demeanor before Vernon came to the unit, before he confessed?"

"Before?"

"Yes."

"Well, I can tell you this. Yes, he was appealing. That's what you do. But in the end, Donnie Ray owned up to his actions; at the time, he'd given in to some dark force. He accepted what he did was wrong, and he was working with his advisor to atone."

"So, he'd accepted it?"

"He had. You know, in here we realize that when we go to the death house, pass through that door to the other side, there's only one of two places you'll end up. You're either going to rise to heaven or spiral to hell."

"Right."

"And people may scoff, but a lot of us are working to reconcile with our acts. You know, prepare for our journey. That's what Donnie Ray was doing before he confessed, before his last appeal to the board was kicked back."

"He was getting ready."

"Yes, ma'am. He was trying to make his peace. I remember hearing him cry like a little kid after his mother walked away from her last visit here."

Denise sat with that for a moment.

"And how was Donnie Ray after Vernon Hamilton's visit? After he confessed to the other murders?"

Darnell stroked his beard as if trying to coax the words. "Almost happy?"

"Happy?"

"Yes, ma'am. He said something about how after all the pain he caused his mother, he was going to ease her suffering after he was gone."

"How?"

"I don't know."

"What did he mean, ease her suffering after he was gone?"

"I'm still trying to figure it out. I guess he was getting spiritual. Maybe he was tired of the roller-coaster ride of all his appeals."

"Why do you think he confessed, after denying it for so long?"

Darnell shook his head. "Maybe he needed to clear his conscience, cleanse his soul. I mean, he seemed upbeat. You know he didn't want his mother to witness his execution?"

"I did. She told me."

"And before they moved him to the death house in Huntsville, he gave away his few possessions. His Bible, his radio. His shoes. That's why I'm talking to you. I figure I owe him in some way."

"Why?"

"I'm wearing his shoes."

"I'm sorry—you're wearing his shoes?"

"We're the same size. Nine. So he made sure I got them. He had some books and sketches. He gave those to other inmates, too. So he was ready to go."

Denise touched up her notes. Several long seconds passed with her looking directly at Darnell before she spoke.

"Tell me, how many people do you think Donnie Ray killed?"

He blinked.

"He killed the girl in Tyler. No doubt about it. He admitted it."

"And the girls in the woods in Clear River?"

"He rarely talked about them. Only to say police suspected him for it, but he told me once that he did not do it. Now, I get that with his appeals for Tyler, he wouldn't want to mess up his shot at a reprieve, commutation to life, you know?"

"Right."

"Now, this may sound funny coming from someone like me in this place, but I honestly don't think he killed them girls in Clear River."

"And why do you think he didn't kill them?"

"I don't know. Just the vibe I got from him, I guess."

Looking at him, Denise nodded, weighing what he'd said.

"Thank you for your help, Darnell."

"Good talking to you. You're welcome, ma'am."

Denise signaled a prison staff member, then proceeded to leave, returning her visitor's chain tag and clearing security.

In her SUV, driving to Clear River, processing all that Darnell had said, she suddenly thought of the old adage a homicide cop had told her about murder investigations.

Things are seldom what they look like.

54

The picture held an awesome beauty for Vern.

The Tetons in Wyoming, summits soaring to the sky like the spires of majestic cathedrals. His eyes crinkled as he lost himself in it, sitting in the waiting room.

Vern hoped this new, unscheduled appointment, coming so soon after his last one, wouldn't take long. A good thing about being here was that big framed photo of the mountains on the wall, because it took him away.

"Mr. Hamilton," the assistant at the reception desk called to him, "the doctor will see you now. Second one on the right."

With an obliging nod, Vern took his hat from his knee and went into the examining room. His physician, Dr. Bill Clark, gestured for him to sit on the cushioned bench next to the examining table. Knowing Vern didn't care for small talk, he got down to it.

"Your recent tests and scans have come back." The doctor's face was serious as he read information from his computer screen. "The results are not encouraging."

"Give it to me straight, Bill."

The doctor was solemn. "Vernon, your condition's deteriorating faster than we expected. I've shared your numbers and consulted with two specialists in Houston."

"And?"

"You don't have years. It's now months."

"Months?"

"Three, maybe four. I'm sorry."

Blinking, the edges of Vern's mustache drooped.

"Are you in discomfort?" the doctor asked.

"The pills and whiskey take care of it."

"You shouldn't be mixing them, Vern."

The two men exchanged a glance, acknowledging the futility. The doctor picked up his prescription pad and began writing.

"I'll increase the dosage."

Vern shrugged.

Slowly pulling the page from his pad, the doctor put his hand on Vern's shoulder. "I wish we could do more."

Vern nodded.

"You have your daughter and grandchild back—some time to put things in order."

Folding the paper, tucking it into his shirt pocket, Vern stuck out his chin, nodded his thanks, got his hat and left. He climbed behind the wheel of his pickup, sighed, then drove off.

Time was ticking down.

Feeling his pulse in his throat, he contemplated the doctor's verdict. Vern realized that, as a cop, he'd made his share of notifications, the worst part of the job. Showing up at the door of a mother, father, husband, wife, son, daughter, partner, relative or friend. Telling them their loved one was never coming home. Confronting the shock in their faces, their screams; steadying the ones who collapsed. A piece of him dying each time.

He thought back to the picture of the mountains. *Some things last forever,* he thought, *but people don't.*

Driving through town, he got gas and made a few other stops, nodding to folks who knew him. Soon he was outside town passing through the gate of Oak Rock Cemetery, following the roadway to his wife's grave. He placed fresh daisies and lilies at her stone, touching it tenderly, a storm of emotion and memory thundering through him.

The arguments, his petty jealousies, his regrets, his sins. *And all the rumors: that I got a temper; that Carrie's quick to anger. And worse. The things they said about your death, about what I did. And the things they said Carrie did.*

It all rose up in Vern's chest.

Music played in his mind; he closed his eyes and he was back with Doreen, dancing in their kitchen, the radio playing her song.

A breeze swept by, and Vern could smell her perfume.

Hearing the song, he thought, *I'll be dancin' again with you real soon.*

Patting her stone, he straightened.

I'm sorry for it all. I ain't perfect. But I'll protect her and our grandbaby with my dying breath, against the lies.

And the truth.

Vern cast a look in the direction of Abby's and Erin's graves. Where the truth was buried. Hyde's confession and execution should've put it all to rest. But the file got out. The story in the *Chronicle* gave it more attention. And it wasn't letting up.

Little by little, Carrie was remembering.

55

Working with vigor, Opal Wells moved through her house, vacuum thrumming.

Dex had taken Junie and Jud to his friend's ranch. The kids wanted to see his horses.

Pushing and pulling the wand, Opal chuckled at having the house to herself. This was how she spent her alone time. Oh well. Maybe she'd have tea and get back to her book later. For now, she attacked every room, every corner, in a full-on cleanse.

When she got to dusting their big screen TV, she thought of Carrie. Opal wished she could have joined Lacey and Grace at Carrie's house a while ago, but she'd had to take Junie to the dentist. That was the day the reporter from the *Chron* was live on network news talking about the case.

Opal was concerned for Carrie, especially after the hurtful fallout online. Carrie didn't deserve it. She was a good person, and that's what Opal had told police when the murders first happened. She told them how Carrie had defended Lanna in the cafeteria when Abby and Erin and the other seniors had picked on her.

Carrie was a hero.

That's what Opal had told Denise from the *Chronicle*, too,

when she interviewed her, right here in her living room, for her big story. No way in a million years should the detectives have ever suspected Carrie. The idea that something happened at the Halloween party with Carrie, Abby and Erin, that Carrie had some kind of grudge against them, was just plain dumb.

Besides, Donnie Ray Hyde was the killer.

Progressing through her house, Opal began straightening closets. Setting aside clothes for donation, she thought of the Benjamin Franklin project she and Carrie did. One of her fondest memories. Opal returned to it the way some people relived glorious moments in school sports. The Franklin project was Opal's game-winning touchdown. Her only A-plus that year.

At the time, Opal's mother, the family archivist-hoarder, was so proud, she took charge of it. "I'll keep this treasure in a safe place, sweetheart." Opal had wanted to show it to the detectives when they questioned her in high school, but her mother had misplaced it. As the years went by, it never reappeared. The other day when the reporter was here, Opal wondered if it might be in a closet somewhere, but her search was futile. Maybe it had been stored with her late mother's things, most of which had been donated or tossed.

Or maybe it was just lost.

Opal went to the big closet in her family's spare room, opening the doors to the nightmare that resided there. It was jammed with some of her mother's things, along with long-forgotten toys, games, discarded appliances—*Why're we keeping this blender?*—and broken tools, among other items.

Shaking her head, Opal created a marshaling area to put in piles for keeping, giving away or throwing out. She began sifting through puzzles, books, records and photo albums. The old records could be worth something to collectors. She'd check. Either way, they were going. The puzzles could be donated. There were at least a dozen photo albums filled with images of generations of relatives. She'd keep them. The laminated pages crackled. Opal looked; some photos were from the early 1900s. Her ancestors stared from them like unhappy ghosts she'd disturbed.

Opal noticed one album seemed thicker. A slim book had been slivered inside. It had an old-style font. Recognition dawned at the words on the cover: *Benjamin Franklin.*

This is it!

Warm memories brought her back to Mr. Fuentes, their history teacher, guiding the class on the assignment: pair up with a classmate and profile a figure in American history. The project could be in any format—video, slideshow, dramatic recording, a book, whatever they chose.

Carrie turned to Opal: "Want to work together?"

"Yes!"

They selected Franklin because no one had picked him yet. They decided to do a book and worked hard on it, researching, writing and laying it out with stylized script, photos and sketches they drew. They went to a printshop, run by a friend of Opal's dad, to get it bound.

It was so good.

Opal opened the book, finding Mr. Fuentes's folded note. *Carrie, Opal: This is beautiful. So well done. Admirable work! A+*

Going through it, Opal traced her fingers over all they'd written about Franklin: his biography, his achievements as a statesman, scientist, inventor, publisher. She smiled at the sticky notes she and Carrie had left on it after getting it graded, basking in it, commenting on what they liked: *This was a good sketch you made, Opal*; or what they'd missed: *Oops, a typo!*

She got to their section on Franklin's work with *Poor Richard's Almanack* and their pages of his witty sayings. She really liked them and reread some.

Necessity never made a good bargain.

He that lives on hope will die fasting.

Early to bed and early to rise, makes a man healthy, wealthy and wise.

There were so many.

Recalling how she and Carrie would meet after class to work on their project, which was around the time of the incident in the cafeteria, Opal read more, smiling.

A penny saved is a penny earned.

God helps those that help themselves.

Lost time is never found again.

The smile melted from her face as she paused at one quote. Beside it was a sticky note from Carrie.

It said: *I love this one!*

Opal remembered how the note was placed—how Carrie had fixed it there after the cafeteria incident with Abby and Erin, just before the big Halloween dance and the murders.

Oh, my God. Here it is after all this time.

Opal put her hand over her mouth, and tears came as she read Carrie's favorite quote.

Three may keep a secret, if two of them are dead.

56

The pickup turned left.

Luke was behind it when he activated his lights and siren, pulling it over.

A cactus-gray Ford Maverick.

He already knew the plate was registered to an address in Sellron, north of town. For the last few days, he'd been subtly scoping out the neighborhood from time to time while on patrol, watching for the pickup for a chance to make a casual, routine traffic stop.

And here we go.

He stepped out and approached. The woman behind the wheel dropped her window. A wisp of pleasant-smelling conditioned air spilled from the interior.

She was alone.

"Good afternoon, ma'am."

"Hi. Did I do something wrong, Deputy?"

"You failed to signal."

"Failed to signal?"

"People get distracted. Could you turn off the engine and let me see your driver's license and registration, please?"

"Oh, gosh." She shut off the motor, then grabbed her purse

from the console. Rummaging, she gave him the items. "Am I getting a ticket?"

"Thank you. Please wait here."

Luke was walking a fine line.

Getting into his car, taking up his radio, starting the process of running her license and registration, he assured himself this would be okay. It would be logged as a legitimate traffic stop and check.

The fact was, before the stop, he knew the driver was Brenda Gwen Jones, ex-wife of Raylin Thurman Nash. Luke knew of the alleged abuse and her protective order against Nash.

What Luke didn't know was if Brenda was the woman he'd struck in the storm.

Recently, he'd played several possibilities in his mind. Maybe Nash violated the order, confronted her that night, and she tried to run off? Maybe Nash terrified her into not filing a complaint?

Making this traffic stop was Luke's cryptic way of checking on her. And if his imagined scenarios were true and she wanted to file a report, he'd help her. It could solve his mystery. He could fess up, and maybe, just maybe, mitigate his situation. It's one of the reasons he hadn't repaired his car, to show he had nothing to hide.

He knew this was wishful thinking. Evidence of his offense existed in that blurry video clip, and time was working against him. His radio blurted a response to his query, which was moot. Luke already had all he needed.

Letting out a tense breath, he went back to the pickup, giving Brenda Jones her license and registration. Putting them away, she noticed he was empty-handed, and a question rose.

"I'm not getting a ticket?"

"No, ma'am, just a caution to be careful."

Sighing, she smiled. "I will, thank you." She moved to start her truck.

"Ma'am, if I may?"

She paused. "Yes?"

"In checking you in our system, I noticed you have a protection order in effect."

Her cheeks reddened, her eyes mixing with regret and unease. Luke realized he was pushing it as he studied her again, unable to determine if she was the woman who he had struck that night.

"Yes," she said.

"Is everything okay on that front?"

"Okay?"

"No recent issues, no problems?"

Now she studied him. As if puzzled.

"Yes. My ex is in compliance, as my attorney says."

"Good, then. If anything comes up, you let us know."

"I will. Thank you."

"Have a good rest of your day."

"You, too. Thank you."

After watching her drive away, Luke got back into his patrol car, sitting still for several seconds, going through his jumbled thoughts. The immediate sense he'd gotten was that Brenda Jones was not the woman he'd struck, and was not being harassed by her ex.

Glad that he'd run down this aspect of his private investigation, he was considering his remaining options when his burner phone vibrated.

It was Derek in Los Angeles.

He'd been attempting to use facial recognition on the blurred video clip from the construction site security camera footage.

"Hey, man," Luke said.

"I'll make this quick, and I won't get technical. It wasn't easy, but I have a face for you."

57

Hugging her stuffed bunny, Emily sang to herself as Carrie rolled her stroller gently back and forth.

They were in the shade, waiting at a bench in front of the old dance hall, when Carrie focused on a far-off vehicle. A pickup, like many in Clear River. She first noticed it driving from Cedar Breeze to the hall; it was behind her, its chrome push bar catching the sun.

Now she grew curious, studying it parked at a strip mall down and across the street. White with tinted windows. Nobody got in or out. Maybe it was nothing. *Or maybe it's a reporter*, she was thinking when a green pickup wheeled into the empty dance hall parking lot next to her SUV.

A woman in her fifties with feathered gray hair got out.

"You're Carrie?"

"Yes." She stood and smiled. "Martha Porter, the manager?"

"Uh-huh." Martha did not return her smile. Glasses atop her head, she stroked her purse's shoulder strap while assessing Carrie. No apologies for the time, after telling Carrie to meet her in front of the hall at 9:30 a.m. "sharp." It was closer to ten now.

"Tell me again, what is it you want?"

Clearing her throat, Carrie began explaining until she was talking to Martha's palm.

"Get to the point—why are you here?"

"I'm trying to reconnect with the town and—" she searched for the words "—I thought I could maybe walk through the hall when it was empty, you know?"

"Ahh…reconnect. That's it." Martha nodded. "To be frank, when you called yesterday and said who you were and all, I was going to say no."

Carrie remained silent.

"But I wanted to meet you myself. Around town, you're somewhat famous, or *infamous*. Whatever."

Not knowing how to respond, Carrie nodded.

Martha's coolness warmed as she bent down to get a closer look at Emily.

"And this is your angel? What's her name?"

"Emily."

"Hi, darlin'." Then to Carrie: "I got work to do in the office, so you might as well come in. *And reconnect.*"

"Thank you."

Martha's keys jingled. As they moved to the door, Carrie turned the stroller, noticing the distant pickup pulling away from the strip mall parking lot.

Likely nothing, she thought.

Martha led her into the dance hall, the air carrying whiffs of cleaner, stale beer and swirling dust specks. The wooden floor creaked, echoing in the emptiness.

Surveying the area, Martha said, "I've managed this place for thirty years. We've had folks like Dolly Parton and Willie Nelson do shows here.

"We do receptions, ceremonies, and there's the big high school party each Halloween," Martha continued. "I remember the one you were at. Sort of stood out for folks because it wasn't long after that the murders happened."

Martha turned to her. "But you know that, don't you?" She stared at Carrie for an icy moment. "Abby Hall was my niece."

"She was? I'm sorry. I wasn't aware."

"We're a big family. I read the story in the *Chronicle*, the one that got all the attention. It underlined the obvious: how you were the only one of the girls to come out of those woods alive."

As she continued, Carrie grew uneasy, sensing that Martha had her own agenda for agreeing to this.

"Some of us felt that you led Abby and Erin into those woods. No one knows why. Sure, Hyde confessed. He's gone. What's done is done. Still, some of us can't shake thinking that you set something in motion the day Abby and Erin died. That you were partly responsible for the chain of events. And you being the sheriff's daughter, and unable to remember, well, it seems questionable. *Even now.*"

Carrie finally found her voice. "Martha, Hyde tried to kill me, too."

"Oh, you remember that, do you?"

"Are you blaming me? I've been tortured by this. Every day of my life. Do you want me to apologize for not being murdered?"

Martha shrugged.

"All we know is that something happened in those woods that day. And you're the only living person who knows." Martha shook her head. "Then, after all these years, you move back with your husband, a deputy. You got your baby here. Even old Vern is hanging on."

"We came back for the time my father has left."

"Point is, you got family, you got a life. Abby and Erin don't have husbands or babies. They can't *reconnect* from Oak Rock Cemetery. But you go right ahead, you *reconnect*. As Abby's aunt, I wanted to say my piece."

Swallowing hard, Carrie pushed back tears.

"I'll be working in my office." Martha swept the air with her hand. "Be my guest, stroll down memory lane."

Martha's steps echoed like a hammer on nails, driving guilt into Carrie's heart. She wanted to leave. Coming here was a mistake. Confused and helpless, she grasped at yesterday's video call with Dr. Bernay, who'd encouraged her to return to the dance hall.

"I know remembering the tragedy continues to be difficult, Carrie," Dr. Bernay had said, "but you've made great strides, sorting through the rumors and speculation, getting to genuine memories. More will come when your mind is ready to release what you've blocked. It's been happening, with the actions you've taken, and events you've experienced since your return. Little by little, your mind is freeing up puzzle pieces of the past."

Suddenly, again, the crime scene photos burned in Carrie's mind. Abby on the ground, her clothes tangled and blood-soaked, her eyes half-open. Erin and the blood-drenched soil, her wild hair, her vacant eyes staring out.

Why were we there? Why did I survive?

Carrie clenched her eyes tight.

Recalling the horrifying images was painful. She felt like a psychological detective, pursuing her own dark mystery. Dr. Bernay was right. By going to the school cafeteria, by talking with Denise Diaz, studying the police files, returning to the woods, she was inching closer to the frightening truth.

I can't run away now. I've got to keep going.

She needed to keep traveling back, revisit the past, untangle the memories and work through the trauma.

Hands shaking, she adjusted them on Emily's stroller while walking slowly along the edge of the hall, her thoughts reaching deep into the shadows, memories flickering in the darkness...

...the Halloween party...first weekend after the cafeteria... She doesn't have a shift at Whataburger, and she's a wicked witch wearing

*green face paint, a long, pointed nose, a black-and-green corset dress…
a cape and hag-hair wig… The music is blasting…a request for a classic, "Sympathy for the Devil," the song throbbing…lights flashing,
strobing, on zombies, vampires, werewolves. Everybody's dressed up…
masked…can't tell who's who…except Abby and Erin…dressed as—
what else?—cheerleaders…matching glitter blouses, vests, shorts, white
cowboy boots…game-day makeup… How pretty they are…talking
with ghouls and monsters…music hammering… Carrie dances with a
werewolf…then a mummy…a demon. She's sweating…it's so hot…
needing fresh air…going out…into the night…into the parking lot…
low laughter rising in a cloud…the pungent smell of marijuana from a
huddle of movie killers. She goes far from them…to a secluded corner
before…a whispered call from the darkness…*

"Carrie! Over here! Carrie!"

*Glitter twinkles from between two parked pickups…the cheerlead-
ers are alone…waving to her in near panic… Abby and Erin…urging
her to them…*

"Carrie! Hurry don't let anyone see you!"

*Not mean-girl voices…but still, her guard goes up. She nears…
What do they want? Is this fallout from the cafeteria?*

*"Carrie, we were looking for you…" Their eyes glistening under the
makeup…they're afraid…or acting like it… Abby checks for privacy…
Erin cups her hands to her face…removing them… "We've heard something so terrible!" Behind the makeup, something's got Abby and Erin
scared…*

"You must swear to God you won't tell anyone!"

Keeping her guard up…she's wary… "What's going on."

*"Carrie…oh, my God…" Erin's got alcohol on her breath…upset,
fanning herself… "It's so scary it might not be true. We have to show
you."*

"Show me what? What're you talking about?"

Another waft of alcohol…they're terrified.

"Meet us at the woods…"

"The woods? Now?"

"*Tomorrow at three…you can't tell anyone…keep it secret until we know…don't use your phone…absolute secrecy…swear…*"

Shaking her head… "*No, no, you're getting back at me…setting me up…*"

"*Oh, God no! Nothing like that!*"

Are they drinking vodka?

Abby seizes Carrie's wrists. "*Carrie! You have to be there!*"

Yanking her wrists free…the moment surreal—the wicked witch and two cheerleaders.

"*Carrie, it's deadly serious! You have to meet us at the woods tomorrow!*"

"*Why?*"

"*It's about your dad.*"

58

Things are seldom what they look like.

The words kept bubbling up in Denise as she walked Harvey in the park, his long leash clinking and tail wagging. He loved being out.

So did Denise.

She'd had a busy day at the paper. She'd worked on a story about a new dental practice. Then a story on a construction company donating playground equipment. And then she'd rushed to the Loop to report on a crash between an 18-wheeler and a van. No one was hurt, but traffic got backed up for an hour.

And between her stories, Denise assessed her recent death row interview with Darnell George Sharp. It had been several days. Still unsure what to make of it, she hadn't yet written anything new on the murders.

Today, whenever she found a free moment, she checked the comments and social media posts coming in on her investigative feature. It continued to be a mixed bag, some saying Donnie Ray Hyde was evil and got what he deserved; others saying he didn't kill Abby and Erin—Carrie did it, and the sheriff's office covered it up. Still others pinwheeled into conspiratorial nonsense, about links to the White House and aliens. And the usual characters chimed in, like FactorRex31, who kept insisting: Chron is dead wrong.

Sitting on a park bench in an off-leash area, Denise unhooked Harvey, then tried in vain to decompress. But, like any good reporter, she was never off the clock on stories that mattered. Taking in the evening breeze, she considered the chronology of the murders.

Vern Hamilton visits Hyde on death row, leading to his confession. Hyde's fellow inmate says Hyde is almost happy after confessing to killing Abby and Erin, giving away belongings and saying he was going to ease his mother's suffering after he was gone. Hyde's mother says that after her son's confession and execution, some of her financial difficulties got straightened out.

The old maxim from the detective rose again.

Things are seldom what they look like.

Watching Harvey gnawing on a stick, Denise's dissatisfaction ate at her.

Something's not right about this, she thought. Yielding to impulse, she took up her phone, scrolled through her contacts and clicked on a number. Harvey trotted toward her, stick in his jaws, just as her call was answered.

"Hello?" a woman said.

"Mary-Ellen?"

"Yes."

"It's Denise Diaz, from the *Chronicle.*"

"Oh, yes, hello."

"I'm sorry if I got you at a bad time, but I want to ask you a few things, if that's okay?"

"All right."

"Well." Denise paused when Harvey placed the stick on her lap, wanting to play. She tossed it, and Harvey left to fetch it. "I recall you telling me how after Donnie Ray's execution some of your financial matters were cleared. Like a godsend, I believe you said."

"That's right, an answered prayer."

"Mary-Ellen, can you elaborate a little? Like, what were those matters, and how did they come to be resolved?"

Like a sad wind over a field of faded dreams, a long mournful sigh sounded at the other end of the line.

"As I said, my husband, Jack, gambled, drank, had run-ins with the law. When he died, he left me with debts, mostly back taxes, liens on the house. A world of trouble on top of what I had going with my boys. Then, after Donnie Ray was killed in Huntsville, I got a letter saying the county discovered it had made some kind of error years ago and my property tax issue was forgiven."

"Who was the letter from?"

"I'll get it."

Denise heard Mary-Ellen moving through her home, rustling papers. "Here it is. Cecil Pratt, County Commissioner. It says something about a miscalculation, property improperly assessed, a retroactive application of something called a homestead exemption, going back a few years, all amounting to forgiveness of the amount owing and a reimbursement coming. About fourteen hundred dollars."

"Do you know Cecil Pratt?"

"Goodness, never met the man."

"Was there any indication this good news was coming before Donnie Ray's execution?"

"None. In fact, I thought the county was fixin' to seize my house and put me on the street."

"Mary-Ellen, can you take a picture of the letter and send it to me right away? I think it's interesting."

"Sure."

"Thank you. Again, I'm so sorry to trouble you."

"No trouble. You've been kind and respectful, Denise."

As she ended the call, Harvey barked, and Denise tossed his stick again. He fetched it and she threw it a few more times, until her phone pinged with the photo of the letter from Mary-Ellen.

Denise read the one-page letter, eyeing the official's name: *Cecil Pratt, County Commissioner.*

She searched online and found his bio: Cecil Floyd Pratt, county commissioner, married to Eunice for thirty years, two sons, one daughter. Served in the US military, then in the reserve, then became a deputy sheriff, then elected sheriff. He was then elected commissioner and reelected twice more. Belonged to gun clubs, volunteered with the Boys and Girls Club, the Make-A-Wish Foundation, was a member of local Kiwanis and Rotary.

Denise tapped her finger on the screen.

Here was Cecil's photo from the time he was sheriff. He stood next to a US flag, white Stetson firmly in place, dark suit, white shirt, dark tie.

That made Denise think of something.

She searched the names Cecil Pratt and Vernon Hamilton together. Various references emerged showing them as senior members of state and regional sheriff and police associations. Then Denise searched for photos.

Several popped up of Cecil and Vern together, including one from a few years back showing Cecil with his arm around Vern's shoulders. Both grinning from a podium. The caption read: *Long-time compadres Cecil and Vern together at the conference in El Paso.*

So Vern and Cecil were old friends.

Compadres.

59

There she is.

Captured in fleeting seconds of blurred security video, staring in horror. Frozen in the single frame, her face filled the monitor of Luke's laptop.

Using every tool at his disposal, Derek had skillfully extracted from a blizzard of dots, a sharper, colored enlargement. The woman appeared to be white, in her midtwenties, with high cheekbones and almond-shaped eyes. Her dark hair was partially matted from the rain, and strands snaked off wildly as she rose from the ditch.

"Luke?" Derek's face asked from the small upper-right corner window of Luke's monitor. "Did you get it?"

"I'm looking at it. I— Wow. This is incredible."

"It's the strongest image I could pull from the footage. I did some enhancing and adjusting. I sent you a secondary image I worked on as well."

Luke clicked on an enhanced full-body photo of the woman in the rain. Head to toe. Pink shirt, jeans.

Here she is.

The woman I hit. The woman who may or may not be alive.

Seeing her made it real, overwhelming him, quickening his pulse.

"Luke?"

He was at a loss.

"Luke, buddy, are you okay? Are we okay doing this? Is this part of an investigation?"

"Sorry, yes. It's okay. It's something I'm looking into quietly—it might be connected to a crime, but I'm not sure yet. I really can't thank you enough for this, Derek." The truth of that night trembling over him, he asked: "So what's next? Who is she?"

Derek half laughed to himself. "So far, we have a face but no name. But I'm confident our photo is strong enough to query databases to help determine who she is."

"Can you do that and still keep it on the q.t.?"

"It'll be a challenge."

Derek explained how facial recognition worked: a subject's features were compared against millions of others in a range of databases. Computers then provided a list of candidates for a potential match. But a human examiner analyzed them to determine if there was a match.

"Sounds time-consuming," Luke said.

"It can be," Derek said. "And since this is not a formal investigation and we're doing it under the radar, it becomes dicey."

"Right," Luke sighed.

"I have contacts across the country."

"But I don't want to get others involved until we know exactly what we have."

"Don't worry. I got friends who owe me. I'll take care of getting it queried through national databases, DMVs, missing persons, military, deceased identification, criminal histories, parole, corrections, everything. All on the down-low."

"What can I do?"

"You can be the amateur examiner, manually checking our images safely against the local databases and open-source sites you have easy access to—wanted, missing person databases, whatever."

"I can do that."

"I'll get things moving on my end. Buddy, I gotta go."

"I appreciate this."

"No worries."

Derek's face vanished, leaving Luke alone with the image of the mystery woman.

Staring at her pulled him back to that night. Blood pulsed in his brain, elevating the reality of the instant he'd struck her. The sickening thud, her face streaking over his windshield.

He swallowed hard. She definitely wasn't Brenda Gwen Jones, Raylin Nash's ex. So he could rule her out.

Whoever she was, Luke begged heaven to let her be alive.

Searching her face for answers, he felt time running out on him. Yes, he'd been monumentally stupid about the way he was handling this. Stupid about everything. Ensnared by panic, paranoia, post-traumatic stress, fear and guilt, he'd taken too many risks and let it go on for too long. Sooner or later, someone was going to find out.

His palms were sweating, just like they were when he killed the young mother in LA.

He fought to think. There was another aspect here. Records from the cell tower warrants showing cell phone numbers should be coming in soon. He opened the full-body photo of the woman in the rain. Then, from the kitchen table, through the window, he glimpsed Carrie's SUV arriving.

Closing his laptop, he went to the front door. She'd gotten groceries. He hurried out to help while she got Emily from her car seat.

"Hi," he said.

"Hi. You take her; I'll get the groceries."

She passed the baby to him. Luke kissed his daughter, then

joined Carrie. "Let me take some," he said, one-handing bags while holding Emily.

After they got everything into the kitchen together, Luke set Emily down to play with toys. He glanced at Carrie. Rooted where she stood, the full grocery bags before her on the counter, she stared in silence at nothing.

"Carrie?"

She didn't move.

"You okay?"

Without speaking, she waved off his concern.

"Carrie, what is it? Tell me."

She took in a shaky breath.

"I went to the dance hall today and…and…"

"What happened?"

"Memories came back." She buried her face in her hands. "Awful memories about Abby and Erin."

"What memories?"

"I can't—I can't."

Luke looked at her for a long moment.

"Carrie, I know I've been distracted." His voice was soft. "Like I've checked out, and I haven't been supportive when you need me."

She stared at him in silent confirmation, inviting him to continue.

"And these new patches of remembering that have come to you, especially after the execution and all the media attention—I know things have been hard for you, and we haven't talked, and I'm sorry. *For everything.* You know you can talk to me."

Carrie nodded, and soon her shoulders shook as she cried. Luke held her as Emily stared up from the floor at her mom and dad.

At that moment, Carrie's phone vibrated on the counter, the screen blooming with a text from Opal Wells.

Hi Carrie: It's Opal. Sorry I missed coming over before. Want to meet for coffee soon? I came across something you should see.

60

Housed in the main floor of a historic stone building, Mom's Cookin' Diner was known for hand-breaded chicken-fried steak, homemade lemonade and apple pie.

Not much had changed inside in the years Carrie had been away.

It still had the white-and-black-checked floor, red-vinyl swivel stools at the counter, and roomy booths. The air smelled of cooked bacon and coffee. The walls were covered in framed yellowing news pages about historic events, including a "yes, it's real" wanted poster of Bonnie and Clyde.

The lunch rush long over, the place was quiet, except for a Patsy Cline song drifting from the kitchen amid running water and the clatter of dishes. A man with keys dangling from his belt sat alone at the counter working on his cheeseburger while scrolling his phone. An older couple was having pie in a booth near the window.

Opal Wells had only just sat down in a booth in a far corner when Carrie arrived. She stood, greeting her with a hug.

"Thanks for coming. I'm sorry I missed visiting you with Lacey and Grace."

"That's okay," Carrie said as they sat. "How're you, Dex and the kids?"

"Doing fine. Junie just lost her first tooth."

"Oh, my."

"And you? Emily and Luke?"

"We're good."

Touching Carrie's hand, Opal's expression turned serious. "How's your dad doing?"

"He says he's not feeling any discomfort."

"Well, that's a blessing. All things considered."

A server emerged, hair piled high, butterfly tattoo on her neck. "What can I get you ladies?"

"Just coffee, thanks," Carrie said.

"Same for me."

"Okey doke."

The server left, and Carrie leaned closer, lowering her voice, struggling not to betray her unease at her friend's request.

"Opal, why were you so anxious to meet? What do you have that I should see?"

Opal looked at her, taking a moment, as if deciding how to answer. No one was near them, but she spoke softly.

"Okay, I know that when it happened, with you, Abby and Erin in the woods, you couldn't remember much."

Carrie nodded, tensing a little.

"And since you moved back, you've been trying to recall things—I know that from reading the *Chron*."

The server returned, setting their coffees down with creamers and sweeteners on the side. "Anything else?"

"That's it for now, thanks," Opal said, waiting for her to leave before resuming. "I debated whether to come to you with this. I wrestled with it before deciding."

"What is it?"

Opal reached into her bag and took out the slender Franklin book, placing it on the table.

"Our project," Carrie said with a measure of relief. So that was it. Unfolding the note, she smiled at Mr. Fuentes's comments and their grade.

"That was my first A-plus. You got a lot of them, but it was a big deal for me, so you let me keep it at my house."

Carrie began turning the pages.

"My mom put it away. It got lost. No one really ever saw it again, until the other day. I found it tucked in her things while I was cleaning."

"We did a good job." Carrie admired the pages. "It looks great." She shook her head. "Look at our notes we made after. We were picky."

"Go to the section on *Poor Richard's Almanack*—remember the quotes?"

Scanning the list of Franklin's brief insights and thoughts, Carrie now knew that Franklin had gleaned many from earlier writers and philosophers. Taking her time, she began reading through them.

"Look at this one." Opal tapped a nail to the quote with a yellow sticky note beside it, made loose by aging. "Your favorite."

Carrie read: "'Three may keep a secret, if two of them are dead.'"

Carrie blinked at it; the way someone might blink before realizing the speck on the horizon is actually a freight train bearing down on them.

"Carrie—" Opal's tone was hushed "—I don't know what to do about this because of the timing. I mean, you wrote this note just before—"

Carrie read the note, neatly printed in blue ink with an arrow pointing to Franklin's words: *I love this one!*

Opal leaned a bit closer. "What did you mean, that you loved this quote?"

Carrie gave her head a shake. "I don't remember."

"Carrie." Opal's voice was now a whisper. "Three of you

went into Wild Pines, and two are dead. You wrote that you loved this quote at that time. Why?"

The blood drained from Carrie's face. Swallowing, she waved her hand.

"I don't know. It was a stupid coincidence, I guess. I don't remember. I'm not even sure I wrote that note."

Their eyes met over the book.

"It's *your* note, Carrie."

Opal turned the book, flipped to other yellow sticky notes, some curling from time. "Mine are in black cursive; yours are lighter, blue printing."

"What's your point with this?"

"This quote, your favorite, was the one I was trying to remember," Opal said. "When I found it, it started bothering me. Like something in all of this was left out."

"I don't understand."

"I mean, at the time, I told police I was one hundred percent certain you would never hurt Abby and Erin. I told the reporter from the *Chron* the same thing when she came to my house."

Opal paused.

The freight train was getting closer.

"Of course, I couldn't tell police back then about this quote you loved, because I couldn't find the book. I never told the reporter either."

"What are you getting at, Opal?"

"I was with you in the cafeteria. Most all of us were at the Halloween dance, then the murders. Then I find the quote you liked around that time. You know, it's the timing." Opal's eyes were glistening.

"What're you planning to do?"

"I don't know."

"Who have you told about this?"

"No one but you."

"Opal, listen to me. Hyde confessed to killing Abby and

Erin, and trying to kill me, too. He's dead. It's over. Why're you trying to make some connection to me and a silly note I wrote in high school?"

Opal shook her head, eyes narrowing, her voice dropping to a tremulous whisper.

"Abby and Erin had a vileness about them. Maybe deep down, some people were thinking, in their secret heart of hearts, that maybe..." Opal's voice got smaller "...maybe they got what they deserved."

Carrie's jaw dropped. She scanned around them for assurance that no one had heard, keeping her voice soft.

"Oh, God. No, Opal! Don't say that. That's not true."

"You know it is."

"Opal, listen, please," Carrie said. "I think you're overthinking this, making too much of it. There is no point to this. It's over. Maybe you should let me keep the book."

"No. I'll keep it." Opal slid it to her side of the table, shoved it into her bag, then stood to leave. "I'm so sorry about all of this. I'm very troubled."

"Opal, please."

"You're my friend, Carrie, and I felt you needed to know about this, to help you remember, maybe."

"Yes, but it's a coincidence, a sad, stupid coincidence."

"Maybe. But, Carrie, I don't know what I'm going to do."

"Just let it go."

"Carrie, it's hard for me to keep things inside, *especially the truth*."

"Opal, please, you can't know the truth because—"

Watching Opal walk out of the diner, Carrie suddenly felt the impact of the train, the earth shaking, the booth seat under her dropping, then her stomach morphing into a cinder block pulling her insides down into a bottomless chasm.

61

A damp towel draped over his shoulder, the bartender put a sweaty glass of Dr Pepper, crowned with shaved ice, on Denise Diaz's table.

"Thanks, Roy."

Before leaving, he threw a glance over his shoulder, then winked in subtle acknowledgment.

Afternoon was fading into early evening at The Old Stirrup bar. Denise had left the paper for the day but hadn't stopped working. Following Roy's glance, she cast a quick eye to a table far across the bar.

She shifted her focus back to her notebook, her phone and the call she'd made earlier to Cecil Pratt. His deep voice still played in her mind. She didn't have time to drive to Kilgore for a face-to-face interview. So, a few hours ago, she cold-called Cecil from the newsroom. When she got him, she adhered to her bird-in-the-hand rule, learned from experience. When you reach a subject on a sensitive story, go for broke because it could be your only shot.

"Commissioner Pratt?"

"That's me."

"Hi. Denise Diaz. I'm a reporter with the *Clear River Chronicle*."

"Well, hello, Denise Diaz of the *Chronicle*, calling from Clear River." Cecil exuded political charm over the line. "What can I do for you today?"

"Could I have a moment of your time to ask you a few questions?"

"This an interview?" He chuckled.

"Yes, sir, an on-the-record interview."

A beat.

"A short one, then," he said. "What does this concern?"

"A letter you wrote."

"I send off a lot of them, part of my job. Do you have specifics?"

"It was recently sent to Mary-Ellen Hyde."

Denise paused to let him digest the name.

"Yes?"

"It deals with an improper assessment of her property taxes and a retroactive application of a homestead exemption." Denise provided the date.

"Okay. We send those out from time to time." Rustling seeped into his end of the call. "Ms. Diaz, it's getting late, I don't have the letter in front of me, forgive me, but I'll—"

"Mr. Pratt, this won't take long. Surely you have the means of retrieving your copy. I could send you mine?"

Cecil didn't speak, so she continued.

"Sir, I'd like to provide you the chance to comment for a story I may be writing, concerning this letter with your signature."

"A story about the letter?"

"Yes, sir."

In the seconds that followed, the temperature of his voice dropped.

"I see."

He sighed the sigh of a pissed-off man.

While waiting, she could hear movement then muffled voices

IF TWO ARE DEAD   283

as he grunted for someone's help. Seconds later, he came back on, his tone cool.

"I have my copy. Seems a straight-up correction of property assessment and homestead. I don't have much time. What is your question?"

"The letter you signed was sent to Mary-Ellen Hyde, shortly after her son Donnie Ray Hyde was executed in Huntsville."

Pratt was silent.

"Sir, as a former county sheriff, do you know Vernon Hamilton, a former sheriff for Clear River?"

After hesitating, he said: "Absolutely. We know each other from our former careers and work for various organizations."

"Would you consider him a friend?"

Pratt hesitated again.

"I really don't understand what you're suggesting—"

"Sir, are you aware that Donnie Ray Hyde confessed to two additional murders after Vern Hamilton visited him on death row? And not long after that, Hyde's mother received your letter alleviating her financial situation."

In the seconds ticking by, she heard his breathing.

"Look, I confirmed I sent a routine letter on an adjustment of property taxes. As for your, whatever it is you're suggesting, I have nothing to say."

In the silence after the call, Denise had sat motionless at her desk in the newsroom, gauging her thoughts. Instinct told her she needed to keep digging, but most critical: she needed Vern Hamilton's reaction.

After leaving the paper, she'd driven to Vern's house. His pickup was gone. He didn't answer the door, and she didn't have his number. Denise called Irene Weaver, an assistant at the sheriff's office, who was often a good source. She'd have the retired sheriff's contact info. Maybe Irene could relay a message to him, if she hadn't left for the day.

"Hey," Irene said. "I was just stepping out the door."

"I'm trying to reach Vernon Hamilton. Have you got a number for him?"

"I do." Irene looked it up and recited it, adding, "I understand Vern's not big on answering his phone. But I overheard Bob say they were meeting at the Stirrup. That was about twenty minutes ago. You might try there."

Now, alone at her table, sipping Dr Pepper, Denise listened to the music in the bar, Don Gibson lamenting lost love and loneliness, which fit her mood.

Time went by and other songs played.

All the while, she kept a vigil on Bob Ellerd and Vern, who were sitting at a far table. Not wanting to address them together, her strategy was to get Vern alone. After a little over an hour, they'd finished their burgers and beers, paid the check, and were getting ready to leave.

Denise settled up and headed for the parking lot, waiting near Vern's Ford.

As he made his way to his truck, she saw a flick of recognition as his eyes found hers. They knew each other from the press conference after Hyde's execution, and because of her stories on the case.

"Hello, Denise."

She stood straight, tapping her phone and notebook to her thigh, ready for battle. This was her shot.

"Hi, Vernon. Do you have a moment to talk?"

"Must be important for you to wait in the bar like you did."

She half smiled. "Yes."

Vern raised his head sightly, the brim of his hat barely above his eyes, gleaming like polished bullet tips.

"What is it?"

"It's important and has to be on the record, Vernon."

"For what, Denise?"

She didn't know if Cecil had tipped him to her call about the letter.

"Donnie Ray Hyde, you, his mother and other matters."

The edges of his thick silver mustache drooped as he studied her, his expression unreadable.

"Go ahead."

"On the record?"

"Get to the point."

"First, you go see Hyde on death row, resulting in his last-minute confession for Wild Pines. Not long after that, his mother is surprised with unexpected relief on back taxes, with a letter signed by Cecil Pratt, a former sheriff who knows you."

"You insinuating a connection?"

"Before approaching you, I called and spoke with Cecil Pratt."

She let that hang in the air before adding, "He confirmed sending the letter. I have a copy of it on my phone, if you'd like to see it?"

"No. Just what're you gettin' at?"

"Appearances."

"Appearances?"

"How this all looks, with events that appear to happen as if by accident, but by pure chance have a connection. I mean—" Denise softened her voice "—for years, your daughter was the *suspect*."

Vern stared at Denise for a long, silent moment, then turned his gaze to the horizon, like a man looking back on his life. Shaking his head slowly, he climbed into his truck and drove away.

62

Patrolling his zone in North Division, Luke's radio crackled as dispatch cleared him for his lunch break.

He drove another five minutes along the highway, slowing at an aging building of weatherworn clapboard. The faded sign hanging from the awning identified it as The Bend in the Road. About a dozen trucks and service vans stood in the dirt lot, affirming its status as one of the best roadside diners in East Texas.

It was tucked in a heavily wooded rural corner amid a sprinkling of businesses, like Zeb Hock's Filling Station and Sondra's Handcrafted Saddles.

Luke went inside.

Deciding on takeout, he got in line and ordered a cheeseburger platter to go. Then he checked his phone and inserted his earpiece for his radio.

All quiet.

While waiting, his thoughts went to Carrie and his nagging guilt for failing to support her. Everything was taking a toll on her. And her recent coffee with her friend Opal had left her unsettled. But Carrie wouldn't, or *couldn't*, open up to him about it. Thank God she was still having remote sessions with her psychologist, because she was holding something inside. Maybe about the murders, or her dad, or something un-covered in the aftermath of the story.

He didn't know what it was. She wouldn't tell him.

"Twenty-one! Cheeseburger platter!" the man in the white apron called out. "Here you go, Deputy. Enjoy."

Collecting his bag and soda, Luke returned to his patrol car for his personal laptop. He headed to the picnic tables, find-ing an isolated one in the shade at the edge of a dense woods, affording privacy.

Setting up, satisfied the connection was strong here, he cued up the enhanced image of the woman he'd struck and got to work as he ate.

Following Derek's advice, he resumed his investigation as an amateur analyst, without the benefit of facial recognition tech-nology. Manually, he checked her face against those in the on-line archives he had access to. Last night, after Carrie went to sleep, he'd stayed up working first on local databases of missing and wanted persons. He also checked the sex-offender registry.

Face after face smiled, stared or, at times, glowered back at him. But they were the wrong sex, race, age. They weren't even close. His search had yielded nothing. That morning, he'd gotten up early and started again, branching out, check-ing the public records for Clear River police. Again, his results were negative.

Now at the picnic table, he was extending his search beyond Clear River and the county to every open-source site, starting with the neighboring county to the west, intending to work his way around the compass points. As he ate, he scanned as fast as he could.

Faces flowed, and as he eliminated them one by one, he came to realize the enormity of what he was attempting. Texas saw close to fifty thousand missing person reports filed every year. And Luke was working under the assumption his mystery woman was missing, or possibly wanted.

What if she doesn't fall into one of those categories?

And he was searching without the aid of technology. It was a needle-in-a-haystack challenge. He had no choice about whether he would see this through. When he started, he'd had nothing but a blurred memory. But with the security video and Derek's help, he now had a face. He was counting on Derek's expertise, his sources, their access to a vast number of data banks to help him solve this mystery.

For now, the best he could do was keep searching.

And there was the cell tower warrant.

I have to believe I'm getting closer.

Closing his laptop, he collected his wrappers and soda can into the bag, dropped it in the trash, then headed for his patrol car.

Walking across the lot, Luke was unaware that for the entire time he sat alone at the picnic table, he'd been watched through high-powered binoculars. They were held by a person in a vehicle that had pulled off the earthen back road bordering the dense forest strip.

Aimed strategically and focused, the long-range binoculars allowed them to observe Luke and his surroundings clearly.

Even the screen of his laptop.

63

Joan Thompson cast a curious eye at Carrie while inviting her into her office at Clear River High School.

"Have a seat," Joan said. "Sofia suggested we meet."

"Yes, I took English lit with her here. Thank you."

Joan nodded. "I understand it was before my time at the school, and around the time when—" Joan stopped. "Well, it was a long time ago." She smiled. "Sofia said you're considering our pre-K program for your daughter, Emily?"

"Yes." Carrie nodded to Emily in the stroller. "I wanted to get a start, learning about it."

Joan slid on her oversize red-framed glasses and flashed a smile at Emily.

"Hi, honey." Joan bent down. "Such a sweetheart. Of course, she's too young for admission now, but many parents inquire early. Let me outline a few things for you."

"Yes, thank you."

Joan sat at her desk. "Our pre-K is at Clear River Elementary, next door. But it's administered from here, for now."

For the next few minutes, she went into the virtues of the program: the full-day schedule; teacher-to-student ratio; employing early-childhood specialists. Carrie was only partly listening. Her pulse had picked up—she corralled her thoughts because things were moving faster for her. She'd finished work at home early, thankful her boss in California, who'd seen much of the recent national news coverage on the murders, was allowing her time when she needed it.

Like today.

Carrie was grateful to Sofia. Unable to see Carrie at the school, Sofia had quickly arranged for her to meet with Joan. *Just the person for you*, she'd said. But the truth was, going through the security procedure for a meeting about Clear River's preschool program was a cover.

Carrie had another motive for revisiting Clear River High School.

"…all to say…the goal of our program is to serve students and parents as best we can."

Joan clasped her hands on her desk, signaling she had finished.

"Thank you so much for this," Carrie said, standing to leave.

"Certainly. We can always look into possible advance placement for Emily when she's older. Get in touch if you have any questions."

Joan moved to open her door. "I'll take you back to the front office, to sign out."

"Can I make a small request?"

"Of course."

"Would it be all right if I left alone?"

"Oh. Well, I'm supposed to escort visitors to the office. Is there a problem?"

"On my way out, I wanted to stop at the common area."

"The common area?"

"Yes, to see the memorial display."

"I could go with you."

"I, well, I'd like to see it alone, if I could."

Blinking behind her big glasses, Joan took a moment, raising her chin as realization dawned.

"Yes, I understand. That should be fine. Be sure to sign out at the office and return your visitor badge."

Classes were still in session. The locker-lined halls were empty. But before Carrie got far, her phone vibrated with a message that lifted her eyebrows. It was Pearl.

Hi honey. Having fun in Melbourne. Got a newshound passenger friend who says something's happening with the case in Clear River. What's going on? Is everything OK?

Hit with a wave of guilt, a lump rising in her throat, Carrie answered.

We're OK. There has been a development. Hyde confessed. It's over. We can move on. Let's talk when you get back.

Carrie hated not being forthright with Pearl, but she set her regret aside. As she pushed Emily's stroller down the smooth, glossy floor to the common area, her breathing quickened. Dr. Bernay had been right—visiting locations linked to the murders had proven conducive to unlocking memories: the cafeteria, the woods, the dance hall. Little by little, Carrie was recovering puzzle pieces.

And one of the worst—Opal's allegation—bored into her heart.

She stopped at the glass case of the memorial display. This was her second time seeing it, but her first chance to study it, another key to the past. There were Abby and Erin, with their pretty clothes, smiling their bright-eyed smiles, forever beautiful in their photos. Between them, a plaque gleamed, turning it into more of a shrine, Carrie thought as she read the tribute about promising lives "cut too short," "to remain forever in our hearts."

Not a word about Carrie.

Is it because I got to live?

Are the answers here, with Abby and Erin?

Now, standing at the display, staring hard into their faces, their eyes like falling stars, Carrie's mind swirled into a whirlwind pulling her back…

…to the dance hall parking lot…the party music thudding… Abby and Erin glittering in the darkness… "Meet us at the woods…tomorrow at three…you can't tell anyone…it's about your dad…"

Carrie gives no answer…shaken, suspicious. Why meet in the woods? Returning to the party…music hammering…devils and demons dancing…she stays until it's time to leave. Her dad will be waiting in his truck. She threads through the departing clusters of monsters… a flash of glitter…

Abby, resolute, mouths, Three tomorrow, *moving away… Erin, resolved, makes certain Carrie sees three fingers… What do they know about her father? Carrie nods to Erin…she'll go, but she doesn't trust them…*

She finds her dad's truck, climbs in… He turns to her, the wicked witch sitting next to him…studying her…as if detecting unease… "Did you have a nice time?"

And suddenly she thinks of his arguments with her mother…doors slamming…him leaving…in Principal Taylor's office holding his hat, the earth shaking… The casket descending into the cold, cold ground… Now, sitting next to him…yes, definitely, she decides, she will meet Abby and Erin in the woods…she'll keep it secret…

"Carrie? Did you have a good time?"

The wicked witch turns to him. "I had a great time, Dad."

64

I discovered something disturbing about the murders in the woods that you should know.

Denise read the email again on her phone.

When she'd first glazed over it earlier, she was between stories. Distracted, she was ready to reject it as just another one of the nonsensical comments in response to her feature on the murders of Abby and Erin. But Denise stopped short of dismissing the email when she saw it was signed by Opal Wells, a school friend of Carrie's she'd interviewed.

And Opal wanted to meet.

Intriguing.

Denise recalled Opal as a bit peculiar, even a titch flaky, but it would only take a few minutes to find out what she'd "discovered." Denise agreed to meet at the IHOP across the street from the *Chronicle.*

Now, putting her phone in her purse, Denise stepped inside, surveyed the dining room, found Opal alone in a booth and joined her. The server offered menus, which they both declined, then brought over a couple coffees.

"Thank you for seeing me," Opal said.

"Sure. But I only have a couple minutes, so maybe we should get to it. What have you discovered?"

"Something's come up. I feel I've misled people."

"I don't understand."

"I have to clarify something about the murders."

Denise studied Opal's face while splashing cream into her coffee.

Opal retrieved something from her purse, a book, and before opening it, explained the Franklin project and the comments she and Carrie had written on sticky notes. She turned the book to Denise, pointing: "'Three may keep a secret, if two of them are dead.'"

Denise raised an eyebrow.

"See Carrie's note, about loving this one?" Opal said.

Denise shrugged. "Okay. Well, Franklin did say those things, Opal, and your project was about Franklin."

"It's the timing, Denise. When she wrote that, it was right after the incident with Abby and Erin in the cafeteria, leading up to the dance and the murders. Don't you see? No one knows why they went into the woods. Three girls go in, and two were killed."

Opal tapped the sticky note, letting her words rest with Denise before continuing. "In my interview, I told you I believed with all my heart that there was no way Carrie would've hurt those girls."

"And now?"

"I don't know." Opal blinked. "I've come to you because morally it's the right thing to do. I can't live with myself knowing this and saying nothing. I know Hyde confessed, but—but you have those case files. You know more about this case than anyone."

Denise sat thinking as Opal leaned forward and dropped her voice lower.

"And something else. After it happened, some people were

whispering that there was a vileness about Abby and Erin and that maybe they deserved what they got."

Denise froze, her concentration intensifying. "What people?"

Opal didn't answer.

"Was it Carrie?"

Still no answer.

Denise said, "Why not go to the police with your book there, and your interpretation of it?"

"No." Opal shook her head.

"Why?"

"A lot of reasons, but mainly because Carrie's husband works in law enforcement. It would be awkward."

"May I have it?"

"I'd prefer to keep it. I told you what I know. You saw the evidence."

"Opal, you could've written the note yourself and stuck it there this morning."

Opal's mouth opened; her face whitened. "Why? Why would I do that? No, no, I didn't."

"Okay, okay. But in my work, I have to be wary of every bit of information that comes my way."

Taking it all in, Denise reached into her bag for her phone. "Let me take a few pictures."

65

It was after sunset when Denise finished walking Harvey.

At home, she filled his bowl with fresh water, petting him as he lapped it up. Then she fixed herself a glass of diet cola with crushed ice, went to her kitchen table and set up her laptop.

She'd had a long day at the paper, but it was time to resume working on the one story that mattered most to her.

In the park with Harvey, lifting her face to the calm evening breezes, she'd assessed what Opal had told her earlier that day at the IHOP. Now, in her kitchen, swiping photos on her phone, she studied the key Franklin quote.

Suppose, for a moment, everything Opal told me about Carrie—this quote, their project, the context—is true.

Harvey nuzzled Denise's lap, and she stroked his head as she thought. Taken with what her recent investigation had yielded, she was confident something was taking shape, so she reviewed key points.

Bottom line: after an altercation at school, three girls go into the woods for reasons no one knows, but only one comes out.

Three may keep a secret, if two of them are dead.

Carrie was the suspect but was not charged—not enough

evidence. *She moves away and the case goes cold. Donnie Ray Hyde emerges as the suspect. Again, not enough evidence.*

Denise took up a pen and jotted some notes, old-school, thinking.

Then Vern's diagnosed. He's terminal. Carrie moves back to Clear River. Vern sees Hyde on death row, resulting in an eleventh-hour confession and financial relief for his mother, through a friend of Vern's.

What else is there? What am I missing?

Sipping ice-cold cola, scrolling the case, opening files. Searching and thinking, tapping her pen.

She delved again into some of the case file reports and crime scene findings. No gun was recovered at the scene. No casings. One report hypothesized the scene might have been staged to look like something else. In his confession, Hyde said he gathered the casings, took items from the dead girls, then got rid of them and the gun.

"What do you think, Harvey?"

Denise pushed on to other reports, coming to one for footwear impressions. They found those consistent with Abby's, Erin's and Carrie's shoes. But there was a partial, larger than those of the girls, consistent with a size eleven, which was attributed to footwear worn by Donnie Ray Hyde.

Shoes. Hyde. Shoes.

Something was pinging in the back of Denise's mind.

Small at first, then it got louder.

Darnell George Sharp.

Hyde had given Darnell his shoes because they were the same size.

Nine.

66

Across town from where Denise was having a breakthrough on the murders, Vern sat alone in his study.

After taking some of the stronger pills his doctor had prescribed, he sipped his favorite bourbon, ice clinking in his glass. With the clock winding down on his mortality, he thought hard, taking stock of his life.

The walls of plaques and citations were proof of a successful career. And next to his computer, photos of Doreen, Carrie, Luke, Emily—frozen forever in frames from Walmart—were further proof of a life well lived. His eyes crinkled. He almost smiled before taking another sip of bourbon.

But thinking of that reporter, Denise, the edges of his thick, silver mustache drooped. She was good at her job, like a dog with a bone—asking Hyde's mother about her finances, talking to Cecil Pratt, then asking a lot of questions.

Troubling questions.

He turned his glass contemplatively on his desk.

It's all coming apart.

He stared into his bourbon, telling himself that he'd tried to do what needed to be done.

What was right for my family.

Looking at Carrie, smiling at him from the framed photos, he took another drink, feeling it flow through him. It might've been the whiskey and medication, but slowly he saw Carrie's face dissolve into…that of a witch…pulling him back…to that night…

…*driving his pickup to the dance hall after the Halloween party…the music thumping…kids in costume everywhere. Emerging from ghosts, vampires and monsters, Carrie the wicked witch climbs into the truck… pulling off her hat…sitting there, with her pointed nose and cape, staring straight ahead… Something is wrong…*

"Did you have a nice time?"

Seconds pass…music thumping… Carrie staring at nothing before turning to him…

"I had a great time, Dad."

He doesn't believe her…something's not right—she radiates with tension…she's trembling…tears glistening and streaking her cheap green face paint… The darkness comes alive in his headlights…sparkling… two glittering cheerleaders walk around his pickup—later he'll remember them as Erin Eddowes and Abby Hall. They're staring at Carrie… telegraphing secrets…eyeing him with intensity…

67

It was late as Lacey worked on invoices at her home office.

She always kept hard copies as a backup.

Her stapler clicked. Empty. Checking her drawer to refill it, she frowned. Out of staples. She walked through the house to Clay's office. Lacey had lost track of time. Clay was in the garage, working on his cars in preparation for the upcoming swap meet in Louisiana.

Searching his desk drawer, she found a box of staples, the kind that fit all standard staplers. After loading hers, she noticed Clay's computer monitor was open to a news story from the *Los Angeles Times*, with the headline: **LAPD OFFICER JUSTIFIED IN USING DEADLY FORCE.**

Lacey began reading the screen.

An LAPD officer will not face criminal charges in the shoot-out that killed a fleeing multiple-murder suspect...

It was an older story. Not long, with a feature that invited readers to click to:

THE DA'S REPORT CLEARING OFFICER LUKE CONWAY

On Clay's desk, she saw a printout of the LAPD's procedures on the use of confidential informants; a section Clay had highlighted said: *The use of informants by LAPD personnel is limited to those non-uniformed personnel.*

A handwritten note on the page asked: *Did he kill a CI?*

Near Clay's keyboard, his tablet showed photos of an SUV with some damage to the front. Lacey was blinking at it, wondering if that was Luke's car, when there was a diffusion of light.

"What're you up to?"

She turned to Clay, then held up her stapler.

"Borrowed some staples."

Clay nodded.

"What is all this?" She indicated the screen. "It's about Luke?"

He sighed and slid into a chair, rubbing the back of his neck.

"Yeah. Listen, Lace, this *has* to stay confidential. There's likely nothing to it."

"What is it?"

"Well, Luke's been acting a little secretive since he got here."

"Secretive?"

"Something happened with him a while back on River Road, in that storm. We think he hit someone and failed to report it."

"Really?"

"Yeah, he was off duty, coming home from the Stirrup. This is before Carrie moved back. I mean, he's told everyone he thought he saw someone on the road, and that maybe he hit debris or a branch. His car's damaged. But we know he quietly checked hospitals and canvassed residents."

"And?"

"Nothing yet, but Bob's asked me to keep an eye on him." Clay nodded to the monitor. "He had his trouble in Los Angeles. I guess Bob wants to be sure he's okay for duty, that he's stable." Clay rubbed his chin, adding, "We know Luke has some PTSD issues from what happened in LA, so we just want to watch out for him, make sure he's okay."

Shaking her head, Lacey cupped a hand to her cheek. "Carrie's been through so much. Now this. Oh, my God."

He pulled her to him. "I'm sure it's nothing." He shook his head. "But you have to swear that what I've told you does not leave this house."

She nodded.

"I need you to swear, Lacey."

"I swear."

68

"Don't sit. I'll make it quick."

Sheriff Bob Ellerd was unsmiling after waving Garth Reeger and Luke into his office at the start of their shift.

"Got a call from the lawyer for the provider on our cell tower warrant." He glanced at his deputies. "She says we should receive all responsive records within a couple days, ahead of the judge's deadline."

Luke nodded.

"And," Ellerd continued, "I also got a call from a lawyer for the contractor. He wanted to know the status of the investigation, seein' how it's been months now."

Ellerd shot a look at Reeger, who gave off an uneasy vibe while adjusting his stance.

"I told him we're working on it and we're hopeful for new leads." Ellerd's chair creaked when he sat. "Let's hope this cell phone warrant shakes out something." Ellerd released a long breath. "That's it. Get out there and get to it."

Garth gave Luke a cold stare.

Seeing them leaving Ellerd's office, Clay Smith tried to read their faces for any indication if the news was good, bad or worse. Reeger said nothing and left. Luke acknowledged Clay with a nod, watching him enter Ellerd's office and shut the door, catching the beginnings of their conversation.

"So, Clayton, you needed to talk before you go to Louisiana…"

Luke went to his car. Calls were stacking up in all zones. It turned out to be one of those days, with Luke taking call after call. A silent alarm; a traffic hazard; assisting deputies in the neighboring county.

For a quick lunch, Luke went to the Sonic Drive-In and got a burger and fries, which he ate in his car before handling new calls. He resumed work with checking on a disturbance, then the welfare of an elderly woman.

Ellerd's update on the cell phone records had left Luke anxious. On one hand, those records might provide an answer. On the other hand, it could lead to the disaster he feared—*that the woman is dead.* Luke had used every chance he had to look through databases for the rainstorm woman, but his search was futile. Even with Derek's expert help using the technology, Luke was beginning to believe it was a long shot.

Two new calls came his way: a theft complaint, which turned out to be a misunderstanding; then another suspicious vehicle, which turned out to be a courier.

Later, Luke was northbound on the highway when a blue SUV shot past him well over the speed limit. Activating his radar, he hit his lights and siren, pursuing the vehicle until it pulled over.

The driver, a woman, was alone. She lowered her window.

He held his focus on her for a moment. She was white, in her midtwenties, with longish dark hair and high cheekbones, giving him pause.

Could she be…?

She appeared upset.

"Did I do something wrong?" Her voiced quivered.

"I got you at thirty over the limit."

"Oh, no, I'm sorry."

After passing Luke her license and registration, she told him, through tears, that her aunt had died and she was driving to her uncle's place in Dallas.

He nodded politely and stepped away.

Running her name, he learned she lived in Galveston and had run a red light in Houston a year ago. Otherwise, no issues.

I don't think it could be her.

He returned her license and registration along with a $265 speeding ticket—he'd seen many young women try to cry their way out of an offense. On hearing about the ticket, her jaw dropped. Her tears gone, she snapped the documents from him.

"Please drive safely."

"Yeah, right."

She drove off.

Luke's lights were still flashing when he returned to his patrol car and got behind the wheel. Before pulling back onto the highway, his burner phone vibrated.

It was Derek.

We've got her!

Luke's screen split with the photo of the face Derek had extracted from the video, and a sharp new photo of the face of the same woman. Luke's stomach lifted.

Definitely the same woman—God, it's her!

Derek's follow-up message said: Joyce-Anne Gemsen, age 28, from Oklahoma.

Luke studied the two photos, marveling at Derek's work when he received another message.

Reported missing out of Oklahoma City.

69

That same afternoon, while Luke responded to calls, Carrie was working at home.

She'd revised concepts for the Los Angeles Metro campaign, which she was leading, summarizing next stages. Nearby, Emily played, watching *Sesame Street*. Later, while Emily napped, Carrie joined a video conference. But during the meeting, Carrie had battled to stay focused on the Metro project.

Opal's allegations had shaken her.

As Carrie struggled to concentrate after her work session had ended, her computer chimed. She'd received new photos and a message from Pearl, who was staying in Perth, Australia, before sailing for Bali.

Hi Honey: It's been a beautiful cruise so far. But I can't help worrying about what's going on in Clear River. Vern won't answer me. Is he OK? Are you OK?

Keeping things from her aunt broke Carrie's heart. Pearl had been like a mother to her, but Carrie wanted her to enjoy her time on the other side of the world. All she could manage was: Don't worry. Enjoy your cruise. We're doing fine. Everything's OK.

Her thoughts swirling, Carrie clenched her eyes.

In recent days, since visiting the dance hall and returning to the school, she'd recovered more fragments of her memory. Different, seemingly disparate pieces were forming a picture.

A horrifying picture of the truth.

The only way I can complete the picture is if I—

The doorbell's chime yanked her from ruminating. Going to the monitor for the front door camera, she recognized Denise Diaz on the step, tapping her phone to her leg.

Carrie knew what was coming, knew full well why Denise was standing at her door.

I can't run away from it.

Carrie opened the door. Not wanting to wake Emily, she kept her voice low. "What is it, Denise?"

"Hi, Carrie. Listen, sorry to come here without warning, but we need to talk. I need your reaction."

"To what?"

Denise looked around. "Do you want to do this here?"

"Yes, and I only have a moment. My daughter's asleep."

Quickly, Denise explained how Opal Wells had reached out to her, what she had claimed.

"Yes, so?" Carrie said, failing to conceal the worry behind her eyes.

Repositioning her grip on the strap of her bag, Denise raised her phone and showed Carrie photos. Franklin's quote filling her screen.

Three may keep a secret, if two of them are dead.

Denise swiped to the handwritten note praising it.

Carrie knew the printing was hers.

"Carrie," Denise said, "given the timing of this note, given the context of your confrontation with Abby and Erin prior to the murders, and given how your injury hampered your memory, I need to know, *on the record*, what is your reaction to this?"

The vein in Carrie's jawline pulsed.

"We were kids at the time…"

Carrie's face was ashen; she was staring, not at the present, but as if she were seeing the past.

"Excuse me?" Denise asked. "Is that your response?"

"Why are you doing this? Hyde confessed." Carrie bit her bottom lip. "You can't read anything into that dumb note because it's a coincidence, just a silly coincidence."

"That's your reaction?"

"I really can't remember much. I'm sorry."

"Then let me ask you about your father's visit to death row to see Hyde—"

Carrie shook her head. "I think I hear my daughter. I have to go."

"But, Carrie?"

"That's all I can tell you."

Carrie retreated into her home and shut the door, and Denise returned to her car.

Before starting the engine, she looked at Carrie's house for a long time, thinking that she was closer to exhuming a secret about what really happened in those woods, hopeful she might see the answers she was looking for.

70

"Hi, this is Mark Kallin from John Jay College in New York, returning your call."

"Thank you for getting back to me, Professor Kallin."

Denise snapped to a fresh page in her notebook.

Since returning to the newsroom after her doorstep interview with Carrie, she'd made a flurry of calls. In between talking with sources and double-checking details, she'd kept an eye on Lynn's empty office, watching for her editor's return.

Denise wanted to talk to her. She had a good story and wanted to get started writing. She was saddened by what it would imply, but she had collected key facts, and it was her job to report them.

Her call to Mark Kallin, a criminology professor, would strengthen her piece. As the author of a number of books, and a person who'd testified in major cases, Kallin was a leading expert on the psychology of false confessions. Denise took a few minutes relating her latest findings to him.

"Interesting," he said. "I've heard about this Texas case."

"What do you think?"

"Well, we know people make false confessions."

Kallin listed reasons ranging from a suspect's mental and

emotional state, to their age, to being stressed, traumatized, depressed or coerced.

"What about to help someone else?"

"Absolutely," Kallin said. "Some people intentionally make a false confession to protect others. And given the context you've provided in the case of Donnie Ray Hyde, with his impending execution at the time, it's not inconceivable for him to have made a false confession to benefit his mother."

Denise tightened her grip on her pen as she jotted down Kallin's words, asking a few more questions before ending her interview and thanking him. Then, looking for her editor, she saw Lynn at the aquarium, checking her cherished blue bettas, guppies and tetras.

Denise went to her.

"Hey," Lynn said, "I have a fun story for you."

"Can we talk in your office first?"

"So serious. All right."

Inside, Denise closed the door, and Lynn sat down and picked up a slip of paper.

"Before you start," Lynn said, "the story is twin sisters who turn ninety-nine next week. We need an upbeat feature on them, with a bit of history of Clear River through their eyes."

"Sure, but I got something new on the murders."

"Right." Lynn removed her glasses and rubbed the bridge of her nose. "You've been chipping away at it. What do you have?"

Denise went through it point by point: Carrie had been a suspect; Vern visited Hyde on death row, resulting in his confession; and Hyde's mother had received financial relief through a friend of Vern's. "It can't be a coincidence," Denise said. She continued, telling Lynn about Professor Kallin's take on Hyde's confession. She then brought up Opal Wells and the Ben Franklin quote, showing Lynn photos of it on her phone.

"Remember, no weapon or casings were found. No strong physical evidence," Denise said.

IF TWO ARE DEAD   311

Lynn nodded.

"And there's the shoes," Denise said.

"The shoes?"

Denise related how crime scene reports in the files indicated a partial shoe impression attributed to the killer, which would be Hyde, as being size eleven.

"But Hyde was a size nine. I called the TDCJ—they confirmed size nine from his inmate records. I called his mother, then the funeral director who handled his remains. Again, size nine. Also, Hyde's fellow death row inmate, Darnell George Sharp, claimed to have received Hyde's size nine shoes."

Lynn nodded slowly. "Good work. Outstanding. It's almost there."

"Almost there? What do you mean?"

Steepling her fingers, Lynn touched them to her lips.

"You raise good questions. Questions that challenge the validity of Hyde's confession. You cast doubt on the official story of what happened in the woods and who killed Abby and Erin."

"But?"

"What you have *proves nothing.*"

"You want me to drop it?"

"No. Not at all. I didn't say that." She held up a finger. "We need one more thing."

"What?"

Lynn checked the time. It was midafternoon.

"Go to Will Young."

"The DA?"

"Yes, present the facts of the *Chronicle*'s investigation to the district attorney. Put all your cards on the table. Like you did for me. Get his reaction on the record."

"Then?"

"Then, no matter what he says, we go with your story."

71

Joyce-Anne Gemsen.

Her name echoed in Luke's mind.

Driving home after his shift, he pulled off the road near Fawn Ridge. He felt drawn here, to the place it happened—aware of the small dent, scrapes and spider-thread crack on his headlight cover that were still present.

A testament to his crime.

Pulling out his personal laptop and burner phone, he called Derek, thanking him with an undertone of nervousness.

"For sure, buddy," Derek said. "Don't worry, I'm keeping it all under the radar. No one knows. I'll keep looking for you, send you what I get. You keep trying with open sources—you can use what I've just sent."

"Appreciate the help."

Opening the missing person poster Derek had sent him, he devoured every key detail.

Joyce-Anne Gemsen.

Date of birth put her at age 28.

Height: 5'3"
Weight: 118 pounds

Hair: Brown

Eyes: Hazel

Sex: Female

Race: White

Scars and Marks: Multiple ear piercings. A small tattoo of a rose on her inner right forearm.

Clothing at time of disappearance: Faded, torn jeans, a white Rolling Stones T-shirt with large tongue logo, a powder blue zippered hoodie, a white ball cap, white Adidas running shoes.

Remarks: Joyce-Anne Gemsen was last seen walking to the ramp for I-35. Video security images show her leaving the Starving MotherTrucker truck stop near Pauls Valley, Oklahoma.

Until she ended up here, in a storm, flying over the hood of my SUV, landing in the ditch and vanishing.

The time and date of her disappearance and the driving distance from Pauls Valley were consistent with Joyce-Anne being in Clear River. Luke replayed the construction site video, watching the rain-streaked flash of pink, then Joyce-Anne rising from the roadside before disappearing. And there were the headlights of an approaching car, which had prompted Luke to leave.

Reexamining what he knew, thoughts freewheeling, he went to the description of what Joyce was wearing when last seen. No mention of anything pink.

But Luke knew she was wearing pink the night he struck her. He remembered the flash at his windshield as well as the fragment of pink fabric he'd pulled from his grille. And the construction site video confirmed it.

Heaving a breath, he shook his head, looking at the poster's contact section: *If you have any information concerning the whereabouts*

*of Joyce-Anne Gemsen, please contact Garvin County Sheriff's Office,
the Oklahoma State Bureau of Investigation, or your nearest FBI office.*

Luke had to assume investigators had already exhausted every
avenue, checking for the location of Joyce-Anne's phone, if
she had one. They would've checked her use of credit or bank
cards, searched nearby security cameras and combed through
databases.

Thinking about Derek's suggestion on open sources, Luke
searched Joyce's name online, finding news reports out of Oklahoma City. There were several from TV and radio stations.
Reading them quickly, he saw few new details. But the major
newspaper, the *Oklahoman*, had something in-depth. An interview with a lawyer representing Joyce-Anne Gemsen's boyfriend.

The boyfriend had cooperated with investigators and submitted to a polygraph, which showed him to be truthful and
have no role in Joyce-Anne's disappearance.

*"My client admits that an argument they had at the truck stop about
money upset Joyce-Anne. She exited the building and began walking toward the interstate ramp before vanishing,"* the lawyer told the paper.

Luke processed the information.

*So how does she go from Pauls Valley, Oklahoma, to this spot in
Clear River County, Texas?*

And most important, is she still alive to answer that question?

72

When Luke got home, Carrie kissed his cheek.

She was holding her purse. Emily was playing with her toys on the living room floor.

"What's up?" he asked.

"I've got to go out." Carrie lowered her head, scanning the contents of her purse. "I put lasagna in the oven. It'll be done when the timer goes off. There's Caesar salad in the fridge. I cut up meat and vegetables for Emily. Warm it, and feed her when you eat."

Blocking her and angling his head, Luke gently held Carrie's shoulders, surveying her reddened eyes, her dampened cheeks.

"Honey, what's wrong?"

"I just have to run some errands."

"Now? I just got home."

"Yes."

"Carrie, what is it? Is it your dad?"

"I have to pick up some things." Stepping around him, she went to the door.

"Carrie?"

"I won't be long."

Standing at the door, watching his wife drive away, concern

prickled at Luke. Turning to Emily, who was chattering and playing, happy as could be, he lifted her into his arms, hugging and kissing her, worry clouding his eyes.

The streets of Clear River blurred.

Was moving back home a mistake?

Driving across town, Carrie brushed at tears, her head throbbing as she took in old, familiar buildings—city hall, the post office, the courthouse. Dr. Bernay had been right. Coming back had unblocked memories, and Carrie was piecing together details of the murders, getting closer to the truth. Dr. Bernay was also right about it being painful.

More painful than Carrie could ever have imagined.

After Luke and Emily finished dinner, he washed her face, then changed her. She played while he put things in the dishwasher. Luke figured—no, *hoped*—Carrie would be home soon. Waiting, he put his burner phone and laptop on the kitchen table and resumed working on Joyce-Anne's case.

Questions webbed in all directions: *What was it about money that she and her boyfriend argued over that forced her to walk to the interstate? Would the cell tower warrants provide any leads? Will those records connect to Joyce-Anne's phone? Why didn't I report this right away?*

Luke was going in circles.

It's because of LA. I was so ashamed and worried about my PTSD that I messed up. If this nightmare ever ends, I'll get help. I can't shake what happened in LA. It's destroying my judgment. It's like a war's going on in my head.

It was underscoring all his failings, including his failure to be a good husband for Carrie at a time when she needed him most.

How could he have been such a horrible, selfish person?

God, please tell me I didn't kill Joyce-Anne Gemsen.

Luke closed his laptop and thrust his face into his hands.

★ ★ ★

Carrie parked at the entrance to Wild Pines Forest.

The same entrance where she'd met Abby and Erin that day so many years ago.

The last day of their lives.

Carrie turned off the motor and gazed into the dense, dark forest. The truth was in there.

Like a monster.

Waiting for me.

She could hear it, feel it, panting, salivating, inviting her to confront it.

The facts, the scenes she could resurrect, replayed like a high-speed movie.

The cafeteria…three may keep a secret…the Halloween dance…

"Meet us…it's deadly serious… It's about your dad…"

But I didn't trust them. What did I do before going to the woods? The screams…birds screeching…running into the river…

It's waiting.

In there.

The truth.

Carrie opened her car door. She got out, stood beside her SUV. Rooted.

Unable to move.

I can't. I just can't go in.

She stood there sobbing, great heaving sobs, hearing nothing, seeing nothing but the shrapnel of her own terrifying past…until…

A hand on her shoulder.

Carrie turned to Luke.

There he was, holding Emily.

She stepped into his arms, hugging them both.

73

Denise's story ran on the front page of the *Clear River Chronicle*, and it dominated the digital edition.

It began like this:

> *The homicide case of two teenage girls—Abby Hall and Erin Eddowes—closed after an executed killer's last-minute confession to their murders—could be reopened.*
>
> *"We can't rule out anything, even reopening the case. New information brought to light warrants serious review," said Will Young, Clear River County district attorney.*

Young had made his comments after assessing revelations about the case uncovered by the *Chronicle*.

The story continued with the background of the case, then went into an early theory held by investigators, which arose from the fact that certain items—IDs and articles of clothing—were missing from the scene, perhaps taken as trophies. It was because of these facts that investigators first suspected the murders could've been staged to look like a serial killer's work by someone with knowledge of homicide investigations. Carrie was the daughter of Vern Hamilton, Clear River County Sheriff.

The story detailed Carrie's liking of a Ben Franklin quote and how it had taken on an ominous meaning in the wake of her cafeteria confrontation with Abby and Erin. And the article gave new context to condemned killer Donnie Ray Hyde's confession, the result of a recent death row visit by Vern Hamilton. Denise questioned the veracity of Hyde's confession when stood against his mother's "godsend" financial relief, relayed after Hyde's execution by a former colleague of Vern Hamilton's. Hyde's confession could've been a false one, according to Mark Kallin, an expert on the psychology of untrue confessions.

The article noted the lack of a gun and casings at the crime scene, and little physical evidence other than footwear impressions. It pointed to the inconsistency between Hyde's shoe size and the partial impression found at the scene.

A series of photos accompanied the story. Among them: the Franklin quote alongside Carrie's sticky note; forensic shoe impressions; TDCJ records confirming Hyde's shoe size; the letter Hyde's mother received indicating the discovery of a tax error in her favor; photos of Abby and Erin, showing what they were wearing on the day of the murders; photos of Carrie and Vern; and a photo of Vern and Cecil Pratt.

The article also went into Carrie's family history and the death of her mother, Doreen Hamilton, at home. It explained how the tragedy gave rise to community rumor about Doreen's turbulent relationship with her husband, Vern, prior to her death. The cause: a broken neck from falling down the stairs after a brain seizure, according to the report by the medical examiner, who was a friend of Vern's.

The story drew upon several interviews, including those with Mary-Ellen Hyde, Cecil Pratt, Opal Wells, Vernon Hamilton, Carrie, and relatives of Abby and Erin.

The article ended with a comment from Abby Hall's aunt, Martha Porter.

"We always believed we knew who killed Abby and Erin. The mystery is, why?" Porter said. *"And only one person has the answer."*

74

Throughout the night, Carrie's subconscious tormented her sleep, forcing her to wake before dawn.

Anticipating something awful, she went to her computer and opened the *Chronicle*'s site.

The headline bloomed: **DISTRICT ATTORNEY TO REVIEW DOUBLE MURDER CASE.** *Oh God.*

Her hands flew to her mouth, stifling a shriek, after reading the story. The allegations fueled her worst fears.

Her world was on fire.

She took even breaths, knowing what she had to do.

She cleaned up quietly, dressed quickly. Hearing the baby stir, she collected Emily and got her ready.

Then Carrie heard Luke in the bathroom starting the shower. Pressing her lips together, she sent him a text before leaving with her daughter in her arms.

Hot water prickled Luke's skin; steam clouds rose with his thoughts of Joyce-Anne Gemsen.

Last night, after Carrie had gone to bed, he'd stayed up studying the missing Oklahoma woman's case. This time he focused on the security camera images of her leaving the truck stop.

Critical information can sometimes be found in plain sight in the background.

He surveyed displays for snacks and drinks, posters for lotteries and local events, but nothing stood out.

As he got dressed, Luke saw that Carrie was already up, likely with Emily in the kitchen.

"Carrie?"

No response.

Doing a check through the house, he realized Carrie and the baby were gone.

It was concerning. Carrie had been under increasing strain, prompting her to leave the house yesterday, refusing to talk to him about it. He'd found her at the forest after he'd used a luggage tracking device they'd put in their cars in case of theft.

Now, picking up his phone, he saw Carrie's text.

Gone to talk to dad about the story.

Story? What story?

Of course. He recalled her saying at the forest how Denise Diaz, the *Chronicle* reporter, had recently come to their home again. He didn't know why. Carrie wouldn't discuss it. But the reporter's visit had clearly upset her.

Opening his laptop, he found the new article and devoured it, not believing what he was reading. The allegations, the speculation, the rumors, the implications—it all hit him like a sledgehammer to his gut.

This is bad. She's gone to see Vern. Maybe she needs a lawyer? Or at least a husband who can help her.

He studied the story and photos again, then read some of the early comments.

Another excellent article. What will happen to Carrie?

Does the Chron have it right this time?

Such a tragedy. Good reporting but so tragic.

Luke thought for a moment, then texted Carrie: Stories can be wrong, honey. Let's talk.

Seconds after he'd sent it, his phone rang.

"Luke, it's Fowler. We need you to start early. Something's happened."

75

The sun had risen; it was shrouded in silver and charcoal clouds by the time Carrie arrived at her father's house.

She'd called along the way, but he hadn't answered. His truck was in the driveway. Carrie used her key to unlock the front door.

Inside, the shades and curtains were closed, the air stale with a hint of Irish Spring soap and Vern's cologne.

"Dad! It's me and Emily!"

No answer.

"Dad!"

Holding Emily, she split a curtain, letting in some light when she heard a rustling in the living room.

"Dad!"

A grumbling led her to the living room, where she found him on the sofa under a blanket. He groaned in protest when she opened another curtain. Light illuminated a bourbon bottle, a glass and pill bottles on the coffee table.

"Are you okay?"

"Fine." His voice was raw. He stood slowly, coughed, scratched his chin, then winked at Emily. "Be right back."

A moment later, the door to the hallway bathroom closed. Nerves rippling through her, Carrie busied herself cleaning up the bottle, glass and pills, starting coffee. She got Emily's high chair, placing it next to the counter. After hefting her daughter into it, Carrie cut up an apple and banana for her.

She stopped.

The print edition of that morning's *Chronicle*, bearing that terrible headline, was unfolded at the end of the counter. Vern, being old-school, still had it delivered. He returned from the bathroom. Her eyes lifted from the paper, meeting his, and her voice quivered. "Did you read it?"

Vern's face betrayed nothing as he lowered himself into a chair next to his granddaughter, his shining eyes gazing upon Emily with all the love they could hold.

"She looks more like you every day, darlin'."

"Dad," Carrie said, her tremoring evincing her determination. "Was Hyde's confession false?" She stabbed the paper with her finger. "This story says I did it. Tell me the truth. You must know."

He turned to Carrie, rubbing the edges of his mustache, steeling himself to unlock whatever he was keeping from her. He inhaled, let it out.

"I found a gun in the woods that day. A Glock. It was one of mine."

"Oh, God." Carrie steadied herself at the counter.

"I told no one. No one knows." Vern looked off. "Ben Mc-Graw and Eve Trainor put things together—your run-in with Abby and Erin at school, then the dance hall. Ben and Eve went hard at you. But with your injury you couldn't remember."

He paused before continuing.

"What they had was circumstantial. No evidence," he said. "We don't have to register firearms in Texas. So they had no link to my personal collection. No reports of a missing or stolen gun. I didn't list all of my guns on insurance, so the records were inconclusive. They did have a partial, unidentified, larger shoe impression at the scene, but the DA said they had nothing strong enough to sustain a charge."

Staggered by what her father had revealed, Carrie sat in a chair, staring at nothing, her mouth opening slightly.

"Do you know what this means?" She held her head, then added, "You said you found the Glock—where is it?"

Letting out a slow breath, Vern found the words. "Far from here. I threw it in the San Jacinto River. It'll never be found."

A soft cry escaped from Carrie.

"Were there casings, too?" she whispered.

Vern shook his head. "I never found any that day, nor did our crime scene people."

"Wait," Carrie said. "The story, the files Denise showed me, said some of Abby's and Erin's personal items were taken. Did you find them?"

"No. You probably don't remember getting rid of them. I figured you staged things. You always were so interested in my crime scene books."

Absorbing the details, Carrie returned Emily to her chair, bracing as a tidal wave of truth swept over her. Shaking her head, Carrie sat at the table, raking her fingers through her hair.

"The truth was always lying right there, right in front of me. The thing I did. The horrible thing I did. Of course I wouldn't let myself remember that. *But what does this make me?*"

"Carrie."

Vern placed his hand on her shoulder; she shoved it away.

"Why did you do this, Dad?"

Sadness filled his eyes.

"I was protecting you. You're quick to anger, like me."

"Like you?"

As this new horror landed in front of her, Carrie stared at him.

"How did Mom die, Dad?"

Vern swallowed as if in pain.

"She died because of me."

He turned to the staircase, replaying it in his mind.

"We were arguing at the top of those stairs. She was mad

at me. She took a few steps down and froze. Her head shook, spasmed, and she collapsed down the stairs. I reached for her, but I was too late. It happened so fast."

Carrie's voice creaked in anguish at hearing this account for the first time.

"It's the truth, Carrie. I swear, I didn't touch her. But my twisted, stupid jealousy at her success, at feeling like other men, her clients, were getting more of her than I was, angered me. That argument killed her. Your mother died before my eyes, and it was my fault."

Vern took a moment, and Carrie saw her father as the haunted, dying man he'd become.

"I'll never get over losing her. And I couldn't lose you, too. That's why I protected you. To make sure you would have a life."

Carrie shook her head, trying to fit the pieces together.

"But it's all a lie. It was me. You should've done the right thing and turned me in. You covered it up, obstructed justice, broke the law."

"I got my death sentence. I don't have much longer. It's down to months now."

They looked at each other.

"Carrie, you were never going to know about the woods and the gun. It wasn't supposed to happen this way." He seized the *Chronicle* and tossed it. "It all came apart. Hyde was a suspect. Hyde was a killer. Hyde was going to be executed. Putting it on him would've put it all to rest."

"But now…" Carrie wiped the tears from her face. "I have to live with this monstrous thing I've done. I should confess— I—"

"No, Carrie, no—just—"

"Just what, Dad? Live a lie?"

"Carrie, listen to me."

"No! I need to figure this out."

She got Emily from her high chair, collected her things and left.

76

Dark gray clouds had enveloped the horizon by the time Carrie arrived home.

Luke had already left for work.

Steadying her nerves, clinging by her fingertips to what was normal, Carrie changed Emily. Then she put on Emily's favorite recording of *Sesame Street* and set her in front of the TV with her toys.

Outside, distant thunder rolled through the air as Carrie stared at Elmo. With his friends, he sang, in his falsetto voice, *"If you're happy and you know it…"*

Carrie hugged herself, her world crumbling around her.

I'm a monster.

I blocked what I did—couldn't bear remembering. The district attorney will review everything. I'll go to prison. I'll lose Emily, Luke. They'll charge Dad in his dying days.

I'll be executed!

Elmo sang, *"…shout hoo-ray…"*

Her insides twisting, Carrie fought to breathe. Outside, thunder crashed as she reached for her phone. Hands shaking, she found a number, pressed it. The line rang.

"Dr. Bernay's office, how may I help you?"

RICK MOFINA

"I'm Carrie Conway, a patient. May I speak with her?"

"I'm sorry. Dr. Bernay's unavailable at the moment."

"It's a bit of a crisis. Could you connect me, please?"

"One moment."

A soothing piece of classical music played; Carrie waited until the receptionist came back.

"Dr. Bernay has been with another patient at a hospital since early morning. She advises that she'll call shortly."

"I really need to talk to her."

"Yes, she'll call as soon as she can."

"Thank you."

Squeezing her phone, tapping it on her knee, Carrie was hit with thoughts of what was coming—media, police questioning, charges. Emily giggled watching Bert and Ernie discussing friendship.

Carrie jumped when her phone rang.

77

Bursts of wind lashed at the trees, strong enough that branches had snapped and crashed onto the highway ramp where Luke was posted.

The storm had hit with sudden and relentless fury.

Not a good day for the sheriff's department to be short-staffed. Luke had been sent to divert traffic from the ramp, situating his patrol car at the entrance, emergency lights wigwagging.

As sheets of rain thrashed his windshield, Luke was pierced with guilt because he wanted to help Carrie. He hoped she'd found some comfort in visiting her father. Thinking she might be home by now, he took out his phone, thankful he still had service. He made a few swipes and taps at his tracking app for her SUV.

Carrie was home in Cedar Breeze.

Good.

Wanting to check on how she was doing, he started, then abandoned, a text. *No, I need to talk to her.* But his call went to voicemail.

He didn't leave a message. Maybe she was busy with Emily, or maybe there was no service in their suburb? He'd try again in a bit. He then radioed dispatch for an ETA on the road crew.

"They've got calls with downed live wires, so hang in there."

"Ten-four."

In the wake of the update, Luke got a text from Reeger.

We got the warrants. Only yielded a couple numbers. I checked
them. One was yours. A couple other numbers popped up but
they dead-ended. Nice try but nothing. I'll send them to you.

Frustrated, Luke wondered how thoroughly Reeger had
checked. Then, while waiting for the road crew, Luke decided
to make use of the time and availability of service and got out
his personal laptop. He didn't want to contact any of the investigators in Oklahoma, but he'd hit a wall with open sources.

Again, he went to the news story he'd found and video images from security cameras at the truck stop near Pauls Valley.
Studying the background, he wondered about the reason for the
argument that led to Joyce-Anne Gemsen walking away; he wondered how she got to Texas and ended up wearing a pink shirt.

Searching her name online again, with the key words *truck
stop*, he found an older news story. It was from an Oklahoma
City TV outlet. He hadn't seen this one before.

He played it: the reporter, Chuck Fortune, was standing in
front of the truck stop.

*"Gemsen and her boyfriend, Dylan Lee Crowders, stopped here
after attending…"*

Luke's internet signal faltered; the news report froze. He
tapped the play button and the story jumped ahead.

*"…sources close to the case say witnesses in the truck stop heard the
couple arguing about…"*

The video froze again. Luke tapped Play, but the video refused to cooperate.

Attending what? Arguing about what?

Lightning suddenly lit up the sky, followed by a pounding
of thunder and loud cracking.

Luke turned to look, cursing as a tree toppled.

78

Dr. Bernay had been fast getting back to her, Carrie thought, looking at her ringing phone with some relief.

But the caller ID came up as Always Charming.

After hesitating a moment, Carrie decided to answer. "Hello?"

"Carrie, it's Lacey."

"Lacey. Hi."

"Hon, are you okay?"

Carrie released a small nervous laugh. "Not really."

"I'm at the shop, finishing with a customer. Would you like me to come over before this storm gets worse?"

"No. No, thanks, Lacey, but you don't have to."

"Well, is Luke, your dad, or anyone, with you now?"

"No."

"You shouldn't be alone with this business in the *Chronicle* coming out. It's just—I just don't know what to believe."

Carrie's voice trembled. "I really shouldn't talk much more. I'm expecting a call."

"Oh. I see."

Those three words held a world of meaning, as in—*maybe a call from a lawyer, telling her not to talk about anything.*

"I just find it hard to accept that this story's true," Lacey added.

Carrie didn't answer, and seconds passed. Heavy, silent, seconds.

"I really should go, Lacey."

"Just listen, hon. You've got everything on your shoulders right now, with *this*, your dad, Luke and Emily. And that bird-brain Opal saying what she said. Lord, you may be feelin' like everyone's against you. But I can come right over. Clay's out of town. I can be there, to help in any way. You just know that."

Barely keeping herself together, Carrie realized how since her return, Lacey and Clay had been nothing but kind to her.

"I do. Thank you, Lacey."

Ending the call, Carrie watched Kermit whispering to Elmo the difference between loud and quiet. Outside, the sky turned to night, artillery-like thunder rattling windows, rain streaking down the glass…like blood…pulling her to her father's revelations about finding the gun…*remembering…the dance hall…*

"Meet us…tomorrow…keep it secret… It's about your dad…"

At home before going to the woods…she didn't trust them…taking a Glock from his collection…stuffing it in the pocket of her hoodie…its weight assuring…she had control…she didn't trust them…they said it was about her father…

I took Dad's gun and went into the woods with Abby and Erin… I did…

Her phone vibrated, then rang in her hand.

"Is this Carrie Conway, spouse of Deputy Luke Conway?"

Carrie swallowed. "Yes."

"This is Clear River County Emergency. Ma'am, I'm sorry to inform you that Luke Conway has been injured—"

"Oh, my God!"

"—he's been taken to Clear River Central—"

"Is he— How bad was he—"

"I have no further information. He's at Clear River Central.

We advise if you're traveling there to exercise due care because of extreme weather."

Carrie picked up the baby, got her things, put on both of their jackets and hurried out the door.

79

That morning at the *Chronicle*, Lynn Grant was on her phone in her office with the door open.

"Yes, Sue, you've got the east... Carol Trent's got north... Right, keep us updated." Seeing Denise arrive, Lynn ended the call. "I gotta go."

Lynn hung up, then greeted Denise in the newsroom.

"Hey, kiddo," Lynn said.

Denise set her take-out coffee down on her cluttered desk. "Heard you on the phone—what's up?"

"Lining up our stringers for this storm, could be a doozy. And, on another matter, congratulations."

Light applause emerged from other newsroom staff, eliciting a small smile from Denise. She pulled off her jacket, picked up her coffee and raised it in a toast, bowing her head slightly in salute to her colleagues.

"We're a team."

Lynn said: "That was another great story. The *Chronicle* can run with the best of them. In fact, the networks are calling again."

"And look at the reader response since it went live at midnight." Kelcey was scrolling on her computer. "Listen to these posts, Denise: 'Stunning story.' And this one just popped up. 'What's going to happen to Carrie when the DA reopens the case?'"

"That'll be for us to find out and report." Lynn clapped her hands together. "Right now, we've got a storm coming and work to do. Marco, come see me for a sec."

Lynn returned to her office with the young reporter close behind. Denise stepped to the coatrack, hanging up her damp jacket, and Kelcey followed her.

"Denise, not all the comments are good. Some of these trolls and haters are relentless. Listen to this one: 'Will the *Chronically Terrible* ever get it right? Next week it'll be the governor who did it.'"

Denise shrugged. "Comes with the territory, Kelcey."

"Well, I think you deserve a Pulitzer."

Denise smiled, touched Kelcey's shoulder, then went back to her desk, stopping in midreach for her coffee as she noticed the brown envelope sitting on her keyboard. It was addressed simply with block letters printed on computer paper, cut to a credit card–sized slip and taped to the front.

DENISE DIAZ
REPORTER
THE CLEAR RIVER CHRONICLE

No postage. No return address. Odd that it hadn't come through the mail. She picked it up and pivoted to her colleagues.

"Who put this here?"

"I did." Marco, notebook in hand, had just come out of Lynn's office. "I get in early, come through the back door. It was wedged in there. Figured it was fan mail, or crackpot conspiracy stuff." He chuckled.

Looking at it, Denise reached for her scissors, sliced it open and shook out a folded sheet of paper. The letter, in bold uppercase, printed in single space from a computer, took up the top half of the page.

FOR YEARS MY WORK STOOD AS LEGEND. FOR YEARS I BAFFLED AND PERPLEXED PO-LICE. FOR YEARS, I MYSTIFIED THE WORLD, HOLDING PEOPLE IN FEAR, DRINKING IN THEIR REVERENCE WHILE REMAINING SI-LENT.
YOU TRIED TO TAKE IT AWAY.
FIRST YOU GAVE DRH CREDIT. NOW, YOU'RE GIVING CC CREDIT. YOU INSULT ME. YOU WILL SEE BY THE TRINKET I SHARE, THAT I AM THAT I AM AND MY WORK CON-TINUES.

Denise felt something else in the envelope. Sliding it out, her scalp tingled as the face of Abigail Elissa Hall stared at her from a Texas driver's license.

80

Standing at her shop window contemplating the storm, Lacey bit her bottom lip.

Her call with Carrie had left her unsettled. Carrie didn't want her to come over.

But sometimes people facing a crisis are too embarrassed to accept help when they need it.

Lacey decided to call Clay.

He was at a swap meet in Louisiana. She didn't like bothering him, but this was important. Maybe, if he wasn't busy, he could offer advice. It rang several times before he answered.

"Hi, Lace."

"Hi. Got a minute?"

"Sure, I found some good parts for the Nomad, original brake kit with the right rotors."

"Good, you've been looking for that awhile."

"This stuff is in great condition. What's up?"

"There's a new story on the murders in today's *Chronicle*, and it looks bad for Carrie."

"Yeah, I saw it online this morning. It puts everything on her. It must be crushing for her and Vern."

"It is. I just spoke with her."

"How'd she sound?"

"Terrible."

"What'd she say?"

"Not much, she was upset."

"What do you think about the story?"

"I don't know what to believe. I don't know what the truth is. I don't think she did it, and in my heart, I feel I should go to her house to support her."

"Support her?"

"She's my friend."

Clay didn't respond.

"Should I go to her?" Lacey asked. "What do you think?"

"It might be best to stand back."

"Stand back?"

"Until things settle. She's facing a world of trouble, with this story, Vern and Luke. Give her space."

"But that's when friends should help. And she doesn't have many friends in this town right now."

"Well, you asked me, and I think just hold off, see how this thing plays out with—"

Interference snapped and hissed.

"Sorry, Clay, what did you say?"

"I said, just hold off, see how it all plays out with the DA and everything."

"I'll think about it. I'll let you go. Good luck at the meet. Love you."

"Love you, too."

Lacey lowered her phone and searched the rain for answers on what she should do.

Stand back. Stand back.

With her conscience attacking her, Lacey didn't know if she could take Clay's advice. Her thoughts of Carrie shot back to high school. Lacey's heart breaking when Carrie's mother died. Going to the funeral to support her. Remembering how Car-

IF TWO ARE DEAD   339

rie was ostracized in school as the daughter of the sheriff—they called her the Narc, Five-O, Undercover. Lacey was there the day Carrie defended Lanna when Abby and Erin's crew bullied her in the cafeteria. Then the murders. Carrie had nearly died. She thought about Vern getting sick, his terminal diagnosis. Carrie's husband, Luke, killing a woman in Los Angeles, his strange behavior here with Clay watching him.

And now today's story accusing her of murder.

It's like Carrie's been cursed all her life.

As the storm thundered, Lacey wondered, *Is Clay right? Should I stand back?*

Can *I stand back?*

81

Carrie strapped Emily into her car seat, then got behind the wheel. The rain was coming in torrents now.

Before leaving, Carrie buckled herself in and took a breath, then used her car's hands-free app to call Luke, praying to hear his voice.

It rang and rang.

No answer.

She backed out of the driveway, the wipers slapping at high speed. Wind gusted. She tightened her grip, driving with caution. There were no other cars on the road in her neighborhood.

Keep it together. You have to hang on for Luke.

She turned onto River Road, the narrow rural strip that led to the highway and into town. Desolate in the near gloom, void of traffic, the storm lashing, she kept a slow, safe speed, glancing at Emily in the baby back-seat mirror.

Just us out here, sweetie, Carrie thought.

Then, in her rearview mirror, she spotted the rain-blurred headlights of a car in the distance. It gave her some comfort to not be alone on the road. But fear needled her with the emergency dispatcher's call echoing in her memory, launching a million scenarios.

Maybe Luke's been shot. Or he crashed. Or he's been struck in a traffic stop.

Carrie tried reaching him again.

It was futile, her worry giving rise to images of Luke in a hospital bed or on a gurney, his body covered with a sheet, her world crumbling...*my husband...my dad dying...the truth of what I am...*

Tears rolled down her face, every drop washing hope away. She needed to talk to someone. She thought of Lacey's offer. But no, she wanted Dr. Bernay.

Why hasn't she called back?

Collecting herself, Carrie needed to act, needed to determine what had happened to Luke. She called Clear River Central Hospital.

"May I help you?" said the woman who answered at Admissions.

"My husband, Deputy Luke Conway—" Carrie's voice trembled "—he was injured and taken there. I'm on my way. Can you please tell me how badly he's hurt?"

"I'm sorry, ma'am, but our policy—"

Static interrupted the call.

"I'm sorry, I didn't hear," Carrie said. "Your policy?"

"Ma'am, our policy does not permit the release of patient information over the phone."

"But I'm his wife!"

"I'm sorry."

"Can you confirm he's there?"

"I'm sorry, ma'am, I can't do that either."

"Well, can you at least tell me if my husband is alive?"

"I'm sorry, ma'am."

Hanging up, her hand flying to her mouth, Carrie cursed under her breath, fear and anger propelling her to do the obvious. She called Clear River County Emergency. A dispatcher answered, and Carrie, her voice charged with emotion, explained the call about Luke.

"One moment," the dispatcher said amid an urgent burst of typing. "What was the time on the call you received from us?"

Carrie gave her the approximate time and the dispatcher checked. In the background, she heard radio transmissions, scratchy voices, the noise of the storm, then silence as the dispatcher came back, static weakening her voice. Carrie strained to hear, tapping the console's volume to full.

"What?" Carrie raised her voice. "Please repeat that."

"Negative. No call was made by us—"

"No, there was—"

The call dropped.

Cursing, Carrie was about to voice a redial when a wall of water splashed on her driver's side window as the car from behind passed. It cut in front of Carrie, creating a curtain of water, overwhelming her wipers. Intense tail and brake lights glared in the pall, forcing Carrie to reduce her already slow speed.

"What're you doing?" Carrie said aloud.

The car ahead switched on its hazard lights, flashing, as it continued decreasing speed, narrowing the gap between them.

Maybe something's wrong? Someone needs help, or they want to warn me that the road ahead is flooded?

She tried looking ahead, then checked her rearview mirror, unable to see clearly from the rain.

The car ahead continued slowing until its rear bumper nearly touched Carrie's, forcing her to slow to a crawl.

82

Withstanding the earsplitting growl of chain saws and the whine of a heavy-duty wood shredder, Luke watched as downed trees were reduced to chips spewed into the bed of a waiting dump truck.

One tree had fallen close enough to startle him.

Thankfully, the road crew had arrived sooner than expected, clearing the ramp quickly. Rain pelted Luke's hat and reflective safety jacket as the crew boss shouted above the roar.

"Just need to sweep!"

Workers set out with brooms. Minutes later, the boss signaled to Luke: "Good to go!"

Luke shouted his thanks.

The wind and rain remained strong, but the intensity had decreased a bit, he thought, walking back to his car.

Allowing the crew to marshal its team and head along the ramp to the next job, Luke then moved his car. Once he was parked off to the side, he got out and opened the ramp, waving traffic through. He got back into his patrol car, radioing dispatch that it was now clear.

Wiping his face, he noticed his personal phone had text messages from Carrie.

You OK?

Are you hurt bad?

On my way to the hospital.

Hospital?
His brow furrowing, he tried to catch his breath, water drip-ping onto his phone screen, his mind racing.
What's going on?
Then his car's dash-mounted monitor beeped with a text message from dispatch.

Call your wife, Luke. She called us insisting she'd been told you were injured. She also called Central, convinced you were taken there. We've been unable to call her back. Storm causing prob-lems.

He typed: 10-4. His throat tightened with tension, concern coiling in his gut. Grabbing his phone, he tried calling Carrie.
No answer.
He texted her: I'm OK. Was out of my car. Call me.
Who would have told her I was hurt?
He swiped quickly to his tracking app, glancing at her car's location. She was in Cedar Breeze. Good. But she must've been so upset by today's story. What could've happened after she went to Vern's?
All right, if he couldn't reach Carrie, he'd better try Vern. But before he could call, his phone rang—the caller ID had a Los Angeles area code. *Is it Derek?* He answered.
"Luke Conway? Carrie's husband?"
"Yes."
"Dr. Anna Bernay in Los Angeles. Is Carrie with you?"
"No, she isn't."

"Carrie gave me your number as an emergency contact. She called me with an urgent request to talk. She may have been experiencing some distress, and I cannot seem to reach her."

"How recently did she call you?"

"Half an hour or so. I was with a patient. If you see her, could you please have her call me?"

"I will."

He lowered his phone, cursing to himself, thoughts shooting in all directions.

This is bad. I should never have gone to work, should've made her talk to me.

Turning back to his phone, he glanced at his tracking app again, but he looked more closely this time.

It pulsed, showing Carrie's car was not at home but on River Road.

And it's not moving.

Had the app stopped updating? Something was wrong. He reached for his radio, raising dispatch. They stood by for his transmission.

"I need to do an emergency welfare check on River Road."

A few seconds of static passed, then: "Ten-Four."

Luke activated his lights and siren.

83

Luke's heart thudded with the panicked swiping of the wipers, his patrol car's siren howling, as he headed to Carrie's location.

Cutting across the county, his brain churning, Luke berated himself for not confronting what had befallen them.

Today's story was gasoline on the burning fire of their lives.

As the storm roiled, Luke felt all of their tragic events were converging. Siren wailing, he was moving fast, making good time along US 59. He then covered a couple miles of state highway before getting onto the narrow stretch that twisted through the countryside. He rolled through the mix of rural properties and forests, nearing the new Fawn Ridge subdivision. Rain blurred the billboards that promised a dream community for families.

Something blazed on the road across Luke's path.

Tensing, he braked.

Gusts had driven a broken branch tumbling into the ditch. Luke took a breath and resumed making his way along a gentle curve on River Road. That was when he saw it.

A single vehicle.

Carrie's Ford Escape.

On the opposite side. Parked on the shoulder, the rain making it difficult to see the interior from his angle.

Okay, take it easy.

Luke slowed. His lights strobing, he made a U-turn, pulling up on the shoulder, stopping behind his wife's SUV. He radioed dispatch with his position and status.

Getting out and walking to the car, relief washed over him as he spotted Emily in the back, strapped into her seat, her crying insulated by the car and the storm.

But with the next few steps, Luke's stomach dropped as if the ground under his feet had given way.

The front seats were empty.

He opened the passenger door to Emily's crying, the hint of Carrie's perfume. Her purse on the passenger seat.

He stood there in the rain, surveying the empty area, his pulse hammering a spike of fear deep into his gut.

84

Denise set the letter and driver's license back down on her desk slowly, as if they might explode.

She took some pictures with her phone while Lynn and the others in the *Chronicle* newsroom gathered around her, reading the message, staring at the license.

Curious, Marco reached for the items.

"Stop!" Denise said. "Don't touch them!"

Marco's hand shot back.

"Dear Lord." Kelcey covered her mouth with her hands. "Is this for real?"

"Meh. A hoax," Marco said. "A nutjob messin' with you. Probably a fake license."

Repositioning her glasses, Lynn leaned closer, studying the items. "What do you think, Denise? You know the case."

"The files listed Abby's license as one of the items the killer took from the murdered girls, possibly as a trophy."

"How did this envelope arrive?" Lynn asked.

"It was wedged in the back door," Marco said. "I brought it in this morning."

Lynn set her glasses atop her head, thinking.

"Nobody goes anywhere," Lynn said. "Don't touch anything, do anything or call anyone. I'll be right back."

She went to her office, closing the door behind her. The staff eyed each other, the license and the letter for a moment as Lynn spoke to someone on her phone.

"I still think it's fake," Marco said. "What's with the 'I am that I am' weirdo phrase?"

"It's from the Bible," Denise said. "The sender's revealing his mindset."

"What?" Marco said.

"It's from Exodus," Kelcey said. "What God told Moses."

Raising an eyebrow, Marco listened as Kelcey went on.

"Something about God's eternal, absolute existence and power over all things."

"Look at you," Marco said.

"Bible studies at my church," Kelcey said.

"All right, listen up," Lynn said, emerging from her office. "Chandler Hayes, our attorney, said we should regard this as evidence. So as not to be seen as obstructing justice, we should alert the sheriff. I'm calling Bob Ellerd."

A short time later, Detectives Mallory and Cobb arrived in the newsroom.

After asking a few initial questions, they snapped the latches of an aluminum briefcase, opened it, tugged on blue nitrile gloves and got to work.

First, they examined the message and license, making notes, their poker faces betraying nothing. They photographed the items, logging and placing them in evidence bags. They used a portable fingerprint reader to collect everyone's prints. They took photos of the newsroom, the rear door.

Then they used Lynn's office to individually question each staff member present. They went through the timeline, asked about reactions to stories about the case, whether anyone had any idea who may have sent the letter, and the status of the strip mall's security cameras.

"They were damaged in the last storm," Lynn said. "Maintenance hasn't fixed them."

When they got to Marco, he said he always came through the back. "The story got posted online at midnight. I'm the first one in at seven thirty. I park at the back for the shade. Is it a crackpot faking things?"

"We'll have to process it," Mallory said.

Questioning Denise took things to a different level for the detectives.

She knew and they knew.

The message was real. It was from the killer.

"This changes everything, doesn't it?" Denise said.

"We can't say for certain. We need to take a good hard look at everything," Mallory said.

"You know and I know, it's real. Your file lists Abby's license as missing from the murder scene—and now, after my story, it surfaces here."

"Are you planning to do a story on this?" Cobb asked.

"Absolutely."

"We can't tell you what to write, but can we ask you to hold off for a bit?" Cobb asked.

"Why?"

"Give us time to examine this, authenticate it, investigate further," Cobb said.

At that moment, Denise heard the vibrations of Mallory's and Cobb's phones. As they looked at them, she observed the near imperceptible crease at the edge of Cobb's mouth, then he traded a glance with his partner.

"We need to go," Mallory said.

"What is it? Is it related to this?" Denise asked.

"You'll find out soon enough," Cobb said.

A few long seconds later, shrugging on their jackets, the detectives thanked everyone, then left.

Kelcey's phone rang; she took the call.

"All right." Lynn clapped her hands. "We did our duty. Denise, we should discuss how to approach—"

"Excuse me!" Kelcey waved her phone. "You won't believe this! It's Paul Leeson calling, the freelance photographer I dated a few times."

"Wow, that's news," Marco said.

"He's on River Road, near Fawn Ridge. Says there's all kinds of police activity around an abandoned car, that a deputy told him it was Carrie Conway's car and she's missing!"

Lynn turned to Denise, who was pulling on her jacket and collecting her things.

"I'm on it!"

85

The horror had cleaved Luke, splitting him apart.

He was the functioning cop, albeit shaken.

But inside, the flawed, guilt-ridden, terrified husband was screaming: *My wife's missing!*

On the surface, Luke held fast to his professional calm, taking action. In the time since he'd found Carrie's car, he'd alerted dispatch, setting procedures in motion. Units arrived in an ongoing concert of sirens and lights.

Luke stood by Emily at the back of an ambulance, its doors open, paramedics assessing her. She appeared unharmed. Other deputies responded, taking Luke's initial statement, asking about Carrie's phone, whether she had a dash camera, starting a search of the area.

"No dashcam, and her phone's gone," Luke said, giving them her number. "I tried locating it, tried contacting her. Nothing. Could be off; the SIM card may have been removed. I got nothing. Try the service provider."

The rain had let up and the clouds had parted, allowing moments of sun as more resources arrived and time swept by. Carrie's car and the surrounding area were cordoned with tape, sealing it as a potential crime scene. Nonessential officers were directed to cleared areas so as not to contaminate the scene.

Traffic was detoured through the new subdivision, but as word spread, curious people parked and walked to the scene to watch what was transpiring.

Detectives Mallory and Cobb emerged to lead the investigation, taking Luke aside. He passed them his phone with Carrie's texts, indicating she was told that he'd been hurt and taken to hospital.

"I think that's where she was headed," he said. "But I was never hurt." Luke surveyed the area for the millionth time. "Someone wanted her out of the house. Who would've told her I was hurt?"

Mallory studied the texts while Cobb continued questioning Luke.

"What was her demeanor?"

"The last few days she's been struggling with her memories of the murders, and Vern's illness. I think today's *Chronicle* was the final straw."

"What do you mean?"

"Maybe she was having a breakdown," Luke said.

"In mental distress, confused?" Cobb asked.

"Yes."

"Do you think she would walk away, harm herself?" Cobb asked.

"No. I don't know. I mean, she had the baby with her. Before this happened, she tried reaching her therapist in California."

Mallory returned Luke's phone.

"Yeah, she could've been lured with a fabricated emergency," Mallory said, "to get her out of the house."

"But why? Who?" Luke asked. "Someone out for revenge because of the *Chronicle*?"

"We can't speculate," Cobb said. "Might be some other things going on."

"What *other things*?" Luke said.

Cobb threw a silent, knowing glance to Mallory. The detectives hadn't revealed that a disturbing package concerning the murders was sent to the *Chronicle*. They needed to protect their case, especially now that new elements were surfacing.

"What else do you know?" Luke demanded.

They didn't answer his question.

Mallory's phone rang, so he stepped away, taking the call. That's when Luke noticed news crews and people collecting far off behind the tape.

"Luke," Cobb said, "at this point, we don't know who, or what, has any bearing. Our priority is to find Carrie. Is there anything else you can think of that might help?"

Biting back on his bitterness, Luke nodded to the Fawn Ridge development nearby.

"Try their security cameras at the job site trailer."

Mallory ended his call and made his way back over to Luke and Cobb. "Dogs are on the way," he said. "So is support from Clear River PD, Search and Rescue."

"Good," Cobb said.

"Let's put up a drone and get a canvass going," Mallory said, indicating the distant older residences. "We'll make an appeal for any dashcam footage, although I don't think many people were out in the storm."

Cobb pointed with his chin to the TV cameras and news people. "We'll need someone to talk to the press."

"What the hell's going on?"

They turned to see Vern approaching after lifting the tape.

"Bob called me, said Carrie's missing." Vern scanned the scene, her SUV, then searched Luke's face for answers.

"She tried to reach me," Luke said. "I found her car here."

"Where the hell is she?"

"There's no sign of her," Luke said.

"Oh, my God."

"Did you see her today, Vern?" Mallory asked.

"I did. Early this morning. She came to my house. She was shattered by the story in the paper. I tried to calm her down." Vern noticed his granddaughter in the ambulance with paramedics. "Is Emily hurt?"

"No, she's okay," Luke said.

"Thank God for that." Vern felt a knot in his stomach, then said to the detectives: "What're you doing to find her?"

"Everything we can," Cobb said.

Spotting Ellerd, Vern went to him to press for more action on the search.

Mallory and Cobb huddled with arriving deputies and detectives, coordinating the canvass and search of the construction development. That's when Luke felt his burner phone vibrate in his pocket.

He stepped next to the ambulance, keeping Emily in his sight, and answered. It was Derek in LA.

"Hey, buddy," Derek said. "I got more on the missing Oklahoma woman."

"Derek, this isn't a good—"

"Only take a sec—they were arguing about money—" A bark pulled Luke's attention; a K-9 team was arriving as Derek said, "The couple had gone to a street market, she was upset about the boyfriend's spending on—"

"Derek, thanks, but it's not a good time. I gotta go."

Luke ended the call overcome with self-reproach.

Is my obsession with myself and my mishandled investigation of the woman somehow the reason we ended up here? With Carrie missing? Oh, God, what have I done?

The dog team was from Clear River PD. The German shepherd's leash clinked as Luke heard the handler, Officer Candida Stowe, explain to a deputy, "The heavy rain can hamper things. But we'll see what Caesar picks up."

Stowe let Caesar get to work, poking his snout in and around

Carrie's SUV. Vern had moved away to speak with Ellerd, but now he returned to Luke's side.

"I pushed him to do everything they can," Vern said. "DPS is bringing more people."

Luke and Vern observed Stowe and Caesar moving along the shoulder, scouring the wet ditch. Other crime scene people suited up to process Carrie's car. Ensuring they were alone, Vern turned to Luke, dropping his voice.

"What did Carrie tell you?" Vern asked.

"What do you mean?"

"After the story came out, after she saw me. What did she tell you?"

"Nothing," Luke said. "She wouldn't open up to me. She said she had to see you. Then I got called into work. We never spoke, other than her texts." He showed Vern the messages. "Looks like she was lured."

Staring at Luke's phone, expressionless, Vern nodded.

"Who would do this, Vern?"

"I don't know. I don't like this."

"I think Mallory and Cobb know something," Luke said, looking at his father-in-law, asking: "What did she tell you? You said she was shattered by the story?"

Vern looked at Luke.

"She was filled with guilt."

Luke said nothing, wondering how their lives had come to this point. Then, hearing a woman calling his name, he turned around to face the crime scene tape, where Lacey was waving to get his attention.

Luke spoke to a deputy, who allowed Lacey inside, directing her where to walk. She gave Luke and Vern hugs; then she stared in disbelief at Carrie's SUV and Luke's patrol car behind it, then Emily with the paramedics.

"I can't believe Carrie's missing."

"Did you see her today?" Luke asked.

Shaking her head, holding Luke in her gaze for a moment as if deciding how to answer him given what she knew, Lacey said, "I called her this morning about the story."

"What did she say?"

"Very little. She was very upset."

"Did she tell you where she was going?" Vern asked.

"No. I offered to come over, be a shoulder to lean on, but she declined. Later, it bothered me, and I decided to see her. That's what I was doing now, when—" She turned to the scene, the growing crowd behind the tape. "Dear Lord."

Collecting herself, Lacey looked at Emily. "Luke, do you want me to help take care of her?"

"Hold on." A crime scene tech stepped up. "No one else touches the baby until we search and swab her. In case anything was transferred to her."

"Oh," Lacey said.

"Lacey, thanks," Luke said. "But I think you should wait outside the tape for the detectives, to tell them what you know. Maybe you could help us with Emily later."

"Okay," she said before leaving.

Time ticked by. Crime scene experts continued processing Carrie's SUV. And they attempted to capture tire and foot impressions from the earthen shoulder.

Nearly two dozen trained, experienced volunteers with Search and Rescue services had arrived. Guided by deputies, they set out on strategic searches of the Fawn Ridge site, building by building, as well as the roadside, fields and forests, for any trace of Carrie.

Sheriff Ellerd came to stand with Luke and Vern. "This is a god-awful thing that's happened," he said. "The FBI is offering support. Have you received any ransom demands, anything like that?"

Luke shook his head.

"We're doing every damn thing we can to find her." Ellerd

nodded to the tape where newspeople had clustered. "I'll give them a brief statement, make an appeal for any information."

Watching Ellerd go to the makeshift podium, heaped with microphones and recorders, Luke spotted Denise Diaz from the *Chronicle*. Making eye contact with Luke and Vern, Denise gestured—she needed to talk to them.

As if we'll talk to you, Luke thought, nudging Vern.

They gave Denise the cold shoulder.

Under intense news camera lights, Ellerd provided the press a bare-bones summary. He took no questions, even though reporters peppered him, wanting to know if police would rule out any link between Carrie's disappearance and the *Chronicle*'s story.

No one in the news group was privy to the package that had been left for Denise at the *Chronicle*, allowing her to protect her bombshell exclusive.

As the media briefing wound down, Luke recognized people among the bystanders who'd turned their focus to him. There was Clara Price. Then he felt the glare of the man who lived next to Price, Raylin Nash, the guy who'd allegedly abused and threatened his ex and was the subject of a protective order. Just as Luke was wondering if he should ask the locals for help, Mallory and Cobb materialized beside him.

"Luke—" Mallory indicated the locals leaving the press conference "—you had previous interactions with Clara Price and Ray Nash, who live nearby?"

A new fear slithered up Luke's spine.

Is this how it all comes crashing down?

He swallowed.

"Yes. After I thought I saw someone in distress near here, in that storm a few weeks back. I asked if they saw anything."

Cobb and Mallory traded a quick look.

"Is there anything you're not telling us?" Cobb said.

Again, Luke swallowed.

"No."

A dog barked. Stowe returned to the detectives with Caesar. Soon, Ellerd and other deputies joined them for an impromptu status meeting.

"Given the conditions, and Caesar's work," Stowe said, "I'm confident there's no scent. Carrie likely left in another vehicle."

"A possible abduction," Cobb said. "We can't assume she'd have gone willingly, leaving her child and purse, especially if she was lured out."

"We've got nothing from Search and Rescue or the drone so far. This location is out of range of the Fawn Ridge security cameras," Ellerd said. "We'll soon be towing her SUV for further processing."

The sky thundered as a DPS helicopter flew by to help with the search.

Long after the minutes evolved into hours, Ellerd put his hand on Luke's shoulder.

"There's little you can do here, son." The sheriff nodded to Emily, now in Vern's arms. "You guys should get the baby home, wait for word there. We're going to keep working."

Luke watched the DPS chopper thudding over the area.

He watched until the sun sank and light faded, along with his hope of finding Carrie.

86

For Luke, leaving the scene on River Road was a failure like...
Los Angeles...standing over her, his hands dripping with her blood...

Carrie cannot die. Luke would never let go.

But hours had passed, and in the gloom, pulsing with emergency lights, watching Carrie's Ford loaded onto a flatbed, Luke retreated. Not to give up, but to gear up.

For the fight of his life.

Finding his wife.

By evening, the intense activity of the investigation had enveloped Luke and Carrie's home. Lacey was there, watching Emily, while Luke and Vern, their faces tense with grief, cooperated with detectives and deputies.

Amid tapping on laptops, subdued phone conversations and crackling radio transmissions, Ellerd, Mallory and Cobb directed efforts. They communicated with forensic and cyber techs, people still searching the scene, and other agencies following leads in the expanding case.

Luke had answered their questions. He knew how these situations unfolded, that a clock could be running down on Carrie's life. Guilt ate at him for Carrie, and for still not telling anyone about Joyce-Anne Gemsen. *What's wrong with me?* He had to think; he had to do something. He'd go out into the night and search for his wife.

But where should I go?

Hope pinged in the back of his mind, chiming with threads to answers—but he couldn't connect them. Not yet. He considered the location of Carrie's car, how fate had placed it near where he had struck Joyce-Anne, the missing Oklahoma woman.

His thoughts accelerated.

Something's emerging.

Luke got out his laptop, phones and notes, and withdrew to a private corner, his brain whirling. The location and his cryptic investigation had yielded the cell tower warrants and phone numbers Garth Reeger had sent him. As expected, Luke's number was there, but Reeger had said the other two numbers dead-ended. Luke scrolled through them on his phone.

I haven't even checked them yet.

Luke opened the missing person poster. Studying the array of photos, he was drawn to the still images taken of Joyce-Anne in the truck stop near Pauls Valley, Oklahoma, where she'd vanished.

Luke looked at the snack displays, the posters for events, recalling Derek's latest enthusiastic call at finding more information. *What did he say?* Prior to the truck stop, the woman and her boyfriend had gone to a street market, then argued about the boyfriend's spending.

Spending on what?

Luke's thoughts went back to the roadside press conference, seeing Clara Price and Ray Nash, the detectives asking him about previous interactions.

Is there anything you're not telling us?

And that reporter from the *Chronicle*, gesturing like she needed to talk. Luke opened up today's story, scanning it, going to the photos, to those showing Abby and Erin. Abby in the shirt her family said she wore the day she died.

It was pink.

Tapping on Luke's shoulder startled him.

He turned to Vern.

"We need to talk."

Luke closed his laptop, pocketed his phones, went with Vern to a bedroom and shut the door behind them.

"I don't know how to tell you this, so I'll just tell you."

Luke steeled himself, expecting to hear they'd found Carrie's body, listening as Vern began, revealing that he had only months to live. "Before I leave this world, I'm going to tell you the truth." Vern then related everything that he and Carrie had discussed—the truth of what had happened in Wild Pines Forest. The truth about Hyde's confession.

He'd stunned Luke.

"You're telling me, Carrie killed Abby and Erin and you covered it up; you're telling me everything in the paper today is true?"

Vern nodded. "Yes."

"No, no." Luke shook his head. "I don't believe any of what you're saying."

"This is why she blocked the memories."

"No, I can't believe this. Carrie's not a murderer."

"It might've been self-defense. And, here, now, she may have run off."

"No. She wouldn't leave Emily. Her purse was still in the car. Vern, she was lured, lured by someone smart, someone calculating."

"Or maybe she hitched a ride. Walked off. I know she was feelin' guilty and confused."

Tears welled in Luke's eyes. "No damn way I believe this, Vern."

"What I'm telling you is based on what I know. And I am tellin' you this, Luke, so you're braced and prepared for what may come—" he nodded outside "—whatever they find."

Luke gripped the side of his head, feeling like it was about to explode.

"I can't stay here."

He strode from the bedroom, headed for the front door, leaving a wake of staring investigators.

Outside, everything was slipping away.

He refused to believe what was happening—what Vern had confessed.

It can't be. It just can't be.

Luke's life was disintegrating, his world crumbling.

Flailing, falling into an abyss, he steadied himself against one of the cars parked at his home. Alone in the cool night air, his brain a firestorm of emotion, he forced himself to think.

Think.

Because the answer had to be there, somewhere—the clues were swirling and sparking like embers as the key elements blazed again.

Carrie's last location, the missing Oklahoma woman, arguing after going to a street market, security camera images, phone numbers from warrants, pink fabric, pink shirt.

Hold on.

Check the phone numbers.

The warrants had captured a number of users in the area on the night of the construction site theft, and later, on the night Luke had struck the missing woman. Reeger said they had yielded nothing.

But I never looked.

Raising his phone, Luke found the numbers Reeger had sent. There were three, including his, according to the notes from the service providers.

Luke tried the one number that was in the area the night and time of the theft from the construction site. He got a recording.

"We're sorry. You have reached a number that has been dis-connected or is no longer in service…"

That one was probably a burner that dead-ended.

The last number, a burner, according to Reeger's notes, had been captured on the date and time of Luke's incident.

Luke called it.

It connected.

He heard it ringing on the phone line, but at the same time he heard a faint ringing near him. Confused, he lowered his phone and ended the call. The faint ringing stopped.

Weird.

Sounded like it was close by; a muffled ringing coming from one of the cars parked at his house.

He tried the number again.

Again, the faint ringing started. Listening intently, Luke moved toward the sound. After the storm some people had opened their car windows.

Luke listened.

Moving among the parked vehicles, the ringing grew louder until Luke stopped at a car.

87

The ringing continued.

Luke stood transfixed.

Lacey's Mustang.

In a heartbeat, from the swirling embers of disparate facts, his mind retrieved, sorted and assembled them, making it clearer than ever.

Luke hurried into the house and got his laptop, alerting Ellerd, Vern, Mallory, Cobb and Lacey.

"You all need to come out here."

With the others gathered in the driveway, Luke began quickly but calmly conveying everything, starting by confessing how he'd hit a woman, damaging his SUV.

"I left the scene, failed to report a hit-and-run."

Eyebrows went up and faces tensed as Luke gave his reasons for embarking on his rogue investigation of Joyce-Anne Gemsen, the woman he'd struck. Showing them images and facts on his laptop, detailing how they fit together, he then called the burner phone number that the warrant had revealed.

As it rang in Lacey's Mustang, her jaw dropped.

"Hold up," Mallory said. "You're confessing to a crime no

one knows anything about, and making some kind of leap in logic. How does this prove anything?"

Nodding big nods, Luke continued.

"Before she went missing, Joyce-Anne Gemsen and her boyfriend attended a street market, otherwise known as a swap meet, near Pauls Valley, Oklahoma," Luke said. "About a six-hour drive from here."

Luke showed them the grainy construction security video of Gemsen rising from the ditch in the rain near Fawn Ridge, wearing pink. Then he told them about the pink fragment he'd plucked from his grille.

"Do you have that piece of fabric, Luke?" Mallory asked.

"No, I tossed it. But listen to me, Gemsen was here, and so was Lacey's phone, at the same time," Luke said. "I couldn't find Joyce-Anne—that's why I thought I was imagining things. But maybe she escaped and was recaptured in this Mustang here? This is how it connects."

Luke turned to Lacey.

"We were all high school kids when Abby and Erin were murdered, weren't we, Lacey? I went to Rosedale Eastern, but Carrie, you, Clay, Opal—you all went to Clear River. In fact, you and Clay were in the cafeteria that day, and you went to the Halloween party, like the story says. You and Clay were there."

Lacey began shaking her head. "I don't understand any of this, Luke."

"You said you called Carrie today; you were on your way to see her. But what if you flagged her down? She'd stop for you. Get out of her car for you."

Luke paused.

"Did the story trigger something in Carrie? Did she finally remember something about you and Clay? Did she remember the truth, Lacey? Is that why you needed to see her?" Luke nodded to the Mustang. "Did you text her from the burner phone, lure her out? What is it that she knew about you and Clay? *Where's Carrie? Where's Joyce-Anne Gemsen?*"

The eyes of the investigators fell on Lacey.

Frightened, bewildered, she brushed at tears.

"No, Luke. I don't know anything. It's Clay's car. He's out of town with his truck. Mine wouldn't start, so I took his Mustang. And it's Clay's phone, but yes, it's a burner. But he said he'd used it for undercover work, part of his applying to be a detective and stuff, and—"

"What?" Luke said.

She turned to the others. "Clay said they were watching Luke because he was acting suspiciously after he damaged his car."

Ellerd weighed in. "Clay was never undercover. And we were not watching Luke. Although, hearing what I'm hearing, maybe we should have been."

Ellerd then nodded to Mallory and Cobb.

"Lacey," Mallory said. "We need you to tell us all you know."

"This can't be happening." Her voice broke.

"Where's Clay?" Mallory said.

Lacey managed, "Baton Rouge, at a swap meet."

"We'll alert police there to pick him up," Ellerd said, "and we'll get a warrant for your car, the phone and your home, which we're going to seal as soon as possible."

Shaking her head, Lacey's voice was a whisper. "I only wanted to help…"

"As for you, Luke," Ellerd said. "We don't yet have a case against you, a victim or a scene. Only your admission. Until we sort this out, I'm going out on a limb here. You're not under arrest at this point. This is my call. I may pay for it later, but because of exigent circumstances, and what you may know to help us, we'll take you with us into investigative custody."

88

Carrie woke.

I'm alive.

She blinked, her breathing keeping time with her heart. Struggling through the weakening vertigo, she knew she'd been abducted.

How long have I been here?

Shifting on a reeking mattress, she felt a subterranean dankness. She was adjusting to the weak light seeping from the letter-sized, chest-high slot in the thick, insulated door. It resembled a mail slot and was part of a one-foot square portal in the door. The door was locked from the outside. She was confined in a room no bigger than a public bathroom stall. In one corner, packaged sandwiches, junk food and bottled water. In another, a plastic bucket with rolls of toilet paper, wipes and sanitary products.

Emily!

Scrambling to her feet, Carrie tried the solid heavy door in vain, shouldering against it. It was locked from the outside. Slapping it, placing her head to the slot, she cried out.

"Where's my baby? Help! Please!"

After pleading for several moments, Carrie listened.

The silence was absolute. No life elsewhere. Nothing. As if her small prison were isolated in a nether region. Turning, slamming her back to the door, she slid to the floor, sobbing.

Why is this happening?

She'd been abducted but didn't know by whom.

The sequence leading up to it came to her in snatches: being told Luke was hurt, putting Emily into the car, rushing toward the hospital. The storm raging, a car slowing so close in front of her, forcing her to stop on the shoulder.

Carrie had waited, the car's hazard lights flashing with urgency. Her wipers thrumming in the rain.

Then the driver's door opened.

A lone figure got out wearing a dark hooded poncho with a ball cap. The rain's intensity made it impossible to see details about them as they approached her like a specter, gesturing for Carrie to lower her driver's window.

Reasoning there might be danger ahead, or someone needed help, Carrie opened her window. Instantly, a stranger's hand thrust toward her, gripping a phone—no, not a phone—clicking, sizzling at her neck, convulsing, her muscles rendered helpless.

A Taser—she'd been Tasered.

She was taken from her car and put into the car ahead—the peel of tape, gagging her mouth, binding her wrists. A hood was placed over her head and she was immobilized, fearing for Emily. Taken prisoner in darkness, fighting to breathe against the crushing force of the tape. Driving and driving, finally stopping. Steadied, a viselike grip on her arm, blind under the hood, being guided slowly inside somewhere smelling like a gas station.

No words were spoken.

As she slowly descended steps into the cold, a door opened, the tape on her wrists was painfully removed and she collapsed on the mattress. After she'd removed the hood and her gag, she must have passed out.

Now, rubbing her mouth, the impact jolted her.

Where's Emily?

Where's Luke?

Carrie took stock. Afraid, helpless and cold, she reached for the blanket at the foot of the mattress. Tugging it, she realized it wasn't entirely a blanket.

Clothing tumbled from the folds.

A note was fixed to them.

Remove your clothes. All of them. Put these on and you will not be hurt.

Examining the clothing, Carrie saw it was worn jeans, a shirt, underwear and a bra.

She swallowed.

Looking more closely at the shirt, she noticed stains.

Dark, reddish brown.

Dried blood.

89

Trembling in a dreamlike trance, Carrie dressed in the blood-stained clothes.

Foul, ill fitting, they felt wrong against her skin. Shuddering with waves of revulsion and horror, she was stabbed with a question.

What happened to the woman who owns these clothes?

Fearing she might never see Emily again, Carrie choked back a sob, then froze.

A tiny, weak noise sounded in the darkness.

She turned to her door, moved her head to the slot. Holding her breath, she listened with every fiber of her being. Seconds slipped by, then, finding its way out of the gloom like a wounded animal stumbling from the forest, the noise came again. Faint, pained.

"Hello…" The soft voice of a younger woman.

"Hello?" Carrie responded, louder, stronger.

"Can you get me out of here?" the voice begged. The voice broke into a rasping sob. "Please!"

"Where are you?"

"Locked in a room."

"Me, too. I'm Carrie, who are you?"

"Joyce-Anne." She sniffed; her voice got stronger. "Joyce-Anne Gemsen. I'm from Oklahoma City."

Oh, God, Carrie thought, her heart racing.

"What happened, Joyce-Anne? Where are we?"

"I don't know."

Joyce-Anne sobbed. Carrie did, too, thinking of Emily.

"I was with Dylan, my boyfriend," Joyce-Anne struggled to say, "at a swap meet in Pauls Valley. He bought a car part with the two grand that we'd saved for our wedding. We fought about it. I stomped out of the truck stop to the highway. I'd had some tequila, a little pot, and I wasn't thinking. I was so pissed at Dylan. I was stupid. But pretty soon I wanted to go back. I waved down a car, never got a good look at the driver, but he was nice, at first. Said he saw us in the truck stop diner and he'd take me back.

"The liar kept driving. I told him to take me back, but he reaches over and I felt this shock at my neck. My body spasmed, then I couldn't move. He put me in the back, under a blanket, taped me up. He drove and drove and drove. I was in and out of consciousness. At one point he stopped, took my shirt and forced me to wear another shirt, a pink one. Maybe to disguise me. I don't know. When I struggled, he shocked me again. He was rough about it, a freak. We drove and drove again. I was angry. I wanted to fight back. I was loosening my bindings. When I got free, I jumped out. God, it hurt. I've never been so scared. It was raining. I ran right into another car. I flew over it, hurt my head, legs, ribs. It was so painful, but I was out of my mind. I crawled from the ditch, ran down the road, praying for a car to help but—but—"

"It's okay, take a breath, it's okay."

"The car that stopped was him again. Now I'm here. I don't know how long it's been. God, we've got to get out!"

"Okay, okay. Where are we?"

"In Hell."

"Joyce-Anne, who is he?"

A long moment passed.

"He calls himself 'The Other,' and his voice is chilling. He's a monster, makes me wear clothes of dead women, saying it cleanses my spirit, prepares me—" She paused, before a terrified whisper. *"He does things to me."*

A sharp noise from above, metal clanking on metal.

"He's coming!"

90

Carrie heard movement like someone descending the stairs, then a shuffling.

Close, very close.

Suddenly the small square portal was unlocked and opened.

Light beyond it brightened.

Moving nearer to the portal with trepidation, Carrie discerned a figure, sending a new bolt of fear through her. The figure was wearing a black hood—the top was four-corner square, like a box, like an executioner's hood. It draped down over their chest and back. Arms in long sleeves, hands in black gloves.

Adjusting her focus, Carrie saw across to the other portal, opened to Joyce-Anne's face, webbed with matted hair. Not believing the outrage of it all, Carrie seethed and exploded.

"Where's my baby? Let us go! We can't identify you! Unlock the door, walk away, let us go!"

The figure turned to Carrie.

A long moment passed, followed by some movement, digital clicking.

A low, robotic, monotone voice, sounding like the personification of doom, filled the space. Carrie knew the person must be using a voice changer—she glimpsed the small box of an amplifier clipped to their chest.

"You wish to be freed?" the voice said.

"We can't identify you."

A long moment passed.

"Where's my baby?" Carrie's sobbing overtook her. "Please, let me see my baby, my father, my husband again. Let us go, you have the power."

"I will release both of you. You have my word."

Joyce-Anne squeaked with a sob of disbelieving hope.

"You will?" Carrie said.

"I will release you to begin your journey."

"Thank you—" Joyce-Anne shook, trembling "—thank you."

The figure slammed the portal doors.

"I will release you into eternity."

91

In the hours that followed, the sheriff's department, supported by Clear River police and DPS, began pulling together a joint-forces operation.

They set up a command post in the corner of the Clear River Mall parking lot, which was messy with tree limbs and debris scattered by the storm.

For her part, Lacey, who hadn't been arrested, was helping investigators, but insisted her attorney be present.

Still, efforts to locate Clay—by his phone, by security cameras near the Baton Rouge swap meet, and by his bank or credit cards—had been unsuccessful. A check of the motel where he was supposed to have stayed turned up nothing. A check for new social media postings concerning Clay, or the swap meet, yielded nothing.

A bulletin identifying Clayton Smith as a person of interest had been issued, alerting law enforcement in Louisiana and Texas.

By midmorning an unmarked police vehicle, posing as a wireless repair truck cleaning up after the storm, was sent to watch the Smith residence. In Clear River County, investigators awaited the warrants needed to search the Smith property and seize any evidence. To expedite the process, they stressed a life-and-death situation, otherwise, exigent circumstances.

When the warrants came, the sheriff's team, along with Clear River SWAT and DPS, started rolling in a convoy to the property. One of the vehicles at the rear was Ellerd's, and he'd allowed Vern and Luke to observe and possibly assist.

Deputies and a nurse had been assigned to stay with Emily at Luke's house.

As the police vehicles progressed through the edge of town, Luke saw how the storm's strength was evinced in the aftermath of toppled trees, broken windshields and damaged roofs. Traffic was moderate. Along the way, they met pickups, some with fractured windshields; a flatbed tow truck transporting a vehicle; service trucks and the heavy equipment of road crews clearing downed branches.

Adrenaline pulsated through Luke. He hadn't slept, his insides vibrating and nerves tingling. He was certain Carrie hadn't killed anyone.

Now, as they neared the property where Clay and Lacey had welcomed them as a colleague and friends, he feared a looming horror.

Luke had no more answers.

All he had left were prayers.

92

The Smith house filled the binoculars of Clear River's SWAT commander.

Lacey's Cadillac was out front. Broken tree limbs and leaf-laden branches were strewn about the driveway and yard.

The binoculars then found a Ford F-150 near the house, indicating, as the undercover scouting van had reported earlier, that Clay appeared to have returned from Baton Rouge.

Out of sight were SWAT members of the first squad, concealed in positions tight to the house. The focus followed along the narrow paved roadway, twisting through the pine woods, where a few small trees had snapped, finding the garage and exterior carport.

The binoculars swept back to the house.

The subject—who many knew personally—possessed firearms and was to be considered dangerous. The commander made a final round of radio checks before green-lighting the first squad to move on the house, executing a forced rapid entry.

In seconds, team members slammed through the front, back and side entrances, weapons at the ready, moving tactically from room to room. Closets and storage spaces were checked; so were ceilings and walls, for body mass.

"Nothing here," the squad sergeant radioed the commander, who turned to Luke and Vern. "House is clear. We'll hit the outbuildings now."

At that moment, the second squad's sergeant issued a dispatch on the radio.

"We have movement."

Clay Smith exited his garage.

Leaving all the doors open, he stepped around fallen limbs to examine the cars he kept in the exterior carport for possible damage. The storm had tossed branches up on the vehicles.

In a heartbeat, heavily armed SWAT members materialized, putting Clay face down on the ground at gunpoint.

"Hey! Hey! What the f—!"

Clay was handcuffed, patted for weapons and read his rights.

"Is this a joke?"

Mallory and Cobb emerged, along with a surge of deputies and officers, who began a search. A drone was launched to examine the property from the air. Clay, hands secured behind his back, spotted Ellerd, Luke and Vern among those gathering at the scene.

"Bob, what is this? Some kinda drill? What the hell?"

"Look at me," Mallory said. "Do you know the whereabouts of Carrie Conway and Joyce-Anne Gemsen?"

"Why would I know that?"

"We spoke to Lacey. This isn't the time to obstruct us—you should cooperate."

"Cooperate with what?"

"Account for your whereabouts in the last twenty-four hours?"

"I was in Louisiana. I just got home from a swap meet in Baton Rouge."

It wasn't long before the investigators had obtained keys to all the vehicles on the property. Clay glanced around at deputies searching the cars in the carport, then the Nomad in the garage. Craning his neck and squinting, he saw others searching Lacey's Cadillac and his pickup parked at the house. Through the pine trees, Clay saw them search around his pool. Others were combing the woods.

"You got warrants?"

"What do you think? You want to cooperate?"

"Go for it. I got nothing to hide." Clay then stared at Luke, and his eyes narrowed. "I'll tell you this: if there's anyone you should be looking at, it's him." Clay stuck his chin out toward Luke. "Ask him why his car's damaged."

"Where's Carrie?" Luke said.

Clay shook his head, eyeballing the others. "You believe this guy?" Then to Luke, "Didn't you kill someone in LA? Then your daddy-in-law gets you hired on here, where you act like you got something to hide."

Luke swallowed.

"I've been watching you ever since you got here, Luke."

As radios crackled with updates, a deputy stepped from the garage, where Clay's prized Chevy Nomad had been searched.

"Nothing so far."

Clay's smirk faded when the dog team, Candida Stowe and Caesar, came forward. Earlier, Luke had given them Carrie's shirt for a scent. Caesar went directly to the garage.

Tail wagging, snout poking here and there, Caesar circled the Chevy Nomad, then yipped. Stowe turned to the investigators: "Can we move this car?"

The car was moved from the pristine garage, revealing two floor plates, each about the size of a coffin lid.

Caesar barked, sniffing the plates. Stowe hefted them open to a grease pit, like those in auto shops. It was a narrow trench over which a car is driven to be serviced. Caesar moved down the stairs, his yelping echoing as Stowe followed, disappearing from view.

A few seconds passed. Then there was the sound of clunking, a squeak and thudding, then Stowe saying, "We've got something here!"

The others started for the pit before Ellerd stopped them.

"We don't want to contaminate anything further." Then he yelled to Stowe. "Take a video!"

"Carrie!" Luke cried out.

There was no response.

Stowe surfaced with Caesar, phone in hand, investigators huddling around her with somber expressions as they viewed two cell-like cubicles, each containing a mattress, bucket and food.

Otherwise, the rooms were empty.

93

Carrie woke in darkness with loud droning in her ears.

Surfacing to consciousness, remembering.

Her prison door opening.

Her hooded captor charging in, clapping a damp, pungent, sweet-smelling cloth over her face. Twisting, struggling, until she passed out.

Now, awake and still a prisoner, her mouth was taped again, making it hard to breathe through her nose in the stifling heat. The air reeked of rubber, oil and gas. She was on her side, sweating, face pressed into a hard, foul carpet, shoulders aching, hands taped behind her.

The heat.

Back-to-back, crammed in with another body.

Joyce-Anne.

Humming of wheels.

Carrie believed they were locked in a trunk and were moving.

Being transported.

Jostling, Carrie felt Joyce-Anne's trembling fingers, brushing hers, squeezing hers. Carrie squeezed back, offering comfort, which was acknowledged by a weak groan.

Are we being taken to our deaths?

Their captor's words echoed in Carrie's mind.

I will release you into eternity.

And his appearance, wearing the dark hood of an executioner.

I've seen that hood before.

In her father's study, in his textbooks on homicides and serial crimes, she'd seen a sketch of the Zodiac Killer, the unidentified murderer in the San Francisco area over half a century ago, who was never found. He'd worn a black executioner's hood, according to a surviving victim.

And Carrie's captor, his voice changer, his robotic menacing speech—that was familiar, too. With her body aching, sweating against Joyce-Anne's, she started to remember. All of it... the hood...the soulless machinelike voice...unlocking...like changing a channel...recovering memory...

"Meet us...absolute secrecy... It's about your dad." But Carrie *doesn't trust them...so before going to the woods, she takes a Glock from Dad's collection...hides it in the pocket of her big pullover hoodie... Meeting them at the edge of the woods...walking into the forest...only the three of them...*

"Why are we here?"

Abby and Erin are anxious.

"A guy at the party swore the body of some girl, a runaway from San Antonio, is here," Abby tells her.

"Murdered!" Erin says. "I'm trembling a little."

Traveling deeper, branches tug at Carrie's sweater.

"Murdered?" Carrie's tone is full of disbelief. "This is nuts. There's nothing here."

"He swore we'd find her in here," Erin says.

"Just call the police," Carrie says. "I don't like this."

"I know it's scary," Abby says.

"So scary," Erin adds.

"But let's be brave, witness it first for ourselves?" Abby says.

"Why would you want to do that?"

"If it's true, then we tell your dad, which is why you're here as our witness," Erin says.

"If it's true," Abby says, "then we'll be like heroes, and everyone will want to hang out with us."

"That's what this is about? To be more popular?" Carrie halts. "You ever think why this guy would tell you this? If it's true, why would he tell you? It's nuts."

"Well, if he's lying, nobody knows we got hoaxed. It's not like they'd believe you, Narc," Abby says, stopping at the spot where long ago lightning had split a tree, turning it into something of a Wild Pines landmark.

Erin and Abby survey the area.

Nothing. No body.

"Guess it was a joke," Erin says.

Suddenly, in her broiling stinking prison, Carrie spasmed, the worst memories hurtling to her...it is no joke...there he is, approaching them from behind a tree...wearing the big black executioner's hood... Abby laughing... "Oh, very funny! You're the guy from the Halloween party... Ain't no bodies here..."

Standing before them...a robotic voice crackling... "There will be."

"What? What is this, really?" Erin says. "It's a joke."

Standing...staring...the emotionless voice crackling..."I serve The Other." His hand, half-hidden behind him...he's raising his arm... aiming his gun...stepping closer...so fast...

Abby turns to run but he shoots her...she drops to the ground...

Erin screams...and in a swift sweep the killer recovers the shell casing... Erin turns, flees, but he fires and she goes down...

Carrie remembers her gun...clawing for it...running, fumbling... hearing more shots...she drops the gun... Running through the woods... running for her life...the ground under her vanishing...she's in the air... falling... The river swallows her and she's flailing...fighting for air in the violent current, bouncing between the rocks...smashing her head... Waking in the hospital...her father looking down at her...

Carrie had found the truth.

Dad got it wrong.

She'd remembered it all.

I didn't kill Abby and Erin.

It was the hooded monster who killed them.

And now he's going to kill us.

Tears and sweat rushing down her face, Carrie thought of Emily. She'd lose her mother. She thought of Luke and the pain that would visit him. She thought of her father. She'd never get to say goodbye.

She'd die with the world thinking she was a murderer protected by her father—her dying father.

Sobbing softly, she began praying...

Now and at the hour of our death...

94

Clay held Mallory and Cobb with a gaze as cold as a headstone.

Hands still cuffed behind him, leaning against a police vehicle, his eyes were vacant, as if he'd left for another world.

The detectives had taken him aside, pressing him hard for answers. Minutes slipped away. How long had they been at this? They were losing time.

"Did you hear me?" Cobb motioned to the garage. "Why do you have confinement rooms?"

"Who was imprisoned?" Mallory said. "Where are they?"

Clay gave them a slight grin.

"Those rooms are my underground shelter. Safe space in preparation for catastrophe."

"No!" Cobb said. "No more bullshit."

Clay nodded slowly. "I will exercise my right to remain silent and request to have an attorney present."

Mallory and Cobb turned to Ellerd, Vern and Luke, who were watching at a distance but close enough to hear. Clay's response detonated Luke's emotions. Swelling with anger, he rushed at Clay.

"Where's Carrie?" he yelled in his face. "Where is she?"

Luke's body arched in the grip of the others holding him back while he shouted. "Where is she? You sick—"

Clay remained silent.

Aided by deputies, Ellerd and Vern pulled Luke away, back farther than before. Luke doubled over, heaving deep, ragged breaths.

Did he kill her? How can this be real?

Looking over at law enforcement teams undertaking the investigation, he saw Stowe and Caesar continuing to work the scene. Luke knew by the dog's reaction that Carrie had been held here.

Underground in that tomb.

His heart pounding, Luke stood straight. Pressing his clenched hands to his forehead, his thoughts were like fireworks, shooting in a million points of light.

We're this close.

In desperation, he looked at Clay's garage, the carport, then the garage again with the confinement cells connected to the pit.

Grease pit.

Raylin Nash had a grease pit. Luke thought harder. Nash had a tow truck. *Orange.* They'd seen a tow truck on their way to Clay's. *Orange.* Luke looked at the carport. When Luke last visited, Clay had six cars in the carport. Now there were five. The tow truck had a car on the flatbed. Luke's heart jumped.

Oh God! That's it!

He flew to Ellerd, Vern, Cobb and Mallory, pulling them away.

"It's the tow truck!"

Not understanding, puzzled, Cobb said, "The tow truck?"

Luke spoke fast and clearly. "On our way in, I glimpsed a tow truck going in the opposite direction."

"Yeah, an orange one," Mallory said.

"With a car on the bed, an old blue Dodge, I think," Luke said.

"A Challenger. I saw it. Definitely a Challenger," Mallory said. "I figured it was storm-related."

Luke shook his head at the theory.

"No. Raylin Nash has an orange tow truck. It was his." Luke pointed to the carport. "Clay's missing one of his cars. Nash was hauling it. That's where he put Carrie."

Raising his phone, Ellerd made two calls, speaking quickly. Then, to the others, he said, "We've got people in the area, moving on Nash's place for the truck. Stand by."

His heart thudding, Luke tried to breathe evenly as he watched people working at the garage, taping it off, forensic people suiting up. Still others searched the woods while a drone flew overhead. Far down the road, blocked by patrol cars, he caught the flash of TV camera lights, where news trucks and media people had collected.

Luke's jaw muscles tensed as he glared at Clay in the distance, thinking back to their first conversations. Clay's fascination with killers who were never caught. Now this nightmare, this revolting reality—*with Carrie's life!*

Ellerd's phone rang, and after a short conversation, he gave everyone an update. "Nash is not on his property. No sign of the truck or the Dodge. We'll put out an alert."

95

Harris County deputy Nora Silva came out of the restroom at McDonald's and went to the counter.

This was her meal break, but she had little time. She was on her fourth straight shift of stressful never-ending days, patrolling her district at metro Houston's northeast edge.

She needed coffee.

While waiting, her radio sounded an audio tone alert. Silva slid in her earpiece, focused on the call.

It was a general broadcast arising out of Clear River County. An alert for a Ram 5500 flatbed tow truck, orange, likely transporting a 1970s blue Dodge Challenger. Subject linked to a kidnapping. Details to follow.

Silva grabbed a muffin with her coffee, got into her marked white Ford Police Interceptor and consulted her computer. The alert subject was Raylin Thurman Nash, a person of interest in the disappearance of Carrie Conway, spouse of Clear River County deputy Luke Conway. Arrest on sight. Subject considered dangerous. His face appeared with his driver's license, and she checked other details.

Wow, Silva thought just as her personal phone vibrated. She looked at the latest text, new info about her sister's upcoming wedding in Las Vegas. Husband number two. *Hope this one's a sure bet*, Silva thought, smiling.

Break was over. Back to work.

Rolling out of McDonald's, Silva was keeping the alert in the forefront, but she had calls to handle. She headed to a follow-up on a burglary. A little community outreach. Stopped at an intersection, she bit into her muffin and took a hit of coffee, then did a double take.

What is that?

An orange flatbed tow truck, moving in the direction of the highway ramp, sped in front of her. An older blue car on the bed.

"No way! Is this my guy?"

Turning right, Silva accelerated, pulling close to read the truck's driver's side door, RTN Towing, Clear River.

"Jackpot."

Silva dropped behind the truck and alerted dispatch, activating her emergency lights and siren. The truck kept going.

"Don't make me chase you," Silva said aloud. "Stay off the ramp." The truck pulled over. "Good choice."

The driver appeared to be the sole occupant.

Calling in her location and status, Silva got out.

Approaching the truck, keeping to the left rear, hand on her weapon, she ordered the driver to shut off the motor, extend his hands out the window, open the door from the exterior and exit.

Silva drew her sidearm, aiming it at the driver's door.

The driver complied and Nash—*yes, he matches the license photo*—stepped out wearing a black T-shirt emblazoned with a large grinning skull.

"On your stomach, hands behind your back."

Nash, who had tattooed arms and a stubbled face, eyed Silva.

"Excuse me?" he said. "What did I do?"

"On your stomach," Silva repeated from behind her gun.

"Was I speeding, Officer?"

"Get down. Now!"

The sirens of approaching HCSO units grew louder.

Nash sneered, then did as she'd instructed. Silva handcuffed him, patted him for weapons, found his wallet and confirmed his ID. Helping him to his feet, she read him his rights. She locked him in the secure rear seat of her car.

"What did I do?" Nash said over the patrol car's radio sputtering transmissions. "Is it my ex? Because I'm late with a payment? Tell her I got the money."

Other units, including those from HPD, arrived and Silva joined them. Amid flashing lights and a symphony of radio dispatches, Nash watched. They rummaged inside the cab of his truck. Some crawled under it. Others climbed up onto the bed and searched the car. A pry bar was passed up to a deputy, who popped the trunk. After scrutinizing the trunk's interior, he shook his head.

"Empty."

"Hey, this is a Plymouth!" someone shouted, examining the front. "A Barracuda, not a Challenger!"

At the same time, Nash's thoughts flipped back to a new stream of dispatches flowing from Silva's radio.

"… HCSO…to Clear River County…seeks confirmation… suspect vehicle of kidnap hostage…transported in tow truck… stand by…"

Kidnap?

"…confirmed…1974 Dodge Challenger…blue…from Smith residence…"

Hostage?

Stunned, Nash tensed. He didn't want this. He hadn't asked for this. His breathing quickened, trying to figure out what to do. Whatever he decided, he had to do it fast.

Silva was coming back to the car.

She got in the front and turned to him, holding up a phone that was recording.

"You're still under Miranda—now we need—"

"I'll tell you what I know if I can make a deal."

96

Death was certain.

Either from the extreme heat of their metal prison, or other means. Salty sweat stung Carrie's eyes.

Prayers were futile. *Take action.*

Never surrender. Never give up.

I will not let this hellhole be my coffin.

Long before the thrumming had ceased, she fought back. Contending with the bumping and shaking as they traveled, Carrie scrambled for Joyce-Anne's bound wrists, feeling for the duct tape binding. Using her fingernails, Carrie scraped at the tape, probing for the end.

Drenched in sweat, battling dehydration and heat exhaustion, she scratched the tape, searching.

It became impossible as they slowed onto a rough road that had them jarring and jogging. Then they stopped, and the humming was replaced with the overwhelming mix of hydraulic grinding, roaring, squeaking and clanking.

But Carrie refused to give up.

Reaching down deep, she continued picking at the tape until—*finally*—she found the end.

Slowly she worked, her wet fingertips slipping, gaining more until she had a few inches. Tensing, she gave it a sharp jerk and tug.

Amid the clamor came the first peel of the tape being unwound.

Hope soared.

Working faster, she uncoiled Joyce-Anne's wrists. Joyce-Anne, in turn, helped free Carrie's hands. They pulled the tape from their mouths. Gasping, contorting, shifting and twisting, they freed their ankles.

Suddenly the hydraulic groaning grew louder—*nearer.* Their dark world quaked with the tremble of metal crunching. Something cracked. A seam of daylight creased their prison as they ascended, screaming for their lives. But their pleas were lost in the thunderous noise.

They were lowered.

Movement ceased.

The uproar around them continued as they kicked, pushed and banged against the walls of their prison.

97

Luke ached for Carrie.

He'd clasped his hands behind his head, pulled his elbows together in an effort to ease his torment, as he waited at Clay's garage for an update out of Harris County.

We're losing time.

Investigators continued processing and searching Clay's property. Down the winding lane, more news crews had arrived. They sought an official briefing. Speculation was swirling online, and media helicopters thundered overhead—one landed at a clearing nearby, picking up a news team.

Against it all, Luke heard Mallory's phone ring. The detective answered, keeping the phone pressed to his ear, a palm covering his other ear, nodding, asking a few quick questions. When he ended the call, he turned to Cobb, Ellerd, Vern and Luke.

"Nash delivered a Challenger in the Houston area. On the way back, he picked up a Barracuda and was hauling it to Clear River."

"What about Carrie?" Luke asked.

"No other details yet."

"Where in Houston?" Ellerd asked.

"They're texting me the location." Mallory's phone chimed. "Got it! We have the address. Everyone's moving on it now. Let's go!"

98

Bill Hardy concentrated on his job in the air-conditioned cab of his thirty-five-ton excavator.

The behemoth's 500-horsepower diesel engine roared as Bill pivoted his machine. Deftly handling the controls with the skill of a surgeon, he lowered the claw, closing its jaws on an Audi, plucking it like a toy from the yard.

This was a step in a process continually replayed at Green Auto Revivers, a salvage and recycling company at Houston's edge. A large operation, it stretched over dozens of acres. Ranges of neatly stacked, flattened and cubed cars towered alongside various heaps of components, all rising like latter-day monuments in a graveyard. But Bill saw it as a place of rebirth because the metal was shredded, then processed to be used in new cars or appliances.

This Audi could be someone's new fridge soon.

Keeping it in the claw, swaying gently, like a baby in a cradle, Bill swung the Audi toward the baler. Carefully, he lowered it into the steel-walled compression box, large enough to hold two cars.

Then he turned to another control console in his cab, tapping it to begin the command sequence. With a loud, smooth, hydraulic groan, the massive thick steel door cover lowered slowly, until the Audi was swallowed. Bill then engaged the main push cylinder and side push cylinder, applying more than four hundred tons of synchronized compression. The Audi's death throes came in a cacophony of crunching and snapping.

In less than a minute, a metal bale, in the shape of a cube, about four-by-four feet, was pushed out of the press box, ready for stacking and, later, shredding.

Bill reached for his thermos, enjoying ice-cold lemonade, and thought about the roll of cash in his pocket from Ray, his pal from Clear River.

Ray had come to the yard earlier today with a rush job.

Bill looked over at the blue Challenger Ray had hauled in. Drained and stripped, ready to go. Ray insisted it be processed today after paying Green Auto's recycling fee.

"I might not get to it. I got a backlog," Bill had told him.

"I need it to go today." Ray put six hundred dollars in Bill's hand. "Off the books."

"Was it used for drugs from the border?" Bill joked, then saw that Ray wasn't smiling.

"Do it today."

Bill stuffed the money in his pocket and grinned. "I think we can manage, partner."

Bill replaced the top on his thermos, then wiped his mouth. His backlog done, he moved on to the Challenger. Diesel growling, his excavator approached where he'd staged it after unloading it earlier that day from Ray's truck. Bill noticed that he'd creased the rear when he first moved it.

I musta been a tad overzealous with Ray's deal. Not that it matters now. Bill chuckled to himself.

Because now, manipulating the controls, he lowered the claw, the jaws clamping tight around the Challenger, hoisting it and turning smoothly. The diesel whined, and the excavator's tracks clanked as Bill guided it to the baler, the Challenger rocking gently in the jaws of the claw.

Positioned at the baler, Bill eased the Challenger into the steel compression box. Moving to the control console, he initiated the sequence. With an earsplitting hydraulic groan, the steel door cover began lowering over the Challenger, until it disappeared. As Bill engaged the main push and side cylinders, he glimpsed flashing lights in his periphery.

Police vehicles materialized, converging on the excavator, sirens wailing with the grinding and crack-snapping of the Challenger being compressed as the sequence completed.

"Shut it all down now!" a voice commanded from a bullhorn. A police helicopter hovered above, news choppers close behind.

Bill cut the power to his excavator and the baler as everything unfolded with furious urgency. Officers swarmed the yard, scanning and searching vehicles. Police ordered him from his cab at gunpoint, handcuffing him, patting him down, reading him his rights.

Stunned, Bill looked to the distance, saw the panic-stricken faces of his boss and his boss's boss, the white shirt and tie managers, running from the office toward him.

Then an officer got in Bill's face. "Where's the blue Challenger that was delivered today?"

Emerging from the group were law enforcement people from Clear River. They encircled Bill, demanding, "Where're the women?"

"Women? What?"

"Where's the Challenger from Clear River?"

Swallowing hard, Bill pointed his chin at the metal cube that had been disgorged from the baler.

A dog team was brought in, working hastily as news helicopters recorded the scene from overhead.

The German shepherd sniffed around the entire cube, which was still warm to the touch. A liquid substance trickled down the tangles of one side. Tail wagging, the dog barked. The handler turned, nodding soberly at the indication of a human presence in the brick of metal.

Staring in disbelief, the earth trembled under Vern's feet. Choking back a breath, wiping tears from his eyes, he looked to Luke beside him.

He wasn't there.

Overwhelmed with an aching terror, Luke had fallen to his knees, confusion and horror filling his face.

Raising his head to heaven, he screamed out.

"CARRIE!"

Luke's cry lifted skyward, into the whipping winds of the helicopters, his agony captured by news cameras pulling in for dramatic footage.

One chopper, with a Houston network affiliate, had flown over Clay Smith's property, where it picked up a crew. The TV reporter invited Denise Diaz, who knew the most about the story, to ride with them to Houston.

Flying from Clear River to Harris County, the journalists, using a combination of sources, texts and an onboard police scanner, kept up with the unfolding drama. The unbelievable sequence was clear—police feared Carrie and Joyce-Anne Gemsen, a missing Oklahoma woman, had been abducted, held hostage, then bound in a vehicle transported to Houston to be crushed and shredded.

Now, circling the scene above Green Auto Revivers, the TV reporter stared at their camera's small screen.

"Did you hear the scanner?" he said as their camera pulled in on Luke. "It's horrifying!"

Her hands and the chopper making for a jittery view, Denise, using binoculars, studied the scene of Luke on his knees near the cube, as police transmissions indicated Carrie and Joyce-

Anne had been killed. Bouncing suddenly, Denise's view shifted and she glimpsed movement at the base of a rust-colored heap.

"Hey!"

Focusing, steadying, Denise clearly saw two people—*two women*.

"Hey! It's them!"

She alerted the others. The camera operator locked on to them, going live.

Carrie and Joyce-Anne, stumbling, staggered out of the wreckage, clothes filthy, remnants of tape trailing, stepping toward investigators, who rushed to them.

Paramedics steadied and comforted Joyce-Anne.

Luke took Carrie into his arms.

They held each other for a long time, and Carrie, in his embrace, reached for Vern, squeezing his hand before moving to hug him as hard as she could.

99

With Luke holding her hand, Emily toddled to the door, peeking into Carrie's room at Rose Stone Hospital.

Seeing her daughter from her bed, Carrie blossomed with joy.

"Hi, sweetie!"

Carrie opened her arms and lifted Emily into them, rocking her in a tearful hug.

"Oh, sweetie. I love you so much!"

It was now evening. Earlier, Carrie had been treated for shock, dehydration and exhaustion, among other issues. But she was doing well. Medical staff wanted to keep her overnight for observation. Luke moved a chair close to her bed.

He caressed Emily's back as Carrie spoke, a trembling hand covering her mouth.

"He wanted to kill us. We were friends. *We were in their home.* How could Lacey not know?"

Luke stroked his wife's hair.

In the time after the horror ended, Carrie had talked to Mallory and Cobb, who'd indicated Clay had trapped her in the underground confinement rooms, which had been partially insulated to muffle screams. Investigators from Harris County,

DPS and the FBI had crowded into her room at various points, and she had told them everything.

Now Carrie searched Luke's face with a new understanding, seeing him differently.

"They told me what you did."

"I'm sorry I kept things from you, from everyone."

"They said it was because of you that they were able to stop Clay, that you put it all together just in time."

When a knock sounded at the door, they both turned. Vern was holding his hat in his hands.

Luke stood. "I'll give you some time."

"No," Vern said. "Stay."

"Please, take the chair."

Groaning as he sat, his voice barely above a whisper, he said, "I thank God we didn't lose you."

Carrie reached for his hand.

"It's clear that I've been wrong about that day."

Carrie clasped his hand tighter.

"I mean, dammit. Clay? He lived two lives. He wasn't even a cop when it started. But all this was going on right under our damned noses. Maybe I had blinders on, maybe because I was thinking of you. I don't know," Vern said. "I'm so sorry, Carrie, for all you've been burdened with for all these years." Shaking his head, he swallowed at the ugliness of their hard years. "I pray you're free from it now."

Carrie gave him a weak smile.

"What I did was wrong," Vern said. "I was protecting you, but I broke the law. I'll face the consequences, set things right, before I leave this world."

"Daddy." Carrie pulled him to her and Emily.

100

Leaving Carrie's room, Luke went down the hall to talk with investigators. Some were from Oklahoma.

He wanted to speak with Joyce-Anne. He'd learned that while Clay had held her captive, he'd sexually assaulted her several times. Arlo Gemsen, a barrel-chested man, stepped into the hall from his daughter's room. After a quick introduction, Gemsen, eyes burning with anger and sadness, looked Luke over.

"So, you worked with Clay Smith and you never knew he was a monster?"

Luke absorbed the question like a deserved gut punch that winded him mentally. Forces of nature, he thought. For Gemsen's question was as crystalline as lightning, but the answer, as elusive as a falling star.

"No, sir. No one knew."

"And you struck my daughter with your car, then left the scene?"

"Yes, sir. It's complicated, but yes, sir, I did."

Gemsen pushed down on the emotions seething in him, thought for a few seconds, nodded, then went back into Joyce-Anne's room for a moment.

Then he returned.

"Okay, she'll hear you out."

Small lacerations laced Joyce-Anne's face; her hair was pulled into a ponytail with a pink scrunchie. An IV tube was fixed to her left arm. Her mother, Katherine, sat in the chair beside her. Luke noticed a Bible on the bedside table.

After introducing himself, Luke related everything he'd done to find Joyce-Anne after the night of the accident.

"I'm sorry for hitting you and leaving without reporting it," Luke said. "We might have found you sooner."

Joyce-Anne and her parents were silent until her mother said, "If you had acted faster, Deputy Conway, and did the right thing from the start, we wouldn't have come this close to losing her."

Luke swallowed hard.

"I'm sorry for all of it."

Joyce-Anne put her scraped hands together, touching her fingertips to her lips. Eyes welling, she nodded.

Arlo Gemsen indicated the door. "You can leave now. This is not easy for us."

101

Several days later, Lacey pulled her rented car into the parking lot of the Clear River County Detention Center.

She sat behind the wheel, staring at the stone-and-brick building.

Ever since Clay's arrest, she hadn't slept. Her world was a hurricane of shock, anger, pain and confusion.

For nearly two days Cobb and Mallory had questioned her, as if she were somehow involved. With her attorney, she co-operated, even submitted to a polygraph. Eventually cleared of suspicion, Lacey was not charged. But she was not allowed back into her home while it was being processed for evidence.

It didn't matter—she never wanted to return.

Ever.

They couldn't confirm how many women Clay had killed over the years she'd known him.

Over the years she'd loved him.

Fate had lifted a rock, revealing that the man she'd given her heart to since high school was a miscreation.

The Texas deputy serial killer.

That's how the Dallas and Houston press served it up.

TV news cameras and reporters were everywhere.

Sarah Curtis, one of the women who worked for Lacey, took her in, helped her buy what she needed, helped her make arrangements for moving on. Then word got to Lacey, through her lawyer, that Clay had requested she visit him in jail.

Now, as she sat in the parking lot, with no media in sight, memories rushed through her: high school, their wedding, her first store, Clay making deputy. At the same time, she imagined the terror of the women he'd abducted and held prisoner on their property.

Tormented a few feet away while we laughed at dinners, celebrated Christmas and birthdays, made love.

Another great find, Clay would tell her driving home from a swap meet.

The underground cells in his garage.

Cobb and Mallory had shown her the photos. *Tell us what you know, Lacey.*

Sitting in the car now, reeling, she thought of all those women and their families.

Women I knew.

Erin, Abby and Carrie.

How many others?

Lacey picked up her phone and began writing the note. She'd drafted it in her heart a thousand times, words she wanted to send to all the families—and to Carrie.

I don't ask your forgiveness. I never knew...

The words on her screen blurred.

Then, one by one, in reverse, they disappeared as she deleted them, her desire to erase her life with Clay taking over.

They don't need to hear from me.

Staring at the detention center, she accepted a fact as hard as the steel bars inside.

She would not visit the *thing* in there.

Clay had ceased to exist.

We no longer existed.

Sitting a little straighter, she glanced at the rearview mirror and her luggage in the back. She'd told her lawyer that she was getting a divorce, selling the house and her salons, and moving to Austin, where she had a cousin.

Lacey started the motor, then pulled away in her rented Ford Escape.

Escape, she thought. *That sounds good right about now.*

102

The mystery cloaking the murders of two teenage girls that haunted this small East Texas community for over a decade ended with the rescue of two kidnapped women and the arrest of a sheriff's deputy living the double life of a serial killer.

"What do you think?" Denise stroked Harvey, who was nuzzling her lap. "A long lead, but it's a big story."

She sipped from her glass of diet cola with crushed ice, and continued proofing her article at her kitchen table.

It had been over a week since Carrie and Joyce-Anne's rescue and Clay Smith's arrest. Lynn had cleared Denise to work on the piece.

"Write it as long as you want," she told Denise. "We've always owned it, and we'll deliver the definitive story."

Lynn had deferred all national media interview requests for Denise, freeing her to go flat out on her work. Nearly everyone Denise had approached spoke to her, except Clay. He'd refused all media interview requests. Still, Denise got exclusive access to some of the investigative aspects once it was known that Clay would plead guilty for the murders of at least sixteen women. With Clay's permission, she talked to his attorney, his pastor and the psychiatrist who'd spent two days with Clay assessing him. As a result, Denise had learned several facts no other media outlet was aware of.

Since childhood, Clay, whose intelligence was above average, felt different, alone, consumed with dark, disturbing thoughts telling him that he was superior to mortals. At an early age, those forces evolved into a separate entity living within him, which Clay called "The Other." The entity demanded Clay commit unspeakable acts to be a worthy servant.

He gravitated to law enforcement to learn skills that would better serve The Other. Before becoming a deputy, one of his first major "operations," as he called them, was to lure two popular girls from his high school into Wild Pines Forest with a fabricated story of a body. He'd already studied textbooks on crime scenes and forensics. In homage to the Zodiac, he'd dressed as an executioner for his operation to sacrifice Abby and Erin, a couple stuck-up mean girls, to The Other. He collected evidence, took trophies and left a good scene. The fact that three arrived in the woods that day and one survived didn't dissuade him.

Even if she'd remembered details, he'd been disguised, took precautions. No one would know. The risk was even gratifying, especially when he'd stalked Carrie in California, knowing he could sacrifice her whenever The Other demanded it.

Living on the edge was thrilling as Clay continued serving The Other over the years, collecting and sacrificing subjects, his power growing. And like Jack the Ripper, like the Zodiac, he knew he would never be captured. Other lesser lights, like Bundy, Green River and BTK, had made errors.

Clay basked in the glory of living in two worlds. On one side, a mild-mannered, community-minded cop, with no one having an inkling of his omnipotence, the power he possessed. But over the years, his work became sloppy. Returning to base with the Oklahoma project, the subject escaped from his vehicle. Fate allowed him to recapture her but only after she'd been struck by—of all people—Carrie's husband, Luke. The mortal fool had bumbled his way to The Other.

But, Clay stressed, he had helped with the downfall.

Now that it had ended, Clay admitted his mistakes. He was proud of his early work in the woods, but its status changed when Carrie moved back and Hyde confessed. Then came the news story, shifting blame from Hyde to Carrie. It was an insult to The Other, an affront demanding action, prompting him to send an enlightening note and evidence to the news reporter, solidifying his stature and glory, while continuing his work.

The truth was, he'd panicked. Errors were made.

Now, on some level, he was relieved he'd been stopped. It was somewhat cathartic. He had nothing to say to the families of those he'd killed and hurt. No one could comprehend his being. As a dispatcher of death, he welcomed his own execution, as his destiny to reign over his subjects in eternity.

Denise shuddered but kept reading, scrutinizing other aspects, ensuring she addressed everything. Getting to the end, she pressed Send, shipping the article off to Lynn.

She sat back in silence, reflecting in the quiet on the darkness of which she had written.

It seemed the world wanted to know more. Denise had not yet responded to the many interview requests from networks, big outlets, even some from Europe and South America. And there were scheduled calls with her publisher for her planned book on the case.

But all that could wait until tomorrow.

Denise reached for her diet cola, which had diluted from the melting ice. She went to the kitchen to fix a new drink. Harvey followed her, nudging her leg. She freshened his water and got him a treat.

Kneading the tension from her neck, her phone pinged.

A text from Lynn.

One helluva story.

103

Carrie gazed from her passenger window as they drove along the country road a few miles from town.

She turned to Luke at the wheel, then looked over her shoulder to her dad and, beside him, her aunt Pearl, who'd flown to Texas to join her family. Pearl was hurt Carrie had not confided in her while she was away. But Pearl knew the whole story now, and she was here, bringing with her understanding and love.

She reached up and squeezed Carrie's shoulder.

Emily was sitting between Vern and Pearl, buckled in her seat, humming happily. Luke turned and they passed under the ornate arch over the entrance to Oak Rock Cemetery. They all got out, with Carrie taking Emily's hand, and as they walked across the lawn, Carrie took a deep breath.

It had been a month now.

In that time, the *Chronicle*'s story had hit on everything, setting things straight. Carrie accepted apologies from Abby's and Erin's relatives. People in town were warmer, kinder. Carrie tried to get word to Lacey, but it was futile.

It's as if she died, too.

Yet another victim.

In the weeks that followed her abduction, Carrie had spoken with detectives, many from other cities, working on the case.

Carrie continued her sessions with Dr. Bernay. There were new challenges now, of course. The Clear River district attorney was preparing to indict her father and her husband.

In Vern's case, they were looking at charges that included tampering with evidence and obstruction. Kilgore and Livingston officials were looking at charges related to Hyde's confession. In Luke's case, he'd left the scene of a serious accident and failed to report it, a felony.

Court dates would be set as their cases moved through the system. Their lawyers each said their actions, being directly linked to a monumental case, could provide mitigating issues and warranted suspended sentences. Still, Luke, facing an indictment, was suspended without pay until his case was settled. He'd found work with campus security at Clear River College.

With her family coming together, Carrie believed they were strong enough to face whatever was ahead, drawing on the recent positive news for Vern. His doctor had got Vern into a trial for a new experimental treatment that could possibly give him another few years. Pearl would move in with Vern to help her brother and be closer to Emily and Luke.

Arriving at her mother's grave, Carrie placed lilies, daisies and baby's breath at the headstone. In the moment of quiet, Emily toddled around her grandmother's marker, her little fingers brushing the granite. Vern's eyes crinkled and he smiled along with everyone else.

Then Carrie glanced across the green lawns in the direction where Abby and Erin were buried.

I have all the answers now.

Later, their visit over, walking back to the car, Pearl and Carrie discussed the family barbecue they were planning.

"Let's stop at Reddick's," Carrie said. "We'll get some pecans for a pie."

"I like the sound of that," Vern said.

Carrie stopped, took Emily into her arms and turned for another look at her mother's stone.

In that moment, the baby waved goodbye and Carrie was catapulted back to her mother's kitchen, helping her make pie... her mother...

...working at the sink...the radio playing a favorite song, Solomon Burke's "Cry to Me." She's excited, calling, "Vern, get in here!" Carrie's mother and father dancing, filling her world with love, like a dream.

★ ★ ★ ★ ★

Acknowledgments & Author's Note

In bringing *If Two Are Dead* to life, I drew upon some of my experiences from my time long ago as a reporter.

Let me begin by underscoring that this is a work of fiction. I've taken immense creative liberties with police jurisdiction, technology, and the geography of East Texas and California. I am not an expert on any aspect. Many of the towns, counties and law enforcement agencies and procedures, as well as other entities in this book, are made up.

However, one element of the story was inspired by something that really happened.

Years ago, while covering a death penalty case, I traveled more than once to Texas. I reported from Houston, San Antonio, Austin, Lufkin and Huntsville, driving across a good portion of the state to interview people, including a killer on death row.

I never witnessed an execution.

But I got a firsthand sense of one.

In the course of my assignment, prison officials offered to take me through the execution protocol step-by-step as if I were the condemned. They took me into the "Walls Unit," giving me the perspective of an inmate facing execution, including walking me into the execution chamber. There, while listening to the procedure being explained, I leaned against the gurney where so many had paid the ultimate price for their crimes.

You never forget something like that.

Many things may have changed since then, but I recalled my time in Texas to give my imagined story the ring of truth.

Writing can be a solitary job, but in getting this book to you I benefited from the hard work and support of so many people.

My thanks to my wife, Barbara, and to Wendy Dudley, for their invaluable help improving the tale.

Thanks to Laura and Michael.

My thanks to the super-brilliant Amy Moore-Benson, to the extraordinary Lorella Belli, and the outstanding team at LBLA in London; to the talented Leah Mol; and to the incredible editorial, marketing, sales and PR teams at Harlequin, MIRA Books and HarperCollins.

It seems like the idea for this story and its evolution into the book you hold in your hands came so long ago. While the bulk of the tale was drafted at my desk at home, the story never left me. In the months it took to complete, parts of it were written in New York City, Toronto, Halifax and San Diego, on trains and planes, in airports and hotels.

This brings me to what I believe is the most critical part of the entire enterprise: you, the reader. Those of you familiar with my stories are aware that this part has become something of a credo for me, one that bears repeating with each book.

Thank you for your time, for without you, the story remains an untold tale. Thank you for setting your life on pause and taking the journey. I deeply appreciate my audience around the world and those who've been with me since the beginning who keep in touch. Thank you all for your kind words. I hope you enjoyed the ride and will check out my earlier books while watching for new ones.

Feel free to send me a note. I enjoy hearing from you. I have been known to participate in book club discussions of my books via Zoom. While it may take some time, I try to respond to all messages.

Rick Mofina

www.rickmofina.com
www.instagram.com/rickmofina/
x.com/rickmofina
www.facebook.com/rickmofina